Praise for the Freak Scene Dream Trilogy, including "The Flowers Lied"

"There was a time when (rock) music was the living pulse of a generation, when wanting to be a rock critic was a credible dream. That is the era of the Freak Scene Dream Trilogy, an ambitious and ultimately successful attempt at recasting the coming-of-age-in-the-wake-of-the-sixties-experience in innovative but authentic language, Kerouac in the 21st century. It jitters around in ever-accumulating fine detail that traces young love and desire and the pure true heart of the era, the music. It was a pivotal time, and Volume II, 'The Flowers Lied,' captures it."

DENNIS MCNALLY, author of "A Long Strange Trip: The Inside History of the Grateful Dead" and "Desolate Angel: Jack Kerouac, The Beat Generation & America"

"If Lester Bangs had ever published a novel it might have read something like this frothing debut by longtime music journalist Michael Goldberg... Readers from any musical era will come away with a deeper appreciation of how nostalgia can shape our lives, for better and for worse."

COLIN FLEMING, Rolling Stone

"Goldberg presents us with a beautiful evocation of the Seventies where the music wasn't just the soundtrack to our lives but the auteur of them. Writerman, our hero, drinks and drugs and dances to the nightingale tune while birds fly high by the light of the moon. Oh, oh, oh, oh Writerman!"

LARRY RATSO SLOMAN, author of "On the Road with Bob Dylan"

"Michael Goldberg is comparable to Kerouac in a 21st century way, someone trying to use that language and energy and find a new way of doing it."
    MARK MORDUE, author of "Dastgah: Diary of a Head Trip"

"Penned in a staccato amphetamine grammar, its narrative is fractured and deranged, often unsettling but frequently compelling, an unsparing portrait of the teen condition: assured then despairing, would-be sex god then impotent has-been, from erection to dejection, an only child battling the wills of his domineering father and interfering mom in the anonymous, suburban fringes of Marin County."
    SIMON WARNER, author of "Text and Drugs and Rock'n'Roll: The Beats and Rock Culture"

"Aspiring rock journalist Michael Stein (aka Writerman) returns in the second installment of Goldberg's Freak Scene Dream Trilogy, picking up the narrative where he left off and fumbling his way across the countercultural landscape of the early Seventies like some less jaded, wannabe-hippie version of Holden Caulfield. This slightly-older-but-not-necessarily-wiser Stein, along with his inner circle of equally confused post-adolescents, is more fleshed-out as a character than in the previous (though superb) 'True Love Scars.' As a result the scenarios he finds himself thrust into, not to mention the occasional disaster of his own making, ring with an additional authenticity that will leave anyone who lived through the same era nodding with recognition. Some will even fidget uncomfortably in their seats, as I did—credit to Goldberg's keen ability to channel his/our own misspent youth while sketching a series of remarkably believable portraits.
    "Among the more memorable scenes: a hamfisted attempt to get his rock journalism published in the college newspaper, even more awkward attempts to get laid (that include at least one success, with his best friend's girlfriend, no less, in a

gondola at the top of a Ferris wheel), getting thrown out of a Neil Young concert by one of Bill Graham's goons, navigating a surreal Halloween party while peaking on LSD, and kibitzing with a popular Lester Bangs-esque rock-crit. Along the way we get cameos from Bob Dylan, the Rolling Stones, Captain Beefheart, the New York Dolls, Slim Harpo, James Brown, John Fowles, Sartre, Dostoyevsky and Godard. Settle in, crack open a bottle and/or spark a doob, and get ready for an emotional rollercoaster ride. Oh, and don't touch the Thorens."

FRED MILLS, editor, *Blurt* magazine

"Just call it a portrait of the rock critic as a young freakster bro, coming of age in the glorious peace-and-love innocence of the Sixties dream, only to crash precipitously, post-Altamont into the drug-ridden paranoia of the Seventies, characterized by the doom and gloom of the Stones' sinister "Sister Morphine" and the apocalyptic *caw-caw-caw* of a pair of ubiquitous crows."

ROY TRAKIN, Trakin Care of Business column

"So who is this protagonist anyway? Holden Caulfield meets Lord Buckley? Speaking in a crazy-assed, hell-fucked jargon, yet choosing his words so carefully it seems like his words are choosing him? And exactly what's happening here? Coming of age in the era between the Beats and the Punks? Licking the combination plate of sex, drugs and rock 'n' roll? Balancing on the tightrope between horniness and empathy? Carrying a torch along the route of Teenage Heartbreak Olympics? Revealing a threesome among guilt, blame and accountability? Tripping on the power of shared musical obsession? Naïveté serving as a gradual learning experience morphing into sophistication, layer by layer. Caught between Dylan's suggestion, 'Take what you have gathered from coincidence,' and Freud's observation, 'Being entirely honest with oneself is a good exercise.' Excuse me, what was the question again?"

PAUL KRASSNER, author of "Confessions of a Raving, Unconfined Nut: Misadventures in the Counterculture"

"'True Love Scars' reads like a fever dream from the dying days of the Summer of Love. Keyed to a soundtrack of love and apocalypse, Writerman pitches headlong into a haze of drugs, sex and confusion in search of what no high can bring: his own redemption. Read it and be transformed."

ALINA SIMONE, musician, author of "Note to Self" and "You Must Go and Win"

"A gonzo look back at misspent youth in the 1960s… It's a crackling good read, filled with humor, pathos, drug use and Dylan references (seriously, I think there's one on every page). Goldberg's freewheelin' style captures a certain late Sixties/early 70s vibe (think the autobiographical writings of Lester Bangs) that makes 'True Love Scars' a pleasure through and through."

TYLER WILCOX, Doom & Gloom From The Tomb

"There never was a Seventies. They never existed. You could, however, construct a reasonably functional Seventies love-doll, inflating it (you guessed right) with canned or frozen Sixties sexual effluvium. Fill it fat, saggy or shapeless—your call. CAREFUL: there will be some broken glass and flammable scum. Shards of chthonic Romance—whew—as radioactive as Godzilla. Only the BOLD need apply. Whoops—beware!—Mr. Goldberg has been there first, and 'had' her first. Reader-side litrachoor is often a matter of 2nd in line. Bon appétit!"

RICHARD MELTZER, author of "The Aesthetics of Rock" and "Tropic of Nipples"

"A crazy fever dream of a coming-of-age novel, featuring a young man who falls in love and subsequently goes off the rails on a crazy train. The narrative voice is really distinctive, and it definitely took me a few pages to get used to it, but I wound up getting caught up in the crazy musical flow of it all and was carried effortlessly through the pages."

BRENDAN HALPIN, author of "Forever Changes" and "Donorboy"

"[His] passion for the counterculture and the music that informed it shines bright in Goldberg's semi-autobiographical novel, 'True Love Scars'... the novel is a whirlwind tale of a young music fanatic's [Writerman] quest for true love, high times and "the authentic real" (not necessarily in that order). ... [Goldberg] narrates most of the tale with a retrospective viewpoint, which enables the reader to empathize more with Writerman's youthful mistakes and sometimes naïve viewpoints. Writerman is wiser now, but he wants us to see how it all went down, because there's meaning in the journey. ... Goldberg develops a unique voice as he flashes back and forth, mostly between 1965 and 1972. The literary gold is in the details. The novel is filled with colorful references about the bands and songs that bring out the halcyon days of that influential era. ... True Love Scars is deeply dialed in to rock's dichotomy of enlightening powers versus stoned party time."

GREG M. SCHWARTZ, PopMatters

"Michael's written quite a series of novels about the early Seventies and the death of the Sixties and the rock 'n' roll dream. I think they're very good. I've never seen a novel talk about Feminism and the Seventies like his Freak Scene Dream Trilogy does. Plus he's a total rock 'n' roll geek. He knows everything about everybody. Believe me, every detail from Captain Beefheart to the New York Dolls. Bob Dylan is God. And a straight guy with a raging sexual agenda searching for his 'Visions of Johanna chick.' It's a terrific read."

TOM SPANBAUER, author of "Faraway Places," "Now Is the Hour" and "I Loved You More"

"Goldberg's virginal sex scenes unwind at the same racing-heart-awkward-self-conscious-anxious pace one can almost remember from those good old, bad old days when the forbidden fruit was all one ever wanted..."

M. SELDOF, Ragazine.CC

"Michael Goldberg reminds us of the difficulties of remaining true to our own visions amidst the powerful exigencies of young adulthood. He paints crazy intimate portraits of the excesses and eccentricities of the sexual revolution. And he speaks to us in the voice and language of the brave microculture of his youth. In this, he opens a door to the rough adolescence of our own 'grown up' disillusioned macroculture. All the dreams and wishes and bright energy buried therein is still brawling for a release. Our inner teenager still wonders what the fuck we think we are doing. To hear a voice from this realm is a blessing. Goldberg makes of himself a channel from that forbidden country. Through his recounting, we remember how we learned to love, how we learned to listen, and how we learned to do whatever it is we do best."

JOLIE HOLLAND, recording artist, whose albums include *Catalpa*, *Escondida* and *The Living and the Dead*

THE FLOWERS LIED

The Second of the
Freak Scene Dream Trilogy

a novel by
Michael Goldberg

Neumu Press
P.O. Box 6740
Albany, CA 94706
insider1@neumu.net
www.theflowerslied.com

ISBN: 978-0-9903983-4-9

To my beautiful wife Leslie,
the love of my life. You make every
day the "authentic real."

THE FLOWERS
LIED

Turn on, tune in, drop out my ass.
It was a utopian pipe dream.
                    —THEODORE LARDUSKY

ONE

1. KING EDITOR

THE SOLID-ASS OAK door has a cardboard sign taped to it, and hand written in that ye old England kinda script: "Lawrence Roth, Jr., Editor in Chief." It's fall 1972, start of my sophomore year, I guess a week after I meet *Thee* Freakster Bro, you know, Jim Costello, a week after I meet Harper and we fuck in my dorm room, yeah a week after all that, maybe even a week and a half since the start of school.

And this is one of those days. A Days of the Crazy-Wild day, a day when something extraordinary happens, a day that matters.

Or anyway, that's what I think. That day.

I'm waiting there in the hall for my 11 a.m. one-on-one, you know, to discuss my first record review of the year—a review of Captain Beefheart's *Clear Spot*.

Soon enough I'll tell you about Beefheart, and *Clear Spot*.

Patience. Gotta have patience, man.

Well that's when Roth opens his door wide enough to stick his oversize bloodless head out. Gets his gaunt bloodless face in the opening between the oak door and the doorframe. Hollow bloodless eyes look me over, and he aims that snooted nose up towards the ceiling. Opens his mouth and talks how he talks. Quiet no affect bloodless voice tells me to wait.

Closes the door quick as he opened it.

I stare down the second floor hallway of the Steinbeck Building, and it recedes in semi-darkness, the overhead lights are turned off so the only light comes through windows at either end, and from some of the classrooms. Near me I see the scratched fir floorboards, and the wood-framed doorways, each door has a frosted glass upper panel. Only built the goddamn goddamn place seven years before that day I stand there, but same as so much at The University, built it to resemble some old Ivy League deal. Old grand Harvard or Yale or Oxford.

As if you can make a new building have the gravitas of 100 years of that peculiar mix of class privilege, earned reputation and Fort Knox amounts of money.

Fucking ridiculous, same as so much in this world, man. Look beneath the surface of the surface, nothing there.

Already it's 11:15. I stand and I wait, and I wait and I stand. I wait. I stand. Fuck, man. Stand. Wait. Are you getting that feeling of frustration, same as I have? Yeah, feel that, fucking feel it. It makes you feel same as shit, right? And I got to wait, got to put up with whatever Roth throws at me 'cause of this rock critic thing. I need Roth. He's the gatekeeper.

If I want my writing to see print he has to dig it. Yeah I got something at stake, and he *has* to use my Beefheart review. My whole trip on the line, and I hate how it feels. Answer to no one, that's who I wanna be. Life on my terms, that's who I wanna be. Only that's not who I am.

Gotta stand and wait for Larry *Fucking* Roth.

King Editor.

Ghost of 'lectricity. Yeah that's what I call it when I'm lost in my mind, the present gone and I'm seeing the past, a memory. Or sometimes a vision. A premonition of what will happen. Or what could happen. Or what'll never happen.

Ghost of 'lectricity. Summer of '67. I'm 13 and I see Captain Beefheart & the Magic Band play this cool-ass rock festival at the Mountain Theater—up on Mt. Tam where a few years later I went on my first date with this chick Lauren, and me and her talked about Dylan all afternoon—and I don't have a clue. Clueless. The sounds Beefheart makes are way over my head. Well it doesn't last. Soon enough I'm digging the cool psychedelic blues scene of the Magic Band's first album. *Safe As*

Milk. And by the time *Trout Mask Replica* arrives in '69 on Zappa's Straight Records label I'm a serious fan.

Trout Mask Replica.

Oh man, epic two-disc freak out, and you know the story, and if not, get a clue. Howlin' Wolf voice Dada poetry free jazz clarinet laid top o' grimy oil and dirt blues rock. Zoot Horn Rollo's glass finger guitar trip-out melts a hole in my brain. And if Hugo Ball or Tristan Tzara had a rock band, had that Howlin' Wolf voice and a clarinet, well that's Beefheart.

Eleven-thirty, and another five minutes gone by, and another five, and no sign the oak door gonna open. Only way I know he's not croaked in there, smell of his stink-ass tobacco and that Paul Whiteman big band shit he plays. It's either Whiteman or Fletcher Henderson or, worse still, Benny Goodman. White man big band's not even music. At least if a human gonna listen to some big band, go for Basie or Ellington or if you're total hip retro-futurist dig Gil Evans. He's the modern shit for sure. No moldy oldie crap for Gil. The records he made with Miles—*Birth of the Cool,* and *Miles Ahead* and *Sketches of Spain* and *Porgy and Bess*—and his own trip—*Into the Cool* and *Out of the Hot* and *The Individualism of Gil Evans*—major brave new world.

If King Editor listened to some cool jazz brew same as that he might start to become semi-human. Might start to feel blood in his veins. Maybe even discover he got a soul. Maybe. But no. Roth sits in his office and does the overwhelming big important editing trip with sapped-out white man big band playing, tries to tap along with his left foot as if he has rhythm only he has as much rhythm as a parking lot.

I hear those white man swing sounds coming outta Roth's office and Roth has the imitation Mark Twain pipe going. I smell the noxious odor of some kinda foul tobacco burning, smoke leaking into the hallway.

Larry *Fucking* Roth's bag is the *New Yorker*, the magazine my folks worship. My folks have a subscription for same as forever, and read every issue. Cover-to-cover. Only they're always behind —at least three months, maybe more. So you can never talk to them about anything current 'cause they've not got to that issue yet. My parents, man, always three steps behind the eight-ball.

I've waited close to 45 minutes. Hate to need the motherfucker. But how else I gonna get recognized as a brilliant genius writer if I don't get words in print? Roth's the only editor I know. He probably hates my review, and this is his way of getting his jollies. What the hellfuck is he doing in there? I mean other than stinking up the place with that goddamn goddamn pipe. Not on the phone, not with that white man big band crap. Could be taking the dreaded red pen to my review. Either that or he's jacking off.

Se Palucher, what Harper said.

Roth wouldn't make his beloved cock-tease Suzie Foxxe wait, and you should see that snoot-nosed editor around her, nodding and smiling and Suzie this and Suzie that and *you've got quite the talent Miss Suzie*. She's got long bleached-blonde hair and a figure that matches the name I got for her: Foxy Lady. Only a sophomore and already she's his "editorial assistant," and yeah I know the kind of assisting Roth wants from her. King Editor be rolling out the red carpet if Suzie Foxxe had a meeting scheduled. I bet most of his meetings with her take place at that cozy French restaurant in town, *Le Coq,* where he tells her how brilliant her boring-ass dance column is, and those two drink champagne, stuff caviar and snail *hors d'oeuvres* into the vacuum suck of their parasitic greed-ass mouths.

Yeah, and I'm pissed. So when I've waited an hour, 14 minutes and 59 seconds, that's it, I open King Editor's door.

He doesn't hear me, head nodding to those square-ass sounds. Sits behind a huge mahogany desk nearly fills the tiny office, a desk grand enough for Maxwell Perkins. He's wearing his imitation Jack London monstrosity of a hat.

Lives in his own world for sure.

He's reading a book, leaning back in his chair, chuckles in that high-pitched way of his—what you'd expect from an old biddy—his shiny Thomas Wolfe black policeman shoes up on the desk. Moving the toe of his left shoe but he's missing the beat of the awkward white man rhythm.

Made me wait while he read his goddamn goddamn book.

"What the fuck," I say.

Hellfuck startle him, and I see the cover. "The Years With Ross." He struggles to get his feet onto the floor, knocks over his mug. Coffee everywhere. On his manuscripts, and pooling under his big black manual typewriter, and drips onto the fir floor. Stands, looks for something to blot it only there's nothing. Stands with that stupid hat, and he's Walter Mitty, arms out, slender hands in front of him, shakes them at me, skeletal fingers apart. His left eye blinks out of control. His bloodless face pale, his bloodless voice so whisper-quiet I gotta read his bloodless lips.

"Do something!"

I do what any stand-up freakster bro would do. I split Roth's office, run down the dark hallway, make my contribution to wearing out the fir floor boards, and into the men's room, and fuck, the paper towel dispenser is empty. Push open the door to the first stall. No TP either. Second stall, either someone is in there or the door is jammed. Third stall, try to remove the roll but the dispenser is locked so I start to unroll one-ply TP and wrap it around my hand.

Oh yeah that's gonna work.

And that's when I lose myself in the moment. In the moment where all that matters, get that roll of TP out of that locked dispenser. Lost in that moment, man. So I kick the thing, and there's some give. Raise up my leg again, slam my heel against that dispenser and it comes loose from the metal stall divider, falls to the floor.

I pick the metal dispenser box up, got it in both hands, throw it hard, and same as one of those comic book deals, you know, one of those words same as "Bam!" or "Zap!" or "Pow!" floats there in the air, a visual sound effect of what's going down, and the thing hits the floor and the metal door pops open. Cool.

I get that roll of TP, get it in my left hand, and hold it high above my head.

Yeah, motherfucker. Fuck yeah. Trumped it. Return of the Last Dude Standing. I've got the golden chalice. I've got Sir Lancelot's sword. Oh man, and I am so high, adrenalin pumping through me.

When I get back to the office Roth is backed away from the desk but still standing. Quick-as-The-Flash I'm blotting up coffee on the desk and the floor, cleaning up the mess. *His* mess. When I'm done Roth looks as if he's considering whether to add me to his butterfly collection.

After a too long silence he hangs the Dudley Do-Right hat on his brass coat tree.

"This is quite upsetting," he says. "Very disturbing, a most unfortunate circumstance to occur before the outset of our meeting, *Mr.* Stein."

Mr. Stein. That's a joke. Roth calls everyone who writes for him, *Mr.*, well *Mr.* or *Miss,* I mean he calls Jim *Mr.* Costello. He mocks us, that *Mr.* deal. He knows none of us are *Mr.* anything. He knows we're a bunch of lay-about stoned freaks.

"If I were a superstitious man," Roth says. "And I were you, *Mr.* Stein, and I had handed in that particular review, followed by this cretinous incident, I'd be quite troubled."

I pull the door closed so it's the private scene. Roth there looking like he's outta the Stone Age, 1942 or something. Imitation Steinbeck brown corduroy coat with the leather patches on the sleeves. William Shawn sweater vest over a collar shirt. James Joyce wide-stripe tie. Hemingway khakis. Roth, man, he doesn't know who he wants to be.

"The symbology, *Mr.* Stein. The *symbology.*"

He sits on the other side of the desk in this grandiose wood and leather chair with a wingback rising behind him and to either side—his editorial throne. There's maybe a couple feet between the back of his chair and the two bookcases and filing cabinet along the rear wall.

King Editor reaches for his James Joyce spectacles. Gets the tortoise-shell frames off the desk, cleans each lens with a white handkerchief, puts 'em on so they sit low on his bony nose.

"I should expunge you from *The Paper*," he says. "Barging in here. Just the kind of thing a freshman would do."

Well it's past time for some Zen White Wall Meditation. Something I learned from Sarah, she was my high school girlfriend, and I still miss her so bad. But anyway.

Gotta imagine I'm looking at a pure white wall. Super slow inhale, exhale, *white wall white wall white wall. One.*

"Sophomore, man," I say.

"Yes, next year, a sophomore. Perhaps by then you'll learn some manners."

White wall white wall white wall. Two. "No, man, I'm a fucking sophomore RIGHT NOW."

Left eye blinking fast. "*Mr.* Stein, really, I won't tolerate such language."

Hard to keep the focus. *Three.* "Freshman, sophomore, no difference. Green as the grass. Well have a seat, and *try* not to dislodge anything else."

Blood dripping down the white wall. *Four.* "*You* spilled your coffee, man."

"Not another word, *Mr.* Stein."

There's maybe a foot clearance on each side of the big desk, and one small wooden chair, a child's chair, between the doorway and the back of the desk. I stuff myself into it, knees higher than my thighs. The low back digs into my spine.

"Quite a conundrum, wouldn't you say, *Mr.* Stein?"

Fuck the White Wall Meditation, goddamn chair in my back, shifting about for a comfort zone. In the glass ashtray Roth's pipe smolders. And there's a stubbed out cigarette got lipstick on the filter. For sure left by Foxy Lady.

"Mind if I smoke?"

I lean forward to relieve the pain, hurts my back in a new way to look up at Roth, and that's when he snaps to a razor sharp focus. He picks a book up off his desk, and under it, my review—plenty of dreaded red ink, but somehow it's not soaked in coffee.

"The book is 'On the Road,' *Mr.* Stein. I'm sure, judging from your review, you know it well."

Yeah sure I know "On the Road." You kidding? I first read it back when I was a high school sophomore, and these days it's my bible. I've made a study of Jack's Method, came up with my own version. What I do, put on a record, crank the volume, run to my desk, and let the words flow straight from my unconscious onto the page.

"I'm sure you're not aware of this," Roth says. "Being a freshman, green as the grass and all, but Jack Kerouac wasn't a writer. He was a charlatan. And a drunk."

Well fuck it, and that was when I realized King Editor was the charlatan. 'Cause Kerouac was one of my idols, and not only that, I mean Meltzer, the great R. Meltzer, this writer of rock books and rock criticism plus rock lyrics for the Blue Öyster Cult, he worships Kerouac. He sees Kerouac same as Charlie Parker. One time Meltzer wrote that those two, Kerouac and Parker, were "universe-blazers, stripminers of personal pneuma, and easily the finest (most consistently exciting) soloists."

Yeah Roth doesn't know Meltzer, same as he's not hip to Kerouac. King Editor's not hip to nothing come floating down the river since Joyce, and Joyce's *big* book been published in 1922. Fifty years before that day I sit in Roth's office.

Oh, man, Roth puts down Kerouac and I can't say shit 'cause I need Roth. Big band Benny Goodman drips onto the rug. Roth, man, lame as the puke-ugly marbled tiles in the entryway of my folk's house. Roth talks in his quiet bloodless monotone, his voice so low, and I have to lean in again.

"Oh yes, Kerouac put words on a page. Doesn't make him a writer, *Mr.* Stein. The masses will go for practically any fifth-rate mountebank pushed on them by the admen, themselves scoundrels of the worst sort."

"You got it wrong, man."

Yeah, looks as if he wants to put me and a chloroform-soaked rag in a killing jar.

He starts to read from "On the Road," his voice has the

heavy sarcasm, reads this grooved-out stream-of-consciousness run-on sentence. Goes on half a page about Dean driving, Sal on the passenger side, and Mary Lou in the back. This be-bop jam of a graph that keeps goin' and goin' and you can't believe it's possible to write same as that and yet there it is, and it really is beautiful and mad and free, Coltrane blowing his most overwhelming total heavy traffic late night improvisation, writing that takes you into the stratosphere. Oh man and glory be, hellfuck goddamn to write same as Kerouac.

"Detritus!" Roth says, and drops the book on his desk. He tosses my review at me. Every page covered with his comments, written in impossibly small print with the dreaded red pen.

"Give me rewrite," Roth says, and oh boy he thinks that's funny.

Our meeting's over. He picks up an oval hand mirror with a silver handle and holds it up, runs his bony fingers through his hair, adjusts his Joycean tie.

"I could use a new tie," he says. "Don't you think? Perhaps in the vein of Nabokov—black with white polka dots."

Back at my dorm room, light a Pall Mall, time to assess the damage. My review lays on my desk, soaked in the dreaded red ink. Roth, man, he doesn't understand what I'm doin'. This isn't some highfalutin *literary* critique for his let's-put-on-the-white-gloves *New Yorker*. What I write is down and dirty Meltzer-style gonzo rock writing. I need a real editor, not King Editor. I need *Creem*'s "Rocket Reducer" Harsh, or Greil Marcus or better yet, my rock critic friend, Sausalito Cowboy.

2. EXTRA LARGE

SAUSALITO COWBOY, AND BUCKAROO too. You know them, right? OK, well, I fill you in. First the Sausalito Cowboy, and soon enough we get to Buckaroo. Sausalito Cowboy has to be at least 24, and I was 16. When I met him. I wouldn't normal hang with an old fart, only I don't care how old he is 'cause Sausalito Cowboy is in all the rock mags. Sausalito Cowboy's my one connection to that world where I want to live.

Rock Star World.

You know the deal Fitzgerald wrote about the rich, *they are different from you and me,* well when I read that I didn't think of Rockefeller, or a bank president or whoever runs General Motors. I thought of John Lennon driving around in that Rolls painted all psychedelic groovy. Neil Young at his 140-acre Broken Arrow Ranch standing on a ridge looking out at the Forever Infinite Pacific. Roger Daltrey, jeans all worn got holes in the knees stepping out of a black stretch limo, and he could afford a million pair of new Levi's but he doesn't give a fuck.

If I get rich, that's how I'm gonna be.

Fitzgerald wrote how reckless the rich are, Daisy at the wheel of Gatsby's car hit and runs down Tom's mistress leaves her dead on the road as if the laws don't apply to her or Tom or Gatsby. But what's most different about being rich is you can be free. Don't answer to nobody. That's rock 'n' roll. Sleep all day, stay up all night. Whole fucking life can be Sal and Dean driving to Mexico in search of Nirvana. Well rock critics get to hang with the rock stars, smoke reefer with 'em, split a six-pack. You get a day pass. Yeah, how I saw it back then, rock critics might as well *be* rock stars.

'Course that was before I met Sausalito Cowboy.

Sixteen when I write the letter. But before I write the letter, I buy the magazine. *Peak* magazine, and what's important about *Peak*, in the first issue there's a call-out for writers. If you have *something fresh to say about the New Culture* you're their kinda freakster bro.

So there I am, man. They're talkin' about me.

I send in a letter about being 16, and what rock 'n' roll means to me, and a couple reviews I write in my best Meltzer rip-off style. Two weeks pass, maybe three, mid-March 1970, and an envelope arrives and in it my letter, same letter I sent, only written at the bottom where there used to be blank space, the Arts Editor wrote me a note, well a sentence.

Nearly a Haiku, a rejection poem.

You're not quite there yet, but thanks anyway, maybe in a few years.

I try to see the positive, *maybe in a few years*, but fuck, I could be *dead* in a few years. I don't *have* a few years. There's a business card with a phone number and a name, Ted Larsen, and maybe this Ted Larsen Arts Editor can help me get to where I *am* quite there. Now. Not some distant few years, but now.

Now, man.

Call the number, and this guy, amused voice deal, answers, "Sausalito Cowboy here, whadayawant?" and it's weird 'cause Sausalito Cowboy is the rock critic I read in *Creem* and *Rolling Stone* and all the rest, and I say, "Sir, can I speak to Mr. Larsen?" and I hear his loud-ass loud laugh, yeah he thinks that's hilarious, but finally it stops and he says, "That's me," and I say, "I'm the 16-year-old freakster bro wrote you the letter, man."

Turns out Ted Larsen and Sausalito Cowboy are the same freakster bro—and I freak. Sausalito Cowboy talking to *me*. Never did find out why he didn't tell me to fuck off. He says I can drop by, afternoons are good, he'll give me a few writing pointers, and by the way, be sure and bring along a pepperoni pizza with mushrooms and olives and heavy on the onions, as a friendly gesture, you know, since he'll be taking time from his busy editing schedule.

"Wednesdays are good," he says. "Come by The Pad, I mean our grand offices, at 1. Number Nine Strawberry Lane in Sausalito.

And.

"Make sure it's an *extra large*."

No way I go alone. Gonna bring Big Man Bobby, you know, loser-ass Bobby who named me Writerman. And this as good a time as any to tell you about him.

Got to give Bobby credit, he's his own freakster bro. He's not same as any other. Never went along with any fad. Never tried to look same as a longhaired freakster bro, not even in the late Sixties. Back then Bobby always wore a button-down light blue shirt and black straight-leg jeans, and the desert boots. He looked kinda same as Benjamin Braddock. You know, the character Dustin Hoffman played in "The Graduate," 'cause of the big nose Bobby has, and his dark brown hair cut short with the part on the right.

Two things I guess I should tell you. Bobby's not big. I mean he probably weighs 120 pounds, 5 feet 5, skinny-ass for sure. And he's not a man, not back then anyway. Same age as me. Sixteen. Me thinking of him as Big Man Bobby, that's a joke. He's always acting same as he's a big deal. He's not a big deal. Later, after he's living up at that junkie rock star's house doing the odd jobs, Bobby really thinks he's a big deal. Bobby was never a big deal. Didn't matter what he thought.

You could think all the straight-as-straight-can-be clothes means he's this straight on the up-and-up deal play-by-the-rules kinda guy. Only Bobby is shady. Crafty too. Bobby does whatever he can get away with, so that straight-arrow look is Bobby's front. And how come I have a friend same as Bobby you might wonder, and I wonder about it now same as you. Don't know why once upon a time I pal around with shady losers same as Polanski and Bobby. Maybe I needed them to help wipe some of the good off me.

The other thing Bobby wears is a black suede shirt jacket he stole off a musician friend. If you can call someone a friend you steal from. Sucker or sap or easy mark. Bobby told me that musician didn't need the jacket 'cause he has more clothes than a person can wear. Said he did that musician a favor taking the jacket. Bobby's better at rationalizing than even me. I dug the fuck outta that stolen suede jacket, I mean until the day we met Sausalito Cowboy. Until then, Bobby stealin' that jacket turned it into some kinda hip outlaw jacket. Later, well, we get to that soon enough.

Wednesday, a bright bright sunny day spring 1970, stop at that Sausalito pizza joint where me and Sarah ate once, spring for the extra large pepperoni with mushrooms, olives, heavy on the onions, the whole deal. Stash the box with the extra large on the back seat of the white Rambler and head for Number Nine Strawberry Lane, the grand offices of *Peak* magazine. Got Bobby on the passenger side and the car radio on KFRC playing "American Woman."

"Find something hip," I say.

Bobby got himself a new short-ass-short haircut, looks even more straight-as-straight-can-be than usual, even wearing the black suede outlaw jacket and his cheap-ass drug store shades.

"Can't you get your folks to spring for FM?"

Bobby thinks my folks are made of dough. He lives with his mom and his younger brother, and they don't have much. He grew up always wanting things he can't have. I don't know where he gets the idea my folks are loaded. Sarah's folks, I mean she was still my chick back then, they've got the dough. My dad does OK, but he's Mr. Stingy, puts any extra dough in stocks. Bobby resents the shit out of me being middle class. Twists the tuner knob, dials past a basketball game and big band shit and Frank Sinatra's "My Way," gets to KYA and the end of "Have You Ever Seen the Rain?"

I got one hand on the wheel, adjust my shades, fuck with my hair, try to see myself in the rear-view.

"I can live with that."

"What the fuck," Bobby says. "You don't *like* Creedence.

You always say they're commercial."

"Changed my mind," I say. "You know that Creedence song, 'Walk on the Water'? That's what I want to do, man."

He gets a Marlboro between his fingers, thumb and index, and when he gets it same as that, he's gonna light it soon enough, no matter what I say.

"What are you talking about?" Bobby says.

Gets out a match book, and I know he wishes he had The Dylan, you know, this lighter I stole off Jerry Garcia the time me and Bobby interviewed him for our fanzine. Supposedly Garcia got that lighter from Dylan himself. That's what he said, anyway. Yeah, The Dylan is another of those things Bobby can't have.

"Walk on the water," I say. "Same as Jesus."

One beat, two, and another makes three.

"And speak to the dead."

Authentic real, I don't know for sure what I mean when I say that speak to the dead deal. I mean in the song, John Fogerty, he's the singer and basically does all the important shit in Creedence, he sings about a walk on the water, and someone or something comes from the other side and talks to him, you know, talks to the character the singer is in the song. And I mean *the other side,* man, we all know what that is, so I figure whoever walks on the water, he's already dead.

Then again.

Maybe whoever walks on the water got the key to the highway, walks on the water to the other side, speaks to the dead, comes back to tell the tale. We all want to live forever, right, I mean if we could, never grow old. Right? *Right?*

Bobby brings the Marlboro up toward his lips.

"Sometimes I don't understand you."

The blue-gold flame rises off the match stick.

"Sometimes that's how I like it," I say. "You got the time?"

He changes his mind, gets the Marlboro away from his face, blows out the match. Drops the dead match on the protector mat beneath his feet.

"Hey man, my car's not an ashtray."

He gets out the Gramps Watch, this silver pocket watch his dad gave him. I call it the Gramps Watch 'cause original it belongs to his grandfather.

"It's 1:16."

"Fuck, said I'd be there around 1."

Number Nine Strawberry Lane, and we discover there is no grand offices. Zero grand offices. Two-story boxy white deal got an overgrown front yard, and too long since it been painted. Upstairs windows got blinds pulled down.

"Something's not right, Writerman," and for once I agree, how can the house with the white paint flake off be the office?

Sketchy for sure.

We know what a real magazine office looks like 'cause of the *Rolling Stone* office, you know, time we rip shit off.

Ghost of 'lectricity. August of 1969. San Francisco. Third Street, down past Bryant, just above Townsend. I'm 16, about a month after I get my driver's license, and it's a Saturday. Park the white Rambler behind the building, a onetime warehouse got old brick walls. Four story, five story, I don't know, could be more. The back door is open, and me and Bobby take the stairs to the second floor. I guess some stoner works late the night before and forgets to lock up 'cause we walk right in, and I swear total authentic real my plan gonna check the scene.

Nothing more, nothing less.

Heavy trip, man, to be where they make the magazine. I read it all the way since '67 when the first issue with Lennon on the cover got printed up. Big-ass lobby, and through a door a huge space with ceilings up in the stars, 7 or 8 foot tall partitions dividing the place into offices, and a big area where they paste the type and the photographs onto pages, and at the rear on the right a door with a glass panel and engraved on it: Jann S. Wenner.

He's the publisher *and* the editor. Jann S. Wenner. So that's his office, and it's locked. There's a big conference room, and a library with a wall of albums and a wall of books. I swear, swear on a pile of my favorite albums, *Blonde on Blonde* and *Pet Sounds* and *Revolver* and all the rest, my plan, gonna check the scene.

We get in there and Bobby all set to get to work. Rip shit off. I shoulda known, he's wearing the black suede outlaw jacket, and the more I see him in it, the more he looks same as a cheap-ass hood. Only I got nothing on Bobby that day 'cause soon enough I'm more than his accomplice. You know, rip shit off.

Before Bobby gets to work, he says what he always says. If Bobby gets dead and buried and they get a tombstone on his grave, these words they'll chisel into it: "Opportunity knocks, you better answer."

Shoulda been one of those decisive moments.

Only I don't think twice. Must've lifted 150 albums from the library, us two with our arms full lugging 'em to the car stash 'em in the trunk. Oh man, 'cause if we get caught, how fucked is that? Don't think I show it, but I sweat it out. I already been in trouble twice for trying to lift records. Yeah, outta record stores. Where the fuck else.

Bobby, man, made for this rip shit off deal. Cool as cool can be, says we go back for some hardbound rock books, and this jazz discography he knows sells for $50 a copy. We both get mint copies of the first issues which we already have but our copies are worn from reading and re-reading. Me knowing Bobby how I do, for sure he took some shit he didn't tell me about. Bobby being Bobby.

I'm freaking the whole time we go back up, and especially after we're in the office again and footsteps echo up the stairs. We're done for, gonna end up in juvey. Only whoever it is goes up to the fourth floor and turns on a radio, and we make our getaway.

So yeah, that's how we know about a magazine office.

That bright bright sun, man, just past overhead, and it's hot on the asphalt, middle of the street front of Number Nine Strawberry Lane. We stand and it's quiet, no cars coming, seems like no one comes or leaves this block, and we look to where the office of *Peak* magazine is, or supposed to be. I have the box with the extra large. Don't have a watch but it must be around 1:30, give or take. I can ask Bobby 'cause he has the Gramps Watch. He's a regular Mr. On Time. I don't ask. Don't wanna ask him anything.

I'm pissed and the reason I'm pissed is I can tell Bobby wants to split. How he's standing, looking at the asphalt, has that same smoke, fiddles with it, and there's maybe five feet, maybe a little more, between us. I look down the street past him, and the sun casts our shadows on the asphalt, and you know how a person's shadow can be way longer than the person, well those shadows look like a giant has some rectangle deal stands next to a short person. I see a long thin stick shadow come out from the short person's hand shadow.

I'm the giant, the pizza box the rectangle, Bobby the short person, and the thin stick shadow his smoke. Authentic real of it, I have six, maybe seven inches on Bobby, but 'cause of where I stand, 'cause of where he stands, 'cause of where the sun shines bright bright up overhead, huge giant long hair freakster bro shadow looms over that straight-ass-straight short-hair short-person shadow.

I see those two shadows, and they tell the story. It's another of those old stories been told over and over. Two freakster bros, one got the good luck, one got the bad. Yeah, in every way I got more than Bobby. Got Sarah, who by then was letting me fuck her, got a bigger house, got my dad still married to my mom, got my dad who got a decent job makes enough for us to live OK, got a car to use, got at least twice as many albums, got going to a good college to look forward to, and so on. Got it all, man.

Back then I always compare me to whoever I hang with, and always I come out on top. Every time. So yeah, look at those shadows and think I see the heavy traffic symbolism. One got the good luck, one got the bad. Wrong. 'Cause what I don't know back then is I have my share of the bad on the way. But the bad hasn't come yet, and that day all I know is I'm special and Bobby's a fuckin' loser.

Only reason me and him are freakster bros is the music. Even when it comes to music we always argue, almost never agree on anything. When I think of it, only one time we total agree. The Mothers of Invention's *Freak Out*. We righteous bond over that record when we first meet in eighth grade. Back then I figure if Bobby's into The Mothers, gotta be cool. Me and him the only ones in junior high ever heard of The Mothers. Well I was wrong 'cause it turns out nothing cool about Bobby.

Give the boxy place one last look before I'm gonna go ring the doorbell. The bright bright sun comes down on that fucked-up flaked paint house looks same as shit. Looks as if it got built in the late Fifties, a rental from the start. Stucco deal, the outside, and shit aluminum frame windows upstairs, and no windows downstairs, and no style.

I've got the guts, I've got the ego-inflated crazy-wild stand-up freakster bro guts, 'cause this is back when me and Sarah total heavy traffic in-love, and life only gonna get more and more groovy. Fearless, how I am. I walk toward the house, Bobby still there in the middle of the street.

"I could wait here for you," he says.

Starts in with his quiet smoker's cough, and I'm fed up with his stalling.

"Whoa!" I say. "I'm sure Boo Radley lives there," aim my index at his chest. "You should be *scared*, man."

Authentic real, Bobby *is* scared.

"Let's just split," he says.

Wow, Bobby is *intimidated* about meeting Sausalito Cowboy. Well fuck Bobby. This is my big break. Sausalito Cowboy my ticket to the big time.

Down the concrete steps, and there's a short concrete path with scraggly bushes need a trim job on either side, and I walk up to the front door. Bobby hops to it, he's scared but more scared if the word leaks he's chicken.

There's a wood frame screen door been painted white a long time ago, rips in the screen and a buzzer to the right of the door. Press the buzzer no sound, piece of masking tape under it, faded black letters: *Out of order.*

Right below on a piece of paper: *UPS, Please leave packages for Ted Larsen, Brandon Williams and Peak magazine.*

Open the screen door and the front door veneer cracked and peeling, and I knock loud, man, figure Sausalito Cowboy gotta be blasting some groovy new LP in there. Some groovy deal he's getting himself ready to review, tell the world all about, hip everybody to the New Trip.

"Fancy digs," Bobby says.

"Shut up, Bobby," I say.

I knock real the fuck loud this time, and muffled, through the fuck-up veneer-crack door, "Hold on, I'm coming!"

"I have to get back," Bobby says, "to my place before it gets dark."

Fucking 1:45 or so and he says that shit.

"You're such a pussy, man."

Bobby's reached his limit, the needle over in the red. Gets himself standing tall as he's able, which isn't tall at all, and gets his voice serious fake tough guy deal.

"Shut up, *Mike,*" he says, and yeah he knows it hellfuck bugs me getting called Mike, but this isn't the time for us going at each other so I say, "OK, Bobby."

I turn to the door, and he goes, "You *listen* to what I say," and I give him the what-the-fuck-now look so he knows *I'm* in the red zone. He tones his voice down two, three notches.

"I'm just telling you we have to split by 4:30," he says. "So I can get home in time for dinner. Mom gets mad if I'm late."

"What a fucking baby," I say, and I was gonna say more, only right in that moment we both shift gears 'cause the door swings open.

3. THE PAD

THERE HE IS, FADED black cowboy hat angled back, on the phone, got the receiver parked between his ear and shoulder.

"That's all you got for me?" he says into the phone, and stands in the doorway working his editor. First inkling I get that even a rock star critic gotta hustle. I figured a rock star critic lets the editors know what he'll review. Never knew 50 percent of being a writer is the hustle.

Until I meet Sausalito Cowboy.

He scopes out me and Bobby. The twice over once deal, sees the extra large, waves us in, and his hand covers the mouthpiece, talks to me same as I'm the pizza boy.

"You can put it over there on the table."

Us two wearing shades and it's dark as a cave.

"*Peak* magazine?" I say, and he nods this resigned nod, you know the deal, when life's too the fuck much, and nothing's going right.

"Look Jann, I'll review the Mountain album. But I'm not gonna say it's good 'cause it mostly sucks."

I step past Sausalito Cowboy into The Pad and he hasn't got any new music going, not playing any music at all. Through the picture window opposite wall down the hill out past all those industrial buildings below Bridgeway, the dark blue Bay. He kicks the door shut with his scuffed-up black cowboy boot.

"Yeah," he says into the phone. "I *know* Felix Pappalardi produced it. Big yawn."

Stands there in all his slummed-out, lazy-ass, overweight glory.

"*Only* if I can use a pseudonym, or you put *your* byline on it."

This is Sausalito Cowboy? Shoulda been the day I get a different idea about rock critics. Only I'm total blown away. All the years I trip out on the groovy ways rock critics write. Finally in the presence. Funky as he is, I see a star. But still, somewhere inside my brain I know rock critics aren't rock stars, they're schmucks. A schmuck with an opinion. Oh, excuse me, a schmuck with an ego big as China or Russia or at least Alaska, and an opinion. Later, much later, years later, I see the authentic real, but not that day.

Here's the authentic real coming at you from my future. His face a pudge, and a sweaty handlebar mustache and a clipped beard, and a pot belly bulges under his stained Commander Cody and the Lost Planet Airmen t-shirt, and over it a brown leather vest looks same as he never takes it off. Lived in, slept in, got drunk in. That brown leather vest discolored from sweat and food and booze. Authentic real, he looks same as that ornery cook on "Rawhide," you know, Wishbone.

Think about it now, I don't know what fantasy Sausalito Cowboy lived in. Parallel universe to King Editor.

He points to a green corduroy couch. We keep standing, don't wanna take off our shades 'cause we think the shades make us cool. He's on the phone, and he listens, doesn't dig what he hears. Takes a step toward what I guess is his desk near the kitchen door far side of the room. There's a table over there, and a typewriter on it. When my eyes adjust as best they can given they're still looking through dark green lenses, I see we're in what was once a living room, only that's before Sausalito Cowboy moved in, before he turned the room into a writer's study, before him and Buckaroo transformed the whole place into The Pad.

Bobby nudges me. "Check out all the records."

Oh fuck yeah.

There's an entire wall of books to the left of the front door, if you stand in the doorway and face the inside, face the couch. He has all the Big Men. Dostoyevsky and Faulkner and Hemingway and Sartre and Thomas Wolfe and Proust and Shakespeare and Camus and Huxley and on and on. He has history books, art books, poetry books, photography books, movie director books. And more. Books on nature and flowers and birds and psychology and drugs and geography and physics and psychics. Science fiction by Heinlein and Asimov and Bradbury, and all the private eye shit by Chandler and MacDonald and Thompson. History of the fucking world in that room.

Got the promo shit too. Pack of Led Zeppelin condoms on a book shelf, snow globe with a plastic Frank Zappa figure inside on the wooden wire spool table front of the green couch, along with piles of magazines, and next to the Zappa snow globe an Alice Cooper bottle opener. I want it, that bottle opener. I dig Alice. "I'm Eighteen" gotta be in the top ranks of teen anthems, up there with "My Generation" and "For What It's Worth."

And yeah, so you understand, this room got the vibe. The serious mojo vibe.

He's still working the phone, doing the rock critic hustle.

"Come on, Jann, give me a break."

He walks across the frayed purple and black oval rag rug that covers most of the hardwood. To his left, that tired-ass couch. He gets to the table with the typewriter, and that table got some serious mojo. It's an old oak table, and a groovy Royal manual sits on the mojo table.

Fuck, this is where he writes the record reviews I read. Sits in a Philip Marlowe office chair. Could be oak too, high back, no arms.

"I could talk to Brandon," he says. "But he doesn't like it either. He didn't even like *Disraeli Gears*."

Well for the first time I got a sense of what it was to be a writer. That day I felt waves of enlightenment. I understood. Only what I understood, it's wrong. See The Pad, see that writer's room, and I understood how a writer needs a groovy writing space, nothing fancy, but it gotta be a place he wants to spend a fuck-ass good long amount of time in, thick in the creative juice of chaos, channel the off-limit unmapped continents of the unconscious, let the live wire poetry of the cosmos course through him onto the page. That room, that day, and I knew it all. I could tell shit happens in that room. Kind of room Kerouac must have worked in or Salinger, that kinda vibe. A writer could turn blank pages to gold in that room.

Only all that I understand that day about being a writer is wrong. What I don't get is it's not the writer's room. It's not the mojo table. Or the Hemingway Royal Quiet Deluxe. Or walls of books and records. Or even a lucky leather vest. It's the writer, the writer with guts to get the authentic real down on the page.

A writer can do that anywhere, man.

Café. Park bench. Kitchen table.

Anywhere.

Bobby sits, green corduroy couch, black cat whose name we find out is Barkadelic, sniffs him. I clear space on the wooden spool table among copies of *Creem* and *Phonograph Record Magazine* and *Billboard*, set down the pizza box. Got my wide-eyed eyes going, check it all out, still lost in the smoke of rock critic glory.

Bobby kicks back, rubs Barkadelic's head and she settles on the couch arm. Bobby lights a Marlboro, doesn't even ask if it's OK. Bobby got chutzpah, gotta give him that. Picks up *Billboard*, and if there's one magazine on the planet Bobby give his right testicle to get a subscription to, it's *Billboard*. Only it costs a fortune.

"Gee, get this," he says, and Bobby is always saying "Gee, get this," as if it's some cool thing to say. "Led Zeppelin grossed over a hundred grand playing Madison Square Garden."

Sausalito Cowboy's got the faded black Stetson, brim angled up, and I see his hairline is way past what you call receding, you know, when you talk about some guy with a receding hairline. Turns out he doesn't have a hairline.

"It's the debut from Ron Nagle," he says, still talking into the phone. "Tom Donahue manages him. Yeah, Jann, *I know* Tom's a friend of yours. Nagle was in The Mystery Trend, remember them? Yeah *I know* The Mystery Trend sucked. This rocks, Jann. It's called *Bad Rice.*"

Raises his hand, gets the fingers and thumb to represent a mouth, open, close, open, close, the silent blah blah blah deal.

"Very funny. No Jann, I'm not talking about my lunch," he says, gearing up for the full-court press. "*Bad Rice* is the name of the album. Hear me out. Nitzsche produced, you know, Spector, the Stones, Neil Young. It's the smart shit, Jann. Really!"

His body slumps in the Marlowe chair, "Alright, just Mountain," and he hangs up. He stands, reaches his arms straight up in a stretch, reaches under the lucky vest pulls at a sweaty arm pit of his t-shirt, falls back into the chair, and looks to where Bobby puffs away right when some ash falls on the couch.

"So who have I invited in?" he says. "And what's with the shades?"

"The Pad is groovy, man," I say, and since he's blown our hipster trip, take off my shades and tell him my name only I see he doesn't know who I am, and Bobby already getting ash on the green corduroy and reading *Billboard* same as he lives here. "I wrote you, Mr. Larsen."

"You're *that* kid," he says. "Tryin' to be Meltzer."

"I guess," and that hand been scratching the sweaty arm pit reaches out. Oh man, he wants to shake my hand. Fuck yeah! I go for the iron man grip, you know the one. If you're a man you gotta have that grip or you're fucked, and even if I'm 16, and in high school, doesn't mean I let that shit skate.

"Welcome to The Pad, *Mike*," he says. "Call me Ted."

Hellfuck, him calling me *Mike,* and I gotta tell him right quick it's Michael, only before I do, coming from the kitchen a voice quiet, slow, Southern.

"Fuuuck thaaat," and he stretches out the syllables so you think he'll never get to the end of his words. "Cah-aaall hem tha Saaaus-ah-litah Cow-*boy.*"

Buckaroo in the doorway, almost a silhouette, the bright bright sun streams into the kitchen behind him. He looks at me through thick black-frame Michael Caine glasses.

"Tha wur-urld fay-muuus Saaaus-ah-litah Cow-*boy*," and raises his arms, holds onto the doorframe, leans into the room. "*Tha-aat's* whaaat his fra-ends cah-aall hem."

And he pauses for a beat. And another.

"All two of them."

He looks at Sausalito Cowboy and laughs.

"Almost got you an assignment outta Jann," Sausalito Cowboy says.

"*Almost* doesn't count," Buckaroo says, and steps into the room, the writer's room, and he's light on his feet, almost a wobble how he walks, same as he's dizzy. Sixteen, and I don't get it. Don't think about how Buckaroo's high flyin'. Yeah, so much I don't know back then.

"I thought rock critics listen to new music all day long," I say.

"Most of it's crap," Sausalito Cowboy says. "Makes me ill, listening to shit music. I leave it to Christgau. He listens to *everything*."

Buckaroo wears a Merle Haggard and the Strangers t-shirt. Restores my faith in my rock-critic-as-rock-star deal. Minus the glasses he's a double for Michael Clarke, the drummer in The Byrds, how Michael Clarke looked back in '65. You remember, right? When first "Mr. Tambourine Man" and later "Turn! Turn! Turn!" were on the radio.

"He *only* listens to new records he's *reviewing*," Buckaroo says. "Otherwise it's the tried and true."

Sausalito Cowboy gets front of this small table, front of the wall of records, and set on that table all by itself same as a totem, The Thorens. It's his turntable, and as he lifts the lid he looks to me and over to Bobby.

"*No one* touches The Thorens," he says. "Except me. Got that guys?"

It's as if the table's a throne and The Thorens is King.

Sausalito Cowboy gets *One Nation Underground* playing, you know, the Pearls Before Swine album with some of Hieronymus Bosch's "Garden of Delights" on the cover. It's the sound of acid, if acid has a sound, that album is. You know when you look down on water in a creek, quicksilver clear sunlight flash, and you see some rocks of the creek bed, tripped-out wild nature of that scene, well that's the sound of the first song, "Another Time," and it's so gentle, guitar notes floating up to the surface into the air, and Tom Rapp's voice, a psychedelic wise man singing of crystal swans and velvet ponds, enchanted glances and jewels in the sky, and this lyric about finding the world outside, inside your mind.

Sound of acid, man.

"Hungry?" Sausalito Cowboy says. "My new friends brought pizza."

"Gee, get this," Bobby says. "I wish I had a piece of this action. *Bridge Over Troubled Water* has been #1 for six weeks, and it's gone double platinum."

Sausalito Cowboy rotates his Philip Marlowe chair, folds the four fingers of his right hand over his palm and aims the thumb at Bobby as if hitching towards the couch.

"Who's your sidekick?"

"That's Bobby, man," I say. "Bobby's gonna manage rock bands—soon as he finds one worth managing. Know any?"

Buckaroo squints behind his Michael Caine glasses, scopes Bobby out, and all the time Buckaroo scopes Bobby he got his face screwed up—quizzical-times-two. Done scoping, Buckaroo steps past the Sausalito Cowboy, close to me talks total quiet confidential. No, not merely the confidential 'cause I also hear the paranoia-on-weed they're-coming-to-take-me-away voice, Southern-style.

"Not a narc is he?"

Man, Bobby never looked more like a narc than right then double-time focused on that *Billboard*.

"Bobby?" I say. "No man, he's a doobie head for sure. Smoke up any weed you got."

That's a lie, flat out. Bobby didn't smoke weed back then. Not 'til later he gets into the reefer madness. Not 'til later we all get into the reefer madness.

Sausalito Cowboy joins in, "Why's he look so straight? And what's with the shades?"

Buckaroo next to me, I smell the reefer he's been smoking, raises his voice too too stoned-loud.

"Hey straight man."

Bobby has that you-mean-me look going.

"Yeah," Buckaroo says. "You. *Straight man*. I'm talking to. You need to grow it out, bro. I thought you were a narc for Christ's sake, especially wearing those shades in here. How y'all expect the musicians to take you seriously, *straight man?*"

Bobby closes the magazine, takes off his shades, gets a cigarette in his left hand, then his right, back forth, back forth. And knowing Bobby, he's getting up the guts to say some shit.

Sausalito Cowboy got an echo of a smile.

"I'd think twice about wearing that jacket, *straight man*."

They think it's funny, call Bobby *straight man*. It is funny. If you happen to be stoned.

"Really, brother," Buckaroo says, and he's still scoping Bobby. "Where you get the jacket? You look like a second-story man."

"Second-story man," Sausalito Cowboy says. "Exactly."

Bobby pushes his fingers back through his hair, only he doesn't have any. Well hardly any. Hair. It's mostly cut off. So he scratches his head, as if he has an itch, him being self-conscious about running his fingers through the hair he doesn't have.

"Bill Graham doesn't look like a *freak*," Bobby says, puts *Billboard* down, and gives a hard look to those two. "*He's* got at least a million bucks in some Swiss bank account. He drives Writerman's favorite car, a Jag. Silver-grey Jag."

Sausalito Cowboy checks the pockets of his lucky vest, at first doesn't find anything, desperate vibe, only he strikes gold, gets out a bent Camel.

"What's Bill Graham got to do with you looking like a narc, *straight man?*"

Bobby digs a matchbook out of his jacket, rips out a match and strikes it. "What it has to do with," he says, and we see the blue-gold flame off that match and his Marlboro lit, and he says, "Doesn't look to me," and holds the match right there, front of him, flame burning the cardboard toward his fingers, "like present company," flame burning down down down the match, "has a Swiss bank account," tosses the flaming match at the ashtray, misses, lands on the table and he jams his thumb on it, picks up the dead match drops it in the ashtray and looks from Buckaroo to Sausalito Cowboy. "*Or* a Jag." Leans back into the couch, cigarette to his lips, the big inhale, has that rip shit off smile happening, trumped the whole scene.

Trumped it, man.

Hellfuck bummers me out. Bobby with his bluster and the match burn on the table and his rip shit off smile. He could really fuck things up for me with Sausalito Cowboy and Buckaroo.

"Yeah," Bobby says. "Tell them how much you want a Jag like the one Bill Graham drives, Writerman."

"I can't believe your Bill Graham fixation," I say.

"Writerman?" Sausalito Cowboy says.

And I try to be cool.

"Some people call me that," I say kinda quiet.

"Second-story man and Writerman," Buckaroo says. "You two gotta be quite a pair."

Goddamn Bobby, now these rock star critics laugh at me too. Such a fucker. Only once they get over laughing about it, they start calling me Writerman, same as it's my name. Total serious deal. Total cool scene.

"Writerman's one to talk about fixations," Bobby says. "Spent a year trying to get his hair like Lennon."

"Yeah, well, Lennon's cool," I say. "Bill Graham *sucks.*"

"You know Graham doesn't even like rock music," Sausalito Cowboy says, and Buckaroo can't believe Bobby thinks a businessman asshole is cool.

"Graham is *only* in it for the money," Buckaroo says.

Barkadelic sits herself down on that pizza box. Sausalito Cowboy's Camel lit, ash falls on the vest.

"Money and *fame,*" he says.

Bobby has that defensive sound, "Bill Graham's into jazz," and what the fuck does Bill Graham digging jazz have to do with anything? "I read an interview," Bobby says. "His favorite album is *Sketches of Spain.*"

Bobby leans forward, smoke between his lips, slaps his hands together right close to Barkadelic, and the cat goes leaping off the pizza box, and Sausalito Cowboy says, "Graham didn't know Miles from Monk when he hustled his first concert."

"Bill Graham got Miles to play the Fillmore," I say. "Both of them."

"Only because Kantner hipped him," Buckaroo says. "Told Bill Miles was cool with the heads."

"*Money* and fame," Sausalito Cowboy says, and that wakes Bobby up. "And chicks. For a while Graham had this 16-year-old babe he was fucking. You should have seen the tits on her. Out to here! She hung out at The Fillmore all the time."

Well that was one of those decisive moments for Bobby.

And is he in, or out? Stand tall for what he thinks, or cave? He looks to me, looks to Buckaroo, looks to Sausalito Cowboy.

"And what of it," he says. "This is America. Everybody dreams of making it rich."

Authentic real hard guy look. Bores in on me, moves to Buckaroo and finally Sausalito Cowboy.

"Bill Graham," Bobby says. "*He* made the dream happen."

Oh man, Bobby trumps the scene all over again, and the writer's room on hold. None of us, not me, not Sausalito Cowboy, and not Buckaroo can argue with what Bobby said, 'cause what he said, authentic real of it, it's the truth.

Me, yeah I wanna to be rich same as the rock stars. Sausalito Cowboy, he wanna be a rich and famous writer. Buckaroo, he wants the fame and fortune too. Same as Bill Graham. We all have our reasons, we all have our rationalizations, we all know we're not in it for the money, we just *want* the money. Too. Don't wanna sell out, but *want* the money. Too. Easy to put Bill Graham down. Easy. He wanted to be an actor, but ended up in the make money business selling rock shows. And t-shirts. And posters.

"You run *Peak* magazine out of here?" I say, and Sausalito Cowboy comes out of whatever distant place that talk of fame and fortune took him.

"There's a bit of a snafu," he says. "Jenkins ran out of dough. The publisher. Everything's on hold."

"Bummer, man."

"Welcome to the magazine business," Sausalito Cowboy says.

Only it really is a bummer 'cause I figure Sausalito Cowboy gonna give me writer tips and soon enough I'm writing for *Peak* magazine.

D.O.A., my plan, man.

Buckaroo got the lost face going, as if he been off in some interior world too, maybe trip on what life be like with Bill Graham's bucks.

Hellfuck if I know.

"You're better off pumping gas than trying to break into the music business," Buckaroo says to Bobby. "You know the odds for a band to make it? Million to one. Actually, more like two million. Or three."

Bobby is happening, how he's got his head up, greedy glint in his eyes. Still high on trumping the scene. Plus nothing Bobby loves more than to talk talk talk the music business.

"Get this," he says. "Maybe I'll hook up with a band that's *already* made it."

Sausalito Cowboy points a stubby finger at the wooden spool table. "Or maybe the next Led Zeppelin gonna fly out my ass," and he snorts, "What's in the box, Writerman?"

"Extra large pepperoni," I say. "With mushrooms and olives and heavy on the onions."

I'd say he lights up same as that huge Christmas tree they

have in Union Square each year, only that would be such a sad
sack square metaphor, even to say it as a joke makes me puke.
No, it's same as Sausalito Cowboy got himself a plum
assignment, or snorts up a line.

"Score! Let me get us some plates."

He's off to the kitchen, banging cabinet doors and drawers.

"Buckaroo?" I say.

And that slow molasses laugh.

"Yeah, one of those names that stick," he says. "You heard
of Buck Owens and the Buckaroos? I wrote a live review when
they played The Palomino in L.A. I guess Buck liked that review
big time 'cause his publicist called me up, put Buck on the
phone and he said he'd made me an honorary Buckaroo."

Up close he's got a couple days of beard going, and the
bloodshot hazel eyes from too little sleep and too much reefer.

"On my driver's license," he says. "Brandon Williams."

I been reading his stuff almost long as I been reading the
Sausalito Cowboy. He's serious into country, and I bought *Okie
From Muskogee* after reading his review. Trip me out, the power
of words on a page. The right words, in the right order,
goddamn goddamn goddamn. Sausalito Cowboy, or Buckaroo
or Meltzer, oh man, I could read their words all of the night and
all of the day. Right then, Buckaroo there in the writer's room,
and Sausalito Cowboy making noise in the kitchen, star struck,
man. How am I ever gonna write the kinda words they print in
magazines? Overwhelming heavy traffic rock critic words.
Those words Buckaroo and Sausalito Cowboy write gotta be
$100 words. At least. Maybe $150 words.

Some of those Kerouac words—priceless.

Buckaroo gets himself comfortable on the couch, leaves
space between him and Bobby, bare feet on the table.

"Pizza better be good," he says.

"What it's going to be is cold," Bobby says.

Yeah, rock critics don't get much sun, sit inside hunched
over their Royal typewriters. Inside. No sun. Everything has a
price. Everything.

"Cold pizza is better than no pizza," Buckaroo says.

"Especially if you have the munchies," and more slow stoned molasses laughter, and he's gonna reach forward, open the box but Buckaroo is fuck-up lazy, man, and fuck-up stoned, and he lies back sunk into the fuck-up couch, waits for Sausalito Cowboy to show with the plates.

"What's with all this cowboy shit," Bobby says. "The hat and that nickname. Is he from Texas?"

"Buffalo, New York," Buckaroo says, and even I know they don't have cowboys in Buffalo.

"What are you sayin'?" I say. "You mean he's same as Ramblin' Jack Elliott?"

Don't hear anything from the kitchen, only I'm smelling the smell of weed mixed into the smoke of Bobby's cigarette.

"It was Meltzer's fault."

I try the Philip Marlowe chair.

"Meltzer's a friend of yours?"

"Pain in the ass is more like it," Buckaroo says. "Meltzer started calling him Sausalito Cowboy. As a joke."

I sit there, Hemingway Royal front of me, fuck, these guys know Meltzer!

"But it's not funny," I say, and I stand, I mean Sausalito Cowboy probably doesn't dig anyone sitting in the Marlowe chair. At his mojo table. Front of his special typewriter.

"Course it is," Buckaroo says. "The joke is, there are no cowboys in Sausalito."

And that's when I see it behind the typewriter. A manuscript. Step in close to the table to see better and on the cover sheet all caps:

THE FLOWERS LIED
BY THEODORE LARDUSKY

"'The Flowers Lied?'" I say.

Buckaroo pulls his knees up to his chest, gets his bare feet off the table and rests them on the edge of the couch seat, arms around his knees.

"His novel," he says. "Four fucking years."

"Wow," I say. "What's it about, man?"

Coming through the doorway with two cans of Bud, a couple of long-neck bottles, paper plates and a roll of paper towels, Sausalito Cowboy sings, "What's it all about, Alfie?" and his voice changes to the Lamont Cranston mysterioso deal. "The *truth.*"

He heads for the wooden spool table, and for sure I catch the smell of reefer. And is reefer the new booze, but I mean these guys drink too, so I guess if reefer's the new booze and booze is the old booze, and what the fuck point am I trying to make, and maybe I've got a contact high, and Sausalito Cowboy says, "Hemingway wrote, 'All you have to do is write one true sentence,' but I say you better make 'em all true."

He sets all that shit on the table. "I'm not going to offer you guys beer 'cause you're under age," he says. "But if you were to happen to drink one I'm sure neither myself nor Buckaroo would turn you in."

Buckaroo lets go of his legs, covers his eyes with his hands, then his ears, then his mouth.

"See no evil, hear no evil, speak no evil."

Sausalito Cowboy pulls a couple chairs up to the table. Gets a Bud and pops the top. Bobby piles two slices onto a plate. He doesn't drink in addition to not smoking reefer on account of he doesn't wanna fog how he thinks. Far as I see it, fog the way he thinks exactly what Bobby needs to get his head outta all that music-biz make-money rip shit off trip, and get in touch with the authentic real. Trip out on the music, man, not the big money the music makes.

Yeah well Bobby doesn't care what I think about his music biz trip, and that's an old story too.

Me and Sausalito Cowboy and Buckaroo get ourselves some pizza, load the cold slices onto paper plates.

"So I'm whoring again," Sausalito Cowboy says.

Barkadelic jumps on the table, heads for the pizza box, but Buckaroo reaches out, closes the lid. Sausalito Cowboy has a slice between his thumb and the other fingers, drips tomato sauce and cheese on his vest. The cat steps onto the pizza box lid, begins to scratch.

"Let's see," Buckaroo says. "As I recall, the Sausalito Cowboy byline has graced reviews in which you've lauded the 'leaden thunder' of Deep Purple's *In Rock*, the 'surprisingly listenable pop sound' of Scott McKenzie's *Stained Glass Morning* and the 'childlike wonder' of Melanie's *Candles in the Rain*."

Buckaroo has a longneck bottle in one hand, slice in the other, paper plate on his lap. "*Now* what shitty record are you gonna foist on your unsuspecting readers? As John once asked of Paul, how do you sleep at night?"

Sausalito Cowboy's too too loud nervous laugh.

"Imagine all those fans of yours," Buckaroo says. "Naïvely trusting Sausalito Cowboy's advice that they pick up a copy, '*post haste*' I believe were your words, of Bread's *On the Waters*."

"Guilty!" Sausalito Cowboy says. "Off with my head! Meltzer's right. We're all whores. Fucking whores. It just gets down to the price," and he's not laughing, and his cold steel eyes bore in on his buddy. "What's *your* price Buckaroo? A gig at *Time*? A book deal? A metallic blue Corvette like the one Spector bought after 'To Know Him Is to Love Him' became his first hit?"

Cold steel eyes shift in my direction.

"Is straight man right, Writerman?" Sausalito Cowboy says. "Are we all in it for the money?"

Oh man, and it's hopeless, we're all doomed, and what can I say? I don't know, don't know man, just don't know. Nothing easy in this world. Nothing easy that matters.

Buckaroo doesn't like the crust, eats his first piece right up to the crust, places the crust on his plate, but that's cool 'cause Sausalito Cowboy digs it. The crust.

"The Devil hasn't made me an offer yet," Buckaroo says.

Sausalito Cowboy picks up Buckaroo's crust, takes a bite as if it was a bread stick, lets out a belch.

"Fitzgerald was a whore for Christ's sake," he says.

I feel the beer.

"Salinger wasn't," I say, and another drink, got plenty more guts. "Kerouac wasn't."

"Kerouac drank up all his talent," Sausalito Cowboy says. "He wrote one good novel. The rest are crap."

You know how we all got quiet when Bobby said what he said about America and making it rich? Right in that moment, the four of us were in silent mourning about the waste of a true and authentic real talent.

For a while the only sound, aside from the gentle kaleidoscopic strum, dazed Farfisa tones and warped slowmo incantations coming from Pearls Before Swine, was the three of us eating pizza, guzzling beer. I guess we all think about wasted talent, I know I do, and are we wasting ours?

"When my novel gets published," Sausalito Cowboy says. "Then I'll call the shots. Like Hemingway."

"When is it getting published?" Bobby says.

Sausalito Cowboy looks past Bobby and Buckaroo, looks out the window, somewhere in the distance, maybe at the Bay.

"It's not finished," Buckaroo says. "He doesn't have a publisher. He's rewritten it three times."

Sausalito Cowboy squeezes his empty beer can hard, drops it onto the table same as a dead thing. "I'll finish," he says, not talking to any of us. Looking off. Yeah, as if he's looking out the window. "I'll *damn* well finish."

"He can't get an agent interested," Buckaroo says.

"But man," I say. "You're a *star.*"

Sausalito Cowboy hears me, and he can't help it, big grin.

"You're *Sausalito Cowboy*, man," I say and he's aglow in my admiration, and that blows my mind 'cause I don't have a clue about ego. Figure freakster bros same as Sausalito Cowboy and Buckaroo don't care what people think, secure in their own self-confidence. Wrong again.

"You want the last beer, Writerman?" Sausalito Cowboy says.

I pass, and he picks up the can, pops the top.

"You're betraying your naïveté," Buckaroo says. "Maybe Santa could drop down the chimney and leave him a publishing deal. Oops, scratch that, we don't have a chimney."

"All they want from me is a rock star bio."

For once Bobby isn't an asshole.

"You have to start somewhere," he says, and I guess that day we both get clued in that a rock critic isn't exactly high on the totem pole hierarchy of writers.

Sausalito Cowboy stubs out the cigarette, picks Barkadelic up off the pizza box, sets her on the rag rug, helps himself to another slice.

"Three Dog Night," he says.

"St. Martins," Buckaroo says.

"Oh yeah," I say. "They publish a lot of rock books."

Buckaroo wipes his hand, the hand he been using to hold his pizza slices, on his cords. "They wanted him to crank out a quickie bio."

Bobby puffs up 'cause now we're on his turf again.

"Gee, get this," he says. "Three Dog Night have charted five Top 40 hits and there's a lot of anticipation in the biz about their upcoming album. Could be a smart move."

Sausalito Cowboy tosses his plate on the table, stands, pizza crumbs falling on the rug.

"Fucking bullshit. Thanks for the pizza, guys. Gotta get back to whoring."

He walks to the mojo table, takes a seat. Only he doesn't start to write, looks past the Hemingway Royal and his manuscript, out toward the Bay again, only somehow I know he's not seeing the Bay.

"You know what they say," Buckaroo says. "About a writer without an editor?"

I lean forward. "What do they say, *man?*"

Sausalito Cowboy laughs his too too loud sarcastic-meets-the-cynical laugh, and Buckaroo laughs his slow Southern molasses laugh.

They laugh at me.

"Nothing," Buckaroo says. "No one says anything about 'em."

4. PEACH BRANDY

SURVEY MY ROOM AND it's major lacking in mojo vibe quotient. Truth of it, my room got the negative mojo vibe. It's not a writer's room. The particleboard desk got minus-zero mojo and same for the Smith-Corona. Still, this is the room I've got. If I'm gonna write, if I'm gonna deal with King Editor's dreaded red ink, this is where I do it. Only first I gotta get the booze to be an authentic real writer.

AUTHENTIC REAL *GREAT* WRITER.

Great writers always have the booze. Hemingway, Fitzgerald, Joyce. Kerouac, Faulkner, Poe. Bukowski, London, Melville. And so on. Only I don't dig the booze. Well times change, and I gotta change.

So onward to Liquor King, baby.

Some evil genius locates Liquor King a few blocks south of the campus in a former 7-Eleven, a squat-ass rectangular building painted dirty gray with a parking lot on the side and a big sign up high flashing "Liquor King" on/off on/off on/off in too too bright too too loud too too red neon. As if they need to draw attention. This close to campus you could hide the place in a cave and everyone would find it.

I'm 19, and in California a person gotta be 21, so I've never bought booze. No problem there on account of my fake ID. Polanski did me a solid. Happy Birthday, Writerman, and for once the inauthentic fake beats the authentic real.

Inside the fluorescent lights cast a sickly green fog. I walk fast and confident right up to this greasy-haired surfer type behind the counter, and my voice deepest deep and gruffest gruff.

"Bottle of peach brandy, *buddy*, Pall Malls, and some Zig-Zags."

Liquor Store's a skinny motherfucker, got his head in a book.

"Hold on, brother, gotta finish the page," Liquor Store says, and that gives me an edge up.

He gotta be 22, 23. Hawaiian print baggies, rubber thongs and a light yellow t-shirt with a faded Iron Cross on it. Sure he has a name, but I don't know it. Liquor Store, that's his name. Shoulda called him anti-Semitic motherfucker. Where do surfers and bikers get off wearing the Iron Cross when it's red with the blood of six million?

Up close Liquor Store has the clean-shaven smooth-ass baby face and Hitler Youth eyes. He's reading Kierkegaard's "The Concept of Dread," another edge up 'cause I know that book, read excerpts in philosophy class freshman year. Liquor Store's into it. Mesmerized by the hocus-pocus.

When he speaks he has the breathless brainiac sound. "He's a *genius*. He said anxiety is the dizziness of freedom, and freedom succumbs in this dizziness. Heavy cosmos, brother. Never saw it *that* way. Explains plenty."

"Fascinating," I say, and I'm using my edge, fired the first putdown. "How 'bout getting me my booze, cigs and papers, and once I'm out of here you can re-arrange your world view all you want."

Liquor Store emerges from his Kierkegaardian trance.

"Peach brandy, huh?" and now he has the edge. "That's a joke, right brother? I have a fine Korbel goes down smooth."

In certitude lies victory, gotta keep cool, talk tough, and I'm Philip Marlowe. Yeah, the Philip Marlowe of great writers gonna pin Liquor Store's ears to the wall.

"Need a hearing aid, fella?"

He slows to quarter speed, no hurry for a chump asking for peach brandy.

"Something wrong?" I say. "Is there a secret handshake?"

"Nothin' wrong, brother. Don't get huffy. It's just—*peach* brandy? First time buying?" and I begin to doubt this enterprise. He's gonna card me. "Imagine a sickly sweet syrup that'll get you drunk, but might make you barf before you get there."

Oh he knows I never bought even an ounce of booze. He gotta see I'm not 21.

"Look, if I want a lecture I'll go to class. Got things to do. I'm a serious writer, man.

One beat, two.

"Authentic real of it, people call me *Writerman.*"

"Writerman?" he says. "*Writerman?* Is that like being a writer version of Spiderman? You have a *Writerman* outfit? Big W on your chest? You leave the cape and tights in the car?"

Oh man, he has the Liquor Store *smirk* on his baby face, and that smirk was same as he calls me Mike, only it's worse, it's how he conveys utter disdain, only worse still, the Liquor Store smirk means I'm not worth his disdain, it's as if I've been downgraded to less than zero.

"You have proof you're 21, *Writerman?*"

Oh fuck oh fuck oh fuck.

Zen White Wall Meditation. *One.* "You're kidding?"

"Yeah, I'll need your license."

Two. And I've got two choices. First, my whole body voting for it, get gone baby gone. Only that'll forever blow my scene at Liquor King. Or choice number two, gut it out, stick to the plan. When anxiety sets in, even Kierkegaard would agree, gotta stick to the plan. Pull my fucking wallet from my fucking pocket, and toss my fucking fake license onto the fucking counter.

"Got things to do, *man.*"

"And what would that be, brother? Save some commas from being misused?"

Liquor Store's an SS interrogator in t-shirt, baggies and rubber thongs. Picks up the license, holds it maybe an inch from his left eye, checks to see I have the anxiety times two, gets it front of his right eye. All he cares about is freaking me. He's not even looking at the license. Turns it this way and that but his eyes stay on me.

"I have a magnifying glass here somewhere."

"You know he was anti-Semitic," I say, and that's when we have the stare-down, his blue eyes zero on my brown eyes, and whoever blinks first is a wimp-ass pussy. He's got the iron man stare going, only that's when I use my edge again.

"You hear me, *brother?* Kierkegaard was anti-Semitic."

And the anxiety of guilt seeps into him.

Three. I look through his eyes at my imaginary white wall. He's a ghost, and all I see is the white wall and I can stare at it all night long if need be.

"That's not true, brother," but there's no certainty in his voice.

"Iron Cross is same as a swastika," I say, and that does it— Liquor Store blinks.

"Hey, I don't hate anyone," he says. "I was only trying to help. You drink that shit gonna get a hangover that won't quit."

He hands my license back, and rings me up.

And as I'm about to pass through the doorway and out of his life, "Hey *Writerman.*"

I turn to see he has the Liquor Store smirk going, and he's ready to crack up big time.

"Good luck writing your *Great American Novel.*"

I put the bottle down too hard on my pathetic desk. The bottle is dark brown, has a shiny gold foil label and a drawing of an orange and gold peach. Unscrew the tin lid, drink of the holy nectar.

Oh it's righteous. Sweet, but what a kick. Another swig, a bigger swig, this is more like it. I'm master of my destiny. I'M THE MAN! I do as I please and if I want to buy peach brandy I buy peach brandy. Big-ass swig. "Oh I got your number you dizzy-ass Kierkegaardian smirkface loser. Don't mess with me, Liquor Store. *Writerman* answers to *no one.*"

I must have drunk half the bottle before I start typing. Only soon after my preliminary swigs what tasted sweet at first tastes same as fruit gone bad and I'm yelling at the walls.

"Fuck you smirkface. I'll drink peach brandy if I fucking wanna."

Still, I hear the put-down sound. *Hey Writerman. Good luck writing your Great American Novel.* Another swig to clear my head, and still another.

Finally I'm ready to write.

Get a fresh sheet of paper in the typewriter stare at the blank page. The white blankness. Not a word. Cool calm sarcastic put-down sound, *Hey Writerman. Good luck writing your Great American Novel,* and that's when I remember.

I'm not writing my novel.

I journey 'cross the room, get *Clear Spot* playing. Cranked loud, the Captain sings his Dada poetry about some *lo yo yo stuff.*

And I'm shouting at the walls.

"Yeah, baby!"

I'm dancing to the swamped-out rhythm. "Do the fucking lo-ass *gonna booglarize you* boogaloo, King Editor, you bloodless corduroy-jacketed twit, and you too smirkface. Someone oughta throw the both of you into a cell—the same cell. Show you how a real writer does it. A *great* writer!"

Another swig, another Pall Mall 'til it starts to burn the yellow nicotine into my fingers, and I type:

Yeah, man, me and Beefheart, we go way back. Let me tell ya 'bout it.

Rip the page out, crumple it into a ball, and into the trash.

*When future generations look back on the Seventies they will marvel that music as wondrous as that found on Clear Sp*ot—-.

Rip, crumple, trash.

Writing's hard work, and I'm so tired. Maybe coffee and another smoke the way to go. Only it's too late. The Owl—that's the Arts College café—is closed. Hard to keep the eyelids open, but still I type:

In the darkest hours do you wonder if that chick you dig the most is in bed doing her lo yo yo stuff with some smirkface loser? Getting down with him when it oughta be you?

Rip, crumple, trash.

Beefheart yells loud. *Sun Zoom Spark!*

That's when I get it. Words aren't up to expressing what I hear. Beyond words. Words are the sound of lips moving transcribed onto the white blankness. Forget words. A human either mainlines the Captain's sound, or he's a smirkface loser.

Gotta let the sound fill my soul.

I hear the shiver of slide guitar, strings quiver, glass against metal, a high lonesome sound echoing up from life's beginnings. Hear the wisdom of wild nature. Hear the DNA of soul and spirit. When the first side is over I flip it and the title track starts. The Captain sings about running so far to find himself a *clear spot*.

Isn't it what we all need? Clear away the noise, and get to a *clear spot?*

Oh I am so ready to write. Finally I understand. Clear as day, clear as glass, clear as the Captain's *clear spot*. So much to get down on the page. Just one more swig, well, perhaps one more after that last one, and another, and maybe the smart move is to take a short rest before I get down to the real work. I stand, the room begins to tilt, and I'm gone baby gone.

Past noon when I wake. Coffee! I need coffee. Some guy with a hammer pounds away inside my head. I get my Keith Richards snakeskin boots on. Same boots as Keith wore during the '69 tour and at Altamont. Front of the mirror see what a half-pint of peach brandy done.

Down the hall, past the lounge and I step out to the landing. Blasted by the bright sun. And that makes the guy with the hammer get a buddy to join in. Left my shades in the room. Oh I am fucked. Everything gone to shit. My one-night-stand chick Harper disappearing on me, the *dreaded red ink*, that smirkface loser, and my inability to write *one true word*.

Wave of the dizzies, fuck you Kierkegaard, hold onto the handrail, and from down in the quad comes *that* voice. Can't sing but sings all the same. Sings a blues, a Skippy James blues, the one Cream covered in '66.

I'm so glad, I'm so glad, I'm glad, I'm glad, I'm glad.

Down three flights, do my best to forget the guys with

hammers, step out into the bright bright. A blur of guys and chicks walking past, talking fast. Of tentative new love and philosophical debate and the mundane chitchat of what are you taking this semester.

And this guy sings.

Don't know what to do. I don't know what to do.

Ghost of 'lectricity. High haunted voice come at you from 1931. Scratched and distorted. Skippy James. That's what everyone called him. Except Paramount Records. They got it wrong. Got it down as Skip James. Still, doesn't take away from who he is. Greatest of the great blues men. No one does the blues same as Skippy James. And the joke's on us. I mean Paramount records him—"Devil Got My Woman" and "Hard Time Killin' Floor Blues" and "Special Rider Blues" and the rest—but same as a bad sign the Great Depression arrives. No one who buys blues 78s has money to burn. And so Skippy James doesn't record again, not for over 30 years, early '60s, and by then he's a bitter old man.

Listen to those Paramount recordings now, what you hear is a spooked sound that never exists again. Skippy James was cold and hard and mean. He was a pimp, a gambler and a bootlegger. He carried a revolver and a switchblade. Some believe he killed a man, and maybe more than one. All of that you hear in his strange high moan.

"I'm So Glad," nothing glad about it. It's a song about how Skippy James thinks he'll be happy if he gets the chick. He's so tired of weeping, so tired of moaning, so tired of groaning. All because of a chick. All because of the wanting. Isn't it always 'cause of a chick? Oldest story there is. Think about it. If you believe the Bible, and I don't, but if you do, starts right with the first chick. Starts with Eve, and ends with Eve.

"Writerman!"

The mess of him stands and stares through mirror shades.

"Well look what the mangy hound dragged out into this most glorious and sun drenched day," he says, and through my

squint I see Jim Costello, *Thee* Freakster Bro, who I met a week
or so ago, the weekend I arrived at The University for the start
of sophomore year.

"Just the gentleman I need to speak to," he says.

His big hand heavy on my shoulder, and his big grin, and a
reprieve from the lonesome. I go from bummerosity to feeling
OK. He sticks the shades in the bird's nest got bloodshot reefer
eyes worse than the first time I seen him.

"Care to join me for coffee and a smoke?"

And he looks at me.

"You're a mess, old sport," and rubs his belly through his
Black Sabbath t-shirt.

Old sport? Yeah calling everyone old sport as if he's Gatsby is
one of Jim's affectations, along with the way he blows smoke
rings up into the air above his face when he smokes. Jim writes
reviews for *The Paper* same as me, but his main deal, he's a poet.

I know I look same as shit, but he's worse. He's been caught
in a windstorm and that doesn't account for the Sabbath t-shirt,
spaghetti and meatballs smeared on it. He looks down at his
shirt, rubs at the stain as if his stubby fingers can fix that mess.

"Well now—ah—ahem," Jim says. "Been up all night."

And he gives me that same dotted-lines eyes look he gave
me the first day we met.

The freakster bro dotted-lines eyes.

It's a way we look at each other where we stone cold
connect. If one of us gives the other that look it usually means
we're both on the same page. But not always. Sometimes it
means, *hold on bro, even if you don't get it, soon enough you will. Hear
me out, and dig the authentic real of what I say.*

"Writing the Great American Poem," he says. "Ginsberg
will be a footnote after they peruse my iambic pentameter."

Oh man, Jim has the Hemingway Royal, and the words fall
onto the page. He writes the heavy traffic epic poem, and I
write zero.

"So how's the novel going?"

"Goin' nowhere," I say. "Can't get started. It's all in my
head. It's a love story."

"Aren't they all?" he says.

"It's about a freakster bro wakes up to what's beneath the surface of the surface."

"There's your title," he says. "Beneath the Surface of the Surface."

"Now all I need are the 350 pages that come after it."

And I don't wanna talk about a novel I can't seem to start writing.

"My Beefheart rewrite," I say. "It's killin' me, man."

He gives me the I-been-there-bro smile.

"Just the topic I must confer with you on," he says. "Far-fetched as it might seem, the idiot King had the audacity to ask *me* for a rewrite."

He takes his mirror shades out of the bird's nest, gets them on, and he's got a buzz-ass energy same as he drank too much coffee, and I've got it too as we cross the quad.

We walk past the student art gallery, X Marks The Spot, where I had some photos of chicks on exhibit freshman year. The "fuck-me photos." That's what Simone called them. Oh yeah, you haven't met Simone, who became the older woman in my life. Way older. She was 35 and I was 19 when we first slept together. That's not her name, it's what I called her, you know, because she's such a hardcore feminist. Ms. Susan Braveheart. That's her name. I'll tell you about her later. Much later. Anyway, that's what they were.

Fuck-me photos.

Photos where I tried to get these groovy freshman chicks to look sexy. You know, the subtle but provocative temptress vibe. The look that elicits the Male Gaze.

Actually, between me and you, taking those photos were my excuse to meet chicks. Get something going, or at least get laid.

Good luck with that one.

The Owl is between the gallery and the dining hall, one of those faux hipster places with small square wood tables and worn wood chairs, Pollock and Kline and de Kooning posters on the walls along with some huge photo posters of Ginsberg and Kerouac and that photo of Burroughs holding a rifle. Burroughs, man, what a loser. I'd read about how he shot his first wife playin' William Tell in Mexico, and yeah she died.

I mean that was fucked up for sure.

Still, Burroughs can write. And what a voice!

We go into The Owl, get two coffees, and Jim says, "Let's retire to a table, old sport."

We walk across the room, Sam Rivers blowin' on the stereo. "Fuchsia Swing Song." Still in his early Sixties hard bop phase, but there's moments when he breaks free, his solo portends the wild dissonance that came later. Me and Jim agree on a table with a window view of the meadow, and after we sit Jim gets his hands around an invisible sax, fingers fly over invisible keys mimicking Rivers' grooved-out solo.

"Coltrane, Writerman," Jim says. "Too bad junk did him in."

I look at Jim 'cause this is serious. He's off his game. I mean a freakster bro can't fuck up same as that when it comes to the heavy shit.

"It's Sam Rivers, Jim," I say. "You're hip to 'Fuchsia Swing Song,' right?"

He's stricken, man, but reels himself back in.

"Of course, old sport. Slip of the tongue. Sam Rivers it is. Never a doubt in my cranial cerebrum," he says, only he's wrong about Coltrane too. Sure Coltrane was the serious junkie, but it's not clear junk was the silver bullet. Coltrane died of liver cancer.

Jim has his hands around his cup of black coffee, he likes to feel the heat. *Thee* Freakster Bro is buzzing, the buzz of too many drugs and smokes and too little sleep, and he gets some folded pages from his pocket. Unfolds 'em and unfolds 'em again and unfolds 'em one more time.

"The best I've yet written," he says.

Plenty *dreaded red ink.*

"Pure genius," he says. "I compare *Black Sabbath, Vol. 4* to 'The Waste Land,'" and hands me the pages. "The only way King Editor can respond to brave new ideas is circle them with his red pen and scrawl a few question marks. He's a sad case."

While I read it he's smoking and muttering blasphemies

about King Editor. Well what he's going for is a stretch. Still. He's got some mighty brass balls to write about one of the world's greatest poets and one of rock's most marginal bands in the same essay. Before I say a word, it's one of those decisive moments. Well I gotta be honest if we're gonna be friends.

"Jim, he's not criticizing your thesis," I say. "He's got a problem with the, quote, overly dramatic, comic book-style writing, the ornate gothic imagery, the over indulgence of language use, unquote."

Jim wipes his sweaty forehead.

"I dig what you're saying here, man," I say. "But I wonder about this: *Like a bitch in heat who attracts the amorous testosterone-fueled canines who, one after another, mount her, enter her, and, like a rocket exploding, do what males must do.*"

"Hmm, a bit much," he says. "Although it does have a raw vulgarity I find appealing."

"And this, man: *The dark burning red hues of Ozzy's voice, echoing like a giant shouting into a series of enormous caves, communicating a kind of ethereal, almost spiritual solemnity, deep salt of the earth reassurance.*

I drop the pages on the table. "I mean what the hell are you saying here, man?"

He takes a final hit of nicotine, drops the half-inch that's left of the Pall Mall onto the scuffed hardwood floor and grinds it out with the sole of his grody sandal.

"Well I believe the mushrooms had kicked in when I wrote that."

Ha ha, we laugh, and Jim shouts, *Meet the new boss.*

I shout, *Same as the old boss.*

"Yeah, same as the old boss," Jim says. "King *Fucking* Editor."

Overgrown bird's nest and sad-dog reefer eyes. "Wait 'til he gets my rewrite," and he shakes out another Pall Mall. He passes me a smoke, moves his coffee to the side, rests his arms across themselves on the table, and brings his head down, forehead against his arms, matted brown hair curls onto the table, and I kid you not, he's snoring same as someone blows air through a horn that makes a snore-ass sound, all nostril and snot and air suck through flesh, and the unlit cigarette falls out of his fingers, rolls to the table edge, and falls to the floor.

Out cold.

5. NIGHT OF THE FIRST BLACK STORY

SO THEN COMES THE night my world gets rearranged once again. Me and Sappho, well her real name is Kate but I think of her as Sappho 'cause she's a serious feminist and she looks same as a dyke off the island of Lesbos with the baggy blue jeans and plaid flannel shirts. She went to my high school for a few years and has a dealer boyfriend in L.A., this loser Ned. Yeah we're gonna walk to the campus theater on account of this "The Films of Alfred Hitchcock" class we're in. It's taught by Wallace Wiley. He's a professor and a wannabe movie director. He knows all the heavy duty films. Knows every shot. And the symbolism of the symbols. Even something you don't know is a symbol, Wallace Wiley knows it is.

Wiley preaches the gospel of "auteur theory," which he got from *Village Voice* film critic Andrew Sarris, who got it from *Cahiers du Cinéma* where Andre Bazin and Truffaut and others who became the French New Wave wrote about it.

Wiley digs the whole Truffaut-enamored-with-Hitchcock-as-misunderstood-genius scenario.

I'm high on both.

Auteur theory and Hitchcock. Authentic real, if there's a theory that makes something mean more than the surface of the surface, I'm into it.

The film we're seeing tonight is "Rope." Two smart-ass college guys kill off a third guy—strangle him with a rope—not with any motive but just to prove they can commit the "perfect murder." They hide the body in a wooden chest in the living room of their apartment and invite some people over for dinner including the dead guy's dad and aunt and girlfriend, and the killers put plates of food on the chest like it's a buffet. It's creepy and for the whole 81 minute film you're doing the sweatin' it out thing—are they gonna get caught or not?

Slight ajar, Sappho's door. She has a room on Middle Earth, same as Jim, only she's on the south wing, the floor below mine, while he's on the north wing. I hear a chick's voice from inside, voice same as lightning when it flashes and the white light veins reach out across the whole panorama of the black night sky. Voice I hear is lightning and diamonds, and all the sad colors.

"Bloody massacre," the chick says. "Take me to the depths of absinthe."

That's how she talks. *Bloody massacre* when things are fucked-up. *Take me to the depths of absinthe* when she wants the oblivion of booze or weed. When the beautiful sadness overwhelms her. Oh but you haven't met her, and me neither. I've only seen her in the Hitchcock class.

I knock repeatedly on Sappho's door.

"The postman only knocks twice," I say.

The door swings open and there's Sappho, shiny brown hair braided into two pony tails. She points her finger toward the inside, and her too loud voice. "In!"

Not over the threshold and already I'm talkin' to Sappho about Hitchcock. But quick-like I stop 'cause I see this chick sitting at the back of the room on Sappho's bed drawing.

Oh man.

Oh man oh man oh man.

This chick sits on Sappho's American Indian blanket, draws in a sketchbook and soon as I see her she's all I'm about. Slender chick, her dark brown hair pulled back kinda same as Diane di Prima on the cover of "Memoirs of a Beatnik." And because of how she has her hair right then, forever after she makes me think of the Beats. Her name's Elise. I find that out soon enough. Chick has an Audrey Hepburn face if Hepburn is 18 and has a Beat trip going. Only this chick is way hipper than Hepburn.

Still, her face is so Hepburn. Same angle to her jaw and the smooth curve of her chin and that serious but slight helpless look, lips closed, nose just the right size, introverted and self-absorbed. Can't see her eyes 'cause of the glasses, and I'll tell you about the glasses soon enough, but I know Elise's eyes are vast and deep as the Forever Infinite Pacific and there's a sadness. Maybe we all have a sadness, and if you look hard enough you see the sadness in all our eyes. Or maybe her sadness isn't same as any other.

I call it the *beautiful sadness*.

As I walk to the middle of the room I see the mascara and eye shadow and pale red lipstick. She wears a black turtleneck, and I see the curve of her tits beneath the sweater.

She's wearing a bra. A bra? And not only that, man, the chick isn't doing the jeans and t-shirt trip. She wears a skirt that ends above her knees. *A short skirt.* One of the only girls I seen wear a short skirt at The University. Most of the chicks who wore a skirt freshman year, down to their ankles granny dress trip. Elise wears a dark blue skirt with small green and red and yellow and purple and white flowers all over it. Black stockings. No chick I know wears any kind of stockings. And burnt-orange cowboy boots.

And the glasses. Black oval glasses with the upper corners rising slightly. Those glasses make a lotta chicks the librarian deal, but with Elise it's kinda that poet Denise Levertov, only better. I never read Levertov, all I know of her is one photograph *Village Voice* photographer Fred McDarrah took in 1959. That photo always made me wonder about the Beat chicks. All the chicks—artist chicks and poet chicks and novelist chicks—who had as much to say as Kerouac and Ginsberg and Corso. Don't hear too much about the Beat chicks. Vibe I get, Elise could have been a Beat poet, or maybe a Beat artist like Jay DeFeo.

And I know. This chick is my Visions of Johanna for sure. This is destiny, me and her. What I don't get that day is the bra and the makeup and the turtleneck and the skirt and the black stockings and the glasses—all of it a language she speaks. If I know the language I know this isn't a free love chick. Isn't a Freak Scene Dream chick. Not a chick gonna let a freakster bro get to her easy. I don't know the language.

Later I learn it. Elise makes me learn it.

When chicks go to college, the minute they land got some radar where they do an instant locate-another-chick-they're-simpatico-with deal and bond. Elise was knocking on doors in search of a smoke and the third door was Sappho, and right quick those two smoking up a storm and talking non-stop about whatever it is chicks talk about when there's no freakster bros around. That isn't quite right 'cause I know one thing Sappho told Elise, told her about me. Told her about my rock trip and how I'm a photographer and write for *The Paper*.

"Hey Elise," Sappho says. She sits down front of her desk, which is along a side wall, but she faces back towards the bed. "This is Writerman, the guy I was telling you about, the one who went to the same high school as me."

I'm in the middle of the room, and what should I do? Sit next to the chick, or sit on the floor, or stand? If the chick wasn't there I'd sit on the bed, maybe take my boots off and lie on it and argue with Sappho about what's worse, her Kools 'cause of the menthol, or my Pall Malls.

Yeah, well, Elise is there, and sit on the bed is too close, and sit on the floor is lame unless we're all down there. So I stand, and the thing is, normally I stand, no big deal. Relaxed, not self-conscious, but with this chick I wonder about shit same as what the fuck to do with my hands.

My hands.

I can stick them in my jeans pockets or cross them front of my chest or one hand on my hip but none of that's right. Everything the awkward deal, self-conscious of every move I make or even think to make, and what does this chick think about *me*, and I need to play this one super cool same as Tom, the guy who had the room above mine in that married students apartment freshman year who fucked a new chick every night. I gotta be disinterested. Get the chick to have an interest by my disinterest. Yeah, gotta be cool as Tom.

She doesn't look up from her drawing.

"So what's happening *Writerman*, Mr. Big Shot rock 'n' roll expert," she says. "Bloody massacre, I'm supposed to be *impressed* 'cause you write for the school paper?"

Oh fuck, and what I learn from Tom total vacates the scene. I say nothing 'cause if I tell her she oughta be impressed, sounds lame, and if I say she shouldn't, well I'm putting myself down and you don't wanna put yourself down front of a chick you dig.

"I never met a boy didn't think he was God's gift," she says.

Oh man, another sarcastic chick. Every chick I dug except Sarah was sarcastic. Only the truth of it, *everyone* I know is sarcastic. Sappho and Jim and Harper and that film teacher Wallace Wiley. It's 'cause we know all that shit about Santa Claus and Gandhi and Martin Luther King, Jr. was a lie. Because there is no Santa Claus, and Gandhi and King shot dead, and the Kennedy brothers too, so nobody is giving peace a chance. Nothing coming down any chimneys except soot and rain.

"Whoa!" I say, back off a couple exaggerated steps, damn lucky I didn't sit on that bed, and she looks up. Gives me the why-you-buggin'-me look.

"I don't know what I've done wrong," I say, and I'm not self-conscious about my hands anymore.

"Why not hang a *fucking* 'do not disturb' sign from your neck and be done with it?"

Man, that gets her attention, and Sappho's waving her hands.

"Time-out, kiddies. Elise, Michael's *cool*. Except for his shit diet. Be nice."

So now Elise isn't doing any drawing, not after what I said.

"Bloody massacre. Horny guys like you coming on to me."

Drops her sketchbook on the bed same as everything's doomed and there's no way out.

"Take me to the depths of absinthe. *Kate*, got anything we can blitz on?"

That's when I see Elise's cobalt blue eyes.

"Guys never get it," she says.

Her eyes are different. Not the tired eyes Sarah had when I first saw her, not the innocent eyes when she's my old lady, and not the party's over eyes after I betray her. Elise's eyes, man, artist eyes, and they see more, so much more.

Blue million miles eyes.

That's what I thought soon as I saw them, you know, same as that Beefheart song on *Clear Spot*. "Her Eyes Are a Blue Million Miles." That song. And yeah, those are the eyes she has.

Elise looks so Bohemian beautiful, and everything about her, her di Prima hair, her Hepburn face, her black turtleneck and flowered skirt and black tights and orange cowboy boots, oh man.

Oh man oh man oh man.

"Looked in the mirror lately?" I say.

Anger burns across her face as if she's scarred right under her perfect skin. Sometimes nothing makes me want a chick more than when she's mad and she can't control it, anger intense as desire.

"Isn't easy," I say, "for a freakster bro to just walk on by."

"All I know is where it's *not* at," Elise says. "It's a drag to be prey."

I look at her and see all the chicks who burned me. Sandy, who I dug in fifth grade, she laughed at me when I gave her a Valentine. Elise rearranges herself on the Indian bedspread, and Julie, who I lusted after in eighth grade, who blew me off when I asked her to the Harvest dance. Elise crosses her legs, and Sarah, I begged, man, but she wouldn't give me a second chance. The toe of Elise's boot ticks nervous in the air, and Harper with her disappearing act.

"We each have our cross to bear," I say.

Only that's bullshit. I'm no victim, the past is the past, and I'm gonna stay in this room, deal with *this* chick, and whatever gonna happen, happens.

"Don't lump me with the lousy guys you knew before."

Toe of her cowgirl boot moves faster.

"You oughta know something about me," I say. "Before you

put the walls up."

She sets her glasses on her sketchbook, covers her eyes with her palms as if she can stop seeing whatever it is she doesn't wanna see, but she can't.

Some things are burned into the retina.

Her voice is the quiet pain of 18 years on the planet. Old people never get it. You don't have to be old to suffer. To feel all the shit ways a person can feel. I bet the pain is worse when a person is young. When you're young everything brighter than bright and darker than dark. The only thing the old feel that the young might escape is regret. Well there's failure too. When a person knows the dreams they once had are dead.

There is something about her, she feels things too deep, and those artist eyes, blue million miles eyes, seeing more than most people see, but it makes her beauty more than beauty, and yeah, I still think of it as the beautiful sadness.

Sometimes *I* feel it, and when I do I think of Elise, her sitting on Sappho's bed that first day we met.

"They're always up," she says. "The walls. It's more like I need to take 'em down."

I start the Zen White Wall Meditation. *One.* Maybe I can talk to her, maybe she hears me.

"Bummer, man."

She's defeated, which isn't what I want at all, and I walk over to the bed, get close to the chick.

Two. "Mind if I sit here?"

She rearranges herself, uncrosses her legs, gets so both her boots touch the carpet. She picks up the sketchbook, and her glasses.

"Sit wherever. I don't care."

Three. I look down at her drawing. It's a guy, more a monster than a guy. He has a wolf head, knives for teeth, and razor blades for hands. It's Picasso and Steinberg and de Kooning. Under the drawing she's written, "Man's true nature."

"Takes too much effort to care," and her cobalt blue artist eyes watch me look at her drawing.

If I could write good as Elise draws, I'd be Salinger and Fitzgerald and Kerouac wrapped up in one heavy traffic great writer. And this I know is weird. But right in the moment I see her drawing I make a promise. If this chick can draw good as my heroes write, I'm gonna write as good as she draws.

"My high school boyfriend."

"Must have been love at first sight."

This is when I understand about the sarcastic. Our cool sarcasm is the mask that hides the scars, and with Elise it's the ex-boyfriend, the monster with razor blade hands and knives for teeth, and with Jim it's growing up without a dad and the chicks who gave him the brush off, and with me it's my asshole dad and my pollyannish mom and betraying Sarah and, and, and.

Elise there on the bed. This is the moment. I gotta be present. So close, and her glasses off. I see those freckles on her nose and cheeks.

Without the glasses there's a softness and a different beauty. The glasses give her a cold intellectual remove, and more, they're a shield. Without them she's unprotected, without them she's as imperfect a human as me, and she doesn't have it all wired down tight, and maybe I have a chance.

"I hate to interrupt this budding romance," Sappho says, her voice upbeat as that low tough voice ever is. "Gotta leave for the film, kids."

Moonlight and the occasional street lamp along the path to light our way reflecting off Elise's Levertov glasses reminds me of the distance and the walls and the sarcasm. The trees block the moonlight here and there as we walk, at times we're in darkness.

The leaves whisper their premonition of trouble in the cold wind coming off the Forever Infinite Pacific, and maybe it's the cold wind that makes her start to talk about one of the times she was damaged.

"There's boys who stalk girls," Elise says, which was an odd thing for her to say right then. I thought she was making some kinda obtuse joke, a joke I for sure didn't get.

"You're the kinda chick," I say. "Could drive a freakster bro to that," and soon as I said it, wanna reel it back.

"Stalking isn't a joke, *Writerman*," she says. "Not once it happens to a girl."

The chill I feel and the chill I see when the moon lights her face isn't from the wind. She's quiet, maybe wishes she didn't bring it up. Sappho strides along, sets the pace with her big-ass steps.

"Anyone mess with me," Sappho says. "Kick 'em right in the nuts."

Sappho has a long black wool coat goes down almost to her ankles, and her black engineer boots. After what she said, I never see her boots the same again.

"Creeped me out," Elise says.

"We need to defend ourselves," Sappho says. "Mete out some vigilante justice."

The moonlight on Elise's pale face, and despite the glasses she doesn't have that intellectual remove. Damaged, man.

That's when she tells us the first of The Black Stories.

"Happened a few years ago," she says. "I was walking back to my car. My mom's car. It was night. This was in Santa Monica. I was alone and it was dark. The street was empty. I was 16 and fearless. I'd been to the open mic poetry reading at this coffee house I liked, and after it I was lost in thought about the poem this beautiful boy with long gold hair read about the ocean, and love."

Her voice is a different voice when she talks about that boy. She loses the sarcastic, and her fear and anger too, and what's left is an echo of the innocence.

"It was like he was bleeding," she says. "Yeah, that honest and true, and I could tell the poem was his heart. Oh I don't know. He used the loneliness of the empty beach on an overcast day, walking alone right at the border of where the sand and the ocean meet, as a metaphor for the loneliness of unrequited love."

She tells us she heard the sound of a car, only car around, and looked up and the car slowed and crept along parallel to her. Yeah that creeped her. She walked faster and the car sped up. The back window rolled down and these white trash guys, one sticks his head out, said something to her, and she doesn't even think, I mean she tells us she should have kept her mouth shut.

"I said, 'What do you want?' and the guy in the car, he said, 'Wanna go for a ride, babe?'" and she panicked, she was a statue, and the car stopped. She can't move, man.

"The worst," she says.

The moonlight on us, and there's hellfuck anger in Sappho's voice.

"Some guys are worse than animals," she says.

Elise pushes her hands deep into the pockets of her trenchcoat, and tells us she had no voice. Wanted to scream, couldn't scream. The two rear doors opened and two of 'em got out. She freaked, but in her freak-out she found the strength, broke free and ran. Those two guys followed her. Well Elise is fast, I mean she'd gone out for track in high school. Faster than fast.

"I ran a block and they're still behind me and my heart was pounding like it was going to burst," she says. "And another block and the panic, those two creeps still there, and I see Rexall Drugs, and I run harder, push open the door. I told the lady at the counter where it's at. She looked at me funny, but she could tell. Why would I make something like that up? Told me to go to the back of the store and through a door, back to where the pharmacist worked during the day where I could calm down, catch my breath. I sat there all alone. And I heard them come in."

"If it had been me behind the counter," Sappho says. "Shoot the motherfuckers dead."

"I couldn't stop shivering," Elise says. "The lady asked them what's their business. 'Buy something or get out,' she said. That voice of hers, you knew she had a gun behind the counter and knew how to use it. They asked for a pack of Marlboros and split."

As we walk up the path, Elise could break in pieces. Almost

a different chick than in Sappho's room.

"Creeped me so bad," she says. "I mean that poem I was thinking about was so beautiful and the way the boy read it, there was such a sound to how he put his words together, but then those jerks ruined it. You're never safe. Even if you feel safe it's a bloody illusion."

She never feels safe anymore, she tells us. Never goes anywhere at night alone.

The towering darkness of trees sway in the wind, block the moonlight, and a street lamp lights her face and she tries to keep it together, adjusts her glasses, which is some nervous deal, but still it's the tragic chick beauty.

"Of course that was the beginning," she says.

"What else?" I say.

"I don't want to talk about it anymore," she says.

"It's important to focus on the future," I say, as if I know shit, and fuck, man, I sound same as my mom, can't believe that self-help babble comes from my mouth.

Thank God, I mean if-by-the slightest-of-slightest-chances-there-is-a-God, for Sappho. She breaks the darkness to pieces. Starts in talking about some coconut oil she puts on her food.

"You need it too," she says. "Both of you. Improve your memory 150 percent. It's like carrots, only for memory instead of eyes. And fabulous for depression. Says it's a positive vibe product right on the bottle."

The moonlight on us, Elise looks over and winks at me.

"*Positive vibe product*," she says. "Bloody massacre."

In that moment we're a conspiracy of two, and I make my Casanova move.

"Elise, after the film wanna come to my room? Smoke a joint. It's safe. I swear."

"Sure it is," she says. "A real positive vibe product. *Your room.*"

"Show you my etchings."

She laughs a quick nervous laugh. How Jean Seberg laughs when she's Patricia in *À Bout de soufflé*, you know, Godard's "Breathless," her and Michel in the hotel room and she tells him she doesn't know yet if she loves him.

"*Paul-Emile Bécat* etchings?" she says.

Yeah she knows plenty about art, more than me, and I know plenty. Only I don't know Paul-Emile Bécat, but how she says it, his etchings gotta be more than nudes.

"Wow," I say. "You're a psychic."

"I learned that workin' the carnival," she says, and that's another of those phrases she used all the time, same as "bloody massacre." That's what she said if she somehow knew something it wasn't possible for her to know.

"Kate tell you I'm a photographer?" I say. "Dig to click some pics of you."

"I bet you say that to all the girls. All the fab *chicks* you take to see 'Rope.'"

"You're the only one," I say, "who's gone on a date with me to see 'Rope.'"

"Oh, so now we're on a date. Why am I the last to know?"

Quiet Jean Seberg laugh, no sarcasm, no walls up, no *bloody massacre*. For a flash of a moment she feels the darkness lift, and somehow I have everything to do with it. Oh man, that was a moment. One of *those* moments, when everything falls away, and all that's there is me and her. Writerman and Elise, and the sun shining bright inside us. I wanted the moment to stretch out. Wanted it to go on and on. Writerman and Elise.

Positive vibe product.

6. MY SWEET LADY JADED

DOOM AND GLOOM, THESE two black-billed magpies. It was Sarah who gave 'em names, Sarah, back when we were both 16, who told me they bring trouble. I didn't see them that day me and Jim met Jaded, and I didn't hear them, but they were there. I know it. They sat on the roof of a dorm building, or maybe the dining hall. *Caw caw caw.* Oh they have the best time, consider the troubles gonna befall Jim. And you know what else? They know I'll get mixed up in it, and then there's me and Elise. Have a good laugh on us too.

Jaded comes cruising into Jim's life same as the shiny new ink blue Mercedes 280se Cabriolet convertible daddy got her for high school graduation, chick takes the curves and shows her curves fast fast faster.

    She wasn't Jaded yet, the day me and Jim meet her. Not 'til I know her some. And after that I shoulda thought of her as Poison Ivy. Or *Thee* Black Widow. Or the chick Skippy James sang about, the one where he *rather be the Devil, than to be that woman's man.*

Me and Jim stand in line for the cafeteria, I have my Pentax around my neck, I've been taking photos all morning, and *Thee* Freakster Bro full-bore into his professor of rock trip, an unlit Pall Mall between his thumb and index, lectures me on Black Sabbath. I'm still pissed about his review, and fed up with all his blabber and smoke regards Sabbath. No matter how many times I play *Paranoid* and *Master of Reality*, nothing's happening.

Absolutely nothing.

He's got his back to the front of the line, facing me, starts in on another round of Sabbath hyperbole, begins to unload some smartass theoretical only right in that moment he stops—the world on hold. The chick he's looking at is somewhere behind me, and while his jaw doesn't do the actual drop down, and no visible hearts or cupids with bows and arrows float in the air, there might as well been.

Understand me now, total heavy traffic pathetic how gone Jim is from one look. If I believed in witches and spells and the hocus pocus, I'd say Jaded hexed *Thee* Freakster Bro.

Well I gotta check out the turbulence. I do the nonchalant turn of the head and if I could see the authentic real of it, I'd see a category six hurricane coming our way. Jaded stands there, and she looks like Edie Sedgwick only with henna black hair, and she gives Jim the innocent smile.

That smile was a lie. Small chick, maybe 5 feet 4 inches, dressed all in black—yeah, that should be a clue. Danger dead ahead. Hair straight henna black, and it's longer than Edie wore it, a touch past Jaded's shoulders. Her skin Warhol white. Her lips a dark burgundy. And her eyes, intense deep amber, oh man, even from a distance, I mean she stands five, six people away, and even from where me and him stand, Jim flounders in the depth of those amber eyes.

Man overboard.

Jaded is smart, and cunning too. I can see her work it either uptown or downtown, star in films at The Factory or shop for a Chanel outfit on Park Avenue. Well I feel it too, *the wanting*, only Jaded isn't my Visions of Johanna chick. I know it for sure. *Caw caw caw*, and it scares me. *The wanting*. Out-of-control buzz. 'Cause I shouldn't be thinking about any chick but Elise.

And that was one of those decisive moments. For Jim. Only he doesn't weigh the options, he doesn't have a choice.

"Jim, man," I say. "Hold your horses," and he gives me a look, and that look signals I have it wrong.

"You're my best friend," he says. "I know you're looking out for me. But understand me."

Oh he's desperate.

"I *gotta* talk to her. Now," and then he's gone on down the line, stands before her, and in a rush of words says the most corny line any freakster bro ever said to a chick.

"My dear," he says. "You are absolutely the most exquisite and rarified and lovely girl I have, in my admittedly short residence here on Earth, the good fortune to see materialize before my undeserving eyes."

Well I know *Thee* Freakster Bro blown it on so many levels, the first being those wrong words. This gonna be over before it begins. Jaded stays cool, gets a good look at him, and I figure he'll have to get cleaned up and looking good to get a chick's interest, *any* chick's interest, but I'm wrong. I don't anticipate how a chick could see the potential, see Jim as a project. I'm clueless, and that's *exactly* my point. I mean *chicks*, man, a maze a freakster bro never find his way out of, mystery of mysteries.

Jaded gets a look at the mess of Jim, but she sees beyond all that, even the *Who's Next* piss-on-the-concrete-monolith t-shirt, and I know that doesn't sit well with her 'cause later it vanished from his wardrobe, if you can call the rags Jim wore before Jaded got involved a wardrobe. She hears the blown away nature of things in Jim's voice, and it's Valentine's Day in the cafeteria line. So goddamn sappy what goes on between them. Her voice quiet, and she tries to be nice, which is hard for Jaded 'cause that chick's a bitch. Of course I didn't know it that day, but I know it now.

"Why thank you—," she says.

Empty air follows the "you," an invitation for Jim to introduce himself, which he does, and he makes the move that seals the deal, no hand on hip Jagger routine, no showboat with the cigarette, no James Dean pose. No man. Jim's humble, does a slow bow.

"And you my dear, could you be so kind as to share with me your most certainly beautiful name?"

"Thank you Jim Costello," Jaded says, and honey drips off those two forming a puddle on the floor, and I wish I had the rest of that roll of TP I left on King Editor's desk, but Jim gonna have to clean up his own mess.

"You're so sweet," she says. "It's Jade. Jade Kaufman."

You know even now I'm not sure about her, 'cause one way I see it, call it The Benefit-Of-The-Doubt, the chick authentic real fell for Jim, and for a brief respite all her trouble girl shit gone baby gone. Other way, call it The Cynical Scenario, chick knew from the start this freakster bro she gonna manhandle, and when he was all used up leave him stranded and half dead. Still, if I were a betting kinda guy, all my chips on The Cynical Scenario.

Right then I see something in Jim I didn't notice before. 'Til now I've thought of him as a kind of rock 'n' roll wild man, but I'm wrong 'cause fuck, I mean as he talks to Jaded I can see he's got some Gatsby charm.

"Would you care to join me and my most esteemed colleague, Writerman, for lunch at our table?" he says.

Here we are in a lame-ass school cafeteria, old grease stink comes off the food, cheap-ass folding tables end-to-end, but Jim might as well asked Jaded to step into the Bentley for a ride up Park Avenue in Manhattan, and a left on 57th over to the Russian Tea Room.

Alright, well I guess it's good a time as any to tell this part.

There is a moment, a different moment, before Jim introduces me to Jaded when she gives me the twice over once, and I see something I don't anticipate in her amber eyes. There's an interest. In me. More than an interest. And in that moment, I could have stepped in, and what follows would take a different path. We'd get to the same destination, of that I'm sure, only instead of Jim getting skinned alive, it would be me.

That's when I took the photo of Jaded. I don't know what I said, but she was into it. There was a wildness, and the *danger dead ahead* thing I told you about, that was her face through the viewfinder. Jaded for real dug that photo, and Jim put a framed print on his desk. Well there in the dining hall soon as I click the shutter I let the moment pass, and the moment's gone, and she's focused on Jim all over again. On his invitation to lunch. And it works. Of course she lunches with us and as we get to the part where we eat the cherry pie she remembers some heavy object in the trunk of her car she needs brought to her second floor dorm room in the building me and Jim don't live in, other side of the quad, and if Jim carries it she'll be so very grateful.

Morning after the day Jim met Jaded he didn't show up for breakfast. *Thee* Freakster Bro *always* shows up for breakfast, so I figured it was Jim's lucky night. And more, since it was already 10 a.m. Lucky night, lucky morning, and when I see him next, mid-afternoon, got a smile won't quit.

   He wants to tell me he got laid, only he can't, and he can't 'cause Jaded isn't some piece of ass. Jim in his heart of hearts, whatever that is, thinks Jaded is his Visions of Johanna. Well she isn't. I'm betting she knew from the start. As if it matters. 'Cause Jim, yeah he sure didn't know.

   What Jim does, he manages to make it clear he spent the night there, you know, in Jaded's bed. How he does it, he tells me how beautiful it is in Jaded's dorm room when the sun rises, and the exquisite quality of light that comes in through her windows. Well I tell you man, after he sleeps with Jaded, Jim is reborn, and that haggard desperation gone baby gone.

Meanwhile it's slow motion regards me and Elise. It's excruciating, some kind of water torture, and the harder-to-get she plays it, the more I feel the wanting. Sure the chick talks to me when I hang with her in Sappho's room, or when we're all in Elise's room, but she always has things to do, busy with classes or studying or her drawing. I never get alone with her. Later, I get alone with her, and Doom and Gloom have a *caw caw caw* party around that one. Elise taking it slow with Writerman, and soon enough I'll tell you more.

Jaded dresses same as she stepped out of a *Vogue* photo spread on New York "It" girls, the high-end version of the London-New York take on street fashion, silk blouses with pop art images, tailored bell-bottom slacks, and she even has a few of those groovy end-above-the-knees designer dresses. Man, the mom and dad buy that chick the moon.

Jaded gotta be Jim's first girlfriend, I mean he would never admit it but that's the vibe. By the day after they meet you don't talk about one without the other. It's always *Jim and Jade*. As in, "*Jim and Jade* are meeting us at the movie," or, "Have *Jim and Jade* come into the dining hall yet?"

Authentic real, major bummerosity Jim hooking up with Jaded. And there's two reasons why. First of all, here me and *Thee* Freakster Bro getting to be good buddies, only now he has other priorities. All he thinks about, all he talks about—his whole world Jaded. No telling Jim he's blowing it. She's gonna fill every need he has, and everyone else can take a flying fuck if it gets down to it.

But the real reason it's such a drag is how it underlines what's *not* happening with me and Elise. I mean Jim sleeping with Jaded the same day he meets her, and here it is weeks after me and Elise meet in Sappho's room and see "Rope" together, and I haven't even gotten to hold her hand.

Jaded has her trip total together. She's a health freak. She jogs, does sit-ups and pull-ups and push-ups and works out with weights. Some days she swims laps, other days she rides her bike. And she's on this special diet too, which I get to soon enough.

Perhaps two weeks after me and Jim meet Jaded, the day comes when she begins the makeover. "My Fair Lady" updated, and the roles reversed. First thing she does is get Jim on her exercise program and the radical diet too. No more loading the enchiladas or spaghetti and meatballs or cheeseburgers and fries onto the plastic dinner plates. I don't know how Jaded and Sappho pull it off, but somehow those two manage to get authentic healthy food—beans and brown rice and tofu and loads of steamed vegetables—out of the cafeteria crew.

Freaks me to see Jaded pussywhip Jim.

You know that Iggy Pop song "I Wanna Be Your Dog"?

Jim, man, it's his favorite.

One morning, well, late morning, me and Jim move through the cafeteria line. Jaded doesn't eat breakfast, and that's the reason I get a chance to hang alone with *Thee* Freakster Bro. Load our trays with apples and grapefruit, dry whole-wheat toast, and oatmeal. Yeah, *oatmeal*. Coffee and Pall Malls our only connection to our unhealthy past. And reefer, of course, but not before breakfast unless we pull an all-nighter, which isn't happening on account of Jaded. Yeah, so anyway, we're both on Doctors Jaded and Sappho's Stay-The-Fuck-Healthy Vegetarian Diet.

First time I met Sappho at The University, beginning of sophomore year, she came down hard on me for the greasy sausage and other assorted shit-crap I ate. I mean she's a serious vegetarian, doesn't even go for milk or cheese or eggs. Well if Jim can skip the meat, and since the greasy sausage and all the rest make me sick if I even think about 'em, why not me?

Jim's lost a few pounds, got some muscle, and this is weird, but he looks *healthy*. Almost as if he's glowing. I start to think I'm too harsh on Jaded, maybe she's gonna be good for him. Of course that glow could be due to something other than his Mr. Health routine. Could be 'cause he's getting laid. You think?

Jim's wearing a new styled-out pair of shades, Ray-Ban Wayfarers, and he's proud to tell me they're a gift from Jaded.

"She told me they're the same model Andy Warhol wears," he says, which wasn't true but I wasn't gonna be the one to break that news to him.

After we hang awhile, after I go through my woe-is-me about Elise, Jim does his best to sound offhand. Even behind the ragged beard and Ray-Bans I see the guilt—something is *off*.

"Jade and I are going into town," he says. "Wanna come along?"

One beat, two, and he's looking down into his empty oatmeal bowl and tearing small pieces off his toast, making a pile of them on the plate.

"Jade's going to help me pick out some outfits, old sport."

It's time for me to let a couple long slow beats go by, which in fact I do.

And then.

"Did I hear you right, man?" I say.

I let more space happen, silence, and we hear the loud racket of a big-ass room full of people. Eating. Talking. Trying to connect.

"Outfits?"

Jim, stricken. I give him the dotted-lines eyes, which in no uncertainty telepaths to him the horror, and in addition I give him the you're-putting-me-on-man look, the you-lame-ass-fuck look, the you're-gonna-let-that-chick-erase-every-unique-ass-thing-about-you look, and the look I direct at him also says *hey, man, you go down this road, when Jaded is done with you you're not gonna have a clue as to who you are, and in your mixed-up confusion she'll dump you for a freakster bro who has some fuckin' balls.* Yeah, give Jim *that* look. Give Jim the chick's-gonna-skin-you-alive look.

Inch by inch.

Jim pushes the small pieces of toast around on his plate, and he waits. Knocks a Pall Mall out of the pack, and he waits. Gulp of lukewarm coffee, and he waits. Inch by inch. Well I can't resist a ride to town and a chance to hit Odyssey Records, where I buy most of my albums, and the other record store in town, Craven's. For sure it'll take my mind off Elise. As for Jaded playing dress-up with *Thee* Freakster Bro? This I gotta see.

We load into Jaded's convertible, Jaded at the wheel, Jim riding shotgun and me in the back digging the new car smell and the smooth feel of the tan leather interior. I'd been in my grandfather's Mercedes, but Jaded's seems plusher, as if those German car makers have seriously upped the ante. I mean we're riding in a motorized Fort Knox.

Jim is buzzing, man, his whole body twitching to an internal rhythm as he searches the dial, locates "Jumping Jack Flash," plays air guitar and shouts along.

This was supposed to be a break from my love sick blues, but seeing those two in the front seat seeming so happy together, Jaded groovin' to the beat while Jim does his rock star routine, and I plunge into a hellfuck funk. Why don't I have Elise as my chick, tell me why? Tell me what I'm doing wrong. Only there's no one to tell me.

There's only me, and I don't have a clue.

We shoot onto the two-lane that winds down the hill, past Liquor King and that asshole smirkface, and on into town and soon enough Jaded pulls into a parking space.

"You know Jim," she says, turns off the engine but leaves the power on so we can hear the end of the song. "How about a haircut?"

And I don't envy Jim's scene, no way, man.

"To go with the new outfits," she says.

Inch by inch.

Thee Freakster Bro stops, mid-verse. Oh man oh man oh man.

"A haircut?"

Checks himself in the side mirror, fingers through the bird's nest.

"Lookin' good, don't you think my lovely? Just like Robert Plant. Yow!"

He stands up in the front seat, fist in the air.

"Dazed and confused! I *love* the Zep!! Rock 'n' *Roll!*"

Jaded turns off the power, pulls him back down to earth, smiles her Valentine's Day smile, and rubs the back of his thick neck.

"Pretty *please* Jim," she says. "Really, as a favor to me. Just a little trim."

She pulls him to her, gives him one of those trouble girl kisses with some tongue, and no guy ever said no to that kiss.

Inch by inch, man.

I split out of there, don't wanna see Samson lose his hair, and besides, I have things to do. Odyssey calling.

"Writerman, how's it hangin'?"

Lucky Larry's behind the counter, chewing gum. Lucky Larry owns the joint. The place used to be a bank, has a ceiling gotta be four times tall as me, which puts it upwards of 24 feet. It's huge. Four thousand, 5,000, maybe 6,000 square feet. Huge huge humungous space full of more records than's ever been in one building.

"What's the sounds playin', man?" and I'm scanning the scene, checking out the posters on the walls—Dylan '65 rockin' electric at Newport, yeah that would look good on the back of my door.

What I'm asking Lucky Larry about is this British chick singing this Dylan song, "I'll Keep It With Mine." It's a snow blown winter day how she sings it. The lyrics are a mystery.

I'll keep it with mine.

Keep what *with mine?* And what about *I'm loving you, not for what you are, but for what you're not?* Sometimes a Dylan song is as much a mystery as a chick. That day, me obsessing about Elise, the mystery of "I'll Keep It With Mine" *is* the mystery of Elise.

Lucky Larry puts up with my questions 'cause I gotta be his best customer. "Fairport, bro," he says, and he sticks a price tag on the sealed cellophane of *Music of My Mind.* "Sandy Denny, queen of the Brit folk-rockers."

Lucky Larry wears a well-faded blue t-shirt got a drawing of Nixon's face on it and under that ugly mug, "What, Me Worry?" "You know Joe Boyd, right?" he says. "The producer. Did Nick Drake and the Incredible String Band."

"Heavy," I say, and I want it to be Elise singing, and when the British chick singer sings *I'll keep it with mine,* I want Elise to wanna keep her love for me with my love for her.

"Truly righteous, bro," Lucky Larry says. "Whole album's a keeper."

The reason Odyssey does so well, given the competition from Craven's, is 'cause Lucky Larry is master of the up-sell, and I fall for it every time. On this day I bring The Band's new one, *Rock of Ages,* to the register.

"Great fuckin' album, Writerman," Lucky Larry says. "I was crankin' it earlier today. Allen Toussaint wrote the horn charts. How killer is that?"

"Cool, yeah," I say. "I'm so into The Band, and you know I'm Dylan's biggest fan."

Lucky Larry's face is too too red from all that Green Death he drinks. He always has a 24 ouncer goin' behind the counter, and that stuff is nasty. He takes a drink, gives me the sage nod, the knowing wink, signifying the unspoken understanding between us Dylan *aficionados*.

"I know you are, Writerman," he says.

Man, Lucky Larry has this way of creating suspense about what he's about to say. He leans in.

"And only 'cause I know that about you," he says, "would I say to you what I'm about to say."

He gives me a can-you-keep-a-secret kinda look.

"What you wanna tell me, man?" I say.

"If you want I can hip you to some shit that's even cooler," he says. "The records Robbie and Levon and the other guys stole all their shit from."

Oh fuck, the need-a-record jitters squared.

"You're into Hubert Sumlin, right?"

Yeah, now he has me one down. Hate having to admit my ignorance, but I gotta.

"Well I've seen the name," I say. "But I don't know anything about him."

"Don't sweat it, that's why I'm here, Writerman," Lucky Larry says. "That's the whole point of Lucky Larry's existence," and yeah he's got the edge. "I'm your encyclopedia of rock. All in one self-contained motherfucker, dig?"

Lucky Larry takes a slurp of Green Death.

"The killer guitar on the Wolf's 'Evil' and 'Smokestack Lightnin'' and 'Wang Dang Doodle.' That's him."

Wolf. Howlin' Wolf.

I first heard some of his sides 'cause Voco played him late-night on KMPX, you know, back in '67, and there's an interview I read where Beefheart talked about Wolf.

"Hubert's been playing with Wolf since '54, Writerman," Lucky Larry says.

"Got some of his records, man?" I say.

Lucky Larry acts as if he gotta consider the question, takes his time before answering.

"I might," he says. "Then again, might not."

Dope fiend shit, 'cause where a few minutes ago Hubert Sumlin didn't mean anything to me, now I'm jonesing. I *need* a Howlin' Wolf record—Hubert Sumlin has secrets I gotta hear.

"Well *do you*, man?"

Lucky Larry scratches under his arm, a slow yawn, another slug of Green Death, sticks a price tag on the back of Earl Hines' *Blues in Thirds*.

"Those Wolf albums are hard to come by, bro."

Real slowmo he comes out from behind the counter, and makes his way, and he's got all the time in the world, no one in the store but me, and we get to the aisle with the monster blues section. He pulls out an album, a two-record set, drawing of Wolf on the cover surrounded by the dark symbols of born under a bad sign: skull and crossbones, devil's head, bottle of Jack Daniel's, pistol, switchblade, and a chick with big tits and a lot of leg showing.

"Can't go wrong with this one," he says.

By the time we're back at the counter I have the Wolf twofer, another Wolf "classic," a Muddy Waters best-of, an album by some Appalachian mountain man Roscoe Holcomb who's "just the biggest influence on Dylan," plus the first solo album from that British chick, and the Fairport album with "I'll Keep It With Mine."

The up-sell.

Lucky Larry, man, he's the master. I walk toward the door to make my exit hellfuck guilty, spent way too much dough having also discovered I couldn't go another day without *Sketches of Spain*, you remember, Bill Graham's favorite.

Yeah, well, once I split out of that scene I head straight to meet up with Jim and Jaded, and no way I go near Craven's.

When I get back to Sasha's, this high-end salon named after the owner where Jaded gets her hair done, Sasha is finishing up, blow-drying Jim's hair. Big wow 'cause now he's got for real rock star hair and as I walk over he sings that line that's become part of this *thing* we do, kinda same as the dotted-lines eyes.

Jim sings, *Meet the new boss.*

I'm supposed to reply, *Same as the old boss,* but I'm spacing out.

It's an art piece, *Thee* Freakster Bro's hair. I'm so caught up in his new scene I forget to sing my response. Huge perfect hair, Roger Daltrey perfect hair for sure under the movie star lights Sasha has lit.

"Writerman, old sport. *Meet the new boss!*"

I'm staggered by the change, his rock star hair, and how Sasha cleaned up the beard and 'stache. Finally get the words out, *same as the old...,* which is Jim's cue. He does a mock curtsy, and that's when I look at Jaded standing a few feet from him.

"Isn't Jim handsome?" she says, only she doesn't look at Jim, she looks at me. And I remember the day me and Jim met Jaded, when she was interested in me, when it could have gone different than how it's gone. I'm something she wants. Her expression changes and she gets next to Jim, squeezes his hand, gives me a proprietary look, *fuck-you, Writerman, don't get in my way, he's mine and I do what I want with him.*

"How come you're not saying anything, Writerman?" Jaded says. "You don't care for Jim's new do?"

"Don't we all wish we had an assistant," I say. "I mean assistance, getting our hair styled and choosing our *outfits.*"

Jim goes into a coughing jag.

"It's the Ritz, honey," Jaded says.

Inch by inch.

Disraeli Gears is a boutique with "Fab English gear direct from London." The owner's this chick in a skimpy dress who looks like Twiggy. She's got "After Glow" off the Small Faces' spacey *Ogdens' Nut Gone Flake* playing.

"How *are you,* dears?"

Afflicted *and* affected. She wants to be some hip London boutique chick, which is funny 'cause turns out she grew up in Kansas City. Jagger imitates Mississippi Fred McDowell, and this boutique chick imitates Twiggy. Go figure.

Soon as we get there Jaded's goin' through the racks, checking out velvet capes and paisley shirts and black suede vests. Disraeli Gears works hard at the London trip, but veers towards the retro Mod scene. The walls hung with old framed photos of the Stones, The Beatles, Donovan, Cilla Black, The Animals and Marianne Faithfull from when she had her hit with "As Tears Go By."

Jaded knows the clothes to make the man. Even if the man inside those clothes is feeling his dick shrivel. She hands Jim a lavender shirt with an oversized collar and frilly cuffs, something Jimmy Page would wear under his velvet coat.

"It's totally *you* Jim," she says.

She picks out a black velveteen suit and passes it to Jim who is behind a red velvet curtain in one of the dressing booths.

I kill time checking out the clothes and digging the music— now Twiggy has Pink Floyd's "Interstellar Overdrive" rocking the place.

Jaded hands Jim a black and gold paisley shirt that Twiggy said was designed by The Fool—you know, the London freaks who made clothes for The Beatles' Apple Boutique in '67.

Soon enough Jim steps out of the dressing room.

Shoulda been a drum roll played by Keith Moon.

He has on the black velveteen suit, and it reminds me of Paul McCartney when The Beatles rock out on the roof of Abbey Road, only *Thee* Freakster Bro looks more regal 'cause of that Jimmy Page frill shirt. The black coat has wide-ass lapels, cut a bit long, almost a frock coat. Shiny black Beatle boots. And the capper: he's twirling a shiny black cane with a brass lion's head handle. The lucky cane, man.

Inch by inch.

"Just call me Lord Jim," he says.

And that was that.

7. BOOZE RUN

STILL BUMS ME OUT to think of the Sylvia Plath poster
Elise tacked high above her bed. It's a photo of Sylvia Plath
blown up huge. How it looks to me, Plath was gone baby gone
before the photographer clicked the shutter. She's barely there.
Got mixed-up confusion, and the disinterest, same as how Elise
is sometimes.

Bummerosity, man, humungous photo of a suicide above
the bed.

Elise does look kinda like Plath. Plath by way of Hepburn
and Levertov, and of course the di Prima hair. Then again, Elise
doesn't look like any of 'em. Elise looks like Elise. She has the
beautiful sadness beneath the disinterest and the sarcasm, and
I'm a sucker for sadness in a chick. Makes me feel strong, the
big man, the freakster bro gonna step into the chick's life and
save her.

She's not really there.

Sylvia Plath. Elise. Both of them, neither of them.

Don't know what got into Elise that night. Broken Tequila
Bottle Night, we call it. Me and Elise. Later I call it The Night
of the Second Black Story. Later, after it happened, long after
it's gone.

Me, Elise and Sappho sit on the carpet in Elise's room early
evening. Start of October I think, but it coulda been late
September. So much so fast that year. Elise with her sketchbook
open sketches in that tripped-out hard angle style of hers. It's a
sketch of two hands, well, two hands that are more claws than

hands. The claws have spikes for nails and somehow the claw-hand on the left holds a gun and the gun takes aim at the claw-hand on the right and that one holds a bottle with "Cuervo Gold" written on it.

Elise's room is down the hall around the corner from Sappho's, west wing of Middle Earth, same dorm I'm in. Her windows have a view on the wild green meadow, the meadow I walk by first day I meet *Thee* Freakster Bro. Through her windows I see some of the forest crowding in on the sides and back of The University.

The view from the rooms on the west wing is serene and peaceful in the spring, but it's not spring, it's the end of fall, as fall becomes winter, when the weather is out of control, rattling the glass. Yeah, and those dark forces are same as us, and what's beyond us, something we can't control, me and Elise.

Inside the room it's groovy. I mean the room of a chick I dig, fuck, inner sanctum. Everything of Elise's I wanna know about as if each item is an artifact from some remote culture. Besides the Sylvia Plath deal, she has art posters. Matisse's "Dance" and Modigliani's "Reclining Nude" and Picasso's "Les Demoiselles d'Avignon."

There's a beautiful sadness to Picasso's whores, but there's something else, they remind me of Hester, you know, Hawthorne's Hester, has the letter "A" on her chest as if it's burned there, a brand, and it makes Hester an outsider, and more, someone who can see around the bend, consider a way to live bigger and wider and more free than maybe anyone else in America, and same for Picasso's whores. When you're on the outside you don't play by the rules, and you see the rules for what they are, a cage, only a cage that doesn't even exist. Everyone pretends there's steel bars, and we're trapped, when it's a mirage. No cage. No bars. No rules.

Picasso's whores, one kind of freedom, Matisse's naked dancers, another, and you know Modigliani's chick does anything she pleases. Only deal comes close is Dylan high on meth barnstorming through Europe 1966 with The Hawks—

the lightning bolt sound of "Tell Me Momma" and "I Don't Believe You" and "Leopard-Skin Pill-Box Hat." If there's ever been a sound of freedom, Dylan in '66 was that sound.

Sappho in one of her moods, she's a stone drag, but that's not why Elise wants the booze. Deeper, man, maybe the hopeless vibe seeps into Elise, or the beautiful sadness too intense, or a memory she can't shake. Later I'll know the authentic real of it, but not yet.

Elise sets her sketchbook on the rug, sits down front of the record player, which is on the floor, a Zenith portable like my first stereo, which I still have in my room at home. She has one speaker up on her desk, the other on the floor near the record player. Shit-ass way to place 'em if you want decent sound, but Elise is a chick, and chicks hardly think about that shit. Well, back then anyway.

Billie Holiday's "Strange Fruit" starts up, and since I known her Elise been playing that sad song. Billie sings about the Southern trees and their strange fruit, and the blood on the leaves and at the root. And the black bodies hanging from those trees.

Creeps me out, that's what Elise said about the song, and still she plays it, and it's beautiful the way Millais' Ophelia floating in the dead water of the Hogsmill River, a red poppy at her side, is beautiful. Bare minor piano chords, and don't misunderstand, nothing beautiful about racism and lynching and all the horrors, but Billie's voice, the murky water, her frozen hand, the dead flowers, and the hole inside me hurts so bad, the one no chick's love ever gonna fill, and the blue melody, those trumpet notes descend, and blood drips off the leaves.

Yeah, that's a sound.

Elise stands and sways to the slow, sad death music, and she's the beautiful sadness, sways slow to the rhythm. She wears a black V-neck sweater, so simple and elegant, and her dark blue skirt with tiny green and burgundy and white flowers ends above her knees, and the skirt is simple too. Same as the black tights. She's so elegant in the simplicity, but there's nothing simple about Elise. The chick is layer upon layer upon layer. A psychiatrist could devote his whole career to study that chick, and never emerge from the labyrinth of mixed-up confusion.

That night she doesn't have on the Levertov glasses and it makes me wonder 'cause most chicks think they look more groovy without their glasses, and is this what Elise thinks? I could have missed it, the quick glance, her eyes on me, a yearning, maybe the wanting, and is the serious way she holds her lips closed tight something to do with what she feels? She sways to the music. And this is strange, but I swear it was same as she's not there, man, and I still don't get it. Sylvia Plath when the photographer clicked the shutter, and Elise, transparent, a transparent willow and the wind blows through her.

I sit near Sappho, can't not look at Elise, and I do look, look through her, and how can that be? Sappho has a Kool going, oblivious to the wind blows through the transparent willow, and the willow sways to the slow death sound. Oblivious, Sappho is. Stuck on her own trip, confused internal, bummered 'cause some guy she has a crush on isn't interested. She talk talk talks about it but I don't listen. Oblivious. Sappho goes on and on and on, how she followed him and stood in the hall outside his room scared to knock.

"Kind of obsessive, huh Kate," Elise says.

"I wasn't *stalking* him, Elise," Sappho says. "Little miss stalker expert."

Cheap shot. Sappho sits there braiding her hair, self-righteous and smug, and you know what, I don't care if she's Elise's best friend. When a friend turns something personal revealed in a moment of trust into a weapon and aims it at the one who shared the secret it's a betrayal.

"Stuff it, Kate," I say. "Just 'cause you're miserable doesn't give you license."

I don't wanna hear what Sappho has to say. I have no interest in another victim story. Third guy she has a crush on since school started, and she still has her dealer boyfriend Ned down south.

When the song's over Elise gets back down on the carpet with us. Yeah, sometimes she's there, and this is one of those times. Another drag, Sappho sucks in the smoke, nothing pretty about it, and her face angled up tries to make smoke rings when she exhales—trying to copy Jim's trick—but she can't pull it off.

"Let him choke on a chicken bone," Sappho says, and twists the burning end of her smoke hard into the ashtray. She gets up, throws herself onto Elise's bed.

"Maybe he's shy," I say.

"Maybe he doesn't like girls," Elise says.

Yeah she's back. "Never seen him talk to a girl," Elise says. "Hangs in the cafeteria with those creeped-out druggies. What do you see in him, Kate?"

Sappho rolls onto her back, pulls the pillow over her face.

"So you coming or not?" Elise says.

Sappho voices this my-world-is-empty-without-you sigh.

"Gonna crash," she says.

Elise puts on her trenchcoat, and the brown fedora and she picks up the Levertov glasses, changes her mind and leaves 'em on her desk, and the wanting so out-of-control, oh I feel it. I dig her so, and the high of her and me going out into the cold night together is the *best*.

I'd go anywhere with Elise. You know how that is, when you don't care what you're gonna do long as it's with *her*. If I listen, I'd hear it. *Caw caw caw*. Doom and Gloom. And more, the wind through the branches, the whispers of the leaves whispering the troubles.

If I listen, but I don't listen.

"Maybe I'll slit my wrists like your idol," Sappho says. "Be sure to drink me a toast. Toss the empty on my grave."

"Gas," Elise says. "She sealed the room with wet towels, turned on the gas, and stuck her head in the oven."

"Thanks for the tip," Sappho says.

Elise looks over, conspiracy-of-two deal, me and her. "Pack of razor blades in my desk drawer," she says. "Do it in your room. Blood makes me faint."

"Can't be that bad, Kate," I say. "He's a loser. There's a

million guys out there," and man, I can talk bullshit good as anyone. "You'll feel better in the morning."

Authentic real, sometimes it doesn't get better, not the next morning, not the morning after that, and maybe not any goddamn goddamn morning.

"If I'm still around," Sappho says, and she's up off the bed. We all split Elise's room, walk down the hall and turn the corner and continue 'til we're outside Sappho's.

There's a sweetness in Elise's voice. "See you tomorrow, Kate."

"Have fun kids," Sappho says. "Don't do anything I wouldn't, you two."

"Well then sky's the limit," Elise says. "Depths of absinthe. Where we're headed."

I'm so glad to leave Sappho behind, her woe-is-me gets on my nerves. Dumb-ass dealer Ned down in Pasadena thinks his chick true blue while Sappho skulks the hallways in hopes some other loser will fuck her.

Me and Elise take the path that winds a quarter mile out to the road, the branches of skyscraper redwoods and firs and pines rub hard against each other, nature so alive, and I want it *bad*, to be alive in the moment, *this* moment.

We're on the path, crushed rock beneath our boots, and Elise has a plan. Always a plan. The plan is we hitch down to Liquor King, buy some booze, and drink it. A simple plan. Only it's not so simple 'cause it's night and Elise doesn't go out at night. She needs someone to go with her, protect her from whoever would do her harm. Well tonight I'm the someone. She's enlisted me as her accomplice, you know, make it possible to carry out the plan. I hope she's glad it's me and her and no one else. Glad the someone is me. I *know* it's true.

We walk past the humungous trees, and hear the eerie screams of the cold hard wind. Don't say anything and each moment passes that we stay silent I'm less cool, and more silent moments go by, and I'm not cool, not the hipster rock 'n' roll cat. I mean what to say, what to say, what to say, man? I wish I had a list. Conversation topics. I don't have a list.

The hard cold fury blows strong and Elise has a hand on her hat. I button my wool pea coat, get out the knit cap I keep in my pocket, pull it over my head and down so it covers my ears. We don't get hurricanes or tornadoes, that kinda homicidal weather in California, but in the moment of that moment I put my disbelief about a God or maybe a bunch of Gods aside, 'cause sure seems Zeus is in a bad mood, or could be Poseidon unleashing a death blow.

Get to where we see the road, and a severe gust batters us and the trees fierce enough I'm scared it'll blow a whole tree right over, and right as I reassure myself these trees have been here since long before I was born, up high there's a sound that freaks me. Yeah, I know that sound, a loud lightning bolt *crack* of a sound, the crack of a branch breaking. Oh man, and is this our fate, killed by a falling branch and we're not lovers yet, haven't kissed, I mean I still haven't held her hand.

Fuck it, I'm not going down, no fucking way.

Get hold of her arm, "come *on*, man," get her off the path, her fedora gone. *My hat, my hat!* Push her against the fat-ass trunk of some redwood. *Michael what are you doing to me?* My chest presses against her back, my face in her hair, feel her tremble but she doesn't resist, and I have the guilt same as if I'm wrongly accused of being a thief, yeah the guilt swoops down, and worse, a stalker who has her against a tree. Oh man, in that moment a huge-ass explosion behind us. Fear gives way to relief, and when I turn to look, oh fuck, 'cause it's where we were—big fucking branch.

"Damn, Elise."

Funny how she reacts, I mean she turns her body, struggles to get away but no, it's not to split, she wants to face me, gets her back against the tree and pulls me to her, her voice insistent, *Bloody massacre. Hold me, Michael.* I find her back, my hands between Elise and the rough bark, all of her tight against me, her head on my shoulder, and we don't say anything, hear the wind, hear the branches, and the fast beat of her heart.

Wow, Elise's heart.

Our bodies tremble, two hearts beat, and the sound of fast breathing, my breath, her breath. She holds me so tight as if the tighter she holds me the more I can protect her from her scary world. I don't know how long we stand there, don't know how exactly we get from holding each other against the tree, to where we're out at the road.

"Coulda fucking killed us, Elise."

She's got her hat back on, still trembles, tries to get herself together.

"Yeah, well *so what?*" she says.

Her hand on my arm, she stands close, so cool having a chick need me.

"Can't count on anything but death," she says. "Damn I need to get blitzed."

Mixed-up confusion, man, hangs on my arm, talks her death talk. Fuckin' *chicks,* don't make any sense but no sense.

"You're such an optimist," I say. "What about love?"

I stick my thumb out which is funny, there's no cars, and I haven't heard a single car, no other people, nothing but us and the night and the trees and down the road from where we stand a solitary street lamp near the bus shelter.

"What about it?" she says. "What *about* love? Just another four letter word, Writerman. Like your favorite poet wrote."

She's challenging everything I believe about love, and for a moment throws the whole deal into question. As if it's credible that love is a con job, same as the stars and stripes, same as God. Only a moment man, 'cause if there's one thing that's the foundation of me it's love. I *know* love exists the way I know I've got a heart.

She finds a Kool in a pocket of her trenchcoat, and I get out The Dylan, spark it, flame protected by my other hand, and she leans in. Oh man, and I wish somehow all the formality of Fifties manners, what my mom taught me when I'm a kid, you know, hold the door for the chick, pull out the chair for the chick, light the smoke for the chick, I wish they would add up to the chick loving me.

"I'll put my money on death over love," she says. "Way better odds."

"Come on, Elise," I say. "*All you need is love, love, love is all you need.* If you don't believe in love, what's left?" I need to connect, you know, me to her, her to me. I look deep into where her eyes are, despite the darkness and how I can't see much of them .

"Otherwise," and I stop myself, 'cause it's the wrong thing, but I say it anyway.

"If I didn't believe love exists," I say, "well I'd as soon end it all."

Maybe it was being out there in the dark along the side of an empty road, nothing but the sound of wind through the trees, branches whispering the troubles, no one but me, and she hardly knows me, and yet I saved her life. Minutes ago. Her voice gets quiet, and flat, no emotion.

"I think about that every day," she says. "Not a day goes by."

Not a day goes by, and I still hear her voice, her words. It was so sad, the sound of her saying them. Hear it 'til the day I die, man. I want to cry when I hear that, and I never cry, I'm not the freakster bro who cries, well almost never. I see that big black and white of Ms. Suicide, Ms. Bell Jar Plath, up above her pillow. Every night she lays there on her bed, looks up, sees Ms. Bell Jar Plath. Hellfuck of a scene.

Elise stands alongside the road, her hand grips my arm, smokes her Kool, her pale skin delicate against the night, and I don't feel like crying anymore. It thrills me, so close to her, the two of us out in this crazy-wild night, and I hope Elise feels it too, and more, gives love a chance.

Down the road the bus stop, and the light comes off the street lamp, fades away in the night air.

"Sometimes I can't stand the bummerosity," I say, "of being alone, man."

Oh I'm ready for it, Elise's cold disinterest, and the sarcastic, the perfect putdown, ready for Elise to get gone, not even there, the wind blown through her. Only it doesn't happen. She does feel something, I *know it*. Gives love a chance. Or gives a chance to the slight slim possibility of gives love a chance.

"Yeah, I know," she says. "Bloody massacre."

I look at her curious, 'cause me and Elise right there in that moment have started to talk about the authentic real of the interiors of us two, beneath the surface of the surface. Oh man, and this is it.

"You feel it too?" I say.

She lets go of my arm, drag of her Kool, side of the road.

"I have two younger sisters."

She shivers, and it's more than the cold.

"We shared a room 'til I was 12. After we moved I got my own room, but it was right across the hall from theirs. This is the first time I've lived away. It's been bloody hard, Michael."

Damn I want her to hold my arm again.

"And of course all the moving," she says, but she doesn't talk about it. Yeah she clams up on that one. Only there's something else, gotta be. Beyond the stalkers, and the moving, and homesick.

Not enough for a chick to bet on death over love.

"You have Kate just around the corner," I say, and the cold gets to me through the pea coat.

"Well what about Jim?" she says.

"Music talk," I say. "We can go at it about Stones' B-sides for days. I mean he's great. I dig it when we hang. Maybe how I feel doesn't make sense. I should be used to it. The loneliness. Only child. It's another world where I live, a one-person world. Me."

I look at Elise, want the connection of our bodies connected, sparks flying from her to me, me to her.

"First time I don't feel alone," I say, "was with Sarah, you know, my ex-old lady. High school days."

Her voice doesn't have the sarcastic, doesn't have that walls up sound, it's the deal when a person cares, but there's something else, jealousy maybe. In her voice, in her eyes?

"What was *she* like?"

Oh man. Sarah? And you never wanna tell a chick you want, about a chick you used to have. Never.

"Wasn't like anyone else on the planet," I say. "Take a book to tell you. Maybe if I write it someday I'll give you a copy. *Sign it 'love to you.'*"

And I laugh, man, and say, *"I think I'll write, 'good health to you.'"*

That's a joke, only she doesn't get it. She doesn't have a clue. You probably don't either. My problem, too many references nobody but me gets. "That's from a Blue Öyster Cult song," I say. "It's sung from the point of view of this rock star who muses on how he'll autograph this chick's cast. *I think I'll sign it 'love to you.' But should I sign it 'just to you.'*"

If you have to explain something same as that, forget it, man.

"I don't dig metal bands," Elise says. "Creeps me out."

"You'd dig the Cult," I say. "The lyrics are sarcastic, dark as those drawings of yours. R. Meltzer writes 'em," and no way she knows who R. Meltzer is, no fucking way.

A light drizzle starts up to come down so we give up on hitching, get into the bus shelter, and I don't feel so alone. Even with Elise not knowing the Blue Öyster Cult, and Meltzer too.

Weird how we tell each other how alone we feel and it brings us together. Maybe this is all I can expect. Moments, hours, days if I'm real lucky, when I don't feel alone.

Me and Elise get on the bus and that bus is gonna take us to the other side, where no living creature oughta go. Well, for Elise it's a return trip, but me, never been blitzed how I'm gonna get blitzed, and I know they're on the roof watching, Doom and Gloom. *Caw caw caw.* Heed the warning, only I never heed the warning. Not back then. Always there's a choice, and I wanna think I make the best decision, but that's not what happens. What I think, and what I do, and never the twain shall meet. Or at least often enough they don't. I mean sometimes they do, just not always.

Elise coulda taken me down any river she wanted that night. Down the Styx or Acheron straight to hell, or the Phlegethon where the boiling blood flows or the frozen lake that is Cocytus.

But the one she has in mind, yeah we're gonna ride the rapids down Lethe to the depths of oblivion.

Liquor King, where we're gonna buy some booze, gonna anesthetize ourselves. Gonna get drunk as we can on a fifth of tequila, gonna blot out every bit of the pain and the lonesome and all the horrors, at least 'til the liquor wears off and it all comes back, bigger and badder and worse than we ever known it.

Sit together on a hard plastic seat near the rear door and somehow I have her hand in mine. OK, this is how it happens. The driver has the radio on playing Dylan. Yeah, and of course, had to be Dylan, and we're right close, me and Elise, she rests her hand on my thigh, real casual, next to my hand, and what a rush, her hand touching me, the warmth, the gentle pressure of her fingertips, and I look at her and she smiles, and if her Jean Seberg laugh is a smile, well that's the smile, and I put my palm on the back of her hand, and she turns it, and we're holding hands, a jolt of current, from her to me, from me to her, her thin artist hand, and I'm paralyzed in the high of us so close, and I hear the Jean Seberg laugh that's her smile.

"Huge fuckin' redwood branch," I say. "Did you check out the size of it?"

"At the carnival we had near-death experiences," she says. "No big deal, Writerman." Still, she sure isn't pulling that hand away. The bus driver tries to duet with Dylan comin' off the radio. The driver has a beautiful voice, beautiful as James Taylor or Sam Cooke, and it sounds weird against Dylan's fake Okie drawl. *No, and I ain't lookin' to fight with you, frighten you or uptighten you.* We're so close our shoulders touch, and I squeeze her hand tight and I think maybe I have a new old lady. Thank you Zeus, thank you Poseidon. I mean, if you actually do happen to exist, and if you had somethin' to do with that branch.

We get off and walk in the rain across the paved parking lot towards Liquor King. We hold hands as we walk, I mean this is brand new for me, brand new for her. Elise quiet hums the melody of the Dylan song, and I sing along kind of quiet too, don't try to ape Dylan, sing how I sing, and Elise hums some more, and you know that moment I talk about before, when I don't feel alone? Yeah this is part of that moment. I mean it was so natural, her humming that song and me singing, walking together, her hand so warm in mine, not demanding anything of each other, and was there ever a moment so beautiful I spend with Elise as that one?

8. THE SECOND BLACK STORY

I'M GONNA LEVEL WITH you, there's nothing great about Liquor Store, but he's no worse than a lot of guys, and him reading Kierkegaard so serious first time I go into Liquor King I knew he was a major brain working there to pay for school. If I hadn't been so into my trip, might have understood he was a smart-ass who didn't have my luck, didn't have a grandfather paying his way to a BA or whatever he's after. Peach brandy sucks, and he knew it, and he tried to warn me. But you know what they say about first impressions. I blown it, forever doomed to repeat my mistakes, or make new ones.

We get to the swinging glass door, and I stop singing, and Elise stops humming, and I let go of her hand. That moment's *over*. Gird myself. Time for some Zen White Wall Meditation.

One. We enter, whole place ugly-ass fluorescent bright, the two of us damp from the rain, and that's what's good about being in this booze dispensary, we get a reprieve from the weather. And there he is. Liquor Store. Behind the counter his face has an expression I once saw on kids coming outta "2001: A Space Odyssey," and he's reading "Beyond Good and Evil," picks at a pimple, and that's when he sees me.

"Hey Writerman," he says. "Need another half-pint of the sweet stuff?"

He smirks a dirty smirk, a nod towards Elise, head of greasy blond hair back, sun-baked chin forward.

Oh, he's enjoying this, and it's as if his laugh, his sarcastic laugh, fills the place, a laugh same as Liquor Store would laugh if he watched a fat man slip on a banana peel and land on his back.

"This guy's *way* into the peach brandy."

Fuck!

Suck in a mouthful of air.

White wall white wall white wall. Two. Why's he reading Nietzsche, and the paranoia strikes deep, those Nazi youth eyes, and how blond his hair is, and how Kierkegaard was anti-Semitic, and I've not forgot the Iron Cross t-shirt, though today his shirt says "Surfers Make Better Lovers."

Goddamn smirkface, 'cause now Elise is hip to my peach brandy scene.

Three. I get right front of him, and there's pus and blood where he's picking at the pimple. "You're not gonna have a lot of customers if you give 'em all crap."

"They pay me either way," he says.

"I bet your boss would love to hear your theories on customer relations."

"Words are cheap, Writerman. You of anyone oughta know that."

He got me there, I'm not gonna snitch, and anyway I kinda like the guy. If I had his job I'd handle it how he does. I bet he feels same about his shitty minimum wager as I did working McDonald's summer between freshman and sophomore years. Only there's something else about Liquor Store. You know the sadness in Elise's eyes. Well he has a different sadness. Life hasn't been the best for Liquor Store—his parents were shit or maybe only his mom raised him or I don't know. I could invent clichéd sad-sack scenarios all day long and what's the point? Liquor Store's never gonna be my friend.

"Fifth of Jose Cuervo Gold," Elise says.

He knows she isn't 21, still has doubts about me, but he doesn't card us. Too much trouble, and he knows how it ends. It is tequila we're buying, not peach brandy. I pay, and Elise gets the brown paper bagged feel-good bottle.

I already have the glass door held open, Elise stepping from inside to outside.

"Some parting advice for you, Writerman," Liquor Store
says.

I turn to see he's got his Nietzsche book open, and Elise
turns too, me just inside the door, her in the doorway, the both
of us watching him.

His eyes move off me onto Elise and down to the book.

"In revenge and in love," he reads, "woman is more barbaric
than man is."

Oh fuck you, Liquor Store, and we're gone baby gone. Elise
in the parking lot, me too. Not gonna acknowledge his
smirkface words, yeah that's how I one-up the scene. Outside I
feel the freeze, the wind cuts through my coat, burns my face,
and I want us away from the fluorescent emptiness of Liquor
King, and the barren emptiness of the parking lot.

"You drink *peach* brandy?"

Oh man oh man oh man.

Liquor Store doesn't even have to be out there to stick the
knife in. I should tell Elise the authentic real, how I don't know
shit about booze, and it was the first time, and yada yada yada.
But no.

"Thought I'd check it out, you know, for a kick. See how
bad it really is."

"You waste good money on bad booze?" she says, and
laughs her Jean Seberg laugh, and maybe it's not a good sign.
Not long after Jean Seberg laughs that laugh in the Godard
movie, she gives up Michel to the cops.

"Let's get one thing straight, Writerman," she says. "Don't
bring peach brandy around *me*. A lot of losers drank that shit at
the carnival."

Yeah, gives up Michel, and soon enough he's dead.

"Smirkface in there," I say. "Guy behind the counter—."

There's a look a chick gives a guy, doesn't matter what he
says, isn't gonna fix anything.

Only good thing about our foray into Liquor King was an
abatement of the rain. Well that and the bottle we have. We sit
inside the covered bus shelter waiting for the bus that's gonna

bring us back up to campus, and Elise takes a serious drink and another.

"At first it tastes harsh," she says, and her hand has a grip on the bottle, and my hand on the bottle, my hand on her hand, her hand so warm, the bottle so cold.

"You get acclimated," she says, "and it tastes good. You feel the fire."

With her I don't need booze to feel the fire. "Soon you'll feel no pain, my dear," and it burns my mouth. We pass it back and forth, me to her, her to me. And that's when she tells me the second of The Black Stories.

"I was 15, first time I blitzed on tequila," she says. "Had this boyfriend, he was 18. You saw the drawing. That boy. His house —his parents' house—out at the beach, Malibu," and one hand grips the neck of the feel-good bottle, the other hand on my thigh, thin artist hand, and her hand is the smallest bird, a finch or some kind of baby bird.

Alive. Warm. Safe.

"His parents were in the movie business," she says. "His mom designed costumes and his dad did something with sound."

The constant patter of the rain on the shelter roof. I could feel her tense up as she told what gone down, a tightness where her hand touches my thigh, and more than a tightness in her voice.

"On a bluff overlooking the ocean. Cost big money, that house. Big patio with a pool. His mom and dad were away working on a film. His mom and dad were *always* away working on a film."

Her confiding in me, well it was kinda same as when me and Sarah used to talk, and this is weird, but there was a joy inside me. I used to feel it when Sarah would tell me a secret, even if it was the tragic deal.

The joy of a chick confiding. In me. Finally. And was this love? Well was it? There was another feeling competing with the first one, the feeling of cheating. Or maybe it was guilt. Here

she was telling me this story, and 'cause of that tightness already
I knew it wouldn't end well, and me feeling a joy, how could that
be right? I still wonder about me, and how I feel when shit goes
down, and how sometimes how I feel doesn't feel like it's how
I'm supposed to feel.

"They had a wet bar in the rec room," she says. "Different
brands of gin and vodka, Jack Daniel's, Southern Comfort, two
different brands of scotch, vermouth, lots of wine. We tried
most of it that year."

She pauses, the finch or whatever bird it is doesn't feel so
safe. In the silence we hear the occasional hard "thwat" when
the wind throws rain at the back of the shelter. She looks up at
me, checks how her words are going down.

"You don't have to," I say.

Ready to take flight?

"I want to," she says. "If you have ears for it," and this is a
test, what kind of freakster bro am I? Kind of guy she can talk
to about the troubles, or another shithead who wants to fuck
and run.

"We had a routine," she says. "First we'd go for a swim, then
we'd get blitzed and he'd try to kiss me. Sometimes I let him. He
was a good-looking guy, strong shoulders, on the basketball
team. That day, the last day I saw him, it was hot, sun blazing
down. We went swimming, and afterwards I was lying on a
lounge chair on the patio."

Young chicks don't have a clue what goes down in the mind
of a horny guy, and as she talks I hear her naïveté that day, had
on some teeny bikini, laid out on that lounge, blitzed, and
getting more blitzed.

"You could look past the pool and out at the ocean," she
says. "I was 15, his folks in the movie business and that house
and I thought I loved him. I was star struck you know. He came
out with a couple of glasses and a fifth of this stuff. Jose
Cuervo Gold. Drank too much and passed out. I don't
remember what happened."

I knew what she was telling me, but I didn't get it. I figured
for a lot of chicks the first fuck goes that way. Both drunk and

the guy's insistent, and he doesn't know if the chick's putting up resistance when really she wants it, or says she wanna when she doesn't, or the next day thinks she told him *no*, even when she told him *yes*. Yeah, well, that might be a way of looking at it, but there's other ways it goes, hellfuck darker ways, and I didn't have a clue how it could be from a chick's point of view.

"Bloody massacre," she says, and there was a sick bad scene in her cobalt blue eyes.

"Major bummerosity, Elise," I say, and the ruin of how she feels there in the cold bus shelter, and I gotta make her know I'm a million fucking miles different from the monster boyfriend. I put my hand on her arm. She shakes it off, but then she puts hers on mine.

"I'm sorry, Michael," and she's trying for a joke. "One of those things, Writerman. Sorta like what happened at the carnival," and takes another slug, and another. She doesn't say more about it and it's weird we drink the same kinda booze she drank when what happened happened. As if each time she gets blitzed on Cuervo Gold she has another chance to change the past.

Or relive it.

We get off the bus at The University so blitzed we need to sit inside this other bus shelter that's right there, empty, as if it's been waiting for us two to show up. We get a couple cigarettes lit.

"Bob Dylan's lighter," I say.

I hold the lighter out so it glints from the streetlamp light.

"Sure," she says. "And this is Hendrix's tequila. Straight from his grave. He was blitzed on it when he wrote 'Purple Haze.'"

"No, really," I say. "Got it from Jerry. You know, Garcia."

"If you think you can impress your way between my legs, forget it Writerman."

"No Elise, that's not it."

"Why would Jerry Garcia give you Bob Dylan's lighter?"

Oh fuck, 'cause this is the problem tellin' anyone about The

Dylan. To convince them I gotta confess, and when I do it makes me look same as a cheap-ass hood. Too late to turn back, so I tell her the story, how me and Bobby went to interview Garcia at his house in Larkspur back when I was in high school. How Garcia got out The Dylan to light up a joint, told us Dylan gave it to him only right then Robert Hunter, who was hanging out in the living room with us, spoke up, said, "Hey Jerry, you told me you *stole it* from Bobby." I go on and on, get to the part where the interview is over and Hunter splits and a totally fucked up Garcia stumbles up the stairs and I make my move, and when I'm done Elise is laughing the kinda almost hysterical laugh where you can't stop, only finally she does stop.

"You're too much, man," she says, calming herself down. "Takes some guts to steal Bob Dylan's lighter from the Grateful Dead."

We sit there silent, smoke our cigarettes until they're done, drink from the bottle.

"Elise, look at me," and she turns her head, her face loose and sloppy how a drunk chick gets, hair wild askew, and her lips.

Oh man oh man oh man.

I get her hand between my hands, and if "you're safe" is a way a touch can feel, that's how I hold her hand. Her cobalt blue eyes get wide and she closes them. Gentle as I know how given how loaded I am, how loaded she is, my lips meet her lips, her lips cold from the night, smell of smoke and booze, and soon we'll be in each others arms. Only her body goes stiff and the tightness, and she pulls away.

Real serious, drunk serious, "I *can't*, Michael," total heavy traffic weight-of-the-world serious.

"Look Michael, I don't think I'm the girl."

Oh man, when-blue-turns-to-gray.

"Bloody sorry," she says. "I mean that isn't what I mean, I mean not at all. I mean I can't. Not tonight. I mean, oh damn."

Drunk as I am I don't get it, her mixed-up confusion. Hanging on me, holding hands, and arms around each other, she oughta wanna kiss, and more.

"I don't want to hurt you, Michael."

There's something she hasn't told me.

"Need time," she says. "I like you, more than like. Just can't."

Goddamn goddamn goddamn.

"Kissing's not fucking," I say. "Doesn't mean you gotta marry me if we kiss."

"You don't know me," she says. "You don't, you *don't.*"

The blush across her cheeks. Here the planet been through the free love era, freaks running naked, McCartney screaming *why don't we do it in the road*, and she's embarrassed about what we haven't even talked about yet. A drag of her cigarette, and another.

Drunk as I am I have to be the serious scene and we're looking into each other's eyes, stone cold connect.

"I'll hang in, Elise," I say.

And that was a moment. Her face struggles for control, and she wins the struggle, and the moment keeps going.

"You're a nice guy," she says. "Too nice, Writerman."

That's not true, well I don't want it to be true. Maybe it's true. Tom, you know, the guy I shared an apartment with freshman year, who fucked a different chick every night, he wouldn't spend a minute with a chick who didn't put out. Harper would spit in my face. Well I'm not Tom, and Elise isn't Harper.

"So now that's out of the way," I say. "What you wanna do?"

We've gone through more than half the bottle and if someone punched me I'd feel nothin'. Elise craves potato chips. There's a snack machine on the dining hall mezzanine. Somehow, despite the rain coming down serious drench scene and how boozed-up we are, we get there, tired and soaked, water dripping off us, lean over the railing look down at all the cheap-ass tables on the floor below. Walk around 'til we get to the snack machine, and look though the scratched plastic. Candy bars and chips. And all the rest. She puts her money in, presses the buttons for a bag of Lay's. Nothing.

"Bloody massacre!"

Chicks and machines.

"Let me," I say.

Oh yeah, let the big man take care of it little lady. Very careful I push in each of the buttons. Nothing.

"Hellfuck," I say, and Elise feeds more coins in the slot, pushes the same buttons. She holds the feel-good bottle against her chest, and I pound on the snack machine, and the hard clear plastic cracks.

"Creepy creeped-out machine," she says.

"Fuck-ass motherfuckin' machine," I say.

I look at Elise, water still dripping off her fedora, her face damp and shiny with it, she laughs her Jean Seberg laugh, and even in her frustration her eyes go mischievous and I have an idea, really gonna show her what a cool-ass freakster bro I am. The back of the snack machine is about a half-foot from the wall, and I get a grip, rock it and the upper back of it smashes the wall, rock it out, smash the wall again. Elise sets the feel-good bottle down, gets a grip too. We get momentum, push the thing, and it smashes deeper into the wall, and we lean it out, *bam*, deeper still, and when it comes away from the wall, we push it right over, fucker crashes face down on the cement floor, and the sound of major shit broken.

Oh man, it's hellfuck funny, funniest thing we *ever* seen. We laugh crazy-ass bent over fuck-up drunk tears 'til the paranoia sets in.

She straightens up, her hand on my arm, and her face serious same as when she doesn't let me kiss her. Her hair is still crazy from the wind and rain, her face has the red booze glow and her trenchcoat hangs open.

"Didn't black out," she says.

And this is the third of The Black Stories. I mean I guess you could call it part two of the second Black Story, but to me it's the third.

"With my *boyfriend*, Michael."

That's when she tells me. "You know how I said I used to lay on a lounge chair out by the pool? I used to take my top off.

I let him touch my breasts sometimes and we'd kiss, but that was all. That day I'd taken it off and I was lying there in the sun. He kept looking at me. I didn't like that. He came over. I thought he was gonna kiss me and touch me, 'cause he always was coppin' a feel, but this time it was different. He got on top of me. I told him '*no*,' I told him, '*I don't want to. Stop it. Don't.*'"

She's slumped over, her body broken, "but he wouldn't stop," boozy fuck-up mess, "wouldn't stop, Michael."

She holds on to me and she's shaking.

"He wouldn't stop he wouldn't stop he wouldn't stop."

Under the mezzanine lights she's a transparent willow got her branches broke. I figure she's gonna collapse in tears but what I don't figure on is how her emotions flip from A to Z so fast. Her lips together, done with being the victim.

"I don't *care*," she says. "I don't look past right now," and wipes her face on her coat sleeve, picks up the feel-good bottle.

"I've wanted to do this," she says, "since I first saw this place."

She takes a drink, shoves it at me and I upend it into my mouth.

"Gimme," she says

She's got the bottle, and begins to dance, flits in towards the railing, and back away, up against it, and back.

"Don't think I'll do it, do you?"

I try and sing same as Levon Helm, you know, with an Okie voice.

"Baby don't you do it."

"Dare me!" she says.

"Do what?" I say.

Winds her arm around and back, let 'er rip, and the feel-good bottle spins through the air, tequila pouring out, down it falls, down, down, down, hits the top of a table, one of those dining hall tables, shatters, bits of glass splattering everywhere, and in that moment I understood, man, beyond understanding. The act of free will and fuck the consequences, of I can do anything, *any fucking thing*. The glass breaks the world breaks.

Tear it down to make it new to make it ours.

"Somethin' I picked up at the carnival," she says.

Yeah, we both laugh. She's Jean Seberg, and me, I laugh the laugh of relief a freakster bro laughs when his chick laughs, and that was a moment. The best part, for me, to understand the stakes of what free is, that was big, but no, and it's not when the bottle shatters. Best part comes afterwards.

In the adrenalin rush she puts her arms around me. It starts as a celebratory embrace, but it's more. She doesn't care my pea coat is soaked. Maybe because of what happened when I tried to kiss her, how when she said *stop*, I stopped, she trusts me, pushes her body against mine, and she has feelings for me. I *know*.

9. GOT YOUR BACK, OLD SPORT

THERE CAME A MOMENT when Jim was put to the test. It was less than a week after that blitzed-out night, night of the second and third Black Stories. Me and Jim were at the Neil Young concert, downtown at the Civic Auditorium. That night I got more clues that the Freak Scene Dream scene of the Sixties, you know, what the straights called the counter-culture, was gone baby gone, replaced by junkies and con men and freakster bro wannabes hawking tattered pseudo memories of something they'd never experienced or understood.

Neil had the wasted Charles Manson mountain man deal going, hair shaggy-uncombed past his shoulders, a wrinkled black-on-black striped *film noir* suit jacket, denim cowboy shirt with the tails out, and beat-up boots, but it wasn't his clothes or his hair, 'cause even from afar there was something else same as he'd lost something he'd never get back. He was done tired, that was the vibe, and if this was what success does to a man, fuck, gotta wonder.

Still, one thing gave me hope, and that was his jeans. Old fucker jeans patched with squares of different size and pattern material, some with polka dots, some with plaid, some with checks, same as someone grabbed any scraps of material they had in the rag drawer. Only how those jeans were patched is what Neil's all about, and even in his ravaged corrosion, still he grabs at ideas and images and experience, takes the low down heartbreak chaos of life, and makes art.

I dig Neil the most, beginning in his Buffalo Springfield days.

Back then he's the coolest freakster bro in the band with his fringed Buffalo Bill leather jacket. So so serious bummered-out lanky tall plays a big fat Gretsch White Falcon sings us his lonesome. Sure Dylan made up the whole trip, smart young white guy lays the deep poetry over folk-rock, but while Dylan has the East Coast vibe and by the time *he* plays rock 'n' roll he has that English dandy thing going, Neil's the stoned West Coast free spirit. Neil lays his heart out in those downer chords, not afraid to sing a bad line 'cause he knows the feel is the whole trip, the *sound* of the words he sings, and the off-kilter rhythm that shows up around *Harvest* but been in the works at least since "Mr. Soul," and the ragged-ass electric guitar. Sometimes it's as if Neil hangs on one note for the whole damn solo. So often growing up I felt lonely as the loneliest Neil Young ballad. "Oh, Lonesome Me" or the other one that's equally downered and out, "The Losing End (When You're On)," where he's all sad-sack singing how he'll never be the same, and yeah it's pathetic, but sometimes it's how I feel. Neil's lonesome sound, sound of my own soul.

I got a couple of press passes from Bill Graham's press guy, Zohn, one benefit of writing for *The Paper*, and drag Jim along 'cause Elise doesn't wanna go. Jim hates Neil Young, hates *that stinky organic veggie music.* He knows Neil's a sell-out, but it goes deeper. Jim's a poet, and Neil sometimes being lax in the lyric department major bugs *Thee* Freakster Bro. Worse still, Jim thinks Neil is the quintessential "back-to-nature hippie," and Jim always thought the Freak Scene Dream sucked. 'Course he lived in L.A., so he never saw the real deal, you know, the early Haight Street trip before it all became a cliché of a cliché. Still, it's Neil Young. Maybe Jim's a little curious. Maybe a lot curious.

Jim has on his full English rock star regalia—the black velveteen suit, a crazy-ass psychedelic shirt and the Beatle boots. And the lucky cane with the brass lion's head. *Thee* Freakster Bro never goes anywhere without that lucky cane. Soon as he got it, he stood tall, a new kinda confidence, 'course it could be Jaded gives him the confidence. Getting laid gives him the confidence. That'll put the bop in a freakster bro's be-bop-a-lula. Then again. Could be the lucky cane.

The scene on the sidewalk leading up to the Civic is a river of ragged, longhaired space cadets along with a bunch of us from The University. There are freaks looking to buy a ticket or cop some dope or sell some dope or panhandle cash for a ticket and dope. I swear I see Dealer Cat, the dude who was hanging around the Mill Valley bus depot the afternoon I hung out with Polanski back in 1971, the summer I flipped out. I'm sure it's the same guy. On the sidewalk all frayed and fucked up, and chanting.

"Weed, coke, reds, hash, 'shrooms, weed, coke, reds, hash, 'shrooms."

Jim stops near to where he stands. Dealer Cat.

What Jim sees: Dealer Cat in the zone, the glazed-eyes trip, face booze-red, veins broken, scorched sunburn skin, oblivious to the havoc the elements deal out to his flesh and blood. And he has a serious coke-head sniff.

Jim looks at him, and Jim flashes me a glance, the dotted-lines eyes, and it's same as he discovers he stepped in dog shit, and what those dotted-lines eyes say to me, well they ask a question: how can a human exist in a state same as Dealer Cat?

My dotted-lines eyes don't have an answer to the question his ask. I'm too self-absorbed, can't see beyond my own hyped-up about-to-see-Neil trip, no empathy for Dealer Cat in the moment. I look at him, see a loser. A fuck-up same as all the rest. Yeah, the fuck-up of my vision.

I mean could be Jesus stands there.

Jim takes a few steps so he stands close to Dealer Cat, stands right front of him.

"Excuse me, old sport," Jim says. "But it did cross my mind that perhaps you aren't aware of the volume of your utterances."

Jim has his hands one on top of the other on the lion's head, the cane right in front of him, and he leans on it.

Dealer Cat sniffs some more.

"Any louder," Jim says, "and they'll hear you down at the pig, er, police station on Pacific."

Nothing. No response. Same as Dealer Cat doesn't hear Jim.

Dealer Cat rubs snot off his nose, wipes it on his mud-color poncho, focuses in on Jim best he can, and his face the mixed-up confusion, same as if he says what the fuck?

"Hello!" Jim says.

Jim's dandy trip something out of a magazine fashion spread, and Dealer Cat looks at Jim and he has to wonder, what does this freakster bro want? To buy some shit? But no, that's not it. And Dealer Cat doesn't know why Jim stands there if he doesn't want to make a buy. Doesn't know why Jim stands there talk talk talks at him. Doesn't understand that Jim can't believe Dealer Cat actually exists.

Only Jim doesn't give a shit.

Jim amazed and amused same as he stands before an exhibit at a Ripley's Believe It Or Not Odditorium.

And finally.

"Peace, brother," Dealer Cat says. "All you need is *love.*"

Jim, man, he thinks it's funny what Dealer Cat says.

Even that day I know one thing. Nothing funny about it.

And then right back to the litany.

"Weed, coke, reds, hash, 'shrooms, weed, coke, reds, hash, 'shrooms."

Dealer Cat sniffs some more, and then sneezes and coughs, and sneezes again and somehow a piece of snot lands on one of Jim's shiny new Beatle boots.

And Jim shakes his head and he's mad, gets out a white handkerchief, wipes the snot off his boot.

Disgusted, man.

"The end is near," Dealer Cat says. "*Beware.*"

And me, I don't get it, and Jim doesn't either, and only later do I understand the premonition Dealer Cat's words portend.

But then again, maybe some kinda way I do know.

A premonition of the betrayal.

Jim, disgusted, man.

Me, I have no disgust for Dealer Cat. In my disinterest and

self-absorption. I don't hate Dealer Cat, I'm not offended, not disgusted, no man. Still, I'm no better than Jim. I write Dealer Cat off as another lost soul when I should see the there-but-for-fortune-go-you-or-I of the scene. And more. Should feel for the dude, and understand the tragedy, the sad sad human drama there before us.

And it's not only Dealer Cat, man, it's the whole goddamn goddamn human race.

"I didn't know they bused everyone down from The Haight and up from Venice Beach," Jim says to me. "Why didn't your man Neil play for free in Golden Gate Park? I thought he was a peace/love guy. Turns out he's a shuckster, only in it for the money. Should have called it 'Bank Account of Gold'!"

"*Fuckin'* smart-ass," I say.

He imitates me. "*Fuckin'* sell-out," and to the tune of "Mr. Soul" he sings.

"*Oh, hello Mr. Sell-Out, I dropped by to cash in my cool.*"

I brought my Super8 camera along, and once Neil starts in I start filming. Gonna use the footage for a film class project. Got my right eye against the viewfinder eyepiece, zoom on Neil's face when *bam*, same as a curtain drops, everything gone black. Separate my eye from the eyepiece and there stands this guy who works for Bill Graham, Jeff Grindly. I know his name 'cause he MCs the shows Graham doesn't make it to, including this one. He has his hand over my lens.

"No filming allowed, man," he says.

Grindly is a skinny snake of a man. Uneven greasy brown hair touches his shoulders and a handlebar 'stache. You know Peter Max? Grindly could be his younger brother. Grindly talks with a New Yawk accent no amount of time on the West Coast gonna eradicate.

"Gimme the camera."

Talk about blind obedience, feel the intimidation, and before I think to question it, hand him the Super8.

"We have signs everywhere," he says. "I should throw you out."

"You're kidding, old sport, right?" Jim says, and turns to me. "Relax, Writerman, this misunderstanding will be rectified momentarily."

Grindly focuses on Jim, and on his face a question due to Jim's rock star get-up. Is Jim somebody? Yeah, well, Jim deserves the self-respect due any human, but that isn't the kinda somebody that impresses Grindly. I rub a finger against the pass stuck to my shirt. "We're with the press. You know Zohn, right? Zohn put us on the list. Everything's groovy."

Some freaks nearby turn our way, and I hear a grumbling "Bill Graham sucks."

"Zohn didn't tell you it was cool to bring a movie camera," Grindly says.

"Well," and what am I gonna tell him? For sure Grindly gonna talk to Zohn, and if I lie I'll never get passes into a Graham show again.

"Why don't you return the camera to my friend," Jim says. "And we can all play nice in the sandbox."

The goon's face fades to red. "How 'bout minding your own business, mista? Keep your trap shut. Capiche?"

More freaks near us hear the loud crossfire of our voices, and move closer, and all the while Neil's up there singing "Only Love Can Break Your Heart" or maybe it was "Love in Mind."

"Cool it," shouts this guy who looks like he's playing Rip Van Winkle in some movie, and another cat might as well be Friar Tuck, wearing this long monk's outfit, yells, "You're ruining the show."

Mr. Security has the camera in his hands, turning it this way and that, tries to find the release and get the film out.

"Neil won't care, man," I say. "He's an *artist*."

Grindly gets the camera open, drops the cartridge on the floor, smiles his sleaze-ass smile, his 'stache raises, ugly spark in his eyes.

"No, man!" I say, and from the freaks a collective moan, "Don't do it, *brother*."

He steps on it hard with his black engineer boot, and the plastic shell cracks. My footage of Neil gone baby gone. He holds out the Super8. "We're gonna keep an eye on you. You're a problem, we don't need problems. Capiche?"

He waits 'til the Super8's in my backpack, and he's walking away when Jim says, "The man is a sadist, a sleazebag and, I might add, a royal bag of shit."

Friar Tuck shouts, "Right on, bro," and others make the sounds of unity.

"Fuckin', asshole!" I say.

"Although we could look on the bright side," Jim says. "We won't have to watch your footage of this boring show."

Oh fuck, 'cause I feel a hand grip my cowboy shirt at the neck, and Grindly's in my face.

"What'd you say, motherfucker!?"

The crowd of freaks, I feel their shock at the violence. "Get your hand off me," I say, and he lets go, but he's right there in front of me. Hellfuck hostile.

Jim twirls the lucky cane, and he must have practiced that move 'cause he has it nailed down tight, same as some professional ringmaster. "Don't you have some important MCing to do?" Jim says. "Perhaps in another state?"

The goon holds his body in a way that total makes it clear he grew up on the streets of New York.

"You call me a 'fuckin' asshole,' motherfucker?"

Still more freaks turn our way, and I feel their frustration—the scene contagious as a car wreck. One calls out, "Stop hasslin' him, man."

Another freak yells, "Get outta here, Pigman!" and that's all it takes to start the chanting.

Fuckin' Pigman, fuckin' Pigman, fuckin' Pigman.

And more join in, a chorus of stoners giving Grindly the finger.

Fuckin' Pigman, fuckin' Pigman, fuckin' Pigman.

Jim has his lucky cane in both hands front of his chest, grips it same as a weapon. "This is quite and for certain out of line and inappropriate, old sport."

Louder still, and more join the choir.

Fuckin' Pigman, fuckin' Pigman, fuckin' Pigman.

"Put the cane down, mista," Grindly says. "Back off or I'll take it away from you. Capiche?"

Pigman faces the crowd. "Get back to watching Neil," he says. "Or I'll have every one of you thrown out," and that's the wrong thing to tell Neil's fans. Oh man do they start making noise, yelling for Pigman to stick his head up his ass, that kinda deal.

"Yeah, OK, I said 'fuckin' asshole,'" I say. "What of it?" and he's in my face again, smells of garlic and after-shave, and his bony hard fingers dig into my arm.

"You're out of here," he says, and I try to shake him off only he's same as a leech, and thank God-who-no-way-can-exist for my freakster bro, Jim got a big stumpy hand on Grindly's arm, and I break away.

"I'm not going fuckin' nowhere, asshole," and I face off with my dad in the kitchen, goddamn Pigman doesn't tell Writerman what to do.

Big fucking crowd, all the freaks pissed off, Pigman's turned their groovy concert to shit. Grindly aims his middle finger at my face, "Listen motherfucker! If you don't go with me RIGHT FUCKING NOW, I'll get security to throw you out on your goddamn ass. Just might break your head in the process. Capiche?"

My voice got the shakes, "No, man," and this guy Wolf I know from freshman year, who's tough as a hummingbird but looks same as Attila the Hun, and his biker cat buddy get in front of me facing Pigman, cross their arms as if they're my bodyguards.

The hippie choir amp it up yet again.

Fuckin' Pigman, fuckin' Pigman, fuckin' Pigman.

From the stage Neil says, "There's some folks causin' a ruckus out there. Makes it hard for me to do what I do. We can't seem to stop the war, but we should be able to keep the peace among our brothers and sisters."

"What a hippie!" Jim says, and to Pigman, "Have fun explaining this to Neil. 'Hey man, please forgive me, I had to scream 'motherfucker' during one of your most sensitive acoustic ballads.'"

Pigman's helpless surrounded by what gotta be two dozen angry freaks, so he splits, total vamoose deal.

"Jim, man," I say. "I'm gonna lay low somewhere in the shadows. I'll see you back at the dorms later."

"No way, Writerman," he says, and he gives me the dotted-lines eyes. "No telling what kind of trouble you'll get in without me," and he twirls the lucky cane, nearly hits Wolf. "Sorry, old sport."

I figure things gonna cool out, but before me and Jim can split to safer environs, Pigman is back with the Bill Graham goon squad: three burly fuckers wearing light blue nylon security jackets.

"Get this motherfucker outta here," Pigman says.

Jim twirls the cane. "You know, sir, we're both credentialed members of the press. I don't mean this as a threat, but I can assure you——."

Pigman gets his middle finger aimed at Jim. "Fuck you, Little Lord Fauntleroy," and to the goons, "This shit too!"

Two of the goon squad grab Jim while the other one starts for me. I move to the right but as the goon reaches for me, switch directions, the old fake-out, take off running, and I move fast, man, fast as fast can be, faster still. The security goon is a fat clown, gotta be 300 pounds. Yeah, Writerman gonna lose him for sure, and my ego explodes—fuck, yeah, gonna pull this one off. And I was serious lost in my daydream, vanquish Graham's goon squad, have the last laugh when I crash into another huge-ass goon, fucker got my left arm, twists it hard behind me. "Hellfuck!"

Neil stops playing, unsure what to do, "Please brothers and sisters."

The goons have a good grip on me, and Jim too. Pigman follows behind, cursing. Drag us out of the auditorium, through the lobby, and out to the sidewalk. Pigman silhouetted in the doorway, his skinny body black against the bright bright of the lobby.

"I see you assholes again," he says. "I'm gonna personally beat the crap out of you."

And the door bangs shut with an ugly metallic clang.

"Capiche?" Jim says.

"Capiche!" I say.

It's a black night, fog thick as thick can be, headlights of the passing cars dim as the beams from flashlights with worn-down batteries. Oh I'm in a foul-ass mood. Thrown out of Neil's concert before he gets out his Flying V and howls at the Devil.

Yeah, the fog is thick as the thickest reefer smoke after a human been smoking in a room with the windows shut all afternoon. Thick as what you get when you burn wet wood with the damper shut. Thick as the maze of conundrums you gotta unravel to understand the plot to that film they make of "The Big Sleep."

Oh yeah, hellfuck foul-ass mood, and I'm about to step forward, I mean no point to stand outside the Civic, no blue-coat security guard gonna let us back in, start to take a step, a step into the unknown haze of thick thick too thick fog when Jim's fingers dig hard into my arms.

"Stop, Writerman," he says. "Watch your step."

Him saying that, well I don't really know why I obeyed him, I mean given the hellfuck of my scene, but I did stop. Stopped and looked down at where I would have stepped. Oh, man, bottom half of a broken wine bottle, big jagged stalagmite shards of glass aim right where the thin sole of my Keith Richards snakeskin boot woulda come down hard.

"Watching your back, old sport," Jim says. And this still isn't the moment, we're not there yet.

The fog blowing in off the Forever Infinite Pacific is damp on my face, and the wind makes the cold goddamn goddamn colder. My pea coat helps but still I'm cold and Jim's velveteen suit is worthless.

"I told you Neil was at best a third rate Dylan," Jim says. "Now that I've heard him live, fourth rate."

He straightens his coat collar, smooths out the sleeves where the goons grabbed him. "Everyone knows Bill Graham's an asshole," I say. "You just saw one of his toadies try to be the big man."

Jim shakes out a Pall Mall. "Use your quite exceptional brain power, Writerman," and he lights up, experiences the rush of the nicotine doing its thing. "If you hire a thug to promote your show, than you're responsible when the thug behaves like a thug."

Whatever, I mean our scene is fucked. Outside when we need to be inside. Enough is enough, and all I care about is seeing Young's electric set, and I formulate a plan. Always a plan.

"Maybe there's an open door around back."

"Yes, of course there is, and a bright red carpet all laid out just for you," Jim says. "I would much prefer if we could make our way up to the dorms post haste, and once in the relative comfort of my room, for certain and most adamantly, indulge ourselves with a doobie or three."

"*You* retreat to the dorms, man," I say, and walk away, fast, faster, and faster still, toward the alley that runs along the left side of the auditorium. There's a chain across the entrance, and a yellow "Keep Out" sign hangs from it, but I get over the chain, no sweat. Don't see any doors along the side of the building, and I don't have time to ponder my next move, 'cause Jim catches up. He's got what's left of his burning smoke in one hand, lucky cane in the other, and I reach out my hand, thumb up. "Yow!" I say.

"Rock 'n' roll!" Jim says, and drops the smoke, and we do a Soul Bro shake.

Jim smiles, and it's a different smile, a conspiracy of two smile. The raised eye, the barest near-subliminal nod. "I think you're a secret hippie at heart," he says.

"No way, man," I say. "I wanna be famous. The fake hippies you see around, all they wanna do is get high and get laid."

And then: "Me, man, I wanna get laid, get high, get rich. I wanna know the transcendence. And I wanna be a star."

And then: "But you," I say. "You're the secret hippie. Soon enough you'll walk around barefoot with the love beads 'round your neck, daisy behind your ear humming Scott McKenzie tunes, sit under a redwood with a hookah smoking hash and writing your poems."

We turn the corner, me first, and it's same as we step into a surreal painting, a gigantic diorama made by Dali and Disney. Neil's silver tour bus parked back there emerges from the thick-ass fog lit up by bright bright overhead security lights bathing the scene in a glowing mist.

The bus is a custom job, and through the mist I see an awesome Indian scene airbrushed on the side, a dreamlike tableau summoned forth by Silver Fox and Coyote who sing the world into being. Redwoods, sagebrush, and mountains. Teepees, a fire circle and a waterfall. An Indian chief holding a bow and arrow, a woman and child by his side, and a big-ass big moose, head held high. Flying across intense orange-yellow sunset sky, huge-ass American Eagle.

Above the windshield where the destination should be, where Kesey's bus said "Furthur," Young's says, "Cortez the Killer."

Stand there take in the glory. And the truth of it, nothing in my mind other than that bus. Not even Elise.

"Neil's bus, man!" I say. "Holy Grail, Rosetta Stone *and* Rosebud, fuck yeah."

"Most of us have outgrown cowboys and Indians," Jim says.

"Neil's gonna cool out in there," I say. "Smoke a doobie between sets."

"So naïve, Writerman," Jim says. "That's where he counts his doubloons."

I have a plan, always a plan, always.

"I gotta tell Neil what gone down, man," and I give Jim the dotted-lines eyes, only he doesn't get it, and that's the limitation of a plan I formulate on the spot.

The bus has tinted windows, and the driver's window is open.

Some thick-necked geezer inside has a smoke hanging from his mouth playing blues riffs on an acoustic guitar. "Let's go," Jim says. "Want that gentleman to knock your teeth out?"

"Then split," I say, and this is when the scene amps itself up. The back door of the Civic bangs open same as it's been kicked, and Neil and some guy step out into the cold-ass night.

"How the *fuck* can I play, *Elliot*," Neil says.

Oh man, Neil Young, right there, and those bright bright security lights, even with the fog, a halo of glowing mist surrounds him. He looks hellfuck bad. His matted grease brown hair parts in the middle hangs low-down past his shoulders. Weird 'cause Neil's face is still boyish angelic same as the Buffalo Springfield days, only I can see his skin sickly pale—as if drugs and dark rooms paint it black.

"I *know* Neil," Elliot says, and he's gotta be Neil's manager, I mean I read the liner notes. I know that kinda shit, of course I do.

"I understand completely," Elliot says. "It's *wrong*. We're in agreement. Absolute agreement. I understand, Neil, I really do. I've already taken care of it. Just got off the phone, spoke to Bill himself. He was *very* apologetic. *Extremely* apologetic. I don't think I can quite convey to you *how* apologetic the man was. He sent his regards. And you know what else he said? You'll appreciate this. He said the only three solo artists he'll listen to when he's home are you, Dylan and Miles. His exact words. *Neil and Bob and Miles are my favorite solo artists.*"

Elliot glances at Neil, looks for reassurance, and he wants it bad, wants Neil to nod or smile or somehow indicate that all is well in the world of Neil Young. And that he, Elliot, has it under control. On his face, *please please Neil, just a nod, that's all I need*. Only that doesn't happen, and all is not well.

They walk toward the bus, Elliot agitated and hyped up, Neil calm and centered. Yeah, Neil's mad, but keeps it in check. The power of silence, man.

So much I can learn, gotta keep my eyes and ears open, more important still, gotta keep the brain open. Take in the new info, and modify all the old ideas so they sync up with the new ones. Otherwise a human gets stuck in the past, stuck thinking the world is flat when the new info says for sure it's round. Most people have the World-Is-Flat Syndrome.

Just trying to clue you in.

The both of them oblivious to me and Jim, and I hear the end of what Neil says, *fuckin' bad trip*, and I walk slowmo towards them, and I'm close, maybe a car length away, and my voice loud in the empty space between the Civic and the silver tour bus.

"Neil," I say. "Mr. Young."

Elliot turns himself quick-like so his body is between me and Neil, and calls to the thick-necked geezer, "Bobby Lee, get your ass out here, pronto," and to me he talks calm but firm, yeah he's dealt with this trip a million times. "Neil's tired, man. Maybe he'll sign an autograph after the show," and that's a lie. I know it, Elliot knows it, and Neil knows it. Neil never signs autographs after a show. Never, man.

Elliot between me and Neil, between me and the bus.

"But—," I say.

The thick-necked geezer comes fast, faster, faster still. "Sorry, kid," Elliot says, and Neil's gonna disappear into the bus, and Bobby Lee gonna send us up the alley, and that'll be it, and later I'll have an unsatisfying story to tell about the time I almost met Neil Young. Only that doesn't happen. No, man, 'cause instead this is the moment.

The moment Jim stands tall. True blue freakster bro. Jim shouts it out, fuckin' too too loud, which for once is the right amount of loud.

"*Judas!*" and he imitates Dylan. "I don't *believe* you! You're a *liar!*"

Neil stops and turns and there's a peculiar look to his face, shock merged with recognition, and everything changes, and in that moment the world falls away. No Civic Auditorium, no silver tour bus, no thick-ass fog. Me, Jim and Neil Young, only three people on the planet, and there's connection. It's not two fan boys and one rock star anymore. No, man, three obsessive

Dylan fans stand in the cold, all three of us know those words that come out of Jim's mouth from listening to the greatest live album of all time, a bootleg recording of a 1966 Dylan performance at the Royal Albert Hall, only that word "performance" no way does justice to the cracked lightning bolt sound, and the anger in Dylan's voice.

Dylan and The Hawks in England fueled by speed and alcohol. A rock 'n' roll band using electric guitars, drums, organ, piano and that *voice* to tear the fuckin' world to pieces. In the audience, a fan, one of many who in 1966 digs the old Dylan, and that fan yells "*Judas!*" at the new mod rock 'n' roll Dylan, calls Dylan out for the betrayal he feels for Dylan selling out his folkie fans, trading in the purity of folk for the vulgarity of rock. Dylan doesn't take it, he fights back, *I don't believe you. You're a liar.* And the band starts in, goes for it total heavy traffic to-the-jugular, and Dylan spits out his fucking indictment of the rich and privileged, "Like a Rolling Stone." And more, 'cause Dylan is the role model for everything Neil has ever done. Dylan's why Neil's not afraid to follow his muse, change his whole trip when he feels like it. I mean here he is touring after the biggest album of his career, *Harvest,* and half of what he's playing each night is an album's worth of new songs that aren't recorded yet.

When Jim says those words, "Judas! I don't *believe* you! You're a *liar!,*" Neil knows, he goddamn goddamn fucking *knows*. Oh man, and in that moment I see Jim for who he is, I see the best he'll ever be. In that moment Jim stares *Neil Young* down. Jim a true blue freakster bro. *Thee* Freakster Bro, for sure. And in that moment our bullshit skins slide away, no skin, and me and Jim are there, blood and bones and brains and hearts, the best in Jim reaches out to me and in that moment I don't feel alone.

Two freakster bros, man.

"Sugar Mountain my ass," Jim says, and Elliot is stunned, no one *ever* talks that way to Neil. "My esteemed associate and good friend Writerman here is the guy the Bill Graham goon squad threw out of your show. He's your biggest fan. And you don't give a damn, Mr. Millionaire L.A. hippie. I always knew you were a fake."

Oh man Jim angrier than how pissed he is at King Editor.

"All that bull about 'your fans, your fans' and peace and love and four shot dead in Ohio, like you care. You're counting the money, smoking a doobie in your fancy bus while those thugs pick on your fans. They're probably throwing another fan out right now. Writerman talked me into coming to your show. Swore if I saw you live, I'd understand. Well I *understand*."

Elliot has way more extreme than the quizzical on his mug, can't believe the words unleashed from Jim's mouth, and oh he wants to shut Jim down only for once he can't seem to take control, but when Jim stops to get air, well.

"Look, I don't get your beef," Elliot says, "but Neil has to cool out before the second set. Bobby Lee here will help you on your way."

The vise grip of the thick-necked geezer, yeah he has my arm.

"Shut up, Elliot," Neil says. "Let go of the guy, Bobby Lee. Get back in the bus. These are my fans. My *fans*, man."

Neil looks to me, looks to Jim, and I *know*. "You're missing it, Elliot," Neil says. "They threw two of *my* fans, out of *my* concert."

Neil Young, Neil *fucking* Young, unnerved.

"Hey man, this is not what I'm about," he says, and he's talking to all three of us, only he's not talking to any of us. Neil Young talking to Neil Young, and even Neil Young has the mixed-up confusion. "I'm not one of *them*," he says, and steps forward so Elliot isn't between us. "I leave the business to Elliot, he's my manager, and sometimes things don't go the way I want 'em to go."

Oh man, Neil Young rationalizing his trip to me and Jim— who woulda thought such a thing could go down. "This is a tough business, this rock 'n' roll game," Neil says. "Hard to survive, not become yesterday's papers. I'm not about money, man. Money's no good, get rid of it. Turn it into jobs, turn it into happiness. The more people I employ, the happier I am. I care, man. And what I sing is real. It's no jive."

Jim takes it in, but he doesn't just take it. "So why play for Bill Graham?" he says. "Everyone knows his security fucks with the fans. It's a cop-out, like, *hey, I'm the artist, I gotta let my manager deal with that shit.* Is that who you are? The rock star who means well but doesn't take control of his trip?"

"Oh man, you don't get it," Neil says, and he's torn and frayed, yeah I can see the toll drugs and booze and night after night have taken. "I've played a lot of shows for a lot of promoters. They all suck. They rip you off right and left. You think these security goons are bad, check the scene in Jersey. It's a shit hole business. I can't reinvent the wheel. It's too much, writing the songs, recording the albums, driving in this bus from show to show, getting out there for three hours."

Elliot, he sputters, wheels turn but no traction. "Neil, we *don't* have time for this."

Only Neil does what he wants. "Let's get on the bus," he says. "I can use a beer. How about you guys?" and he walks side-by-side with me and Jim.

"Fuckin' A!" Neil says, and he shakes his shaggy-ass head. "Threw you guys out!"

When Neil's raging electric set is over and we split the Civic, this huge high flyin' high groovin' mass of us, past midnight and the cold gets colder, but the fog is gone, man, and in my stoned state the sky glows bright bright with the glitter of stars and the switchblade sharp light of a half moon.

"Jim, man," I say. "That was righteous."

Well surprise surprise, Neil's got a new fan. "Rock 'n' roll, old sport," Jim says. "Elixir of the Gods."

Only I'm not talkin' the music. And my heart beats fast, faster, faster still, and the cold cold air, oh man I am so high, high off Neil's weed, high off Neil's high flyin' sound, high off the communal vibe that comes from all us Neil fans in the post-concert ecstatic, and I float in the surreal hyper-real tripped-out zone, and I *know*, man. I see through the bullshit, and the truth all there before me. In the midst of my reverie, me and Jim, we *are* the authentic real freakster bros.

We are the *authentic real.*

I give Jim the dotted-lines eyes deal, only nothing comes back. He looks down, brushes some dirt off his black velveteen coat. Turns his body away, not any big dramatic deal, subtle the way he does it, but I know. Jim's not sharing the post-Neil ecstatic so the two of us can truly groove in the bond forged this night.

"No, man," I say. "I'm talking about you watching my back, and standing up to Neil. You know. *Judas!*"

"The right thing to do, old sport," and he total shifts into his Jim routine, raises his fist high, "Yow!" and still no dotted-lines eyes. "We are triumphant, Writerman. Met Neil, trumped the Pigman. Rock 'n' Roll!"

I feel alone, and high as I am, maybe the primo skunk we smoked exaggerates the loneliness. If only I could shake it away, let the high of the night overwhelm me. And I feel something else, feel the wanting for Elise, my whole body aches with it.

Feel the loneliness so intense, and maybe it's never gonna leave.

10. THE SOUND

PERHAPS YOU WONDER ABOUT my rewrite. The
Beefheart review. Did I finish it? Well yeah, in fact I did. What
could've happened, the Sausalito Cowboy and Buckaroo
offering sage advice. Then again, Jim could have helped me get
it revised. Only that's not how it went down, but I'll tell you.

I'll tell you right now.

I go to Elise's dorm room, late afternoon, and she has the
door open, and she always has the door open, at least when I'm
there, and I can't help but wonder if it's to welcome me in, or so
I don't try some major Casanova moves.

Oh man, she's wearing one of her short black skirts with
the flowers, black turtleneck and the matching tights, no shoes,
her hair longer from when I first seen her in Sappho's room,
and the longer her hair gets the more crazy-wild I see in her.

She sits on the rug, she always sits on the rug. Her back up
against the side of her bed. She doesn't have a bed frame, only
the single mattress on top of the box spring. Draws in her
sketchbook how she always does. A wild animal with razor
blade teeth gonna rip apart a chick lying naked parallel with the
bottom of the page.

Her legs straight out front of her, and all she has to do is be
there, and the wanting *so strong*. Elise does nothing but exist and
I hardly can stand it. Did I ever feel this way about Sarah? Did I
ever?

Nothing gone right about the rewrite, and I'm there to
hang out, tea and sympathy as they say in England. Jagger sang
something like that, no, that's not right, it's coke and sympathy

Jagger sang. Then again that's him and Richards having some fun.

First thing I say, not even a "hey, what's happening," no man, I launch into my trip.

"King Editor total doesn't get it," I say. "Such a square, man."

Elise isn't one to be my mirror. She digs me, maybe she loves me, but that doesn't mean she goes along with the party line, whether the party is me or Sappho or whomever. Don't look to Elise for reflected glory.

I have my review with the red ink, and she offers to read it, and she's an artist so she'll understand. Words or the lines of a drawing, no difference, it's all art, and I figure soon as Elise reads it she'll go off on him, you know, King Editor.

A Kool burns away and I smell the menthol. She reads while I stand around. Walk from her desk to the bed, bed to the door, door to the freestanding clothes closet with the mirror. Suck in my cheeks, get my hair so it parts down the middle, perfect John Lennon trip.

She thinks it's funny. Not the review, me in front of her mirror. She's been watching my hipster pose. Could go at me with the sarcastic, but she doesn't, and that's some of what's groovy about how it is, me and her. For now she's cool with my imperfections.

"Sugar coated?" she says. "Or the naked truth?" and I *know*, 'cause if she has to ask if I want soft-core or hard, well for sure I have a problem.

"Gimme the hard stuff, Elise."

She pats the rug right next to her.

"Come sit," she says, and oh man, she can say any words she wants about my words if I get to sit next to her, and I get myself down there on the rug, fuck yeah. She has the pages piled on her skirt, you know, on top of her thighs. I look to where they are, only most of my look is at her legs, where they come out from under the skirt. She has on black tights, and her thighs and the rest of her legs, the smooth curves, perfect black silhouette of each leg.

"Esoteric to the nth degree," she says. "Confusion reigns, my dear."

I'm so close, and if I'm not careful my right hand could slip off of my thigh onto hers. Hard to think about Captain Beefheart. *Those legs.*

"Michael!"

"Sorry," I say. "I was contemplating."

"I see what you're contemplating."

"Pretty skirt."

"Shut up."

She rests her smoke in the clear glass ashtray on the rug. She has the pages in her hands, points to some shit King Editor wrote, spreads the pages so some are on my thigh, some on hers —all these crazy words I wrote about Captain Beefheart spilling onto our laps.

"Don't you want people to get it?" she says. "Understand the deep truths about Captain Beefheart?"

She has this page with the serious red ink and she has me looking close.

"Some of this reads like the transcript of a crazy man ranting on a street corner."

"It's an in joke deal. That's how Beefheart sounds sometimes. You ever heard him?"

"We're supposed to be psychic?" she says. "All of us who somehow lived oblivious to Captain Beefheart until your review?"

And I laugh same as a person who gets caught at something, but she doesn't laugh. Takes my review more serious than I do. Come on, man, all I want in that moment is to touch her.

Only since she's called me on my jive, I have to face up to it. Writerman's trip is an ego trip. Indulgent, insular, self-referential. For my novel, the novel I haven't written a word of yet, well maybe. But it's not appropriate for a review. So much of what I write, well, the sentences go on for half a page wind 'round and 'round loaded up with adjectives and adverbs and metaphors. Try and make sense, oh man, through the woods, down the rabbit hole, take the secret tunnel, up up up to the meadow, crawl in the grass, around the back of the mountain, and onward, ever onward, the journey, always the journey. But a journey to where? Hellfuck I know. Lot of it, man, *I* don't even get what it means.

She looks for this certain page, and in checking the pages that rest on my thigh, she leans against me, and her hands touch me. I feel her shoulder and some of her arm and the side of her leg. I feel her warmth, and that was another of those moments, the moments where life is good as it ever gonna get. Gentle pressure of Elise against me. Her hands brush against my thigh. Her voice sounds the way it sounds when she tells me about the poem that boy read at the open mic, before she goes outside and the two stalkers get out of the car. Her voice is different, echo of the innocence, and I can imagine what Elise was like back when she was so much younger.

"The way you write, Michael," she says. "It could make for a new kind of poetry. There's a rhythm to the way the words sound," and I want to see into her mystic blue eyes, her million miles eyes, and know if she feels anything, if her hands on my thigh are more than an accident, and if she wants to press against me. I want to kiss her, but what I see is Elise serious as serious can be, and if she feels what I feel, no way for me to know.

"There's a sound you've got," she says. "It's quite thrilling."

I look right at her, scanning her face for clues, 'cause this gotta be a put-on.

"I never heard anything like it at the carnival," she says. "Your words are a mystery no one who reads them will ever solve."

And in that moment I don't care about the review.

"You hear a *sound* in my words?" I say. "Authentic real?"

My excitement is her excitement, same as we both wake up right then, too much coffee or nicotine, buzz with her discovery.

"I wouldn't hype you," she says.

A *sound*, man.

Bob Dylan has a *sound!* Kerouac has a *sound!* And the Stones! That's when Elise realizes she has her hand on my thigh, has it resting there as if it's normal as normal can be, and she looks at me, my eyes, her eyes, and I see it, man, and she doesn't move her hand, she leaves it there and she rubs my thigh with her hand.

Oh it's too much.

You know how they talk about people swooning in love stories, well if swoon is a way to feel, it's how I feel. My arms around her, turn my body, pull her to me so her body turns and we face each other, and all the pages slip off us onto the rug, and all of her against me, and she lets it happen. In her eyes she feels it too. I hold her and we're silent, our bodies still.

That's when I make my second attempt to kiss her. My lips against hers and she wants it, only I feel her whole body get that tightness again same as before.

"I can't, Michael," she says. "It's not you, I swear. It's me. It's what happened to me."

And then she's all flustered pulls her skirt down hands in her hair hands pull at her turtleneck so it covers her waistline and she's the serious deal all over again.

She's picking up all the pages trying to get them flat and in order.

"I can't talk about it now," she says.

I'm freaked 'cause how are we ever gonna make love if for starters we can't kiss.

Well that's when she tells me the sound of my words isn't enough. The review has to make sense too.

"A review isn't a poem, Michael," she says. "A review is like those essays we have to write for class. If you could write this in a way that's simple and straightforward and clear, people will get the message."

My eyes, her eyes, I mean we're two lovers who can't speak what's really going on.

"You don't want to push things," she says. "I mean the language."

"I can restrain it," I say. "How I, the words I use."

"You have to take it slower," she says. "Simple is what I mean."

"I get swept away," I say.

"You don't understand at all," she says.

"I understand, Elise."

Yeah, I understand the beautiful sadness, and what the monster boyfriend did to her, and how she's not recovered, and how each step of the way, each touch is so hard for her, the struggle inside between fear and desire.

I understand.

Since I said this was about the review, I'll tell you that the next morning I got up and rewrote it simple and straightforward, not through the woods and down the rabbit hole, and that was that. Fuck the review. All that mattered was me and her were more than friends and we knew it.

There was one other thing that was important. When she said my words had a *sound*, I heard Elise falling in love. It's not that I mistook her love of that *sound* for a love of *me*, 'cause both were going on. She's the one asked me to sit next to her, and placed that slender artist hand on my thigh, and let me hold her. She's the one. Only in my obsession, Elise as my Visions of Johanna chick, and a recognition that she feels it too, there's something important I forget for a while. What she said about the *sound*. My *sound*. A writer would do a deal with the Devil to have their own s*ound*. Yet I forgot all about that part, or maybe I didn't believe it. Later, though, much later, I remember, and I believe, and when I do, finally, when that day comes when I start to write my novel with that *sound*, well that's the start of when I become an authentic real and true writer.

11. BETRAYAL

OUR MEETING WITH KING Editor was scheduled for 10
a.m., only it can't start at 10 a.m. 'cause we're not there. We're
stoned, don't have a watch, don't give a fuck. Got all the time in
the world. Got better things to do, listen to *Exile on Main Street*,
smoke another doobie, but eventual we arrive at King Editor's
office while we're in serious conversation mode. Us two
debating something serious heavy traffic important: whether the
Stones' version of "Stop Breaking Down" is better than Robert
Johnson's original.

"Nothing beats Johnson's recording," Jim says. "It's classic.
And Sonny Boy cut a killer version in the Forties."

"Yeah but the Stones track fucking rocks," I say.

We don't pay attention to King Editor, or Foxy Lady who
sits close to him writing on one of those yellow legal-size pads.
Only one reason Roth got her there, and he's probably gonna
try out his Casanova moves soon as me and Jim split.

Jim is a mess. Hair matted and tangled and that greasy shine.
There's some food, maybe toast crumbs, in his beard. If you
gotta know the why of it, Jaded split for L.A. to help her mom
recover from a boob job. Left *Thee* Freakster Bro on his own for
a week.

King Editor sits behind that humongous desk, and he's
pissed. He has Foxy right next to him as if they been working
on some important editorial business, when authentic real he
wants her close to smell that magnolia-stink perfume she uses
and fantasize about placing his thin-ass bony fingers on the bare
thigh right below where her shorter-than-short skirt ends.

Well this is the moment when Jim sees that low child's chair, the one I sat in.

"Where'd you get this?" he says. "Steal it from a nursery school?" and he kicks the chair hard out of the way, out into the hall, and it slides along the hardwood, wood scratching wood, and there's nowhere for us to sit.

Now if it were up to me, I'd stand. It's not up to me. Jim's already split off down the hall to find some normal-size chairs.

Roth wears a Damon Runyon seersucker suit and you might think he's pissed 'cause Jim kicked his chair, and I'm sure he doesn't dig it, but same as I told you he was already pissed. Before Roth can say something Jim is back with two folding chairs.

Goddamn goddamn goddamn.

Why didn't I get a normal chair when I met with Roth, but no, he presented a tiny-ass child's chair that no adult person would ever sit in, and I sat in it.

Jim hands a chair to me and we unfold 'em, set 'em side-by-side. Roth shakes, how mad he is, and Jim collapses into his chair. He wears one of the Edwardian shirts Jaded picked out for him, this one a bright pink, two inch wide stripes of ruffles come all the way down from the collar to his waist on ether side of the buttons, has sweat spots under his armpits, and the black velveteen pants, yeah he's been wearin' them for days, the pants wrinkled and lint clings to them, and the scuffed-up Beatle boots.

As I take a seat Roth picks up a manuscript, Jim's Black Sabbath review, and waves it at *Thee* Freakster Bro. During the two years I knew him, Roth never looked more ridiculous. Fucking brown and white seersucker and one of his Mark Twain bow ties with a brown and white checked pattern. But it's the hair that hips me to the chaos within. Don't know if he didn't use enough grease, but that shock of hair rising off his enlarged head is almost an Elvis rockabilly deal. But I don't think Elvis or Billy Lee Riley or any of the groovy rockabilly cats.

Somehow the outfit and the hair makes me think Pat

Boone, how Boone looked in the Fifties with the hair short on the sides but high on top. Pat Boone, man, middle-of-the-road asshole who took the rock 'n' roll songs that Little Richard and Fats Domino and Big Joe Turner could only get onto chitlin-circuit R&B radio, neutered the shit out of 'em, and scored the big money whites-only pop hits.

Yeah, pussy-ass Pat Boone.

Roth's left eye blinks how it does when he's madder than mad.

"This, *Mr.* Costello, is contemptible."

He slaps Jim's rewrite down on the desk, and there's a beat of silence loud as a doomed church bell clanging.

I understand the why of King Editor's fury, but that doesn't excuse what he does next.

"*This,* this, uh, uh, *this,* it's an atrocity."

He gives me a look, pegs me an accomplice, and the weed-fueled paranoia sets in. Why's he give me *that* look? What have *I* done?

"*This,*" Roth says, and he picks the manuscript up again and he goes off, talks with the pinched self-righteous sound of the Woman's Christian Temperance Union about all the ways the review is far worse than vulgar. Foxy does her best to keep the serious face, only she can't. Roth is staring straight ahead at Jim, which is lucky for Foxy 'cause he doesn't see she's suppressing a giggle.

Left eye blinks erratic, and he's wheezing. Rolls the manuscript, and *whacks* the desk. Says more shit about the review, how disgusted he felt when he read it, and *whack,* an affront to art criticism, and *whack,* a betrayal of everything *The Paper* stands for, and *whack whack whack.* Roth stands and his head shakes and that hair must have risen another inch or so.

"I should have you expelled, Mr. Costello, *old sport.* Disgraceful," and he coughs, and another, and those coughs turn into a full-blown asthmatic coughing jag. He makes a fist of his free hand, the one that doesn't hold the manuscript, pounds his chest, once, twice and a third time, and the coughing stops and his wheeze starts up again.

I look to Jim, and the arrogance from when we arrived is fading. Jim slumped in the chair, and oh man, if there were a meter in the office to measure the tension, that meter be up at 130 percent. Foxy can feel it, she rises from her seat. She looks to Jim, looks to me, looks to Roth, and she wants to take care of us all, soothe down the scene. Chick needs Al-Anon bad.

"Larry, are you OK?" she says, and pulls at her sleeveless v-neck lavender t-shirt, a shirt that's a size too small, pulls to get the wrinkles out, only there's no wrinkles, that shirt tight the way her skirt is short. Man, the chick has a mountain range under that t-shirt. And no bra.

Me and Jim can't help but look, and her arms so tanned and her face too, and lavender lipstick, and those legs, those legs, those *legs.*

"Is there *anything* I can do for you?" she says.

Roth waves her away. "Sit! Sit!"

Jim stretches out a leg and starts to tap out a beat with the toe of his boot against Roth's desk, *one and two and three and four.*

A seedy Keith Richards facing off a pussy Pat Boone.

Jim silent except for the four-four beat of his boot toe against wood as King Editor's eyes bore in. And all of us, we wait, and wait some more.

One and two and three and four, one and two and three and four.

Finally Jim speaks. "I certainly thought you'd appreciate my rewrite, *Mr.* Roth," and Jim watches the smoke from his smoke drift into the air. "You know, the *humor,*" and straightens his head, looks through the Ray-Bans right at Roth.

And the beat. The *beat.*

One and two and three and four. One and two and three and four.

"What about, as you've said, the need for 'The Critic' to take chances?" Jim says. "To push the boundaries past the conventional, to venture into *the other,* to speak in an *authentic voice,*" and Jim pauses—*one and two and three and four.* "I happened to choose the voice of *Satan.*"

Foxy chokes, and I'm laughing.

"Enough!"

And Roth's left eye out-of-control same as some parasite

alive in his eye socket.

"Stop that infuriatingly bothersome thing you're doing with your foot, *Mr. Costello.*"

"Thought you'd appreciate the *humor*," Jim says.

His foot against Roth's desk. *One and two and three and four.*

Roth's head sunken between his shoulders, got that no neck look, hands at his hair frantic to get it off his forehead, get it back the way it's supposed to be only it gets wilder and wilder.

"Thought *sure* you'd appreciate the *humor, Mr.* Roth."

Still, Jim brings his boot back so it's next to the other boot, and that rock 'n' roll beat is done.

The next thing that happens worth telling is when King Editor smiles the thin smile of vengeance, and picks up *my* manuscript.

"Mr. Stein," he says. "This is superb."

For a moment I smile the smile of an ego out-of-control, and my head floats high into the air above my body, and I feel the self-satisfied glow of success, but quick enough it all goes south. Roth starts in on how well I've taken *his* direction, how important the editor is to the editor-writer relationship, and what a lucky *freshman* I am to have an editor of such genius, who's studied the masters, from Homer to Thomas Hardy, from Aristotle to Joyce. Oh yeah, Roth does a song and dance to his crucial role in shaping every sentence, no, every *word* of my review, and leaves me feeling same as the soggy TP I tossed in the garbage after cleaning up his spilled coffee.

Jim slouches, sullen lips press tight, and he takes what's left of his Pall Mall and throws it to the floor.

"Your tie is crooked, old sport."

The cigarette smoking there on the hardwood. Roth can't see it, but we all smell it burning.

Jim hums that old The Crazy World of Arthur Brown hit, "Fire."

Roth's left eye going haywire, his nose twitching as he sucks in the smoke stink.

Foxy stands, pulls at her t-shirt, leans forward to see what's burning only the desk is too big, no way she can see it, leans forward and gives me and Jim a view, you know, top of the mountain range.

"Do something!" Roth says, but Jim doesn't move.

Roth looks from Jim to me, and what the fuck? I sit there, Jim sits there, Roth sits there his nose twitching out of control, and that's when I take action, crush the smoking butt with the sole of my boot. And grind it into the hardwood.

"It's out, Mr. Roth," I say, and Jim gives me the freeze-out, his puffy face tight, stares straight ahead.

Foxy is back in her seat, back messing with her yellow pad, back to business

"Mr. Stein's review is to go in the next issue, Suzie. We'll place a snipe on the front page, "Stein on Beefheart, Pg. 6.""

Jim been all slumped but now he sits up, his eyes burning through the Ray-Bans right into King Editor, and there might as well been a wall of ice between me and him. His voice pinched and high.

"Shit on Beefheart, Pg. 6."

That's when King Editor sets the trap. There are times when some deal a person like me figures is of no consequence ruins the person's life. Well this doesn't ruin my life, but it causes me plenty trouble. Roth says he wants to run a photo of Captain Beefheart with my review, and do we have one?

The answer is no, *we* don't have one.

But me, *I* have one back at my room, and right-quick I tell Roth. Oh yes, King Editor, do I ever have a photo of Beefheart, in fact I have a half dozen photos of Beefheart, I have more photos of Beefheart than anyone else here at The University, and I'll run and fetch them.

Yeah, too quick. And as quick-like as I tell Roth I have a photo, Jim farts. But before he farts, in the flash of the moment after I tell Roth but before Jim farts, this happens:

Remember, we're sitting next to each other. I turn, give him the guilty eyes. He turns, removes the Ray-Bans so his hard eyes meet mine, and what those eyes tell me is I'm a chump, plain and simple. And he has Liquor Store's smirk on his face, and I *know*. Too quick to volunteer the photo, and the eagerness in my voice, oh fuck, and the quease, yeah, I got it.

Jim sits in that chair, and he hasn't showered since Jaded split, and he smells.

Soon as I say my kiss-ass to Roth, Jim lets it be known to all present what he thinks. That would be the moment he farts. A loud perfect fart sound so much same as the perfect fart I think it might be one of those rubber deals they advertise in the back of comic books, you know, a whoopee cushion. Only this fart is for real.

Hear it, smell it, know it.

Not sure what Jim ate for breakfast, but it wasn't oatmeal 'cause the fart is loud and foul. The odor, same as some rancid, hard-boiled eggs gone bad kinda trip, you know the smell, the air heavy with *eau de shit*.

"How does Jade put up with you?" Foxy says.

I don't care about Jim's fart, all I think about is me. How I've blown it. Mr. Eager Beaver Eagle Scout. Fuck it. I didn't do anything. I played the game. I made my choice and my review is going into *The Paper*.

Stein on Beefheart, Pg. 6.

Nothing wrong with any of it. Jim, he's the one hellfuck his scene. If he wants to write for *The Paper*, he has to play the game. No one gives Jim license to write any sick thing he pleases. I mean he can write whatever, but don't expect to get it published.

Oh yeah, I build a case high as the wall surrounding Troy. And now it's built, and high as that wall is, yeah that's how righteous I am. Jim so the fuck in the wrong, and the anger he vibes at me, bullshit. No betrayal if Roth runs my review. No betrayal if I go get the photo.

And yet...

Jim puts the Ray-Bans back on, stands, he's there in the doorway, and he sings "Jumping Jack Flash." Twirls the lucky cane and points it up at the ceiling and he sings. It's a song about coming up against the hard times, and surviving. He spins around 360 degrees, and steps out into the hall, turns to face us, sings that famous chorus, how he's Jumpin' Jack Flash and life's a gas gas gas, jams the metal ferrule of his cane down hard into the hardwood.

"Suckers!"

And he's off down the hall.

"As I was saying, Mr. Stein, we'll need that photo," King Editor says, and it's as if all that gone down never happened.

Foxy doesn't hide her smile, yeah she's glad Jim is gone baby gone.

Well I can't sit another moment, can't go along with this lame scenario, fuck no, and I'm out that door. *Fuck* King Editor. Goddamn goddamn goddamn. I'm in the hallway, hear Jim down the stairs and I run, get to the stairs, take them two at a time, hit the first floor as Jim leaves the building. Hear him singing *gas gas gas* and I'm out that door too.

"Hey, Jim, man," but he doesn't stop, he walks fast, direction of the Arts College, and I run past, and turn to face him. "Hey, come on," and he stops walking, stops singing, and we stand in the courtyard between the library and the Steinbeck Building. Jim has the lucky cane in his one hand, other hand on his hip.

"That asshole tries to humiliate me in front of you and that bimbo he wants to screw," Jim says. "When he's finished shitting on me, he gives *you* a gold star."

His face has the grim look of disappointment. In me, in life, in the whole of civilization.

"And you brown-nose."

"That's *bullshit*," I say. "Your drama with King Editor has nothing to do with me," and some guy's got a wood-chipper going inside my head.

"You're a big baby, Jim. Your trip won't get you anywhere."

He brings the cane in front of him, plants the metal ferrule in the ground, his hands, one on the other, top of the lion's head.

"I've maintained my self-respect."

His face puffy in the sunlight, the dark-ass shadows beneath the Ray-Bans.

"*I* haven't sold out."

"This has nothing to do with that," I say, but he's right and I *know*.

Curls his lip up into a rebel sneer, Elvis in a bad mood.

"You're too desperate, old sport."

Oh man, 'cause I know, in desperation lies defeat. Fight my anger, and I hear Neil Young's lonesome sound.

"I don't give a fuck about King Editor," I say, but the situation is way more insidious. If you take each path to the extreme, you're either the Weather Underground building bombs to blow up the symbols of the establishment, or you are the establishment, and the roles we act out that day, well Jim's the anarchist waving a black flag at the end of his lucky cane and I'm the good boy. You know, Mr. Rogers.

"I care about my writing, man," I say. "I wanna get published."

I look right at Jim, right at his shades, try to see into his eyes but I can't. What I see is my own reflection. And what I see of me, beyond the long curly hair and the gaunt face and the John Lennon specs, see someone I don't dig.

Yeah, and Jim has it right.

Too fucking desperate. There's tightness in my chest, and I try to will it away. I want so much to be the righteous one, and Jim the immature ass. But it doesn't go away, the tightness, and I remember how I sat in that child's chair, took Roth's abuse, but not Jim, he didn't sit in the child's chair, he sat in a man's chair.

It's hard to fess up, but authentic real, I dug it when Roth laid into Jim. And the rush when Roth said he was gonna run *my* review. Only *my* review. I didn't care what Roth thought of Jim's review. All I cared about was mine. Yeah, I know, kind of shitty.

Jim must feel the guilt, know some of this is his fault. I get a Pall Mall going, and I'm gonna put the pack away, but no, I hold it out for him. He looks at it, looks at me, takes the pack.

"Sorry, old sport," he says and shakes out a smoke. "I get so mad. But you should have stood by me, Writerman. We need to watch each other's backs."

Well now I'm the one who's pissed.

"King Editor is a royal shithead," I say. "But me and you, man, we didn't agree we'd tell him to *fuck off.* Of course we're freakster bros but it doesn't mean I follow you blind off the cliff."

12. THE GLAM TRIP

I DON'T KNOW WHY I go to Jaded's room. It's the day before Halloween and I stand in the hallway, the Stones rocking me, can't get "Stop Breaking Down" outta my head, that out-of-control buzz buzzing me same as the first time I saw her—when I know it's wrong but still I'm gonna do it.

Something alluring she did at lunch. A lure. To lure me here. We left Jim at our table to get seconds. I held the swinging stainless door, and as she walked past she turned, and her hand against my ass.

"I'm writing a paper about 'Tender Is the Night,'" she says. "I hear you're the expert."

"It's Fitzgerald's best," I say. "'The Beautiful and the Damned' is overdone but it *is* a hellfuck portrait of the fall from grace, and 'Gatsby' is perfect, but 'Tender Is the Night' is his masterpiece," and she looked at me how she did in Disraeli Gears, and says in a quiet voice that I should come to her room later.

Hellfuck nerves on fire.

My best freakster bro's chick. Not what Mr. Rogers would do. And sure I'm total gone on Elise, only there I am approaching Jaded's room. Why? If I knew the answer I'd be a millionaire famous as Freud or Jung.

Her door is slightly open, and I see her double bed, and that's when Jim yells out "Writerman! What are *you* doing in this neck of the woods, old sport?"

The two of them in front of Jaded's desk, *Thee* Freakster Bro in Jaded's prissy Louis XIV chair with the curved armrests and the ornate floral fabric. He wears his freshly laundered pink shirt with the ruffles, and the black velveteen pants. Jaded's doing something to his fingernails.

"Well whatever you're doing here, your timing is perfect, excellent really," he says. "You're a witness to the *glamming* of Lord Jim," and the truth of it, I'm glad to see him—saved me from myself. For more than a moment, the dark red she applies to his nails doesn't register, but then I see it.

Jaded all in black, and her face beautiful as Anna Karina in *Vivre sa vie*, only Jaded's lips are fuller and her eyes bigger. I know the glam trip is Jaded's idea.

Jim stands, twists around to look at his hands in the round mirror Jaded has hung over her desk. He sits, looks at me and it's as if his eyes ask, *this is cool, right Writerman, right? Right?!* Well, he gets nothing from me.

"What do you think, old sport? Lou, Bowie or Iggy?"

"Fucking weird, man."

"Michael doesn't *know*," Jaded says.

"You're living the past," Jim says.

They show me British *Vogue*, open on Jaded's double bed, a six-page spread on the London glam scene. I sit there, my left hand on the velvet bedspread, and flash on Jaded's pale skin against the purple velvet. Naked against the white marble.

Ghost of 'lectricity. Mid-October of 1972. The three of us drive up the coast, heading to the City, and the San Francisco Museum of Modern Art. They'd been going at each other all morning, a lovers' quarrel about nothing. By the time we get inside the museum he's so pissed he walks away, hurries himself into an elevator, gone baby gone.

It doesn't seem to bother her. At the landing between the first and second floors she leans her back against the white marble wall in the stairwell. "Marble suit me?" she says, and her hands behind her head, elbows to the sides and her trench coat falls open and her tits push against her tight black cashmere sweater, and the pearls, real pearls around her neck, the white of those pearls and the white of her skin and the white of the marble, and fuck she's gorgeous. On her lips the dark red lipstick. Yeah, marble suits her, and I look and she's naked against the white marble, her pale white skin, white pearls, white marble. I want to kiss her dark red lips, and was that when I knew?

"Come on, Jade," I say. "We should find Jim."

He's in a third floor gallery standing before a huge photo Diane Arbus took of her husband, Allan Arbus, after she left him, and if the Neil Young lonesome were an expression on a person's face, that's the expression. In the moments after Jim put his stiff arms around Jaded and pulls her to him, was that when I knew? I don't want to be there as they make up. He thought all was well in the world with his chick back in his arms, but I see Jaded's face coming over his shoulder, her amber eyes wide open, and no love, man. She looks at me, and she might as well have her hand on my ass.

There were loads of photos in the article, the still from "Performance"—Jagger with the big hair and the lipstick—and one of Lou, heavy mascara and the nails, standing close to Bowie in full Ziggy drag and the caption said they were "recording a fabulous new song, 'Walk on the Wild Side,' that those in the know call a 'gender bender classic.'"

"A role reversal is what it's all about on the street," read the text, "and in the most fashionable and exclusive private clubs in London. Women adopting a severe, aggressive, even macho look while the men go fem with their frilly pink shirts, extravagant velvet pants and coats, lipstick and lace, painting their nails, even cross-dressing. The *now* style is undeniably androgynous. The new age is here, and it's oh so glam."

The whole feminism deal coming down, and what's a poor boy to do?

Well Jim lit up a number and by the time it's a roach they've convinced me. I agree on purple polish, and when Jaded finishes painting my nails, I hold my hands out before me, only they aren't my hands. And that's when I first start to lose it, submerged in an existential disconnect.

So lost, man.

She does my lips with purple lipstick, and gets some white makeup she rubs into my cheeks and below my lips and on my jaw and my whole face doesn't feel same as my face. I stand to get a look at me, and same as the hands aren't my hands, well it's hard to see me in the freak face looking back from the mirror.

Some dorm bathrooms are coed, but the one on Jaded's hall is chicks only. Me and Jim waited outside while Jaded checked if anyone was in there. Through the door I heard Jaded talking, and this chick came out, and it was this chick that guy Tom I told you about fucked freshman year, this sexed-out Rhonda chick who looked sorta same as Joan Baez back '63, '64, same straight dark brown hair, and real stubborn and she hung around our apartment and was total stuck on herself. Right off, first time I met Rhonda, she didn't dig me, she thought she was the coolest of the cool, and I mean she might as well been Liquor Store's younger sister. Had his same smirk, and so sarcastic—only worse.

"Well what have we here," she says, and she checks me out from my purple lipstick and white makeup to my Keith Richards snakeskin boots.

"You make a real cute girl, Stein," she says, and I feel bad as I ever felt around her. "Now I know why you never get any chicks."

Jim gives her the double-barreled drop-dead-motherfucker look. "You have such a beautiful face, my dear," he says, "and from what I can see of it, your body is a true tribute to womanhood. So sad you have the patently pernicious personality."

Rhonda, man, she gives Jim a fuck-you look right back, and to me, "Tell your ugly *girlfriend* the tampon dispenser is right inside the door," and she's outta there, on her way down the hall, gone baby gone.

I guess Jaded been standing in the bathroom doorway watching the whole sad scene.

"Old girlfriend?"

"No!" I say. "Not gonna talk about the bitch."

"She's got a thing for you, old sport," Jim says. "I can *feel* her passion."

So that's when Jaded asks Jim to stand watch in the hall. Oh man, he doesn't dig it, me and her alone together.

"I'll be right outside," he says.

"I know you will, love," Jaded says.

Soon as the door closes Jaded makes her move, gets me sitting so my head is back against the counter on a towel, her fingers in my hair and touching my head, and she gets most of my hair into the sink. Her dyed black henna hair inches from my face and the smell of her perfume. She told me it was called Narcisse Noir, and I bet it was, had this intense sweetness and an animalistic musk kinda smell—Barbara Stanwyck perfume for sure.

"I thought I was gonna help you," I say. "You know, with your paper."

"I wasn't expecting him," she says, and she's right close to me, her chest at eye level. I stretch my legs out, spread my knees apart and she has her fingers back of my neck, working the muscles.

"I've thought about how handsome you'd look with black hair," she says. "If you'd stepped up, said the right words, coulda had me. Day us three met."

She's not massaging my neck anymore. "But Jim."

She puts on disposable white rubber gloves, pulls 'em tight on her small hands. "He was interested," she says. "Didn't know if you were."

She turns on the water, soaks my hair. "You have to take what you want when you see it, Michael. Sometimes you don't get a second chance."

Jaded spreads Vaseline on my forehead and my ears and neck to keep the dye off my skin. Says the gloves remind her of the ones she wore in high school art class back when she was gonna be a painter and she used her hands to apply the paint.

We got to talking about the Abstract Expressionists. I mentioned Clyfford Still and she told me back then she was under de Kooning's spell.

"Still's paintings are an alien virus," I say. "A cold, harsh, inhuman thing. As if he's ripped the surface away and you get a glimpse of the truth, and it's ugly."

"I used to hate Clyfford Still," and she rubs the thick henna paste onto my hair.

"That's how I felt about Ansel Adams," I say. "Before I knew any better."

Maybe it's the tension of me and her alone in the bathroom, of what she'd said to me, of what I'd said to her, but when I say that about Ansel Adams, Jaded laughs her smart-ass laugh.

"Clyfford Still and Ansel Adams," she says. "Can you imagine a joint show? That's like Quasimodo going on a date with Anita Ekberg."

When she's done—my head still back, my hair still in that sink—she gathers up all my hair into a plastic cap, and as she ties a black towel total around my head so I'm wearing a turban, the bathroom door swings in, and so quiet it's not even a whisper:

"Here he comes," I say. "Quasimodo."

"Anita Ekberg," she says. "I like that."

"What are you two colluding about?"

"You know, Anita Ekberg," I say. "'I Shall Be Free #10.' Jade's never heard it."

"I can remedy *that*," he says. "I really have been delinquent in educating you about Dylan, Jade."

That's when Jaded tells me the henna has to stay on four hours, so while they get dinner I'll be stuck alone in her room.

"You can revisit your favorite," Jim says. "'Tender Is the Night.' Jade has a copy."

The unveiling gonna be at midnight, but that's hours away. *Tea for the Tillerman* is on Jaded's turntable. I'm shocked she's into Cat Stevens. I expect a jazz disc, Mingus or Rollins, or if it's not jazz, that first Leonard Cohen record. Something hip. I lower the needle on "Wild World," and that song gotta be why Jaded bought the album. It's about a chick leaving her boyfriend, who cautions her that it's a wild world out there, a hard place for a chick to get by with just a smile.

Yeah, well, Jaded has plenty more than a smile.

I turn the Louis XIV chair so it faces the oval mirror, and there's my reflection. Black towel turban wrapped around my head, pasty skin, Lennon specs, purple lips. Stretch my mouth wide into a freak show grin. Fucking Rhonda, I don't look same as a chick. I'm Lou, I'm Mick, I'm Iggy, and it's the danger zone. I'm the New Trip. Drawn another line between me and the straights, only I have a line between me and the Freak Scene Dream freaks too 'cause none of them gonna get it. What a lot of people don't understand is the spirit of the Bohemian trip, the Beat deal, and the Freak Scene Dream, all of it is about doing your own thing. Me wearing snakeskin boots 'cause *I* dig 'em, not 'cause of what anyone else wears. So why do I wanna copy Lennon or Dylan or Young, and tonight Lou or Mick. Well, I'm not a math equation, I'm a mess of contradictions trying to find my way through the maze, and my heroes are touchstones, helping me sort out my trip.

On Jaded's desk, "Tender Is the Night." Fitzgerald set the opening scenes in Antibes on the French Riviera, and wrote there while he and Zelda lived in the Villa Saint-Louis, about 16 miles south of Villefranche, where nearly 40 years later the Stones recorded *Exile on Main Street* in the cellar of Keith Richard's rented Edwardian mansion, Nellcôte. Keith all junked up, the whole group tax-exiles digging into American roots music to make an album of corroded blues and bittersweet country, stoned R&B and druggy gospel. If they ever make another film based on "Tender Is the Night," *Exile* should be the soundtrack.

The *Exile* cover is a black and white photo, the wall of a tattoo parlor covered with pictures of sideshow freaks. Shot somewhere along Route 66 by Robert Frank in '55 when he crisscrossed the U.S. shooting rolls and rolls of expressionistic black and white, a series of photos revealing the bleak shadow side of Fifties America. Frank tried to get a book of the photos, "The Americans," published in the U.S. but he couldn't get a publisher because his photos were too fucking real, showed an America the straights didn't wanna see. The first publication of "Les Américains" was in France in '58. The French connection, man, first third of "Tender Is the Night" *set* in France, and *Exile on Main Street recorded* in France, and "The Americans" *published* in France. And dig this, Robert Frank meets my man Kerouac on the street in New York, shows him the photos for "The Americans" and Kerouac writes the introduction to the U.S. edition, which Frank finally gets published in '59. Fitzgerald, the Stones, Robert Frank and Kerouac rubbing elbows with the Devil at some lost juke joint on Route 66. I'm obsessed, man, but none of it gonna help Jaded write about the book.

When they get back Jim puts on Coltrane's *A Love Supreme*, and lights a fat doobie, and Jaded pours us drinks from one of those half-gallon bottles of that infamous college kid brew Almaden Burgundy, and right fast we toast "the glamming of Jim Costello and Writerman."

The cool night air blows in past the curtains, that mystic gong, and Coltrane blows a sweet melody, and McCoy Tyner fingers the right chords on the piano, and Jimmy Garrison's insistent four note bass line and Coltrane again, that odd rhythm to the melody from his sax. We're silent, we sit there, and we bear witness. The music takes us beyond the transient surface of our lives, beneath the surface of the surface, not in the jarring way of Clyfford Still but a gentle, soothing narrative brings us deep into the river of one mind, only that's wrong, 'cause it's not the mind, it's beyond the mind, and Coltrane chants *a love supreme, a love supreme*, and he mirrors those four bass notes, and Jaded starts to chant, and me, and Jim, *a love supreme, a love supreme*, we all chant with John Coltrane until his voice is silent, and we're silent too.

"All the religion I need," Jim says.

"Can't you ever stop talking," Jaded says. "Just listen."

Well that's what we did, we listened to the rest of the album, all of us silent.

After some time passes, we settle back into the known world. I look at Jim but he's hidden behind the makeup, and it's clear how a human face—my face, Jaded's face, Jim's face—is a front behind which nobody has a clue. What's under the transient surface of Jim?

I sit there contemplating such things when Jim asks if I'm going to King Editor's annual Halloween party at the Raven's Woods Mansion. Wallace Wiley's gonna premier his 16mm film, "The Deadly Kiss." Everyone who's worked on *The Paper* or is taking a film class or knows King Editor or Wiley or the other professors in the film department is invited. I've planned on taking Elise, but Jim suggests we all go together—Sappho too. That's when Jaded says it's a costume party and she's going as Dick Diver, the protagonist in "Tender Is the Night," and Jim gonna be Lola, the transvestite in The Kinks' song.

"Gonna wear a dress?" I say.

"Party of the year," Jaded says.

"Can't be Lola without a dress," Jim says, and sings:

Girls will be boys and boys will be girls, it's a mixed up muddled up shook up world except for Lola, Lo-lo-lo-lo Lola.

"Do you know what Wiley's film is about?" I say.

"The usual," Jim says. "Death, sadomasochism and betrayal."

My hands on Jaded's smooth white skin.

Through the stoned haze I look into Jaded's mirror. My hair so black, black as night, black as sin. My skin so white from the makeup, white as crushed bone. Lips purple as the lettering on the cover of *Are You Experienced?* The face has the makeup a chick puts on her face, but it's on a freakster bro masculine face, how the chin juts out, and the bits of beard under the white paste. What's weird is how the mask of a chick—the purple outline of lips, the white makeup and dyed hair—is superimposed on my freakster bro face. There I sit, trying to figure out what's male and what's female. Of course I'm a freakster bro, no question, but it's more complex. We're a yin-yang mix of masculine and feminine. What's different is how the makeup brings the feminine to the surface. And it freaks me. Who the *fuck* am I?

13. PARTY OF THE YEAR

THE NIGHT OF THE Halloween party everything is surreal. Before I get to Elise's room I'm serious stoned, and though I know Jim's gonna bring weed and there'll be plenty of King Editor's booze, I have a special stash in my coat pocket. In addition to a few emergency joints there's a packet of coke and a tab of Orange Sunshine. I wanna do blow with Elise at the midnight hour. And the acid?

The Boy Scout motto is Be Prepared.

I'm wearing my fancier duds. Burgundy velveteen bellbottoms and matching sport coat I got at Disraeli Gears, a white tuxedo shirt from the Goodwill, and a purple bow tie to match my lips and nails.

Not a costume, but it's a costume.

All week Elise made a big deal about how she wouldn't wear a costume, said it's stupid for people our age to wear 'em, but I know it's deeper. She's not secure enough in who she is to be someone else for even a single night.

I wish I could say I'm not worried about how Elise will take the freak-out of my glam trip. In Jaded's room it was easy to rationalize, *she's an artist, of course she'll get it,* but when I get to Elise's doorway I'm scared. What if she doesn't wanna have anything to do with a freakster bro wearing nail polish?

The candles cast huge dreamy shadows on the wall, tripped-out shadow shapes of Elise and Sappho's bodies. They're dancing to that Supremes' song, "Come See About Me." I smell the weed and there's two paper cups and the Almaden jug on the desk, and the glass ashtray with two Kools burning up.

Sappho is dressed as a *Playboy* bunny, and I find out later she's Gloria Steinem, back when that feminist chick did her magazine exposé. Ms. Libber herself got on a one-piece black Speedo swimsuit and goddamn if she doesn't have tits out to here. I never knew what she had under those baggy clothes she always wears. Large white bunny ears rise off her head, white puff tail comes off her ass. I don't get it right then, but something's off, how she looks at Elise as they dance.

Elise raises her arms above her head and brings 'em fluttering down on either side of her body and her tits move beneath her tight black V-neck sweater. Blur of flowered skirt, blur of black tights and curvy legs and small perfect feet. Shakes her hair, and it's past her shoulders, candlelight flickers across it as she dances. She turns this way and that, the candlelight on her face and off, and when it lights her face, the beautiful sadness. Doesn't matter her being so gone and so free—it's always there.

She stops dancing and goes for more wine, and that's when she sees my face, or whoever's face—purple lipstick white paste makeup henna black hair—and her paper cup falls to the rug.

"Bloody massacre," she says. "This has to be Jade's idea," and she steps close to me. Purple nails on hands that used to be my hands. "Talked you into it. How'd she do that, Writerman?" and what to say? Can't tell her I care what Jaded thinks. Can't, man.

"It's really really strange, Michael," she says.

Her face has the mixed-up confusion of *who is this guy?*

Time passes slowly.

She stands there silent, checks me out, tries to make sense of it.

And finally. "You've got the guts," she says. "A lot of boys would never do it."

"Gotta take a risk," I say.

She reaches out, her fingers in my frizzed curls to know it's not an illusion. "I know you, Michael," she says. "You're not one of those macho men Kate swears about. You have feelings. Is this the girl part of you, all this?

And that's when she hugs me, and all the uptight fades away. "Yeah," she says. "I like it."

It's different from when we hugged after the tree limb fell, from after she threw the bottle, and after she read my Beefheart review. This is pure, and this is what I've wanted since I first saw her. The weeks of restraint, in the moment of that moment it's over, the longing in our eyes and the pull we feel to touch, and I reach for her, her body against me. We hold each other in the flickering light, and it's natural as nature. But then her body gets stiff and she wants me to let go. I thought I'd done something wrong but no, it's her trauma—an anxiety overtaking her. She needs a drink, she says, red wine in paper cups, and we sit on her bed. I wipe the sweat under my nose, and white make-up comes off on my fingers.

"This shit is freaking me," I say.

I stand before her closet door mirror and I look strange. Not the extreme freak-out of an Andre Kertész warped mirror, but it's wrong how I look, stretched there and here. Step in closer and all I see is my face. Well, *a* face. Face isn't my face, and who am I? Who *is* Writerman? Don't know the face. My ghost skin, white paste make-up, skin white, dead white against the dead-of-night black hair. Purple lips. *Never* get used to purple lips. Glitter purple nails. *Never*. The make-up a mask. Michael Stein, guilty as Dostoevsky's Raskolnikov, yeah well Michael Stein is gone. Writerman is gone. Gone baby gone. Disappeared behind the mask.

This is deeper than the yin-yang male-female trip. The mask of makeup makes me question the surface of my surface. Strip away the costume that is the outside of me, what a human sees when they look at me, makeup or no makeup, you know, all my rock star affectations—snakeskin boots and Lennon hair and the cowboy shirts and The Dylan and some such—well what's left? My consciousness, and it has nothing to do with the surface of the surface. And as I look into the mirror, a new feeling seeps into me.

Writerman, or whoever the fuck I am, is separate from

every other human, only the feeling amplified into an overwhelming alienation. I'm the protagonist in those Camus novels, "The Stranger" and "The Fall," and I see the Hitchcock poster, weird vertigo image of a man falling falling falling in a swirling black and white op art spiral, the man tiny against the scale of the spiral. First time my soul takes a hike, and there in the mirror, the Existential Freakster Bro.

Sappho is over at the stereo asking what do I wanna hear, but I'm dazed, one of my hands between me and the mirror, and I see through the hand, ghost hand, don't know the hand. Her voice from a distance, and I struggle to get away from the mirror, pull myself out of the existential quicksand sucking me down down down into the op art spiral of no return.

Save my soul, save myself. *My* self.

Some of the existential trip falls away, but it'll return, and next time it won't be so easy to pull out, and the Existential Freakster Bro is there, an invisible shadow, only more than a shadow, a version of me without the guilt, the me that doesn't give a fuck about right or wrong, the me that can lie and steal and betray.

"Play what you feel, Kate," I say, and the shadow alienation, the Existential Freakster Bro, stands at the back of the room and watches. I sit down on Elise's bed, our thighs touch, and it's not only me can't control the reverberations of what's going down tonight.

Sappho gets a song going. Organ whirls loud distortion from the crap Zenith speakers. Me and Elise still dazed—her because of the hug and how I look, and me 'cause I seen the Existential Freakster Bro inside me—when from the hall through the doorway imploding into the room comes the ass of a big chick in gold lamé.

She backs in, bent over. Big gold lamé ass. I see it, we all see it. She spins around, stands tall, left hand on her hip, dress too tight, stomach bulging. Shoves her right arm straight out, hand up, palm facing us, and from the crap speakers hellfuck loud:

Stop! In the Name of Love.

Jim, man, and he's Lola, Lola doing Diana, his arm out and we all see his hairy arm pit, a dust ball of hair, and he mimics Diana's moves, the hairy arm stretched out, his big clunky hand up, palm aimed at us for the "stop" line, and then slowmo pulls the arm back, snaps his fingers three times as he lowers that hand to his upper thigh and slaps both hands against his thighs once and moves his body, tries to do it graceful as Diana, but Jim is a big awkward guy, looks same as a big ugly transvestite.

The four of us get in a circle and start dancing, 'round and 'round, singing along, and it's in the high of us dancing that I got this odd feeling, as if something wasn't quite right. I thought it was the shadows dancing on the wall creating a sense that there were others in the room. Well that wasn't it at all.

Jaded.

In the doorway, and it's the lost existential who-am-I all over again. Out-of-control buzz. But I'm not scared, I'm strong, stronger than Michael Stein ever been and the Existential Freakster Bro whispers in my ear that deal Burroughs borrows from Vladimir Bartol, or was it Hasan-I Sabbah?

Nothing is true, everything is permitted.

It's layer upon layer, what goes on as we get deeper into it. In my stoned haze I think I see Jaded wink at me, but I don't know for sure. *Coulda had me. You have to take what you want when you see it, Michael.* I look over at her and what if Elise sees me, and still I do an exaggerated wink. *Coulda had me.* I want Elise but I can't resist Jaded.

She stands in the doorway has on her Dick Diver costume —a man's black suit, white shirt and black bow-tie. Her hair pulled back and hidden under a black derby. One moment I'm sure she winks back, and the next, well not sure at all, or maybe she intends to wink at me. Layer upon layer. And the paranoia strikes deep all over again 'cause I'm sure Elise saw Jaded wink, I mean *if* Jaded winked, 'cause maybe she didn't, and in that moment I feel something else, my destiny gonna manifest.

Tonight.

"I can see you're all having a barrel-of-monkeys' worth of

fun," Jaded says. "But we do have a party awaiting us."

She turns on the overhead light, and we see Jim real good. He has on that tight gold lamé dress and there's falsies or toilet paper, something stuffed in the bra. Jim Costello with tits! And a cheap ill-fitting blonde Marilyn Monroe wig, and his beard and mustache and blood-red lipstick and death-red nails, and curling out the front of that gold dress and all the way up to his neck, mess of brown kinky chest hair. Ugliest chick I ever seen.

He's been dancing in his stockings, but he has black high heels with him, the kind without a back. He tries to slip into them only his feet don't go, the shoes too small, and he nearly loses his balance. Finally he sits on Elise's desk chair, jams his feet into them.

"I'm tired of Almaden," Jaded says. "I wish you had champagne. I *love* champagne."

"Really, my dear?" Jim says. "I thought gin and tonic was your poison, urr, I mean passion," and I can tell, man, Jim wants Jaded to say *no Jim, you're my passion,* but that's not happening.

"There's a lot you don't know about me," Jaded says, and she steps out into the hall, impatient, and behind the makeup Jim has this cuckold look, or maybe I think it now, knowing what happens later.

Jim in the dress tries to keep his balance, and Sappho comes over in her bunny outfit and sweaty makeup—eye shadow running, lipstick smeared—and of course she has to butt in.

"How's it feel to be a woman, Jim?"

"You only wish you knew," he says.

Jaded, man, watching from the hallway, "Don't be mean, Kate. He's a *lovely* girl."

Well it could have fallen to pieces, but Jim pulls a *deus ex machina,* lights up a fat number and hands it to Sappho. Amazing how a joint cools the chick out.

Elise gets on her beige trenchcoat and brown fedora, and we're about to split when Sappho smiles this evil Modigliani smile. If the chick in Modigliani's "Seated Nude" was possessed by the Devil, that's Sappho's smile.

"Gonna be your lucky night, Elise," she says. "About time

you got laid."

Fucking bitch, only it's Elise who feels the blow. There's an awkward silence and a flat out horror overtakes her face. The horror of what the ex-boyfriend did all over again.

"Leave her alone, Kate," I say, and I put my arm around Elise, and her sad eyes look up into mine.

That bitch Sappho gets on her long wool coat, covers up her bunny outfit except for the ears, and picks up a sign she made, a piece of cardboard taped to a yardstick that has "Sexism: the original sin" written on it.

The all of us get out into the hall.

"Gimme another toke, Jim," Elise says.

"It's Lola, Elise," I say. "You know, The Kinks' song."

"I *never* liked that song," Sappho says.

"That's surprising," Jim says. "It seems so *you*, Kate," and he stands there in that gold lamé dress, and starts in with a different song.

I'm a man. I spell m-a-n. Man.

Sappho copycats him, and she's Maria Muldaur, you know, days of the Jim Kweskin Jug Band.

I'm a woman. I spell w-o-m-a-n. I'll say it again.

"Bloody massacre," Elise says. "Now you two got that straight, let's *go*."

Don't know how we got to the parking lot, especially Jim in those heels, but eventually we assemble next to Jaded's Mercedes. Jaded gets the top down, and me and Elise get in the back seat. She presses against my side, and despite the trenchcoat I feel her warmth, her face inches from mine, and her hand, her beautiful artist hand with the long thin fingers, it's there on her thigh, waiting for me to take it. Sappho and Jim are in the parking lot arguing about who gets to ride shotgun.

"I'm sorry about what Kate said, Elise," I say. "You gotta ignore her bullshit. You OK?"

My hand on her hand, and we're holding hands, and oh man, she squeezes mine.

"Oh Michael, that's so sweet," she says. "No one's ever been so considerate of my feelings."

She kisses my cheek, a quick kiss but it's a special kiss, her caring for me, knowing I'm caring for her. I mean my Visions of Johanna chick, man, my *Visions of Johanna,* and I want to tell her everything, about the longing, about the wanting and the love I feel, but I can't think of anything brand new, no kinda poetry that would have that Writerman sound. So I'll say what's been said before, those words that been said by lovers going back to the beginning of time. Authentic real, if a freakster bro means them, and the chick he says them to is receptive, well they might as well be brand new, minted for her alone.

"I love you, Elise."

Oh man. She pulls away, total frownland scene. "*Michael,* I don't want *anyone* to love me. It's better for both of us if you don't confuse things with that romantic crap."

She's so fragile, and have I pushed it too far, and that's when I see the Existential Freakster Bro standing behind the car, watching us.

"It's already all mixed-up confusion, Elise."

"That's life, Writerman," she says. "A riddle of confusion."

I know she digs me, and maybe she loves me, but the *word* "love" freaks her so bad, and I'm not sure why but I fall back on Dylan, what would Dylan say, what *had* Dylan said? So quiet my lips barely move, "No success like failure, and failure's no success at all."

"What's that, Michael?"

"It's nothing," I say. "It's something I picked up over in England."

"Copycat," and she squeezes my hand, and the Existential Freakster Bro takes a hike, and she doesn't wanna be anywhere but there in that car. With me.

You should have seen us packed into that Mercedes. Jaded dressed up in her Dick Diver costume, one hand holding the derby down on her head, the other on the wheel, and Jim big as he is in that tight gold dress and the high heels and that ugly

blond Marilyn wig, up in front holding Sappho's sign, and
Sappho other side of Elise all turned around so her knees are
on the seat and she faces backwards 'cause she's drunk-ass
stoned and she doesn't wanna sit on her bunny tail, her ass with
that puff thing sticking out towards the front right up against
the back of Jim's seat.

"You get in a car crash, Jade," Sappho says. "I'm one dead
bunny."

Jaded was speeding that winding road, taking the curves too
fast and that's when Sappho lost it, fell onto Elise and me, lying
across our thighs, her head in my lap. The wind was blowing
Elise's hair crazy-wild into my face and she grabbed her fedora.
We both looked down at Sappho, oh man, goddamn goddamn
bunny ears all bent weird and her face loopy lipstick smeared
looking up at us. Yeah, Sappho total messed up scene, and I
laugh, and Elise laughs, we laugh the conspiracy of two laugh,
and Sappho laughs too, the three of us laughing, and for right
then all Sappho's bullshit forgotten, or forgiven, or at least put
aside.

We were so free and happy, man. If only we could have
stopped that moment forever. I was still holding Elise's hand,
and I squeezed it tight, and her mouth against my ear.

"I'm so glad I'm with you tonight, Michael."

Jaded drove through the woods, and turned off onto a private
road, a moonlit dirt road, and it was another couple miles to
reach a field crowded with cars. The Raven's Woods Mansion
was maybe a quarter mile from where she parked, at the end of
a dirt road that curved through the woods. Once out of the car
Jim took off his heels, said his feet were in revolt and he'd
rather be barefoot. As the five of us walked, the silence broken
by a frequent litany of swear words when Jim stepped on a twig
or rock, we could see occasional bits of orange and yellow
through the trees, lights strung up on the house.

Huge trees shadow the road, and at times we can't see
anything. *Caw caw caw.* Two black magpies, can't see them, but
they're there, perched on stick-figure legs. Doom and Gloom,

they see us on the road, and they know how it all ends. They laugh, I know it, laugh at the foibles of us people, how full of it we are, how knowing and certain and self-important. *Caw caw caw*. Whisper of the troubles blowing in the wind, through the leaves, each windblown leaf a warning.

14. DELIRIUM OF THE IMMORTAL

THE MANSION IS A magnificent ruin. Paint peeling, smashed windows boarded over, gardens overrun with weeds, and the ivy everywhere, curling up the side of the house, working its way into cracks and under roof shingles. The mansion's an experiment, one that will eventually reveal how long it takes unrestrained nature to bring civilization to its knees.

We get to the front stairs and meet the pumpkins. On both sides of each stair. The stairs lead up to the porch, and more pumpkins. And more. Big luminous pumpkins, candles burn inside, eyes and noses and mouths cut out, glow orange pumpkin faces glare at me, taunt me.

Black cutouts of bats and goblins attached to the house, and huge grey and white spider webs, and on the roof, a mannequin witch. Still, the house a decaying ruin, and without the fake bats and spiders and witches it would be even scarier. Jim sits on one of the rotted front stairs, gets his heels back on, and from somewhere on the front porch, a crazy-ass crazy witch voice:

"Come inside, my pretties, it's time to have someone to eat."

High-pitch, shrieking laughter, yeah, the Devil's friends think something is really the fuck funny. That kinda sound. That kinda fuck-up scary-ass laugh kinda sound.

Me and the chicks walk up to the porch, and that's when more of the weird seeps through my skin. Total Existential Freakster Bro trip, and this is how it is all through the night, moments of existential remove, moments of stoned in-the-moment-I-am-free ecstasy, moments of the face that's not my face mixed-up confusion, moments I'm Writerman at his best, but also darker moments, 'cause during this night there gonna be times I'm Writerman at his worst.

We can hear all the noise—music and voices and crazy-ass laughter—coming from inside the mansion.

"Man," Jim says, trying to get the hang of walking in heels as he joins us on the porch. "*Everyone's* gotta be here."

"What's important is *we're* here," Elise says, and if things been normal I'd know what she said is important. All five of us together, that's what matters. One of those serious deals about being in the moment. That Zen Beat trip. *Be Here Now.* The five of us being here, for us, it's all that exists. Only in the moment of this moment I'm not here and there isn't any me to be here, no me to *Be Here Now,* and that should be a colossal bummer, only it's not. I stand on the porch, and feel the freedom of anything goes. I can do anything behind the mask, and my head gonna explode.

We all get into the entry, and it's a big room and that room must have looked groovy back when someone gave a fuck. Higher than high ceiling with thick crown molding, and the gold wallpaper above the wainscoting faded and peeling, and the fir floors need a refinish. There's people lined up at the big coat closet in the back. Frankenstein's monster and his bride, and Count Dracula and Vampira. Still others in second-hand evening gowns and tuxedos gather front of an octagonal oak table, center of the room, and through a double doorway towards the rear of the wall to our left, the chaotic of the ballroom.

There's two baskets on the oak table. One on the left with a white card in front that says "His" is full of small white cardboard boxes, each tied with a black ribbon. The "Hers" basket has playing cards cut in half, and each half has a safety pin through it. On the "His" card front of the left basket, "Open at midnight, find your other half, meet your true love."

"Oh fun," Sappho says. "We get to play the dating game."

Jim totters forward, struggles against the gold lamé dress, reaches for a box.

"Got your hand in the wrong basket, Miss Lola dear," Jaded says.

"I may be wearing a dress," he says. "But I'm the same red-blooded manly man."

Still, he pulls his hand back empty. "I think we're beyond this kind of silliness."

Only Jaded wants to play, Dick Diver trying her luck, and she picks up a white box, and I see it, man, Jaded making out with some foxy chick in a summer garden dress or a lace negligee or buck naked.

No telling how far she might take it.

Elise stands front of the chicks' basket, and I take her arm, step toward the ballroom.

"Don't take one," I say.

"Why not?" Sappho says, and that evil Modigliani smile. "A tall dark stranger has the matching half, Elise."

Oh man, 'cause right then it's the worst of Writerman. Pounding blood loud in my head.

"She doesn't need anything from you, Kate."

Elise laughs her Jean Seberg laugh, and takes a card.

"Loosen up, Michael, it's *only* a party game."

"Not a game we're gonna play."

"He's *jealous*, Elise," Sappho says.

"Put it back, Elise. I thought me and you—," only she steps away from me.

"Bloody massacre," she says. "I can't *believe* you're for real."

Well that's the first time she gives me the cold eye. Her cobalt blue eyes are the razor blade hands she draws on that ex-boyfriend and they hellfuck cut me.

"Don't put me in a bloody cage, Michael," and she pins the Ten of Hearts to her V-neck sweater over her left tit.

Ghost of 'lectricity. Some guy's klutzy hands unpin the card, cop a feel through the sweater, pull it up over her head, and they fall back on the bed, and *no, no, goddamn no.*

Shake my head violent fast, and if this be the future I don't wanna know about it.

"I don't believe *you*, Elise," I say.

"He doesn't understand you, Elise," Sappho says. "Guys don't get it," and she lays on her libber trip, says I'm same as the other freakster bros, and all of us no different than our dads and our dads' dads, and blah blah blah, how the patriarchal system been in place thousands of years, and every one of us thinks a chick is our property, thinks once a chick is our girlfriend she cooks for us, and cleans for us and spreads her legs for us whenever we get hard.

It's right outta some feminist manifesto.

Elise gives me the freeze-out, tells Sappho she gonna check her coat and she's gone. The Neil Young lonesome sound, and I slip a dumb-ass white box into my coat pocket, and wish a wish.

Sappho sets her sign down, gets her own card pinned to her swimsuit, sticks out her ass at me, the ass that's got the white puff tail under her wool overcoat, and to be sure I get the message, turns her head and her pink tongue jabs from between her lips, and she goes to join Elise in the coat check line.

What happens next, this Phil Spector record comes booming through the house, and Jim tells me Wallace Wiley has picked all the party music, and this is his favorite song. "He Hit Me (And It Felt Like a Kiss)," sung by The Crystals' Barbara Alston. If how the song makes me feel in the moment of that moment were a sound, it's the sound of a huge-ass question mark. No matter how many times I've heard it, once again I'm shocked.

You know the song, right? That classic Phil Spector sound, same kinda sound as "Be My Baby" and "He's a Rebel." These days, when we're so used to bass, drums and two electric guitars, those Spector records sound like they're from another planet. The way he used an orchestra to create a huge-ass rock 'n' roll noise. No one does that anymore.

Booming so loud.

"He Hit Me (And It Felt Like a Kiss)."

The music builds and builds as strings come in total heavy

traffic intense beneath a first person confessional. The singer says she told her boyfriend she'd been untrue, and he hit her. He hit her, and she's *glad*. He hit her, and still she wants him to stay.

And I want to get out of there, out of the entry, peeled gold wallpaper got it in for me, man, wallpaper eyes, and the eyes know the secret language the pumpkins speak. You remember, right, the pumpkins along the stairs and on the front porch. Only to me the pumpkins speak their secret language, and the wallpaper eyes understand, see through the surface of the surface. And what they tell me is something is wrong, this song is a bad fucking omen.

Me and Jaded and Jim stand together, smoke cigarettes on the entryway side of the doorway leading to the ballroom as new arrivals stream past, sucked into the chaotic. Jaded holds onto Jim's arm, her face all screwed up.

"This song is an abomination," she says. "Wallace Wiley is a sadist."

"It's one of Spector's masterpieces, Jade," Jim says. "Don't you think, old sport?"

A fine dust of downerosity is falling on us, every damn thing going south as if there's a mathematical formula at work, each unit of stoned blitzed-out high equal to x-units of hardcore downerosity, and right then Sappho returns carrying her sign. Usually there's almost nothing Jaded and Sappho agree on, but that song, oh man oh man oh man.

"A real abomination," Sappho says. "Wiley's *such* a sexist pig."

Jim's had it with the chick shoes 'cause he gets 'em off and sets 'em out of the way against the wall, as if those heels are part of the decay been going down at the Mansion since time began, or some such.

"To play a song like that," Sappho says. "Worse than sexist."

More and more loud, more and more instruments. The hot heavy air, and a wind blows through the leaves and the branches crack. Falling, falling, and the song, man, we're under the thumb of that goddamn song.

"Hate to admit it," I say, "but for once you're fucking right, Kate."

"Come *on*, old sport," Jim says. "You must appreciate the egocentric audacity of Spector releasing that record in '62. Immediately after The Crystals went Top 20 with 'Uptown.'"

Well Jim's clueless about the impact the song has on these chicks. Me and him might as well be in a museum digging some esoteric painting. You know, ART. Well for the chicks there's nothing abstract about it. Jaded lets go of his arm, and the way she does it, same as she pushed him.

"Jim, that song's about a guy beating up his girlfriend," she says. "It's *offensive.*"

"But Jade, my love," Jim says. "The arrangement, the vocal, and—."

Sappho, man, the chick steps past me, gets so she's facing him, has both hands around the yardstick, you know, her libber sign.

"What if it were a castration song?" Sappho says. "And the guy in the song *likes* it."

And she throws the sign at him, cardboard against his chest, and it fell to the floor. Jim laughs and Sappho assumes a boxer stance, and how ridiculous—her in a black swimsuit, bunny ears rising from her head, fists up, white puff.

Jim laughs all the harder.

"Or how about his girlfriend cuts his *dick* off," Sappho says. "You dig that, Jim?"

That's when she punches him, only she doesn't have any strength. Still, *Thee* Freakster Bro is furious she dared touch him. Picks up the goddamn goddamn sign and breaks the yardstick over his knee.

"Bitch asshole!" and throws the broken sign down where his heels lie.

High on the delirium of the immortal, whoever I am is gonna cool it down. Well it goes same as this. Jim's hand forms a fist, his arm starts to move. Sappho stands where she stands, the sound of her fury.

"What about it Jim? A happy song about castration?"

Yeah Jim is furious, gonna teach Sappho a lesson. As I step between them he pulls his arm back, my foot lands so I face him, and his punch, a punch meant for Sappho, lands fuck-ass hard in my gut. Burning needles and I fall back against the wall, below the wallpaper eyes, and they laugh at my folly along with the pumpkins and somewhere up high Doom and Gloom laugh too, and my hands, palms against the wall try for my balance. Pounding blood loud, burning needles, room spins 'round, and where's Elise? I slide down the wall, come to rest next to Sappho's broken libber sign. Discarded shoes, discarded libber sign, discarded freakster bro.

Jim leans down, sweaty lipstick-smeared face in my face, sticky hand on my arm, and let the phony-ass apologization begin.

"Oh damn," he says. "Writerman! You alright?"

Sappho screams, "Look what you've done. All guys want is money or power or to beat someone up. You, you *pig*."

"We should get you to a doctor," Jim says, and I pull my arm away. "Jade, what do you think?"

No, no, I'm fine, no big deal. I'm the Existential Freakster Bro, I'm Writerman, I'm whoever I am behind the mask, and the stoned blitzed trip, adrenalin of the fight, delirium of the immortal.

"Really, I'm cool," I say, only I'm in no shape for nothing.

"You sure, old sport?" he says, and his pudged-out bearded face lipstick smear too too close. "I never would want to hit you, Writerman."

I didn't believe him, not that night, and not now. Something about his voice, he kept saying he was sorry and his look of concern more mask than the makeup. He'd hit me hard. No way he'd hit a chick, not even Sappho. What if he *wanted* to hit me, his sneak-ass way to get back at me for what happened at King Editor's office, or, and this is pretty out-there I know, but what if Jaded let it slip she dug me, or intimated as to why I'd come to her room.

I lie there, and after some time passes I hear Sappho. "If the happy castration song was playing, would you talk about 'the production?' Well Jim? Would you?"

Where's Elise? Did she see me step in to save Sappho? I get up, hands against the wall, steady steady. Someone's beating on a drum in my head, and all I have to show for what happened is a lump under my hair.

"You disgust me, Jim," Sappho says.

Jaded's face, man, she might as well be yelling *Don't touch my man.* Sappho so stoned she doesn't see it, but I do. Jaded sees me watch her, and I'm positive she winks. Second wink, or is it the first? And something else. Jaded saw me step into the fray, and it excites her—both the violence and me surviving the punch same as it's nothing, well, almost nothing.

Elise is a desolation angel walking toward me. All I see is the half-card pinned to her sweater. All the bad vibes crashing down, and I want to shout *no*, want to rip the Ten of Hearts off her.

You're mine, Elise, don't you understand? Mine.

The Ten of Hearts is a personal affront, an advertisement to every freakster bro. *I'm available, boys, come fuck me tonight, any of you, all of you, with one exception, anyone but Writerman.*

And that Phil Spector record, still it plays, and it's a haunting.

"Bloody massacre. An abomination. Kate, have you heard the words to this song?" and Elise gives me the cold eye squared, same as the song is my fault. "How cruel to play it. Whoever chose it is absent a heart."

The music a thick black smoke pressing down on us and in that moment I'm out-of-control.

"You mean you didn't hear it at the carnival?" I say. "Didn't old razorblade hands, didn't he hand you a Jose Cuervo and sing it to you out by the pool?"

An icy wind through the leaves, crack of the branches, and Elise is stricken. The cracked limbs in the dirt, *don't cry Elise, don't cry.*

"Damn you, Michael," she says. "Kate's right. You guys, you're all the same."

Pounding blood loud, and the punch of Elise's words.

Caught, man, red-handed, in a trap *I* set. And *what the fuck have I done*. Yet I'm glad too. Don't wanna be glad, but I am. I hurt, so she should hurt.

"What I've heard," she says. "It's more than I *ever* wanted to hear. More than you'll *ever* understand."

My body slumps, the pounding blood loud, and that team of guys going at my insides with sledgehammers. Total freeze-out, but I *gotta* talk to her, my hand on her thin arm through the black wool sweater.

"Don't you touch me!"

She jerks her arm, and her pulling it away is another punch. Hurts fuck worse than the one Jim landed. And *my* apologization begins.

"Elise, I so fucked up."

"Fuck you, Michael. I was bloody wrong about you."

In front of us, the chaotic—the ballroom and music and voices. I'm on the threshold, hellfuck of what gone down, needles in my gut, shame of my words, and I take a step, ferry across the Acheron, and leave them all behind.

Crossing the threshold is when the Existential Freakster Bro takes over. I'm strong, and all the guilt and shame and pain gone. I leave behind the petty morality of human kind, rules of good and evil, confront the mass of horny-ass chicks and guys, bodies press in against me, hot and sweaty.

Oh man, huge-ass candelabra overhead and an even more humungous stone fireplace spits sparks from its wall of flames. Move through the room as if I'm a giant, push the dark blur of petty people aside, move toward the illusory nirvana of the bar and booze.

Who knows how long I stand at the bar, and as I stand there I watch myself as my mind examines all that gone down as if it's something that happened to a passing stranger. I watch as I drink the fine cabernet that King Editor blew his dough on when *fuck*, 'cause out of the chaotic comes the whole crowd. Jim and Jaded and Sappho and Elise at the other end of the bar.

Elise is a ruin, her face contorted, her body a wound. I watch as she drains a glass, and another, and one more.

Well that's when *I* get the tab of acid from my jacket pocket, but it's not the *I* that's Michael Stein, it's the Existential Freakster Bro, and *I* place the tab on my tongue. Wash it down with the cabernet, and how long 'til it kicks in? *I* see the wine bottles on the bar, my hand on a bottle, it's *mine*, and *I* watch as *I* pick up the bottle, and another full glass too, and split from the bar, leave them all behind yet again.

Oh it was a scene, man. Push past a guy in a tux and top hat, only he's a she, silver glitter and gold stars cover her face, and under the black tux jacket, no shirt, only her bare skin and I grab a feel and she laughs. Other chicks wear a bowler or a fedora or a beret, some with a thin mustache glued under their little nose or a fake goatee. Guys in dresses, guys in slips, guys in bras and lipstick and wigs. And the guys in the dresses dance with guys in tuxes, chicks in tuxes dance with chicks in dresses, guys dance with chicks and chicks with guys, and I never seen such mixed-up confusion.

Twosomes and threesomes and foursomes. Everyone wearing makeup and those black Lone Ranger masks only these are shiny gold masks and silver sequined masks and red glitter masks and white glossy masks. Everyone hides behind masks, real masks, gender masks, or the mask of their made up face. Surface of the surface, and not a clue what's beneath.

15. SOUL TO SOUL

I'M IN THE CHAOTIC of the ballroom, drinking straight from the bottle, ready for the acid to kick in, when from a distance I see her. Simone. Well, I hadn't started thinking of her as Simone yet. She was still Ms. Braveheart. She kinda reminds me of Liv Ullmann. Same kinda scarf around her head as Ullmann wears in "The Passion of Anna," same kinda troubled emotions beneath the surface of her surface. A stern Swedish pride and what they call good bones.

Turns out she grew up in San Diego, same as Harper, so it has nothing to do with Sweden. She undoes the scarf and her long wavy hair falls past her shoulders, and the moonlight makes a halo around her head. Her face—she's across the room right in front of the windows, but later when I see it up close—it's the face of the angel-whores in the Alfons Mucha posters.

I figure she's at least 30, though when I get the facts direct from her, turns out she's 35. Usually I'm not turned on by older chicks, and this one a teacher too. She teaches the "Women in Film" class, and yeah, I've heard she's a hardcore feminist.

I'm looking across the room at her when I hear Sappho's low voice and, oh no, coming at me one more fucking time, the lot of them, and they all look a ruin, have the tired bummerosity of too long in the rain with no umbrella. The Existential Freakster Bro splits, and I'm me again, Writerman, and I'm pissed. Can't a freakster bro get a fucking break? Well they see who I'm lookin' at and they all start in.

"Isn't Ms. Braveheart a femi lesbo?" Jaded says.

"Of course not, *Jade*," Sappho says. "Look at her with that *child*," and we watch as this freshman I seen at the Arts College hands her a glass of wine.

Elise still has the freeze-out vibing off her. Later she told me she was so pissed right then, but freaked-out too. She said she had such expectations for me and her that night, but we'd fucked it so bad, and she didn't know how to make it right.

We watch Ms. Braveheart kiss the sycophantic freshman, and it's the Robert Doisneau deal, "Le Baiser de l'Hotel de Ville," only the roles reversed. Well it unnerved everyone but me. Sappho says Ms. Braveheart is a "cradle robber," and Jim can't imagine "kissing a teacher," and Jaded doesn't want Jim to even look at her.

"She could be his mother," Elise says.

"That *woman*," Sappho says. "Someone told me she fucked a freshman one time after class. Locked the door, and they did it right in the classroom."

Jim being Jim sings:

Maybe it's a lie, even if it's a sin. They'll repeat the rumor again.

"She did it!" Sappho says.

"I'd think you'd like that, Ms. Steinem," I say. "Payback time."

Sappho lights a Kool for herself, one for me, and holds out her glass, "Gimme more."

I take the cigarette and fill her glass only I pour too much and it overflows onto her hand and some of the overflow drips to the floor.

Only later I remember the red wine drops on Sappho's hand as the moment the acid explodes in my brain a luminous layer of iridescent light above the stoned high of wine and weed. As the drip of wine inflates 'til the Mansion can't contain it, so my brain expands. I am the river unconscious flowing through the human soul. I am Writerman, and finally, *finally*, the New Trip within my grasp as if space and time evolve beyond, evolve to, oh fuck, and I am so close. *Finally*. To live the authentic real.

Goddamn goddamn, yeah!

I raise up my hand, the one holding the Kool, and there's burning purple fire at the tips of each finger. My body still in the ballroom, but my consciousness splits the scene and I'm far far away from Elise and the rest of 'em.

Ghost of 'lectricity. Well this is the part that Dali for sure coulda directed. I see this chick and her body is tattooed with her sins, in black ink, her whole body, in a language that doesn't exist. She's maybe 10 feet from me, and she looks same as Anna Karina in *Vivre sa vie*. Isn't no sorta, kinda deal, not vague how Jaded has a passing resemblance. I mean *exactly*. This chick might as well *be* Anna Karina. Black hair, almost a bowl kinda haircut, bangs right above her eyes, and she's naked. Only for once I'm not staring at a chick's tits. I can *almost* read the words. Some letters appear as regular English, only the words they form aren't words I've seen before, and others, it's as if they're backwards or upside down, and still others form what looks to be a word only it's an illusion of a word.

One moment I'm looking at the chick, and then I'm high in the stratosphere, looking down with x-ray vision on the entire Mansion, and everyone has their sins inked into their bodies, and my own body is down there too. I see me standing in the ballroom, naked, my sins inked into every inch of me. Well it isn't only our sins, 'cause stamped into our skin is who our parents are, and our race, and our gender and more, all the things that make up our humanity. All of us cursed, all of us blessed, all of us human.

Link Wray's "Jack the Ripper," fuck yeah! Crash of rock guitar car out of control reverb-soaked tremolo twang through the guardrail garbage can drums hard against the cliff down down down into the ravine, *and then*, oh man, walking toward me my crazy-beautiful Visions of Johanna, Elise, and I *freak*. She's a vision of all I lack, all I want, all I need. On the threshold between before and after, between the question and the answer. What the *fuck* now? She comes closer still, and leaning in, her mouth against my ear and her breath fills me with her warmth.

That's when she tells me how much it pissed her off when I tried to control her, and my words, when I brought up the ex-boyfriend, made it so much worse. We were gonna have to talk about all that, she says. *Later.*

"Bloody massacre, Michael," she says. "I'm fucked up and I need you. This place creeps me. So many strange people. Hold me. Please."

So I hold her, and she knows it's OK. With me she's safe. Doesn't matter if she's fucked up or creeped out or frozen 'cause of the ex-boyfriend. I accept her, no questions asked. My arms around her, her soft black sweater, and it isn't about sex. I hold her how a freakster bro holds a chick who's in pain, and it's all me giving to her. She relaxes into me different than before. And a current arcs neon bright between us.

That night I understand a Visions of Johanna chick is more than a freakster bro's old lady. Elise is the yin to my yang. I hold her and Elise is *the other.* A chick, man. So different. How she moves, how she thinks, how she feels, how her heart beats.

The taboo of opposites. Freckles dust her small perfect chick's nose. Curve of her chick lips, the thin line when she presses them together isn't giving nothing away. Her blue million miles eyes, don't know what's beyond 'em. A chick, man, *this chick,* a lifetime of secrets and I barely have a clue, but in this moment there is, well I don't want to say it's love, but something along those lines in how she looks up into my eyes.

There in the ballroom flowers flow from her mouth, blood red roses and virgin white lilies and blue passion flowers, flowers pour from her body, from her ears and mouth and pussy, each flower a line from a poem or song or story, the words of Plath and Dickinson and Stein and Bronte and McCullers and Lee, the flowers sing of the beautiful sadness and never have I seen such a thing—not before, not since.

She moves her body slow, man, to Etta James' "I'd Rather Go Blind," and she takes my hand and her wounded animal lips whisper so quiet, "Come on Michael, slow dance me the way I learned it at the carnival."

We're lost in some Fifties dance hall. Those sour New Orleans horns, and in her eyes the reflection of me I see is a version of me so much more who I am than I see on my own. And for once she's a mirror. I'm *somebody* in her eyes, and finally I shake free any last residue of the Existential Freakster Bro, free of self-doubt and confusion, and I'm me, the new Writerman. And then it happens, a river of beautiful sadness flows from her to me. All the fear and dread of what happened in the past, and Etta James sings she'd rather go blind than see the guy she loves walk away.

"I'm so sorry, Michael," Elise says. "I wish we could fix all the bloody leaks."

How we hold each other—so much more than friends.

"You and I, we're always stepping in big puddles splashing muddy water on each other," she says. "I get it all over your boots and you get it on my skirt and then we try so hard to clean up the mess and we fail bloody horribly."

She shakes, and I hold her. It seemed such a long time. Us standing there, me holding her, the warmth of her body.

"Don't know what I'd do," she says, "without—," can't finish the sentence. "Why's it have to be so hard, Michael?"

And that's when I kiss her.

"My oh my, did Cupid's arrow *penetrate* your lovely body, Elise?"

Goddamn goddamn, we fall apart, we're side-by-side. And there's fucking Sappho standing maybe a yard away, looking at us with her Modigliani-chick-possessed-by-the-Devil smile.

Elise has a tight grip on my arm, not a hangin' on me grip, but something about it—I'm the only thing keeps her standing.

"Kate," I say. "For once can you not be such a *fucking* ass."

So much disappointment in the way Elise looks at Sappho.

"Bloody massacre, Kate," she says. "He's my *boyfriend.*"

Well that should have been the end of the night. We should have pulled ourselves together, got the coats and Elise's hat and splitsville right out of that scene back to the safety of Elise's room. Cleaned off the mud from her skirt, from my boots. Seen if we could erase the beautiful sadness, and figure out what it meant for me to be her boyfriend.

Only that's not what happens. I still don't know the details, or even the outline of it, only that right then Sappho's face goes green, and all the cynical drains out of her and she needs to confer with Elise. One of those chick deals, where in the moment it's so important, and later it's nothing. Those two talk quiet, and I don't hear their words. I mean with the music so loud, and the noise of what's gone down with me and Elise louder still. Next thing she needs to talk to me, Writerman, and takes my arm so natural how a lover would.

"Michael," she says. "Something's happened. I need to help Kate."

"What can I do?"

"Please, trust me," she says. "I'll see you tomorrow. OK?"

Well it's not OK, how can it be OK, but I tell myself, *listen to Elise, man, she needs you to let her do her thing. She's asking you to trust her.*

"OK, Elise," I say. "See you in the morning. Cool?"

Oh man, you shoulda seen her face. It's all there in her cobalt blue million miles eyes that she understands I'm trying not to be an overbearing jerk. There's a joy, she can't contain it. It's not that we're back to where we were before we fucked things up, it's on a whole new plane.

Her *boyfriend*, man.

Three important things happen after Elise and Sappho split. The first occurs at the midnight hour when a bell rings to signal for us males to play King Editor's dating game. I have an Ace of Spades, and since Elise isn't there, won't hurt anything to check out the chick who has my other half.

I'm up on the second floor when I see the visions. Red roses in the wallpaper as I walk down the hall. Blood red roses and black thorns, Aubrey Beardsley drawings alive on the walls. Stop and watch the roses blossom and the bees fly from one flower to the next, and you know what else, the walls have framed photographs of the Big Men. Flaubert and Fitzgerald, Hemingway and Zola, Salinger and Tolstoy. And there's more, and all of them, to a man, they have their humanity tattooed into their souls, that's what makes them Big Men, and as I walk the Big Men speak, and they have words for *me*, Writerman.

Hemingway's voice high, not the thick guttural bass I expect. *All things truly wicked start from an innocence.*

Should be freaked, man, photos talking, but in the acid dream it's normal as the flowers alive in the walls, and sins tattooed into skin, normal as the imperfections that make us human.

Tolstoy speaks Russian, and still I grok the scene. *What a strange illusion it is to suppose that beauty is goodness.*

Mark Twain leans out from his frame. *Courage is resistance to fear, mastery of fear, not absence of fear.*

Faulkner so blitzed. *Given the choice between the experience of pain and nothing, I would choose pain.*

And Sartre. *I am no longer sure of anything. If I satiate my desires, I sin but I deliver myself from them; if I refuse to satisfy them, they infect the whole soul.*

The Big Men, trying to break on through, trying to tell me: all of us imperfect, all of us open to temptation, and vanity, and sin, and all the rest. 'Cause we're *human*, and that means we've made mistakes, and we'll make plenty more, but it also means we can be forgiven, and we can forgive. The future doesn't have to repeat the past. How else can a planet of imperfect creatures live together?

Well in the midst of that acid-fueled reverie I come face-to-face with the second important thing. I run into Ms. Braveheart there in the hallway. We both stop. I'm the length of a medium size dog from her, a collie perhaps, and I get a good look. She's for sure a mature woman, no college chick. It's not so much her skin, which is rough and brown from too much sun, or her long Freak Scene Dream hair, which is parted in the middle, curling down on either side the way Sixties chicks used to wear it. It's the attitude she's earned through her extra years on the planet.

And her eyes, the defiant, self-assured eyes of a woman who has nothing to prove.

She wears a white blouse with ruffles, and a fancy black velvet skirt. She checks me out, and how she looks at me, well it's kinda same as when Harper looked at me in the cafeteria, only so much more intense and it makes me feel strange, a chick checking me out the way I check chicks out. Strange, but still I feel the wanting. Out-of-control buzz. She sees my glam trip, and more. She sees beneath the surface of the surface, sees the mixed-up confusion of how I lost my way, and how I'm starting to find it.

She smiles a stoned smile and walks past me, and I turn to look at her, and watch as she walks away. And in her walk the self-confidence I saw in her eyes, a walk that says she doesn't give a fuck, and that walk makes the wanting in me even stronger.

Oh man oh man oh man.

The final important thing that happened that night happens in the attic. The only light is a Tiffany lamp far end of the room. There's someone sitting on a couch near that lamp wearing a tuxedo, their back to me, smoke rising from a cigarette. I collapse on a chair far from them, and I'm so exhausted—gotta be the post-acid crash. Freaks me that maybe my encounter with Ms. Braveheart is a betrayal of Elise.

Goddamn I'm a fuck-up.

Chick finally wants to be my chick, and me lusting for the teacher chick. Think about it for a long time as I sit there smoking a number, my mind working hard to rationalize, and eventual I find a trap door, a way out. It was the acid, of course it was, and the weed and the booze, and anyway, what's the big deal if I *look* at a chick. Looking isn't touching, isn't fucking.

I finish the number and crave a smoke. Damn, my Pall Mall pack is empty, so I walk across the room.

"Could I bum a cigarette?"

That's when I see this person in the tuxedo sitting on a floral love seat is a chick. Jaded? But where's Jim? What the hell is she doing up here all by herself? She shakes a cigarette out of the pack, holds it out. I step closer and she turns and it's not Jaded. *Shodo* turn of her head, same as how she moved that afternoon in my door room. Oh man, chick has a black Lone Ranger mask covering her eyes, and plenty of sins inked into her flesh.

"Need a light?" Harper says.

Already she's changed. Not to how it was later, fall of '73 at Ms. Braveheart's house. In the attic Harper doesn't have the tattoos yet, and I don't mean her sins, no, there's real tattoos. Later. She's thinner, not gaunt but too thin. Her hair is shorter too, but she hasn't dyed it yet. What freaks me are her wrists. I tell you about that soon enough. She doesn't know it's me behind the makeup. Well I sit next to her on the love seat and press my right thigh against hers and she doesn't dig it, not at all, and she wants her space.

"Aren't you gonna light my fire, Harper?"

She strains to see it's me, and then she knows, calls me by the nickname she used that afternoon we fucked, the afternoon that seems so long ago.

"Mr. Rogers? Lipstick?"

I see her hands, and the thin blown glass birds and fish and flowers are dead.

She asks if I have a joint, but sorry to say I smoked 'em all up.

"Got some blow we can do," I say. "Oh, but you don't do blow."

"*Yeah* I do."

"Go with your new look?" I say.

"I'm going to hell anyway."

She's got a small mirror and I have the envelope, pour the coke on the mirror. She uses a switchblade to make lines, and that was the first time I saw her switchblade. It was beautiful deadly, with a black ivory and silver handle. I get a fiver and she rolls the bill into a small tube, hoovers a line, and another. The end of the rolled bill warm from her nose, I suck up two lines, and oh the rush. Yeah, I have energy, man. We put it away, the mirror and the fiver and the blade.

Everything's different with me and Harper, sharing dope how we did, it's as if we're merged, the both of us wired, the both of us horny, and we've got history, the memory of the one afternoon we spent together, and is that the coke?

"Let's see if you've learned anything," she says, and straddles me. Her ass on my thighs, her chest hard against mine and I kiss her, serious, no hesitation, I just go for it and she melts right into me. Here I go again. I know it's wrong, *he's my boyfriend*. Fuck, out-of-control buzz, taste Harper again, and it brings it all back. We stop kissing, and she has a whole card pinned to her tux, a Joker, only that Joker is from a different deck. Harper makes her own rules. That's when I see the scars, dark scars on the underside of her wrists.

"You told me only a coward bails on life," I say.

"I had to know what it's like to die. How it feels as the life drains out of you."

"Goddamn goddamn, Harper."

"Life gets too much hype," she says. "Death ought to get its share of attention. Whitman didn't think death was so bad. You ought to read 'Leaves of Grass.'"

Her fingers touch my purple lips. "You've taken some risks since I last saw you."

Harper's smile, a satiate-my-desires kinda smile, and still I could walk away. Well fuck it, buzz high from coke, shadow of the Existential Freakster Bro cheering me on. Free fuck, man, what I thought. Only I don't know Harper's put me on the installment plan, no money down, 10 months 'til the first payment due.

TWO

1. CHRISTMAS (BABY PLEASE COME HOME)

I STAND ON THE sidewalk and stare at the empty parking lot and wait. Asphalt damp from the rain coming down heavy last night and all morning too, and the redwoods and firs past the far side of the lot still wet, water dripping off the branches. Past 3:30, my parents late, but I don't care. Three months since I seen 'em, but I *don't* care. Don't wanna split for home, and I'm glad for every extra minute, as if each minute here at The University is another minute I'm alive in my own skin.

The University shutting down for Christmas break. My new friends gone—Jim and Jaded split for L.A., and Elise and Sappho too—but think about it, I *have* new friends.

It's goin' OK with Elise. OK but slow. We hang out, and it seems she's trusting me more, but still she's freaked about sex. When I try to push things past a kiss, the specter of the monster boyfriend, and *no fucking way*.

As for Jim, we're still friends, but there's weird moments. Maybe it's the paranoia goes with smoking weed, or what went down with King Editor, and of course there's that punch to my gut. And there's Jaded.

All that's the surface of the surface anyway, could be gone in the snap of my fingers. Who I am still based on my friends as my mirror, reflecting back versions of me. I haven't changed so much from who I was, you know, with Sarah.

The trees are beautiful in the shadows of the dark clouds that fill the sky, those shades of gray clouds, not the white billowy clouds of a summer day and not yet the hard black clouds when the apocalypse is near. These clouds portend storms of one sort or another, and the trees, they're beautiful, but even as I witness the beauty, what I feel is nature without people is so goddamn lonesome.

I wanted Elise to come with me to Marin and my folks' place, but no way. She was sweet about it, *maybe when we know each other better*. She's crashing at Sappho's 'cause she can't go home. You think I have a thing about my folks, nothing compared to her trip. Already I miss her terrible.

I get out the Pall Malls, a symbol of who I've become, of the me that didn't exist recent as last summer, and as I hold a cigarette I see another symbol, the purple nails, and despite the gray of this overcast afternoon those nails sparkle. That glam shit makes me feel rock star special. Have my henna black hair pulled into a ponytail and I'm wearing a black fedora I found at a second-hand store downtown.

For the first time since school started I think of the future, of the coming summer. That day in June gonna come, and what then? We pack everything, not only enough for a three-week vacation, *everything*. This world we made gonna vanish as if it never existed. And what about the who-I-am that my friends mirror back to me? Who *is* Writerman without them?

Yeah, who is Writerman?

Past 4 o'clock, sick green '69 Rambler four-door comes too too fast into the lot jerks me hard out of my ghost town reverie. Dad jams the brakes, sees me across the lot through his side window, raises his hand, a slight wave, and is that a grin? Glad to see me, but of course he hasn't *authentic real* seen me. Drop my cigarette to the asphalt grind it hard. Car does a hard left and he drives slower my direction. Mom through the windshield and she hasn't seen me either 'cause she has that world-is-flat gonna-pretend-Mike-is-still-11 smile.

Maybe it'll be different. There were times I had fun with Dad. Skiing Heavenly Valley up at Tahoe was a blast. Me and him on the slopes. My dad's pretty good, and by the time I was 9 I was a fearless hotshot taking off down Gunbarrel flying over the moguls and when I did crash I'd get my skis back on and back at it. My dad couldn't keep up but I'd wait for him at the lift line and we'd ride the tram together look out at the mountain, trees frosted white, slopes dotted with skiers, me swearing this time I'd make it down without a fall. Once when I was 12 my dad bet me five bucks I couldn't do it and he was right, but only 'cause I didn't wanna ski it slow. Didn't wanna ski it same as a *chick*. No man, fuck the five bucks, I skied it same as a crazy-wild freakster bro 'cause it felt so free bombing fast downhill through the snow, icy air against my face, "Eight Days a Week" blasting in my head.

When I lost my balance, certain I was in for a fall, it was worth it to feel the danger. And in the moment before I hit the snow...

Absolutely free.

Pulls up in the sick green Rambler, rolls down his side window, sees the makeup and oh man, does that thing he does when he's so goddamn mad. Total unaware it's happening, the end of his tongue folds back on top of itself and his teeth dig down into the top of that doubled-over tongue, and it makes his face look total horror show, and next thing I know he yells with that hard voice.

"You look like a damn fag."

Mom tries to maintain her everything-is-hunky-dory smile, only my makeup confirms her worst suspicion that me gone off to college only made things worse.

I don't wanna feel anything. These months at The University I forgot how it was with them, but it's same as I never left, and the pull of who I been in their eyes.

Don't wanna feel a thing.

"Worse than a fag," he says.

It's a dare but I'm not gonna lose control, not gonna lose my sense of who I am 'cause right then I *know*. I'm everything he isn't, the anti-Dad, and I let that anger inflate my body and

I'm strong inside. He turns away, yeah he doesn't wanna lock eyes. He'd be the one to blink.

Oh fuck, and what an idiot to think that sap about me and Dad skiing. It's never gonna be same as that again. Three goddamn goddamn weeks, but I *don't* care. I'm not willing to sell out who I am, too big a price to make Mom happy, and with regards to Dad, no price I pay could ever be enough.

Mom gets out of the car, and seeing me she disappears in a daze, her mind gone on vacation. She's dressed up for a special occasion, tried hard to look bright and pretty to see me. Not even wearing her glasses for a change. Has her auburn hair up in a beehive, and a new yellow dress with white butterflies and a white collar buttoned at her neck, the dress cinched at the waist by a wide black belt with a gold buckle. Fancy black dress pumps with little black bows. All of it doesn't make anything seem bright 'cause of her heartbreak face. Dazed, gone far far away, she's one of those "Night of the Living Dead" zombies, a hug and she kisses me on the cheek and I do the same, and when we let go there's a purple mark where I kissed her.

The ride home is a ride to hell. Dad's driving too fast, has the radio on too loud tuned to the game so we gotta hear these loser sports announcers doing their back forth while I stew over my dad's words. *Motherfucker,* calling me fag how some racist son-of-a-bitch calls a black man nigger or some anti-Semitic jackass calls me Jewboy.

A Budweiser commercial starts in, and that's the trigger for my dad to offer up a tribute to one of the sports announcers, this guy who was a big shot on the 49ers before an injury sidelined him.

"That Steve Lansing," Dad says. "He was some wide receiver. A real man," and his eyes in the rearview, his eyes into my eyes. "He's no *fag.*"

"Yeah he's a *real* goddamn hero, Steve Lansing is," I say. "Same as those saps gone off to Vietnam. Same as Tricky Dick. Real macho men."

"You don't know what a man is, Mike," my dad says.

Mom sits, back straight, neck tense, how she gets when we fight. She gives us her silent deal. Later she'll have it out with him. She'll talk quiet but there's severe power in her quiet words. He'll yell, but his wall of noise won't change my mom's mind.

"December 8, 1941 I went to enlist," he says. "Day after Pearl Harbor. I was 17, said I was 18. That's not why they didn't take me. It was my perforated eardrum."

We've heard his woe-is-me about the perforated eardrum a million times. How he woulda been a big war hero except for his lame ear. He bought one of those brown leather bomber jackets at the army surplus years ago, and he still wears that thing. Pathetic, my dad enlisting. And that fucking bomber jacket. No way would I have fought in Vietnam. I woulda split for Canada if I wasn't 4-F 'cause of those three weeks in the nut house after I freaked out and wrote the bad checks. Man, that's a scene I don't wanna think about.

"Real stand-up guy, Steve Lansing," my dad says. "Hurt his leg. Caught a pass from Tom Basker, snagged that ball, gripped it against his chest and he started to run and Percy Jones tackled him and they both went down."

"Oh, bring out the violins," I say. "Maybe you can get him a goddamn wreath."

Mom reaches up to the sun visor, I guess she wants to angle it so she can use the mirror.

"I swore when I had you, Mike," my mom says, "you would *never* play football."

We're at the summit when my mom sees her face in that mirror, and the purple lipstick on her cheek.

"Not a chance," I say.

"Worried you'll chip your fem nails?" my dad says.

She rubs the lipstick smear as if what I got gonna afflict her if she doesn't get it off.

"I'm not a moron, Dad," I say. "Risk your life for a stupid game."

Dad revs the engine and the car jerks, which I think was what he was going for in that moment.

"Football *is* life," my dad says. "There are winners and there are *losers*."

"Football players are whores," I say.

Mom looking into the mirror, and God-who-for-sure-doesn't-exist only knows what she's seeing.

"Mike's a winner, Len."

Dad's hands tight on the steering wheel and man is he ever white knuckling it.

"Whores sucking the dick of money and fame," I say.

"Mike!" Mom says.

We keep at each other, one of those arguments where neither of us gives an inch, when Dad accelerates into the curve and in that moment, the horror as he realizes he's taking it too fast.

Sick squeal of brakes and the burn rubber stench, and he twists the wheel. There's water or some shit on the road 'cause the car spins. Close my eyes, Mom says "God help us," and this is how it's gonna end, my eyes tight shut, and I wait.

I wait for the big bang, the sick green Rambler crashing head-on into another car, and everything gone black, or the car careening over the edge, and the long silence before the car meets the ground.

Only none of that goes down.

Instead we jerk to a stop. We're in the opposite lane, against the sheer side of the mountain they cut into to make this dead man's curve of a road. We're facing uphill and if a car comes 'round the turn we're goners. Dad's an asshole, but I give him this, he's quick, gets us into our lane. How many lives have I got? I'm not a cat but I sure hope I've got another eight.

It's dusk when we pull into the driveway. Dad, his whole body a clench, walks towards the house. Mom faces me, arms limp at her side, the twilight dulling her bright yellow and white butterflies dress. Tries to get her world-is-flat smile going but it's hopeless.

"I'll make dinner," she says. "Meatloaf and salad and broccoli."

I can't tell her I don't eat meat anymore.

I lie on my bed wearing my pea coat and the Keith Richards snakeskin boots smoking a number. Got a window open and hope the smoke gonna vamoose outta there so I don't have to fight Dad about it. The room so small, cowboys and Indians wallpaper since before I remember. My old stereo, the Zenith all-in-one deal with the turntable and the AM/FM radio—older version of what Elise has—right where I left it on the built-in under the windows. Heat of the joint between my fingers. Brought maybe a dozen records home, could be a baker's dozen, got one playing.

Blonde on Blonde, man, Dylan's Cubist masterpiece, refracts the world off the hard angles of his sound, a sound made from wiry blues-rock and all those Beat words and of course the *voice*. History of the world in the *voice*. Dylan the know-it-all, Dylan the narcissist, Dylan the neurotic. Dylan the hippest cat in the room. I hear the myriad mysteries of a chick in those *Blonde on Blonde* songs. Chicks he wants so bad, chicks that betray him behind the garage door, and the Visions of Johanna chicks messing with his mind. All the troubles Dylan has with chicks, and he doesn't get to the bottom of it any better than me.

I want *Blonde on Blonde* to rescue me from the gray house and this room, my old bedroom, and the goddamn goddamn wallpaper, and take me to that Victorian living room in Albert Grossman's grand old house near Woodstock where Dylan posed for the cover of *Bringing It All Back Home* with Grossman's own Visions of Johanna chick Sally there in the background wearing a red pants suit.

Well it doesn't happen, I'm still on the bed, roach about to burn my fingers. Gotta get out of this place only I'm not going anywhere. My friend Frankie is in L.A. at his artist uncle's place for the holidays, and I'm having nothing to do with Polanski, fuckin' loser. Wish I could get Bobby to let me stay at his pad for a few nights but I don't think we're friends anymore. Bobby thinks he's the big time since he became road manager or personal manager, some kind of manager, for Fleet Fingers.

You know, Jasper "Fleet Fingers" Horton. Not surprised if you forgot about him, I mean he's been outta the spotlight since about '68. Yeah, well, Bobby letting me crash at his place isn't gonna happen.

Ghost of 'lectricity. Summer of '72, summer after my sad-ass failure of a freshman year. My first real job, you know, not fooling around pulling weeds for my grandmother or the chores for my allowance. Behind the counter at McDonald's, the busy work it never ends. I'm there for one reason. To earn dough for a decent stereo. One reason only. Amp and turntable and big-ass speakers.

   On this day, same as yesterday and the day before, same as tomorrow and the day after, I get the apple turnovers, after we fry 'em up and they cool off, into the red cardboard sleeves with the golden arches. They're miniature coffins, those red cardboard sleeves.

   Get those red cardboard coffins lined up on the rack under the heat lamps ready for when customers want to buy 'em. Got on the idiot outfit. Baby blue idiot shirt and baby blue idiot hat, both have golden arches on 'em too. And the black slacks and the polished black dress shoes. I'm behind my register when in walks Mr. Rock Star Manager.

   Bobby and his sidekick, this guy who I've heard of, but never seen 'til right then. The sidekick is close behind Bobby, and the vibe coming off him same as he's Bobby's dog, so right then he's Dog to me. Dog been doing some work for Bobby, probably has something to do with Bobby's shifty side business. Bobby has on Ray-Bans and his hair is longer but neatly trimmed fake hipster look the industry suits go for.

   Bobby's not wearing the second-story man jacket, replaced it with this shiny new black leather jacket. It's a million bucks that jacket, only what's funny, it's the same exact style as the second-story man jacket. The desert boots are history 'cause Bobby got on black pointed rock 'n' roll boots.

   Dog is Bobby junior, only his shades aren't Ray-Bans, they're the cheap-ass drugstore shades Bobby used to wear, and fuck, Dog's wearing the original second-story man jacket—the leather worn through at the cuffs and collar. But I don't care how those two look, what bugs the hell out of me is how they act.

Bobby sees me, says something to Dog, and right away there's nods as good as winks, or some such. Bobby laughs his truncated laugh, almost a cough but it's a laugh, and Dog, oh he works hard to mimic Bobby and laugh along with him. I mean it was as if I'm the funniest thing they've ever seen.

Bobby comes up to the counter and there's no *hey man, great to see you.* He starts in to this chick Nancy there at the register how he wants a double cheese and large fries and a vanilla shake and fucking Dog, he wants same as Bobby, which I can tell irritates Bobby.

"Hey man, how's it goin'," I say. "Still workin' for Fleet Fingers, right?"

"Yeah, it's cool," he says.

I ask about Fleet Fingers, and Bobby stands there nodding his head as if he's listening to some big deal important music. Says nothing, looks over at Dog and those two laugh all over again.

"Bobby," I say. "Maybe we could hang Friday, I'm off Friday."

All of a sudden he's looking around the place super interested in the windows and the cheap fiberglass booths and the sign that lists the food items, and same as he didn't hear me, still doesn't say anything.

"Bobby!" I say, my voice louder this time.

"Busy Friday," he says.

"I got Saturday off too."

Yeah well he has some excuse, says he gotta drive to buttfuck wherever, and their food arrives and Bobby hands Nancy a 20.

"Look Writerman," he says. "Me and my assistant gotta go, give me a call, maybe we'll get together sometime."

There's a knock, and muffled through the door Mom's voice

soft, same as all those times when I stormed off slammed my door and she showed up to talk—listened to all my shit about how it wasn't fair whatever Dad wouldn't let me do, or some sad sack about a chick I dug in junior high who ignored me.

"Can I come in?"

Crush the roach in an empty mug I kept pens in when I used to live there.

"It's a free country," I say. "If you're white and you have enough money and keep a low profile."

She opens the door, me lying there looking at the ceiling, and says something, says it same as a fact, "What's wrong," and why the hell she say it? She heard Dad, seen the makeup. She knows.

She closes the door and goes to sit in the oak captain's chair over by the built-in, below the windows, far side of the bed, smooths her yellow dress, sniffs, and wrinkles up her nose.

"You mean other than I have to be here for three weeks?"

Mom's wearing her ugly glasses. They're oversize with translucent pink frames. Too bad she gotta wear 'em. Those glasses hide how pretty my mom is. I've seen pictures of her from when her and Dad first dated. I swear she looked kinda like Lauren Bacall. I guess she still does. If the years were airbrushed away, and she changed her hair style. And lost some pounds. And dressed different. And, and, and.

"We were hoping being off at school, on your own, things would get less—."

"*Psycho*?" I say. "You thought I'd get it together. Start digging my grave, major in science so I could become a doctor," and I hate having to defend myself, hate my mom so sad, hate this dead gray house, and this room, and the cowboys and Indians wallpaper.

There's disappointment in her eyes, as if all the times she said I was special, blind fucking faith in whatever crazy scheme I was gonna somehow pull off, all of it taken back.

"I don't understand," she says.

"What's there to understand."

I look at the sliding closet door. All those years, night after night, I was certain someone was in there but when I forced myself to turn on the light, no one. All that fear, lying in the dark, wasted.

"Oh Mike," and we're both in the darkness of what used to be my room—only I don't see it that way anymore, all I see is a shit-ass bedroom in a crappy gray house in the suburbs that I hope to split from forever in three weeks.

And I'm so fucking guilty for what I've said, gotta back off.

"Mom, I appreciate what you and Dad have done for me."

All the years I grew up, the bills always paid, plenty of food, and even now Mom getting my grandfather to pay my tuition, room and board, all so I can take drugs and paint my nails and hang out with Elise. Well too fucking bad, I never made a deal about how I spend my time at The University.

"This isn't my life," I say. "This place, and what you want for me."

"What happened that summer—," she says.

And we both know what she means. The summer after high school graduation, the summer I smoked all that weed, went down down down. The summer I flipped out and was in the nut house for three weeks.

Yeah, she doesn't have to say another word. We know.

She leans forward and the way her jaw juts out, even with her lipstick smeared some at one corner of her mouth, I can see why Dad fell for her. Still it's hard to imagine the two of them same as me and Elise all those years ago.

She sniffs again, mixed-up confusion for sure.

"Mike," she says. "Are you smoking marijuana again?"

"Everything's *fine*," I say. "At school I've got the best friends *ever*."

Her voice goes flat, and it's not fair how life beats people up.

"That's nice," she says, and gets up. "The meatloaf is burning."

2. AUTOMOBILE BLUES

IT WAS IN THE boredom of hanging around my folks' gray house, sick of reading, sick of listening to records, sick of Mom wanting everything to be nice, that I decide I need a car.

You have a car, man, you can split. Get gone baby gone. A car is another kind of freedom, and I don't care what Kierkegaard has to say about it, we need freedom same as we need blood in our veins and air to breathe.

I go looking for freedom, and think I find it at Honest John's Used Cars.

Honest John's is a big dirt lot in San Rafael up Highway 101 about 15 minutes north of my folks' house partial in the shadow of the freeway overpass. Far below the rebar-embedded concrete supporting all the fast cars what you hear is a cavernous roar. The car lot's a garbage dump of slumbering junkers, row after row baking in the sun, and a dirty white trailer at the back where the garbage men wait for a sucker they can sell some garbage.

Case you're wondering about the makeup, you know, do I show up looking like a total freakazoid, well the answer is no. Buying a car is enough to deal with without purple nails.

Right quick this sales jerk at my side keeps pace so close his plaid wool shirt brushes against my pea coat and I get more of his Winston than he does, speed rap going about every car we pass.

"Name's Jeffrey Blumenfeld," he says, "but call me Jeff, brother."

Well to me he's Used Car Jeff. Has skanky Black Oak Arkansas hair and a gaunt meth freak pall. You know those losers Philip K. Dick writes about in "A Scanner Darkly"?

We walk past dented Volvos and rusted Chevys and when he isn't hyping the cars he's making small talk about the 49ers' chances to make the Super Bowl. I've written him off, a subhuman leech, when somehow we get on the subject of comic books and discover we both were once serious Daredevil fans.

"I still have issue one," he says. "The origin of the Daredevil story. It's in a plastic sleeve in a box at my parents'."

"I had that issue, April '64, but I gave it to some fair weather. Was that ever a mistake."

"Tell you what, brother," he says. "If we close a deal, issue number one is yours."

So then he tries to hype me on a red MGB Roadster.

"Runs like a charm, Mike. Know what I mean?"

And I hear the echo of the roar.

"It's *Michael,* man."

"Got it," he says, and he moves his palm slow along the hood same as it's some foxy chick's bare thigh.

"Little old lady had this babe in her garage, Mike. Fifteen years!"

"My name's *Michael,* not Mike."

Yeah well that's when I spy the blue Triumph TR4 convertible. Has a few problems. Rear bumper dented and at an odd angle. Paint has that look paint on Volvos gets after too many years. Canvas top ripped has duct tape in places. All the downside registers, but what I see is me and Elise cruising down to Liquor King to buy a fifth of Jose Cuervo or out to the Forever Infinite Pacific for a walk on the beach. And issue number one. Fuck yeah!

A sign on the windshield: Reduced! $500.

"Great car, brother," Used Car Jeff says. "Runs like a charm," and it seems to me the echo of the roar gets louder and he says something but I don't hear it, all I hear is the echo, and someone beating the inside of my head with a mallet.

"Little old lady have this one in her garage too?"

"One owner, Mike, uh, Michael. A doctor, his weekend car. It's a chick magnet."

"That part of the guarantee?"

His left hand is in his jeans pocket, the muffled jangle of coins.

"Our cars are all 'as is.'"

We take her out for a spin, Used Car Jeff driving of course, and it's same as he's my best freakster bro, how we're shootin' the shit.

The car backfires, sounds as if someone set off a cherry bomb in the trunk. He takes a left under the freeway, foot full down on the pedal.

"Feel the road, Mike," he says. "Listen to the power of that engine."

"It's *Michael,* man," I say. "How many times I gotta tell you?"

Forty-five in a 35 zone the car feels fairly solid, round the corner, guns it to 60 on the straightaway and onto the onramp and I feel the shake, and at 70 on 101 South heading toward the City every atom screaming, and I swear, for sure pieces gonna start to fall off.

"Love these cars, Mike," Used Car Jeff says. "Uh, Michael. Real man's car. Nothing pussy."

How the hell I'm supposed to know if the car is right on, or a loser? The engine's kinda loud but isn't that how it's supposed to be with a sports car? And the road, man, it's same as the slightest uneven section or pothole or bump is telegraphed right to my body. I don't know if it's good vibrations, but I feel 'em.

Used Car Jeff shouts above the noise.

"Dig it, brother. They don't make cars like this anymore. Hey, you smoke weed?"

Has a doobie in his hand passes it over. I know this reefer gonna be skank, no way does the sales jerk have the primo deal. Already it's in my hand so I'm gonna try it. I gotta hold The Dylan down below my knees to get it lit and lean forward careful to keep it out of the wind whip my hair back when I sit up straight, take a hit. Bam, this shit stronger than Jim's weed. Used Car Jeff is a sales jerk but he's the man. Can't deny a bro has his hands on this kinda stash.

"Enjoy, man," Used Car Jeff says.

Eventual we get into Larkspur, cruise past the Larkspur Theater has a cool-ass retro double bill of "Dr. No" and "From Russia With Love."

"Man I'd sell my mom down the river to screw Ursula Andress," Used Car Jeff says, holding the joint my way. "The knockers on that heifer don't quit."

He cuts up to Sir Francis Drake and a right toward the freeway, jerks his head at an angle, looks at me quick-like, and if his peep show dirty laugh is a smile, that's the smile he gives me.

"Hey Mike," he says. "Which actress would you screw if you had the chance?"

"Michael, man," I say.

"Right, Michael," he says. "But which chick?"

If I say nothing, maybe he'll get a clue, but his question hangs there between us, and it doesn't go away, and every moment goes by seems to me it gets more the awkward deal. I look down at the dash compartment door, talk through closed lips. I mean I don't wanna share my fantasy life with this jerk.

"Don't know, man."

I take the joint, take another hit, can't talk if I have a mouth of smoke.

"Come on, Mike," Used Car Jeff says, and I give up on trying to correct him. "Has to be a movie star you'd sell your soul to the Devil to fuck."

"Never thought about it," I say.

That's a lie, 'cause I mean I have a list of movie star chicks I've fantasized about starting with Jeanne Moreau and Jean Seberg and of course Anita Ekberg and Anna Karina and all those Hitchcock babes, and Anita Pallenberg and Michele Breton. I mean it goes on and on.

"You're into chicks, right?"

And there's a humungous big question mark in his voice

that questions my manhood, I mean in that moment it all rests on if I have an answer. And the weed forms a web of paranoia. He's paranoid, I'm paranoid.

"*Right?*" he says.

You know that teacher chick, Ms. Braveheart, the one I met up with in the hallway at the Halloween party, yeah she shows up in my cranium.

"Liv Ullmann, man."

"Is that a chick?" Used Car Jeff says.

"Yeah, she's a *chick*," I say. "Haven't you seen any of Bergman's films, 'Persona' or 'Shame'?"

"Foreign babe, huh?" he says. "Oh I get it. I know how your mind works. Those foreign babes game for anything, right? Like Sophia Loren. Let you tie 'em up, the works."

"Ursula Andress is Swiss," I say.

"You into some kinky sex, Mike?"

When eventually we're back on the lot he lays the big one on me.

"Gonna drive her home?"

"Give you $300."

Used Car Jeff's easy smile goes away, and a side of him he's kept under wraps shows up.

"I like you, Mike. I think I can talk the boss-man down to $475—if you buy her *today.*"

"$325."

Oh man, he looks same as he discovered his stash missing. There's a hardness to his face, his anemic lips pressed tight. His dark brown pupils contract to small dots.

"Let me explain the economics of the used car business to you, Mike," he says, and the echo of the roar so fucking loud. "We paid good money for that car," and the echo of the roar and the words from his mouth are one sound and the sound drones on.

I want the car so fucking bad, and Used Car Jeff knows it, he feels it, sees it.

"How about $375? Ask your boss."

His left hand into his jeans pocket, fiddling with those coins.

"You're really fucking with me, Mike," he says. "Taking food outta the mouths of my kids."

Damn I want the TR4 and he knows it's only a matter of time before my desperation takes over. I look at the car, see me at the wheel, Elise right close. Her hair blowing in the wind. Passing me the booze bottle.

"OK, $475," I say. "Hundred bucks deposit. I'll be back before New Year's with the rest. Deal?"

"You just bought yourself a righteous vehicle, Mike," and he goes back to the trailer, comes back with a "standard contract" for me to sign and a receipt for my $100.

I make sure it has the correct VIN number and says the total price and all that. Dotting the "i's," or whatever. Only in my excitement at buying a car—finally, my own car—I forget all about issue number one.

It's past nine when I call Elise at Sappho's house, and soon as Sappho picks up the phone I hear the party goin' on. Sappho's voice too loud and I can't help it, blood loud pounding and my mind going where it shouldn't. Half card pinned over Elise's tit, *I'm available, boys, come fuck me tonight.*

Force my voice into the bright sound of Mr. Optimist.

"Hey Kate, happy New Year. Merry Hanukkah."

"Too bad you're not here," she says. "A bunch of Ned's friends and my high school girlfriends. Elise brought all the Motown," and oh man oh man oh man.

"How's your folks dealing with all that?"

"They're in Florida for the week," and oh fuck, I know Elise is in some bedroom and some monster all over her.

"Can I talk to Elise, Kate?"

"She's out."

"Where the fuck?"

"Temper temper. Ask me nice."

"Come on, Kate."

"They went to buy booze."

"They?"

"I'll give you three guesses, Writerman."

"Don't fuck with me."

"I don't appreciate your vulgarities. Gotta go."

And I'm talking to dial tone, and that's the second time I feel real anger at Sappho. And what I feel toward Elise, the anxious and the jealous and the desperate taking over.

Ruined, how I feel.

I stay home all day Sunday, lay on the living room couch read Dostoevsky's "The Idiot," which is me. First 'cause I let Sappho push my buttons, and second 'cause I hand over 100 bucks on a car about which I know nothing.

Well there's three things I need to make happen to get the car. Need Mom to give me a lift to Honest John's, and I need Dad to give me $375 and add the car to his insurance policy. Gonna need Mom's help to get Dad on board. Before dinner, with Dad out in the garage, me and Mom in the kitchen, I tell her about the car. She complains, says what we both already know, that Dad's gonna bust a nut, although she doesn't use those words.

When I'm a kid, the saddest days are Easter Sunday and Christmas, 'cause pretty much every other kid is out hunting for Easter eggs or opening presents under their tree. Their *Christmas* tree. Jews don't celebrate Christmas, my dad says. No tree, no stocking, nothing.

This year I feel even sadder 'cause for two years I *did* celebrate. I celebrated with Sarah's family. Their Christmas trees were the most beautiful trees I'd ever seen, with bird ornaments and deer ornaments and shiny silver and red and blue and yellow balls and a big glitter star on top.

The last Christmas Eve I spent with Sarah, the tree lights were on and all the house lights off and we—me and Sarah and her brother Seymour and her sister Esmé and her dad—were all in the living room and her mom played carols on the upright and we sang those sappy songs. "Oh Little Town of Bethlehem," "Santa Claus Is Coming to Town," "Silent Night," and "White Christmas." Even sapped out as those songs are, it was the *best*.

Christmas day is surreal at my house. We pretend it's no different than any other day. Everyone on the planet is up before daybreak. We get up at a leisurely nine, and the usual breakfast deal. Dad's in the yard same as every weekend, Mom's cleaning the house, and I'm on the couch reading "The Idiot."

Got *Blonde on Blonde* playin'.

After a while Mom goes outside to talk to Dad, and soon enough I hear his blabber and smoke. Through the window I see Dad do that horror show deal with his tongue, and then it's the two of them arguing on the cement patio other side of the walkway that leads to the front door. There's a brick planter Dad built runs along the far side of the walkway and separates it from the patio. Mom grows begonias there but it's winter, and the flowers are dead.

On the hi-fi Dylan sings his cynic's blues, "Leopard-Skin Pill-Box Hat," where he goes to his chick's house and she's in the garage fucking her new boyfriend, and I tune Dad out. A normal freakster bro comes upon his chick two-timing, no telling the violence gonna happen. Not Dylan. What bugs him is that hat the chick has on.

There's something deep Dylan's saying, more than the obvious, that he's through with the chick. More than his mutant version of the blues, you know, complaining about a chick done him wrong. Dylan has the twist of he doesn't *care* what the chick does if only she would take off her absurd ridiculous hat. A pill-box hat was what Jackie Kennedy wore after the President was shot.

But a leopard-skin pill-box hat, well I could see Edie Sedgwick, who Dylan dated for a minute, wearing one. I could see the chick in "Like a Rolling Stone" wearing one when she's at the finest schools or when she rides on the chrome horse with her diplomat.

Yeah, that hat, that absurd ridiculous hat. It's the object that tells us the whole deal is meaningless. Not where it's at, not at all, man.

After a while Mom comes in, and she's in such a good mood I figure she must have got Dad on board.

"Merry Christmas," she says.

"Thanks Mom."

She cooks some burgers for lunch, and Sappho's voice preaches the consequence of eating one, and how a cow had to die and the cow's blood on my hands. I eat the burger anyway 'cause Mom helping me and in a good mood, I can't hurt her feelings. Sometimes it's not worth it to stand up for what you believe in. Sometimes you gotta take other things into consideration. I don't really believe that, but there in the kitchen I rationalized my way into that scene.

Dad arrives, takes a seat and starts in. "They're shysters, Mike."

"Dad, you don't know."

"It's a used car place, they're crooks."

"I need $375," I say. "And the insurance."

"I won't stop you from buying it, but I'm not giving you one damn penny."

"I gave 'em a deposit, Dad."

"That was a cockamamie thing to do. You're an idiot."

For once I think maybe he's right.

Always a plan, and this time the plan is get the dough from my grandfather. I do something I don't expect. Before I go see him at Mel's Shoes, his store in San Rafael, not too far from Honest John's, I tie my hair back in a ponytail and stuff it into the fedora, skip the lipstick, and get the purple polish off with Mom's stinky polish remover.

Grandfather leaves a salesman in charge and we're off to A & W Root Beer, a couple blocks south of Mel's Shoes. We walk slow, which is how he walks 'cause of how rotund he is, walks slow and his breathing fast and heavy as if he doesn't get enough air. Still, has his head held high as usual, the breeze messing with the hair around the edge of the voluminous bald acreage that dominates the topside of his oversize head.

"I once had a black fedora," he says. "Long time ago. When I was a young man."

The A & W has this huge-ass sign with a big mug of root beer lit up against the pale blue sky. Grandfather buys us each a root beer float. I love those frosted clear glass mugs they serve 'em in. We sit at one of the tables out front.

"So how's the college boy," he says. "They teaching you how to write?"

I love my grandfather so much, man. No one asks about writing except him. Not even Mom.

Wish I didn't have to muddy shit up asking for dough.

He sits there so roly-poly, his bald head and puffed-out face and he gives me one of his whatever-you-do-is-fine-by-me smiles, which isn't the authentic real truth, but in the moment of that moment is some of how he feels. He digs into his root beer float and his smile transforms into an isn't-this-the-best smile.

A lot of the time my grandfather lives Be Here Now not even being conscious about it. He's the one that put the lie to all my hate-my-family shit. I can't hate my family 'cause he is family. Sure glad I don't have the makeup on. Sometimes looking freaky isn't worth it. I don't know if I believe that either, you know, long term, but this particular day I do.

"Since you ask, Grandfather, I need your help on a school-related matter."

My grandfather is real careful not to spill any of his float on his clothes. He takes pride in how he dresses. Before any item of his clothes starts to look worn he replaces it. And his shiny black brogues are *perfect*. Never seen him in shoes that don't gleam same as a Jaguar hood ornament.

So I tell him how I need the dough for a car and why me owning a car is so important, and this and that, and that and this, and some more this and a hell of a lot more of that.

"I was thinking Grandfather," I say. "Maybe it can be a combo extra Hanukah and early birthday present," which is a stretch since I already got a hundred bucks Hanukkah check from him, I mean where you think I got the down payment, and my birthday's not 'til July.

A normal grandfather would see me as a mooch, chip off the ol' mooch block, only interested in him for his dough, which isn't the authentic real at all. It's complicated. It's *always* complicated when a person has bucks. Even if you dig 'em the most, there's an attraction that bucks have, and if a person says they dig a rich human only 'cause they like 'em, and don't fess up to digging the rich aspect too, they're a liar. No way to ignore the dough. The greed factor, we all have it.

"It's a lot of money, Mike."

I have half my float left and I'm gonna be sick if I take another bite of the vanilla ice cream. My grandfather is already done with his.

"You confident it's a decent vehicle?" he says. "Used car dealers have a notoriously bad reputation."

"Dad's gonna check it out," I say, and that's a lie 'cause Dad hasn't agreed to check anything out, hasn't even agreed to add the car to his policy.

I have the serious deal on my face, a special look I use when my grandfather has something serious to talk to me about, the look that says everything he says is humungous important and it's same as I'm taking notes, but since I'm not, that look tells him I'm memorizing every word comes out of his mouth.

I'm worried that if I tell him I can't eat anymore of the float it'll bug him, you know, 'cause Nana is always talking about how kids are starving in China whenever I don't want to clean my plate.

He goes on and on for a time, talks about cars, his first car, first car he bought for my mom, how if you don't maintain a car it can really go to hell, and so on.

"A car is a *big* responsibility, Mike."

"Sure is, Grandfather."

And then I tell him how total full I am, the float was great and all, but I'm *done*. Right then his face is the quizzical, but it passes fast as it appeared, and the truth of it, he doesn't care if I finish or not.

"I'll give you the money, Mike. I'm trusting that your dad

will make sure it's a good one."

You know how sometimes a thing works out exactly the way you want it? I ask Dad about adding the car to his policy, and he tells me the only way he'll do it is first he goes with me to Honest John's and checks out the car *before* I buy it. Don't even gotta ask.

What he's got an attitude about is how I'm gonna look when we go to Honest John's. He saw me the day I met with Grandfather, no makeup, hair in the fedora, and if I clean up for Grandfather, I better clean up for him. I don't even mind so much. I'm sick of the makeup.

"I don't know what's with you and your grandfather," Dad says.

He doesn't dig Grandfather and I know why. Both Nana and Grandfather always looked down on Dad. Started back in Brooklyn when Dad's the leader of the Boy Scout troop Mom's brother was in. Dad comes from a lower class deal. His family, well it's his mom and a step-dad for a while, plus his younger brothers, lived in a cramped apartment in Brooklyn. My mom lived in Brooklyn too, but Grandfather was the successful businessman and they had a big house that from the pictures at least was really something. So right from the start Dad is James Gatz to Mom's Daisy Fay. Only Dad never transformed himself into Jay Gatsby. To this day he's still James Gatz.

Man, nothing Dad ever could do was enough for Nana and my grandfather. It took me a long time to see from Dad's way of looking. Dad and my grandfather, two real different people. My grandfather always reading and learning about culture, and such a generous spirit, and Nana and him took Mom to the art museums and the theater, and Dad never got into any of it, and always worried about money.

Right to this day.

"I guess you ended up with the same blood as the old man," Dad says. "Could turn out to be a curse. Going to be a quite a day when you go bald, Mike."

Oh man does he think that's funny, but for once I keep my

mouth shut.

We're on 101 heading north in the sick green Rambler and I take a hard look at my dad. He's wearing his prescription sunglasses. They're same as his regular glasses, black plastic frames, only difference the dark dark green lenses. His short hair greased back and he shaved. His profile is an echo of the younger man in the black and white photos my mom has in the old albums. Handsome Jewish face Mom fell in love with so long ago. Sometimes I wonder if she doesn't regret not marrying a man with more dough, which is funny for me to wonder about, but still I do. They say money doesn't buy happiness and it sure doesn't buy true love, but if true love fades, a truckload of dough isn't gonna make things any worse.

"Hey, Dad."

I want him to say *yeah?* or something to indicate he's open to a conversation.

"I know Mom got you to do this, but thanks."

He almost gets a smile going, only Dad doesn't ever smile, at least I don't remember one. Something else. I don't wanna think it, but when I cut my hair, the John and Yoko trip, before I fucked everything up with Sarah, I looked a whole lot same as Dad. I mean I'm young, none of the torn-and-frayed life done to him, but still.

His fist comes down hard on the top of the dash.

"I'm not gonna let those sharks screw a Stein," he says, and the thing I forget on occasion is what a stubborn son of a bitch he is.

"That nail polish. Why would you do such a thing?"

Fuck 'cause there's still a little purple on my right pinkie.

"You're never gonna grok it, Dad."

He rolls down his window to let air in the way someone gotta split the claustrophobic of a packed elevator, and I work on my pinkie with my thumbnail.

"You're going to a good school, Mike, and it's costing your grandfather a lot of money."

His hands on the steering wheel do the white knuckle trip.

"How are you going to make money as a writer? I've worked for the City 22 years. Some jobs are secure. Doctor, lawyer, architect. Engineer. Those are solid. The odds in roulette, 37 to one you'll lose. Writer? Putting your life on 13 and crossing your fingers."

Crave a cigarette, but no way. Dad would bust a nut. "Maybe I want to live that way," I say. "There are things a person gotta do and damn the odds. Take a risk."

He takes the off-ramp too fast and he's jamming the brakes.

"No you don't," he says. "You really don't."

That's when I see it, his tongue doubling over, only he's fighting it, fighting it hard, and instead of biting down, instead of the usual horror show, he forces the tip of it out between his lips.

"If you want to *live* you do," I say.

Dad parks close to the road, as if he thinks his car can get contaminated from the junkers. I take the lead, walk too fast over to the TR4. Bright bright sun burns up the patched black canvas roof and the parched hard dirt. Seems to me the TR4's more faded today and the echo of the roar is louder, as if I'm standing over Niagara Falls.

"Sure know how to pick 'em, Mike," and he sees every dent, every patched up rip in the canvas, every scratch in the disintegration-blue paint job.

"You sure it has an engine?"

Used Car Jeff gives a yell from the back of the lot.

"Hey! Mike! Right with you, brother."

"*Brother?*" Dad says.

Used Car Jeff vamooses into the trailer and Dad gets to work. There's an odd metallic pop as he raises the hood. I know nothing about cars but it's dirty under there. While he checks the scene I pace back and forth, circle the car, die for a smoke.

"The guy said they did a major tune-up, Dad. Spark plugs, the works."

"You believed him?"

Bent over the engine, his back to me, the hard edge where

his crew cut ends.

"All of the hoses shot. It runs?"

"Yeah, it runs," I say.

Spits at the parched dirt.

"How's the engine sound?"

"Like a fuckin' engine."

"Don't swear at me, Mike. We can go home right now."

"Sorry, Dad."

He takes another slow walk around the TR4, "Tires are shot, too," and the echo of the roar overpowering loud, so loud I'm *in* Niagara Falls.

"The exhaust pipe, where it connects to the muffler, rusted right through," he says. "You know what that means?"

"Needs a new exhaust pipe. No biggie."

"You could get asphyxiated," he says.

This moment is when the sun extinguishes and the planet goes dark and we all freeze to death.

"I'll get the sales guy," I say.

Dad walks over and I don't know what he's gonna do.

"Mike, when that snake slithers out from under whatever rock he calls home *I* do the talking."

When I return Dad's under the TR4, and all I see is stained pant legs and dirty brown work boots.

"Dad," I say. "Sales guy's here."

Dad keeps doing whatever he does under there.

"Got a cigarette, Mike?" Used Car Jeff says.

I guess he's trying to upscale his image. Still has that scurvy gray face, but he's cut his hair so it's more *Meet the Beatles*. Has on a short sleeve white collar shirt and a royal blue tie, although the top button of the shirt is undone and the tie's not cinched tight, and no tie clip.

Dad stays under long enough it bugs Used Car Jeff. He paces in front of the car smoking my Pall Mall, his free hand in his pocket jingling coins, and it bugs me, the sound of those nickels and quarters and dimes. Eventual Dad eases himself out from under the car, and gets up. He shakes the dirt off his back and his pants. Gets his first look at Used Car Jeff, and he digs how Used Car Jeff looks less than he digs how I look the day he first sees me with the makeup.

"This the *salesman*?"

That's when the echo of the roar fades to nothing, and the whole rest of the time we're at the lot I don't hear it.

"You have the authority to negotiate price?" Dad says. "Or do I talk to your *boss*?"

"Yes, *sir*, I can handle the transaction," Used Car Jeff says. "No need for you to speak to the boss-man. Your son owes another $375, cash or check, and the car is his."

"This car is shot," Dad says.

"For the price it's a steal, sir," Used Car Jeff says. "Any used car, there's a little work to be done."

He steps toward Dad, a grin making itself up outta his lips, and extends a hand.

"Name's Jeff, sir."

Dad lets Used Car Jeff's hand wither by its lonesome.

"Look, buddy," Dad says. "We'll pay you $100 and take it as-is, or you can give it a full tune-up, new tires, replace the exhaust system and I'll write you up a list of what else you need to fix."

Used Car Jeff's brown eyes blink fast, he's sweating, his shirt damp under the arm pits.

"Mike, we've got a deal. I have the paperwork in the office."

Dad steps closer to Used Car Jeff so they're maybe a yard apart, burning up in the bright bright sun.

"Why don't you get your boss, or do *I* need to beat him out of the brush?"

Used Car Jeff retreats, puts another couple feet between himself and Dad.

"You checked out the car, right Jeff?" Dad says. "Before you put it up for sale."

"Runs like a charm, sir."

"Well, Jeff, I'm employed by the City of San Francisco so I know plenty about these things," Dad says. "California has some very high fines that are imposed on used car dealers who sell cars with faulty exhaust systems."

Dad looks at the dirty-white trailer, wipes his hands on his pants, spits a fat loogie in the parched dirt.

"The entire Honest John's Used Cars operation could be shut down for a minimum of two years, Jeff."

I told you Used Car Jeff's face isn't healthy, but right now the gray skin has more than a hint of psych ward green. You know that time at Liquor King when I wished me and Liquor Store could be friends? Well I don't wanna be Used Car Jeff's friend, but I feel for him. I know what it is to face off against my dad.

"Be right back," and he heads for the trailer only he drags his boots in the dirt, a trail of dirt dust floating behind him.

That thing where Dad says he works for the City, well that's true, but his job has nothing to do with any California state regulations, or cars. Usually Dad stretching the truth would piss me off, but not at all today.

"Ten bucks says he'll be in there 20 minutes easy," Dad says.

We stand in the heat, me and Dad both sweating, his forehead shiny and his upper lip too. We have our hands on our hips looking at that trailer same as two cops on a stake out. Time passes, time gone, time lost forever, and eventual Used Car Jeff comes down the stairs.

"This better be good," Dad says.

What happens next is a lesson in delusion, my delusion. I assume 'cause Used Car Jeff looks same as a meth freak that he doesn't have his shit together. No man, Used Car Jeff is a Zen Master whose chosen form of meditation is the closing of deals.

"What have you been doing in there?" Dad says.

"No need for you to get all hot under the collar, Mr., uh, Mr.?"

"Stein," Dad says. "Leonard Stein.

"Good name," Used Car Jeff says. "Jewish name, right?"

"What's it to you?" Dad says.

You know how Dad wanted to join the army and fight in World War II? Nothing he hates more than an anti-Semitic son of a bitch. If his face is a thermometer, well it shoots up well past a hundred.

"Didn't Mike tell you? I'm a member of the tribe too, Mr. Stein. My names Jeffrey David Blumenfeld. My Jewish name's Yariv. Had my Bar Mitzvah right over at Congregation Rodef Sholom, you know, on San Pedro Road."

Dad isn't smiling, but the thermometer drops back to maybe 65, give or take, I mean this is all metaphorical anyway, so just know it cooled him out.

"You're kidding me," Dad says. "Mike was Bar Mitzvahed there."

Fuck, and he gives Used Car Jeff a damn good facsimile of a smile, and tells Used Car Jeff *his* Jewish name is Eliezer. Dad reaches out a hand and those two hands, self-righteous asshole hand and snaked-out liar hand, come together.

"So Yariv," Dad says. "What can we do here to make this right?"

I can't believe it, Used Car Jeff and my asshole dad bonding?

"How 'bout we split the difference, Mr. Stein, uh, Eliezer."

Dad does the math in his head and Used Car Jeff keeps on talking.

"You want to buy the car for $200, your son and I agreed on $475. How about you kick in another $135 and we call it a deal."

High up in the air I see two birds flying off, far enough away I can't be certain of the color, but it gotta be Doom and Gloom, and while I wanna believe I've triumphed and they're leaving with their tail feathers between their stick-figure legs, that's not it at all. I mean their job is done, no need to hang around any longer.

"Deal," Dad says. "You got yourself a deal, Yariv."

Fuck, 'cause that's when I remember Daredevil issue number one, only with Dad right there, no way for me to bring it up.

3. THE FLOWERS LIED

I CALL SAUSALITO COWBOY a few days after Christmas and arrange to drop by The Pad. Haven't been there since school started, and I wanna show him my Beefheart review. What I really want is him telling me I'm a good writer.

Or better yet, a *great* writer.

Reflected glory, man.

I've got other reasons to head for The Pad. I want the high of coolness I get being friends with rock critics.

And I wanna see if they have any groovy records to unload. Lot of times the labels send Sausalito Cowboy and Buckaroo a bunch of promo copies of the same album. Selling the promos helps cover the rent. How Sausalito Cowboy explains it, freelance rock critics can't make shit writing. If a critic isn't gonna work the counter in a record store, or doesn't luck out with a teaching job somewhere, he needs the perks the labels provide. All those extra albums, the cash from selling 'em, it adds up. And there's all expense paid vacations, better known as press junkets, to interview some shit-ass new group, the free food and booze at meet-our-new-artist dinners and cocktail parties, and the unlimited bar tab at showcase clubs.

Even clothes, man. I seen Doobie Brothers t-shirts and a Poco sweatshirt and even a Grand Funk Railroad jean jacket. Of course all the freebies aren't free. Always a price. The labels expect the critics, and there's not that many—maybe three, four dozen across the country who count—to oblige with some good ink now and then.

Not that the reviews sell a truckload of albums. It's the

credibility a rave gives an album. The pithy sentence a label can quote in ads run in the rock mags and underground papers, and on the radio. Whole lot easier to get a WNEW music director to listen to Little Feat if Christgau gives them an "A" in the *Voice*.

Good a time as any to fill you in on something that blew my mind. Dad, man, he may be an asshole, but he came through. Spent Wednesday morning taking the car to a garage to replace the exhaust and tires, and the afternoon getting parts and giving it a tune-up. Musta felt bad calling me a fag, or maybe he finally got it through his head how important it is to Mom we get along.
    Sometimes I don't have a clue about my dad.

I get the patched up top down, fuck, *my own car*, and I wanna smoke a number, but I don't 'cause I'm not so sure I have the shift deal nailed down tight, and the last thing I need is to be stoned and fuck up the gears. Give the car gas, floor the clutch, turn the key, engine starts right up.
    Freedom, man!
    And in my head I'm hearing that old Stones song, "I'm Free" off *Out of Our Heads*, back when the Stones were still doing their mid-Sixties mod trip and Brian Jones was alive and in the band.
    "I'm Free," the one about being free to do anything, any ol' time.
    Got the car in first, release the clutch and I'm off, total adrenaline rush, cool air against my face, and this is the life, onto 101 South, cruising in fifth, what a blast. Got Elise, got a car, got some friends and I'm on my way to see the Sausalito Cowboy and Buckaroo.

Can't wait to take Elise for a ride. Goddamn goddamn. Another couple weeks 'til school's back in session. Yeah, well, gonna call her when I get home from hanging with Sausalito Cowboy.
    I stop to pick up the obligatory extra large pepperoni, which makes me kinda sick 'cause of my vegetarian trip, and soon

enough, Number Nine Strawberry Lane. Walk towards The Pad, hear this groovy British power pop blasting, sorta same as The Beatles only it's not them.

Buzzer still has the tape under it, *out of order,* and seeing that fucked up screen door and the veneer peeling worse, and I'm falling down an elevator shaft, the high of driving the TR4 gone baby gone, an elevator shaft of downerosity.

Oh fuck.

Somehow in the moment of that moment so much depends on if they had the buzzer fixed. If Sausalito Cowboy's buzzer can live again, erosion of fucking everything can stop. I reach out, finger there before it, close my eyes, imagine the buzzer works and how beautiful the world can be again.

If the buzzer works it means everything that's wrong in this world can be fixed. It means Nixon can be impeached and replaced by the new Kennedy, whoever that might be, and the pollution of rivers and streams and the ocean can stop.

If only the buzzer works.

If only.

Press my fingertip against the grimy beige button and time slows, I enter the moment and the moment stretches, oh please let the buzzer work, and I swear, if only the buzzer works I'll believe there is a God.

Well despite the volume of whatever record is playing, I can tell it doesn't work.

Oh fuck, gotta shake the disappointment away, and I knock, and knock again and again, knock hard louder and why can't they fix it? Why does everything gotta be so wrong?

The atrophy of every goddamn goddamn thing.

Music so loud I know Sausalito Cowboy doesn't hear me.

Door's not locked, push it open, lean in, and across the room sitting at the magic table, front of the Hemingway Royal Quiet Deluxe, Sausalito Cowboy sings fuck-ass loud trying to imitate the singer who has a Little Richard-by-way-of-Beatle-Paul scream. And all my bummerosity gone as I witness Sausalito Cowboy, free as free can be, wailing along to that glorious jangle.

Don't cha lie to me.

It's not only a demand to a chick, demand to the whole fuck-up planet. Gimme some truth. Sausalito Cowboy rocks his body forward back, types away on the Hemingway Royal to the beat of that rock beat. I watch him and dig on how gone baby gone he is, total lost in the sound, and I let a beat go by, and another, and loud as I can I shout, "Hey man!"

Sausalito Cowboy turns, but it's probably the pizza smell more than my words lost in fuzz guitars. He says something, turns back keeps typing so I drop the pizza box on the coffee table and right quick Barkadelic climbs on top. I collapse into the green corduroy couch. The big smoked-glass ashtray on the wooden spool table is empty and that's a first, and maybe everything doesn't have to deconstruct.

The song ends and before the next one starts I try to start a conversation.

"Who's this?"

"Big Star. It's the smart shit. Memphis power pop extraordinaire. Give me five maybe 10 minutes, I'm on deadline," and he's back typing.

This spacey song about going to India plays and I flash on that Ravi Shankar album I bought in '67 after I read about George learning the sitar. I dig The Beatles' whole India trip, but then I remember that old Maharishi guy who suckered them and tried to screw the young chicks who came to his ashram to get enlightened, and that wakes me the fuck up. Even The Beatles got conned. The Beatles, man.

Bummer them breaking up.

End of the world, no more Beatles.

Walk over to the Thorens' throne, front of the wall of records. This day the plastic turntable cover is hinged back and I look down at the spinning vinyl. Flash a look to Sausalito Cowboy deep in his writing, and super careful pick up the album cover. The album is called *#1 Record,* and the cover's a photo of this luminous blue-white neon star with the word "Big" in yellow neon inside the star. The audacity, call your group Big Star, and your album *#1 Record.* Guts, man.

We want the world and we want it now.

This is when Buckaroo makes the scene, and there's frustration in his Southern voice.

"He's lu-ost his ma-nd," and walks past Sausalito Cowboy, gets to the Thorens, reaches under the throne where the amp sits on a shelf, halves the volume. "How kin I write about Marty Robbins with this shit play-un, *Cow*-boy?"

Next Buckaroo's at the front door, sticks his head out looking for something he doesn't see. Closes the door sits himself in a chair facing the wooden spool table and his stoned eyes zoom in on the pizza box. Johnny Cash on his yellow t-shirt and under Cash's hard face, "I walked the line."

"Hey, Buckaroo," Sausalito Cowboy says. "I need a closing graph," and he stands, stretches his arms so his finger tips close in on the ceiling and his Asleep at the Wheel t-shirt lifts, huge-ass bulbous belly covered with a thick matt of brown hair, tries to bend over touch his toes but that's a joke, gotta be a foot between his fingers and his boots.

"How 'bout this," Buckaroo says. "With Paul and John's solo efforts lacking the *esprit de corps* of their famous collaboration, you could do a heck of a lot worse than the debut from this faux Fab Four."

"Not bad," Sausalito Cowboy says. "I owe you a beer."

"Now can you turn that shit off?" Buckaroo says.

Sausalito Cowboy ignores him, walks into the kitchen. Buckaroo doesn't mess with the Thorens but dials the volume to zero. Figure he's gonna go back to Marty Robbins but nope, picks up an album that's leaning against the Thorens' throne. It's the first Roxy Music album, has this chick spread same as a centerfold on the cover.

"Can't get over this little darling," Buckaroo says. "You seen this cover, Writerman?"

"Which Brian do you think is fucking her?" Sausalito Cowboy says, coming back with paper plates and paper towels. "Ferry or Eno?"

This is the moment they see the purple polish, the lipstick too, and the henna hair—course they see the hair.

"What happened to you, Writerman," Sausalito Cowboy says. "Get an overdose of Bowie?"

"Right on, man," I say.

They think it's hilarious, my new look.

"These kids nowadays, Buckaroo," Sausalito Cowboy says. "Never know what they're gonna do next," and a squint kinda deal. "You're still into chicks, right?"

"No, man," I say. "Anteaters and baby kangaroos."

After that they stop hassling me. "Check it out," I say. "My review of *Clear Spot*," and I hold out *The Paper*. I have it folded to the right page, big photo of Beefheart. I want Sausalito Cowboy to read it, but instead he drops it on the wooden spool table.

"Captain's in top form on 'Low Yo Yo Stuff,'" he says. "That's the smart shit."

"'Long Neck Bottles' is sublime," Buckaroo says. "Which come to think of it, we have beer?" and he scoops Barkadelic up off the pizza box and heads for the kitchen.

"That cat is big on pizza," Sausalito Cowboy says. "Beats Friskies."

"Come on, read it."

Shifts in his chair so he looks right at me, and his face the dead-serious trip, no lie. "I'm not."

"What the fuck, man," I say. "Thought you were gonna help me."

Gets a couple slices on a paper plate. "I *am* helping you, Writerman, that review's already published."

"So?"

"Waste of time. Your time, my time."

Buckaroo's back with three Buds, puts two on the table.

"Tossed her out," he says. "Time for her daily constitutional."

"Gotta let me give you pointers *before* they run," Sausalito Cowboy says. "Too late to rewrite it. If I tell you the lede sucks, then what?"

This time it's Sausalito Cowboy at the door, looking around.

"Wish he'd get here."

"Who you waiting for, man? Godot?"

"The *delivery*," Buckaroo says, and all was quiet in that living room.

Sausalito Cowboy's voice was reverential. "The *promos*."

I pick the pepperoni off my slice, make a pile at the side of my plate.

"Finish your novel yet?"

Sausalito Cowboy in the midst of chewing starts to cough, and the cough turns into a coughing jag.

"That would be a no," Buckaroo says, and he's antsy, yeah, listens for the sound of the UPS man—him and Sausalito Cowboy in need of a vinyl fix and grocery money.

"So what's it about, man?" I say. "You never told me."

"Think he can handle it, Buckaroo?"

"I don't know, Cowboy. Not sure if Ziggy can take it."

He laughs his slow molasses laugh, and Sausalito Cowboy laughs the laugh that combines the cynical and the sarcastic.

"Hey, man, I brought the pizza."

"Well you know it's called 'The Flowers Lied,'" Sausalito Cowboy says. "It's about the hypocrisy of the hippie dream. That game you and your friends still play."

Once again the room is quiet, as if we each hold our breath.

"It was a lie," Sausalito Cowboy says.

This isn't what I wanna hear. Not from Sausalito Cowboy, not from anybody.

"It was an economic impossibility," he says. "The so-called counter-culture. No way it could sustain itself. Financed by middle and upper class parents. Turn on, tune in, drop out my ass. A utopian pipe dream."

I don't believe him, I mean it's logical, what he says, but I don't care. I *won't* believe. Me and Sarah, we were the Freak Scene Dream. We were the innocence. And the scene down at The University, yeah we're living it. A version of it. Being artists and writers and photographers and poets, digging the symbolic in films and art and music, searching for love and opening our minds with wine and weed and acid. It's *not* a lie.

"Parents paying the rent on all those hippie pads," he says. "Sending their kids a check each month."

It goddamn goddamn *isn't.*

"It was a fraud," Sausalito Cowboy says. "Amazing it lasted long as it did."

They were still jonesing for the promos when I split the fuck outta there.

When I get home Mom tells me I had a call.

"Elise?" Mom says. "What an odd name."

Hellfuck bummer. "Did she say when I should call? How'd she sound?"

"Who is this Elise girl, Mike?" Mom says. "She didn't sound Jewish."

"She's my secret Baptist child bride, mom," I say. "We've got a whole brood of Baptist kids in the trailer where we live."

"What's wrong with you, Mike?" Mom says.

Got my windows closed but the neighbor mowing his lawn sounds loud as a mosquito plugged into one of Hendrix's Marshall amps.

"Bloody massacre, Michael," and to hear her voice again. "This is so messed up down here. L.A. Makes me crazy. Well how *are you*, Writerman?"

"Got myself a car, Elise," I say. "Cool-ass sports car. Convertible. We can drive out to the beach or something. Me and you."

The quiet shyness of her voice in my ear, and that's when I get how intimate a phone call can be. If she were with me she'd have her mouth on my ear for me to hear how she sounds on the phone.

The warmth of her breath, and her lips.

"I'd like that," she says. "Yeah, Michael. A lot."

Her mouth on my ear, and I want her with me, not in L.A. Want my lips on her lips again.

"It's been hard up here," I say.

"Your family?"

"Well sure," I say. "It's not that."

Goddamn goddamn loud mosquito buzz.

"Look," I say. "It's hard being away from you."

So goddamn loud the loudness, and I don't know if she says something. Don't know where her voice is, and her lips.

"Elise, you there?"

"I'm here."

I say what I don't mean to say.

"Look, when I called, Kate told me you were out buying booze."

"So?"

Mosquito bites on my neck, and so fucking loud.

"With some *guys*."

"It's none of your business, Michael."

"I gotta know, Elise," I say. "Is it me and you?"

"I don't know what it is," she says, and that fucking lawn mower mosquito noise fills the room, and my head, everything falling apart, and if she's trying to play it cool, well that's done.

"Oh bloody massacre, Michael. *Damn.* I miss you too."

Four hundred thirty odd miles.

"*So* bloody bad."

Between her lips and my ear.

"It's been a mess being down here at Kate's," and the mosquitoes, but louder still Elise's quiet shy voice, lips against my ear.

I miss you too. So bloody bad.

4. Hi Di Ho

THE NEXT DAY, MID-afternoon, I drive into Mill Valley to Village Music. Got more used records there than anyone ever seen in one place. Well, that's not true. I mean Odyssey has more records, but Village Music has more obscure hipster cool records. And what it doesn't have, John Goddard, he's the owner, knows how to find. Ry Cooder and Jerry Garcia and Michael Bloomfield and there's more including Sausalito Cowboy and Buckaroo call up John when they need to track down a rare disc. An old blues '78, soul classic or a country-western deal.

Village Music, man.

Aisle after aisle of record bins filled with the good stuff. Washington Phillips, Blind Lemon Jefferson and Charlie Patton. Billie Holiday, Bessie Smith and Hank Williams. Woody Guthrie, the Incredible String Band and the Holy Modal Rounders. Little Walter, the Mississippi Sheiks and Sister Rosetta Tharpe. And all the rest. John has a back room that's nothing but singles. Imagine. A whole fucking room.

One time, this is back in the high school days, he let me and Bobby come up to his house in the Mill Valley hills to see his record collection. Nearly all that's in the house is records. He's got rooms same as a library. Freestanding bookshelves only they're custom made to hold records, and mint copies of *everything*.

Yeah, well, that time we went up to his house, that was before he caught me stealing.

On this day I walk in and John's behind the counter, he's got long wild hair and a longer wild beard. Got on a Village Music t-shirt, drawing of Cab Calloway on it with the words "Hi Di Ho."

Hi Di fucking Ho, man.

Reverend Gary Davis on the record player sings "Death Don't Have No Mercy." It's a simple blues, a simple song that says it all.

Well, he'll come to your house but he won't stay long, Look in the bed and somebody will be gone.

"Quite a song," I say. "He's for sure giving us some truth."

John's a big guy, well, I have this impression of him as a big guy—I guess 'cause I looked up to him. No one knew as much about music as John, except maybe Lucky Larry.

He crosses his arms front of his chest, has a no-funny-business hardcore serious face, and I know what he's thinking. He's thinking, *that's that Michael Stein who tried to steal those albums from me four years ago.* Yeah, of course, what else would he be thinking. Well he could be thinking that I look more of a freak than he ever seen me look before, you know, lipstick nail polish henna black.

Try to ignore that look, and feel as if none of it gone down, but it did go down, and I can't shake the sleaze creeping through me. Feel same as a second-story man, total lowlife crook.

"I'm up here for Christmas break, John," I say.

Yeah he doesn't budge, day he die he's not gonna forgive me, and if my freak face bugs him, he doesn't let on.

"Is there a record you want to buy?"

I wrote John a letter right after he caught me, told him how sorry I was, said I'm not the kind of person stabs friends in the back, which obviously is a major lie, but anyway, said I'd never do any shit same as that again and please give me a second chance 'cause I'd hate it if I could never come in and buy records from him.

Got a postcard about a month after I sent that letter, on one side was that Cab Calloway drawing and "Hi Di Ho," and on the other he wrote, "One more chance."

Waited a good long time before I came into Village Music again, which sucks major 'cause it's the only record store in Marin worth a shit. Finally went in, first thing I did, told him again how sorry I was and how I hoped we could maybe pretend it didn't happen and start over.

"Well we can't," he said. "But if you want to buy a record, I'll sell you a record."

Some people, you betray their trust you might as well be dead. I mean the way they feel about you ever after. On this day John still has his arms crossed, same as there's jailhouse bars between us. I'm not sure why I come to his store, guess I have the need-a-record blues. Or maybe I hope he'll be how he was before, wish some goddamn goddamn thing here where I grown up would be same as it was when Sarah was my chick, but nothing's the same. Nothing, man.

"Anything new that's good?" I say.

"There's never anything new that's good."

He looks older somehow, maybe something about his hair or the beard, or maybe there was a tiredness about his face.

"There's this Wanda Jackson album that's been reissued," he says. "I've got it on display over there. *Rockin' With Wanda.* You know her? The Queen of Rockabilly?"

Never heard of Wanda Jackson. Turns out she had some hits in the '50s and dated Elvis. She had a U.S. hit in '56 with "I Gotta Know" and she topped the singles chart in Japan in '58 with "Fujiyama Mama."

This was what I dug about John Goddard and Lucky Larry. Every time they hipped me to something new.

"I'm gonna get this one," I say. "I'll leave it here while I look around some more."

"Take your time," he says, but I know he's watching.

I find a used copy of *The Best of Slim Harpo.*

The Stones covered "Shake Your Hips" on *Exile,* and I gotta hear the original. Slim Harpo is *dead,* dead back in 1970 of a heart attack. Dead at 46. Figure that one out.

It's soothing to flip through old blues albums, as if there's safety in the imagined past those records signify. I don't have to make up my own mind whether Slim Harpo is any good the way I do with a new band. It's understood Slim Harpo is fucking great. I mean the Rolling Stones recorded two of his songs, the other one being "I'm a King Bee," which they cut for their very first album. The Rolling Stones, man. Of course Slim Harpo is great. Same deal for Muddy Waters and John Lee Hooker and Lightnin' Hopkins. And of course the amazing Robert Johnson. Buy their albums and go home, put them on and if I don't dig 'em at first, play them over and over and over until I do.

I figure with one of those legends it's on me to get to where I dig it, get comfortable with a voice that doesn't sound same as any voice I hear before, let the groove work its way into me until it's my groove.

The sound of those records is different, an old sound, they come from a place I can't ever get to. Funny 'cause Slim Harpo recorded "Shake Your Hips" in '66 and I was alive in '66, '66 is only six years before that day I buy *The Best of Slim Harpo,* and yet when I get home and play the record it sounds kinda how Washington Phillips' "Denomination Blues" sounds, old and fucked up, you know, sound of the authentic real.

Those records and a lot of the records I dig, records by newer artists, the Stones and The Band and the Flying Burrito Brothers, none of them are the sound of the nowheresville house I grew up in. None of them are the sound of the suburbs creeping all over Marin County, taking over the old ranches and the hills once covered with weeds. Not the sound of my parents, or shit ice plant all over the hill behind our house, or the soulless plastic America crowding out everything cool. All of those records my escape hatch, man.

John uncrosses his arms, rings up those two, slips 'em into one of his white paper bags a little bigger than a record album that has his Cab Calloway "Hi Di Ho" logo on 'em.

"See ya," he says, and I don't know if he has a change of heart, but he gets a wise-old-man sound to his voice and right in the moment of that moment I don't feel same as a second-story man.

"Good luck with whatever you're studying," he says.

"Thanks, man," I say.

5. ME WITHOUT THE MASK

THE NIGHT BEFORE I'M gonna split back to The University it's around 8 p.m. Mom in the den watching some lame-ass sitcom on TV and Dad in the living room. He's got himself a glass of Jameson, his favorite Irish whiskey, sits on the couch, feels no pain, listening to the copy of *Sketches of Spain* I got at Odyssey, and I can't help but dig the scene. My Dad listening to one of *my* albums. It's hard to believe. Of course he's been into Miles since his college days. He's the one turned me on to Miles. That's also hard to believe but it's true.

I'm grooving on the cool orchestral sound too, and it makes me think the world is bigger than I'll ever know, and fills me with the optimistic.

"You ever gonna travel to Spain, Dad?"

He jerks out of his reverie, and I wonder where was he? Where does Dad go when he's got Miles on? Does he fantasize about some chick he dug in college, or a stock that's gonna jump the moon?

"Hearing *Sketches* makes me want to see Spain," I say.

"Miles," Dad says, has his feet up on the coffee table which Mom would have a conniption if she saw. "Remember when we took you to see Miles?"

Safe ground, the time us three saw Miles in Berkeley, at the Harmon Gymnasium.

"Didn't everyone have to wait forever for him to come out onto the stage?"

"He's an artist," Dad says. "He can do what he wants."

"Yeah, Dad," I say. "I know. I know all about that."

He looks up and no putdown, and maybe this is the first time he gets it. Maybe a little bit.

"Right, Mike," he says. "I guess you do."

I awake to the sun filtered through the curtains and the sweet rush of optimism 'cause today I'll get outta Dodge. Leave my past behind, head into the unknown, and though I'm not actual headed to any literal unknown, might as well be. Today I drive down to The University, and by tonight I'll experience the unknown of where Elise is at. Gonna see Jim too. And Jaded. Even that bitch Sappho.

The house, my old bedroom, Mom and Dad—the all of it will recede into the past, a memory I'll blot out best I can. The University holds the possibility of a different kind of life, the New Trip, expanding my mind in ways I can't fathom and beyond all that, break on through to whoever Writerman really is and who he can be, if only I can shake the worry and fear. I throw back the covers, leap from the bed so excited to get going, load up my car, *my car*, and hit the road.

The urgency to get gone is unbearable. Hurry a shower. Stand in the kitchen front of the sink and spoon soggy corn flakes into my mouth. Mom washed my clothes, folded everything in a neat pile, as if having those clothes all clean and folded can somehow fix what's broken.

I get the car loaded, and go back in the house and into Dad's bathroom and lock the door. I do my lips, do my nails and go into my room. I turn up *Houses of the Holy*. Wait for my nails to dry, and I want the bone-crunching hard rock to drown out the noise of my worries and fears and guilt but it doesn't and no matter how loud it plays, I can't escape.

Lying there I wonder what the fuck I'm doing wearing the stupid make-up. Well I don't need to wonder 'cause I *know*.

This is all about my dad.

It's the physical manifestation of me trying so hard to be *everything* he's not. Only right then I understand the fallacy of that rebellion. 'Cause I don't wanna be the anti-Dad. As long as who I am is defined by who he is, I'm the negative space all around him. Well in the moment of that moment, that's when I know I'm done with the make-up, but I don't wanna take the time to get it off, or give him the satisfaction.

In the kitchen Mom's cutting carrots for a soup. Her hair got done yesterday, and a gray cotton dress that flares out from the waist hangs to mid-calf and over it a white apron. Says "Le Cuisinier." The Cook. Oh man.

"I'm sorry you have to go," and she looks up, sees the lipstick, sees the nail polish. She doesn't say anything about it, she doesn't have to. And for once she speaks the authentic real.

"I can't say it was a nice visit, but I wish you were staying."

And she can't help herself.

"I know it's just a phase."

Yeah, well, everything's a fucking phase.

My arms around her and we hug and it's one of those short mom/son hugs, and she kisses me on the left cheek. I'm glad the goodbyes are almost done.

"I'm not going through a phase, Mom."

"I wish you'd get serious," she says. "About a career, Mike."

"No that isn't it. You want a doctor-lawyer professional you can brag about."

She has some air squeezed out of her kinda look, and the veins of dried leaves cover her hands.

"No, Mike," she says. "I don't really care about that. I just want you to be happy."

Why do I have to start in? "You and Dad look backwards at the way things been only they're not that way anymore," and right then I'm so certain of myself. Never more clear on who I am. If I gotta be the anti-Dad, so be it.

Quietly I sing:

Everything passes, everything changes, just do what you think you should do.

"I don't understand?"

Of course not. That was a language she'd never understand.

"Don't worry about it," I say. "Nothing important, some *stupid* rock song."

"You'll call me when you get to school?" she says. "OK?"

"No, Mom," and she starts to say something, but she stops. There's no way she can make me understand.

"I'll call in a week or so," I say.

Maybe.

I find Dad out in the garage trying to fix his old radio.

"Why don't you get a new one?"

"You're never gonna save a dime," he says.

He's got the radio open and he's using his solder gun to fix a broken connection.

"Hey, Dad," I say. "Thanks for helping me with my car."

He lays the solder gun on the work bench, looks from the radio to me, and he doesn't know how to react. Maybe he'll say something about wanting to help me, something human.

He takes in the make-up and this war starts between the him who hates how I look, and the him who tries to accept me for who I am. He has his tongue under house arrest.

"Thank your mom," he says, and turns back to his fuck-up radio.

Before I drive to The University I stop at the shopping center that's about a mile away. In the car I use a handkerchief to wipe the lipstick off my lips, and in the drug store I buy some stinky polish remover. In the men's room back of the Safeway next door I get the polish off and throw my bottle of polish and the lipstick and the polish remover into the garbage.

You know what else I drop in the trash? Rest of my Pall Malls. In the euphoria of shedding the glam trip I think I can quit smoking. It doesn't end up working, but I don't know it won't, and in the moment of that moment I'm ready for a new beginning.

Wash my hands real good, look in the mirror and see Writerman. My hair still partial black but maybe two inches of brown roots. My hair never been so freaky frizzed and long. It's me, and I like the me I see.

Me without the mask.

THREE

1. LE GENOU D'ELISE

FOR A MONTH, MAYBE longer, the beautiful sadness lifted off Elise, blew off her same as fog. And because the beautiful sadness was so much heavier and deeper than fog, when it blew away Elise was transformed.

In the movies, when a guy and a chick fall in love, the director can use montage to show the passing of time as the romance blossoms or blooms or whatever metaphor you wanna use for how the first month of love transpires. The lovers walk along the beach with their beatific smiles, hold tight to each other scared out of their wits on the roller coaster, and kiss a kiss same as no other.

Well that's how the rest of January and most of February was with me and her. We were so deep in our trip it felt as if her dorm room was our entire world. Sure we saw Jim and Jaded and Sappho most days, and usually showed for our classes, but when I think back to those months, all I see is me and her. She never said the word. Love. She said she didn't believe in love, but I knew.

Still there was a problem. She wouldn't let me touch her beyond the occasional kiss or hug, and sometimes my hand on her thigh. It was a remake of "The Sun Also Rises," only instead of Jake being impotent 'cause of his war injury, it's Brett unable, or never in the mood.

One day in late January we agree to collaborate on a silent film as our final project for the French New Wave class we're taking. We're in her dorm room, side-by-side on the rug, backs against the side of her bed, bottle of Almaden within reach. We decide our film gonna spoof one of the French New Wave classics.

I suggest *Jules et Jim*, thinking Elise can direct, I'll be the Jim character, Jim will be Jules, and Jaded as Catherine. Yeah well Elise doesn't go for that at all. She doesn't say why, but I don't think she likes a love triangle with me and Jim and Jaded.

"I'll only do it if *I'm* Catherine," she says.

"No way, Elise," I say. "I'm not sharing you with Jim, not even in a film."

Well next she wants to know what I think about *À Bout de souffle*, you remember, Godard's "Breathless."

"Well yeah," I say. "*I* could be Michel, and you could be that chick he digs, Patricia, the one Jean Seberg plays. You already got her laugh down."

"Don't say that," she says. "It's *my* laugh."

"Elise, you'd be *perfect*," I say. "All you have to do is cut your hair and you'll look same as Patricia."

"Cut my hair!"

Of course later she did cut it, later she started dressing same as that Patricia chick. Yeah we'll get to that when it happens. But what did start up soon enough was her quoting from *À Bout de souffle*. And it wasn't only Elise. This professor, Andrew Fine, had screened that film for our French New Wave class, and we got him to show it three more times. Oh we dug the hell out of it—me and Elise and Jim and Jaded and Sappho—bought copies of the script and read it aloud. There were nights when we all got blitzed in Elise's room, Jim would quote Michel, and Elise would quote Patricia, and I might quote Michel too. That film was loaded with classic lines. Still, maybe because we dug that film so much, me and Elise decided not to base ours on it.

Trying to decide on a film is hard, and what makes it worse is Elise right next to me wearing a tight black retro sweater and a short paisley skirt that's her one nod to the recent past. Her curvy legs, the legs of the mythic Psyche, stretched out before me.

We'd been drinking, and those legs, and her shoulder right against me, I thought this would be my lucky day, so real casual-like I put my hand on her thigh. At first she total doesn't go for it, *you don't have permission, Michael,* says it's the wrong time, and she isn't in the mood, and that gets us talking about it, me complaining that no time is the right time 'cause she's never in the mood. I don't know what's going on with her 'cause soon as I said what I said, she apologizes and tells me if I still want my hand on her thigh, she'd like that.

"Just keep it right there, Michael," she says. "OK?"

I keep it where it's supposed to be, don't make any Casanova moves, but after we sit awhile drinking more wine and discussing New Wave films, something gets into me, a wild buzz, and I start singing "Riders on the Storm," you know, The Doors' song, sing this one line, *girl you gotta love your man,* over and over.

First time I sing it, she gives me a look, second time she tells me *Michael, stop it,* third time she's so pissed she starts to get up, and in doing so brings her thighs and knees up close to her chest for leverage, and I move my hand off her thigh, but 'cause her knees and upper legs aim at the ceiling, as I pull my hand away the skirt comes with it, and I see all of her pale pink thighs and beige panties.

She gets herself up fast, hurries to her desk, frantic smoothing her skirt. Oh man, that monster boyfriend might as well been in the room with us, how freaked she was.

"I didn't mean to do that," I say.

"I don't *care,*" she says. Her hands shaky, she pours herself another glass of the red stuff and drains it. "I mean I care, I mean I, oh, I don't *know.*"

"Elise, it was an accident."

She stands there awhile, calms herself, gets a Kool going.

"It's *OK,* Michael, really," she says. "I don't *care* about that. It's you pushing and pushing to make what you and me have, oh god, *more.*"

She cools out, but I was frustrated. At 19 a freakster bro wants more than to hang out smoking and talking and drinking with his chick, and me and her don't have anything happening regards sex, and that gets me thinking about those Eric Rohmer films, you know, *Le Genou de Claire* and *L'Amour l'après-midi,* repressed desire and sexual obsession, where so much of the time nothing happens.

"What about *Le Genou de Claire?*" I say.

"They're so boring, his films," she says. "The only thing that happens in that whole movie is when he touches her knee for a second."

"Exactly," I say.

Our film will take place in an empty classroom. Thirty minutes in which nothing happens. The narrator speaking words in a voice of great import, but his words are psychobabble. Everything will rest on the emotional landscape of the actress. Emotional tremors registered in the fault lines of her face. A simple statement. *L'amour, l'amour, y'a que ça. All there is, is love, love.* I look at Elise in front of her desk, pale white of her Psyche legs, and that's when I know the truth of the film, *our film.*

We'll call it *Le Genou d'Elise.*

The part I don't tell her: This film will free her from her fears, and she won't be haunted by her past any more. What she'll see on the screen will be through my eyes, and she'll feel how much I care for and respect and love her. Each frame a caress, and another, and another, and yes, yes, oh fuck, *yes.* She'll be mine, soul *and* body.

And love.

No longer will she deny it.

She's beautiful the day I start filming her. The white polished boots we found at the Goodwill, the faintest-of-faint pink chiffon skirt that ends about a hand's width above her knees, the white lace tunic, the white pearl necklace we borrow from Jaded, and Elise's brown hair, longer still and wavy and clipped back out of her face on each side, her face one of Hiroshige's irises and I'm crashing on the rocks. Yeah she's something that day and this is for me how she's dressed, of course it is. I mean the truth of it, Elise never cared about the film.

Me with my frizzed-out two-tone hair, and my Lennon specs, my plaid cowboy shirt with the sleeves rolled up and the bellbottom jeans and the snakeskin boots. Psychedelic Freak Scene Dream film director, my ego out-of-control, yeah I'm the new Godard, the new Truffaut, the new Antonioni, and Elise my movie star lover, my Anna Karina, my Fanny Ardant, my Monica Vitti.

Each film cartridge lasts 15 minutes. Kodak Ektachrome 160, to approximate the muted color in Rohmer's films. How I shoot, I have the Super8 camera on a tripod. When the film runs out there's plastic clicks. *Click click click click click.*

A wide shot from inside the classroom frames the closed door, the door a symbol, *a portal to the unknown, an entrance into the womb, the classroom as the Garden before the snake and the apple, Huxley's doors of perception, or perhaps the classroom symbolic of every classroom, of every room, of the banality of existence.* The door opens and swings back into darkness, the darkness a symbol of *a cold, alienated world of lonely, desperate people,* and Elise steps into the doorway, *an overpowering bright vision of light in the darkness. Of hope trumping the bleak and inevitable decline of man's existence. Of beauty, of love.*

She's beautiful, but her beauty isn't translating. How she looks in the doorway and how she looks through the viewfinder is so different. So much rides on this film, of fixing what's broken inside, sending her fear away forever. What I see through the viewfinder won't fix anything and it won't get me anything. Not the moving pictures, not the essence of her soul, and not the sexual desire I need from her.

I'm sure it's me. *I'm* doing something wrong. I try moving the lights and put diffusion gels in front of them and bounce the light off the ceiling. I try shooting from different angles, medium shots and close-ups. We spend hours fussing with this, tweaking that, trying to get it right but nothing is working.

Well fuck, it's not me or the lighting or any of that. I don't see her soul through the viewfinder 'cause she's shut down.

It's *her*.

She sits on an oak chair, knees pressed together, hands folded on her lap, dazed, not even there, and I tell her she can breathe. She gets up, stretches her legs, walks across the room and back, and as she comes towards me rubs her hands down her thighs, thin artist fingers smooth her pink chiffon skirt, and the skirt is a shield. Between me and her.

Lately everything's a shield. The cigarettes, the booze, her sweater, her skirt. Everything to keep me from touching. She rubs her forehead, her fingertips press into the skin and she pushes her artist fingers back through her hair and rubs the back of her neck.

"What is it?" she says.

I sit in the wood chair where she's been sitting, and she finds her Kools and I get The Dylan, and she leans down, her chin near my forehead and I look up. Each freckle on her nose floats in the pale of her skin, the flame touches the cigarette and she inhales, and steps back. The lit ember floats in front of her chest, aimed at me.

"It's not right," I say.

"It's exhausting. That camera on me," she says, and she looks for an ashtray but there isn't one, only a paper cup on the floor. Her frustration, about all of it, the hours wasted, my dissatisfaction, and *no ashtray*.

"*Here*," she says, and holds out her cigarette. She's close again, her cobalt blue eyes the razorblade hands and I feel the cut. Such a long day and no *fucking* ashtray.

"Bloody massacre, take it!"

I'm the only one there for her to yell at only she doesn't yell. Her hand jittery holding the cigarette.

"Just *take it*."

I knock her ash into the cup. Hold her cigarette up but she doesn't move.

"It feels like I'm being *watched*," she says.

She unclips her hair so it falls over her ears and brushes her hair to be doing something, anything.

"Yeah, it felt how it feels when you stare at me," she says. "We're in my room and I look over and you're watching."

Her whole body limp as if some downerosity dust blown on her, and she stuffs the brush in her purse. How it is when a person grinds their teeth, that's her hands.

"I wish you wouldn't," she says. "Stare at me."

"There's something in you that's so beautiful, Elise," I say.

My obsession. She clips her hair back so her whole face is visible, laughs a self-conscious laugh, higher pitched than normal.

"It didn't feel good," she says, and is she talking about in her room, or today making this film? It's confusing, the tenses switching as she speaks. "You staring at me like I'm 'The Persistence of Memory' or *Les Demoiselles d'Avignon'* or 'The Plum Blossoms,' some *painting* you dig. I'm not an object, Michael. I'm a girl."

I go to the camera and load a fresh cartridge. I'm sure she sees me, 'cause it isn't some subterfuge. The reason we're here is to make a film, but the authentic real of it, 'cause she's tired or frustrated or her head some other place, she doesn't get it. I look through the viewfinder, and fuck, 'cause I been waiting all day to see this. I start the camera, got a closeup on her face, and take a seat facing her.

What happens next is the reason I've told you all this so far. In Elise's face I see the fear that's keeping her from giving herself to me, and right in this moment her face is the face I want. On film. The authentic real of her right there, in her worry lips and desolation eyes, her broken smile and cracked heart. It's as if she's free associating. She's talking, to me, direct from her heart to mine.

"I worry about the drinking. I can't sleep if I don't get
blitzed. Michael, I lay there and I'm afraid. I feel *so* afraid. It's
hard to breathe. The fear rises out of nowhere, and it
overwhelms me. I used to have nightmares about what
happened, but now it's as if what he did has become an anxiety
that's always in me. At first when I got blitzed I could escape it,
but now I can't. It's always there, Michael."

She stares ahead, her eyes seeing the past, but now it's a
different past. Translucent fingers holding the bottom edge of
her chiffon skirt relax, and her face changes and she laughs her
Jean Seberg laugh.

"That was so sweet when we danced at the party. You held
me and it felt like you'd hold me as long as I needed it. I leaned
against you and I wasn't alone. Yeah that's when I knew I could
trust you, Michael. You're the first boy who's ever cared. You
care more than anyone. If someone came in here right now
with a knife you'd fight him. I know you would. You'd fight to
the death to keep me safe. My life means more to you than your
own. More than it means to me. I can't turn away from that. But
I can't turn to it either. Oh, you can't understand."

She changes again, and her whole body tightens. "When you
touch me I feel so anxious. Like rats biting me or ants crawling
everywhere, and I want to run. It's not you. It's *me*. I can't. I
can't."

We sit there awhile, in the silence of the classroom, and she
speaks again. "You know, Michael, there are times when we're
together and I want you to touch me. Really, I do. But
sometimes even only your hand on my thigh, it starts."

Click click click click click. Both of us freaked. She's freaked 'cause
she realizes the camera's been running. She's captured on film.
Not her words 'cause a Super8 camera doesn't record sound,
not mine anyway. It's her face, and the drama gone down across
it. Me, I'm worried *and* freaked. Worried 'cause I don't know
what's on the film. What if the light was wrong, what if she
moved so her face wasn't in the frame, what if her eyes were
looking down, what if it's a bad roll or they fuck up the

processing or—everything can go wrong racing in my mind. And freaked 'cause of her words. *When you touch me I feel so anxious.* Really really freaked. *Click click click click click.*

It's well into the evening by the time we get the equipment up to my room, and she changes her clothes, and we eat dinner. We make it back to her room, hurry same as addicts through a number and suck down our first drink, but it doesn't take our panic rush towards oblivion to know it's different. The dark shadows on her face. I'm there with her, do my best to be present, but the film, man, *the film,* and did I capture her luminous pale face in the fading light, and how I could see right through into her soul? Did I get *that* on film? *My obsession.*

We sit close at the edge of the bed on the midnight blue comforter, her body limp. She's wiped out, and guilty, and ashamed of what she can't do, for her and for me, but mostly for me I guess, and this isn't what I want. I mean working on the film brought us closer, but here in her room she can't escape the past.

Only I'm gonna help her get past the wolf head razorblade nightmare. She wants my arm around her and she leans into me. I feel her heart beating and her quiet breathing. We sit there, time passes, heart beating, quiet breathing, and still we sit, and faint through the walls from another room Eric Burdon sings "We Gotta Get Out of This Place" to his chick, sings about how there's a better life, elsewhere, for the two of them, and some people walk down the hall laughing their stoned late night laughter.

There's us, and there's everything else, and all I care about is us. We're so close, my arm around her back, my other hand firm on her arm, and we start to talk about it. How she feels *right now,* and she feels OK, and her pale luminous face, she trusts me, and did I get *that* on film? *My obsession.* She isn't freaking and she isn't giving up, my Visions of Johanna, so much trust in her blue million miles eyes. No fear, man, no freak-out.

"Oh Michael, this is *so* excellent," she says. "Why can't we always be this way?"

Her head against my shoulder, her soft brown hair could be alive how it seems to caress my neck, and the side of my face.

"We can, Elise," I say. "The fear is when you look back and let the past take over. Why would you wanna be lookin' over your shoulder?"

"I know it doesn't make sense," she says. "It's a girl thing. I don't care what Kate says, girls *are* different. How my emotions rise and fall, come and go, change and rearrange. I feel good, and it creeps out of nowhere, and I'm in the grip."

Her thin artist fingers take my hand, her fingers rub the top of my middle finger. Compulsive how she rubs it.

"Let's make a pact, Michael," she says. "Our secret, OK?"

Well of course it's OK.

"When I feel it start," she says. "I'll tell you."

"Yeah, you should tell me," I say. "I'll help you, Elise. You'll listen to me and I'll send the fear away. I'm not afraid, and you don't have to be afraid."

We don't get out a knife and make true love scars, but we might as well have, how close and beautiful and true. She puts my hand on her thigh and her hand on my hand, the warmth of her palm and her thin artist fingers on my hand, her love burning an invisible true love scar into me, and we sit that way, and she doesn't freak, and then she moves my hand so it's against her stomach, nearly touching the bottom of her left breast, my hand on her sweater. Well I can tell. My hand hardly there at all, but before she can say it, across her face the wolf head razorblade nightmare, and did I get it on film, did I, how fragile she is, and the fear, did I?

"I'm scared, Michael."

The suicide poet on the wall above us, not even there, and Picasso's whores, defiant outsiders, in silent judgment, and I move my hand back to her thigh.

"Remember our pact, Elise. Take a breath. Stay with me. A deep breath. We're right here in *this moment* and *I'm here*. This moment is the only moment, and this moment will go on forever. Nothing scary about me and you here on your bed."

"Yeah," she says. "Nothing scary. I think I'm OK."

After a while she wants us to lay on her bed, our heads share her pillow, her body against mine, and she tells me about the rest of our pact. She wants me to agree not to try any Casanova moves, not to try and fuck her. She wants me to be with her close how we are when she feels safe and the wolf head razorblade fear isn't there.

We lie there quiet as before, and then her lips against mine, she wants me to kiss her and I do kiss her, not a deep heavy traffic French kiss, no, a sweet gentle kiss, but all the same it's too much, and fear rolling through her, a storm coming off the Forever Infinite Pacific flattening everything in its path, and she turns away.

"No, Michael, I *can't*."

"Breathe *now*. You don't have to go nowhere. Stay with me, stay in this moment, Elise."

"Yeah," she says. "I'll stay with you."

When I wake we're side-by-side, lying on the comforter, still have our clothes on, and she's turned toward me, holding onto my arm. Man, she's beautiful in the morning light, her hair crazy-wild, no lipstick. Her voice the nervous quiet of that night I called her in L.A.

"You're so sweet," she says. "No one ever cared about me like you do. I'm always gonna love you for it, Michael. Always."

Oh man oh man oh man.

It was the only time she said the word "love." I mean in a positive way about me and her. Well I didn't know that then, that it would be the only time.

We're under the midnight blue comforter, and she wants me to lay my head against her stomach. I can't see her pale white stomach, her luminous white skin, can't see any of her in the darkness under the covers, and she guides me, and my face, my cheek and my nose and my ear and the side of my forehead press against the warmth of her flat pale luminous white stomach, and her hand, her thin artist fingers touching my hair, playing with my hair, fingers pushing through my hair and her hand on my cheek, her fingers on my lips, her finger tips sliding over my lips and her fingers push into my mouth, burning a true love scar into my soul.

The film. *My obsession.* The processing lab is in New Jersey, and it takes three weeks. Drives me crazy, man, waiting. *My obsession.* And each time I see Elise show some of who she really is, beyond the surface of the surface, I wonder, did I get that on film, well did I?

2. THE BOOBY PRIZE

SOMETIMES WHEN ELISE FELT the fear, we'd get in the TR4 and drive up the coast, wind along the two-lane blacktop thousands of feet above the huge rocks and the stretches of beach and the Forever Infinite Pacific vanishing out at the horizon. Canvas top down and the wind spit damp on our faces. Yeah it was fuckin' cold but we were *alive,* and it would transform her, as if she'd taken some kind of side-effects-free anti-fear drug.

She'd find some groovy song on the radio—"Heart of Gold" or "Tumbling Dice" or one time it was Van Morrison's "Jackie Wilson Said (I'm in Heaven When You Smile)"—and crank it loud. We felt so close in the car cruising—well I sure felt it.

'Cause of the music there was no pressure to talk, and because there was no pressure, we did talk. We talked about the life or death shit. In that car all the guilt and worry and what-if split, gone baby gone. No past, no future. Only the moment. Something about being in motion—me busy driving, hands on the wheel—set her free. The TR4 was a savior, man, and I was glad I'd done what I'd done to get it.

There are more nights when I stay with her, nights when we pass out on her bed, other nights when she wears her Krazy Kat pajamas and I strip to my t-shirt and shorts and we get under the midnight blue comforter, and some nights when I wake, my face against her stomach, and her thin artist fingers on my lips.

All the time me and her hung out led up to one night. This night. Starts with Sappho's party, and me and Elise total blitzed, and in my stoner glow I'm Lennon and Kerouac and Godard, my nervous system high-wired. I'm the last freakster bro standing, man, guns ablaze. She's not wearing her Levertov glasses, so her beauty is soft-focus boozy, not wise-ass brainy, and in my alcoholic haze she's so Visions of Johanna. The two of us sit shoulders-and-thighs-touching close on Sappho's bed. Such changes since I first saw her all those months ago, as if it's a film I've almost forgotten, I mean so much gone down.

We walk boozy slow down the hallway, and pretty much everyone on the hall laid back or get it on or crashed out. I hear the mellow of Miles' "Shhh/Peaceful" as we pass one door and the sing-song of Garcia's "Candyman" behind another. She holds my arm to steady herself, and sings from Smokey's songbook, her voice a cool soprano.
   I don't like you, but I love you.
   Outside her door, she's finding her key, and does she wanna smoke a number?
   "Bloody yeah," she says. "Whaddya *think*, Writerman."
   She's too blitzed to get the key in the lock, the drunk frustration of simple things don't work.
   "Someone changed my lock!"
   Yeah well she'll show 'em, and plops herself down, her flowered skirt an irregular circle around her. She's an origami flower, the way her body is folded, coming unfolded.
   "Michael!" she says, and her voice gonna get what she wants. "You changed it. Why'd you *change* it?"
   Her hair needs brushing, and her blue million miles eyes search for an answer. She wears a too-big-for-her Egyptian blue wool sweater and under it a cornflower blue t-shirt, and the flowered skirt, the one with miniature red, pink and white roses on black, and the burnt orange cowgirl boots. Such a beautiful mess in her fuck-up dishevel.
   Her voice has that sloppy alcoholic pace. "Bloody massacre, *Michael,*" she says. "Bet yer ass I wanna smoke it. Yer *groovy groovy*

joint," and her hand slaps the carpet. "Right *here!* You sit *here* next to me."

"Give me the key, Elise," and why's it always me wants something from her?

She shakes her head slow, hair falling across her face, tongue coming out a little between her lips. "Nope," she says. "Doesn't work and you don't get it. Like it here. Can see *everyone* going by my room."

The faint sounds of behind closed doors, and we know this is stupid so after she's been sitting awhile, after I've been standing looking down at her, she gives up the key and I unlock her door. Get behind her, my arms under her arms, and I pick her up and I want to hold her. Just hold her.

Once she's standing she pushes her door open. She tries to keep steady, take a step, lift her right cowgirl boot but instead of putting it down in front of her it ends up off to her right, and the left boot too far to the left, erratic stop-start stagger across the room, face down onto her bed. Lies on that midnight blue comforter, a human rag doll, beautiful mess of brown hair, Egyptian blue sweater and flowered skirt.

I'm at the stereo, you know, on the floor near her desk, ask her what she wanna hear. She turns on her side, hair falling crazy in her face.

"Motown! Hear me, Michael. Motown!"

I get The Miracles' *Greatest Hits* on the turntable, get the needle on "You've Really Got a Hold on Me," dig the retro doo-wop sound.

I sweat from the hot of her room, and she sits up on her mattress, pulls her sweater off. She's got her palms on the mattress, on each side of her for support and lifts her calves so both legs and both boot heels stick straight out, Raggedy Anne silly cute. Yeah, she's too much. I grab the bottom of one boot and she lays back on the bed. I pull the boot off, and the other.

It's damn hot, and I take off my Hawaiian shirt, but leave on the dark burgundy t-shirt that's got John Lennon's face, and Smokey and the Miracles are jamming "Mickey's Monkey."

"Come on and dance with me, Elise."

"Light a candle, OK, Michael," she says. "Gimme wine."

She's up, wobbles off balance gonna fall back on her bed but somehow steadies herself, makes it to the desk.

"Wantyata turn off lights."

The Almaden bottle's where it always is, maybe a third full, give or take, take or give, and I'm ready to take right along with Elise. We've drunk too much already, but that doesn't stop us. I've got The Dylan, light a couple of her candles. Her face luminous white, oh man, her bare lips pale, and could Manet paint a face so lovely, or Julia Margaret Cameron make a photograph to compare, and did I get the authentic real of her face on film? Well did I?

She's dancing, and the candle light makes tripped-out shadows of her on the wall, and as the flames flicker and she moves the shadows move. Her arms snake Egyptian, zigzag up in the air, down in front of her, down by her sides, and she shakes her hair. Her Psyche legs descend from her flowered skirt, move boozy cool.

"Hey," Elise shouts. "Let's twist!"

She bends her knees, raises her arms, snaps her fingers. Throws back her hair, closes her eyes and shakes her head jerky fast. Her upper body moves one way and the rest of her moves another, legs doing those fab foxy twist moves. Well all of a sudden she stops, looks down at the rug, her head back and forth slowmo trance kinda deal. There's sweat on her t-shirt.

"Too hot," she says. "Michael, why's it too hot?"

She's close enough I could touch her, and she looks up, and in her blue million miles eyes she's my Visions of Johanna. For real. It's heavy 'cause her eyes tell me I, Michael Stein, *matter*. To Elise I matter. I mean something in her life, and I hope to God-who-probably-doesn't-exist that I have her same as that on film. And more. The wanting, *her* wanting, I see it, and for the first time since me and Sarah were done I know I'm someone. A chick I love cares for me. *Wants me.*

Her blitzed how she is, she has the sentimental splattered all over. Her face changes, and that internal struggle I seen before, yeah that's in full effect. There's something she wanna do, but she's scared.

"Oh, what the hell," she says.

She grabs the bottom of that cornflower blue t-shirt and pulls it up. Her hands shake, yeah she's scared, as the shirt rolls up her torso fast, off her stomach and past her bra and over her head, and her hair falls out onto her shoulders and her back and some hair in her face too. She pulls the shirt off her arms and she's wearing a new black bra.

Oh fuck, man, she's way sexier than that Constance Towers chick in "The Naked Kiss." I still wonder about the black bra, you know, did she get it 'cause she figured it would be sexy for me to see her wearing it?

She could leave it on, but she doesn't want to, and in reaching behind her back to undo the straps she thrusts her chest forward, and oh man, there's nothing sexier than when a chick does something same as that total natural unselfconscious.

"Damn," she says. "I can't get it. Michael, help me."

She has her back to me, and I step close and I can't get it either. I've never been with a chick who wears a bra. Well there's three tiny-ass hooks gotta be undone, and I struggle to unhook 'em, and of course she's impatient.

"Can't you get it, Michael?"

Well eventual I get the bra unhooked, and she takes it off, throws it toward the bed and before she can turn I get my arms around her, my hands on her tits, and electricity of sex burning through me. I thought sure she'd stop me but no way, and I hold her like that, her ass against me, my hands feeling her.

Finally I let go and she turns, and there she is. Oh man oh man oh man.

First time, and it's too the fuck much. Me, Writerman, seeing Elise's tits. They're beautiful gorgeous groovy perfect. Firm and pear-shaped, not too big. Seeing her half-naked, well it makes me think maybe there is a God, 'cause it's hard to imagine beauty on the order of what I see without divine intervention.

Already we've gone way past anything we've done before

and this is gonna be the night, I know it, time for me to serious lay on the Casanova moves, and get her all the way past her freak-out fear trip.

She's dancing, the light flickers on her face, lights up her hair, her tits a blur as she swirls away from the light, away from me, and her body turns around again, facing me, some of her in light, some in darkness. There's wildness in her boozy face, and there's a new kinda freedom in her dance.

Yeah sure she's blitzed, but still. I've been with Elise when she's blitzed plenty times and she never took her shirt off, never let me touch her tits, never came close to this scene, and I stop thinking about the film. I love her so much and I could cry to see her this way.

Elise trusts me.

I take off my glasses and my Lennon t-shirt, and I'm strong, a real man, naked from the waist up. Yeah, Jim Morrison on the beach.

When the album ends I play the other Miracles' disc, *Going to a Go-Go*. We're freeform slow trippin' to a couple tracks but when Smokey lets loose into "Ooo, Baby, Baby," she steps forward, and she's losing it, falls into my arms. I hold her, and we slow-dance so slow how we did at the Halloween party.

Intoxication, man, those strings swell, her against me how she is, her tits warm against my chest. The fast beat of her heart, of my heart.

Finally. Oh fucking Jesus. *Finally*. Skin against skin. *Finally!*

Elise's nipples are hard. Her face and neck are different, there's this thing that happens, she's sweating and there's a faint red that wasn't there before. She looks up at me and I kiss her, pull her tight against me, my hard-on against her crotch, my tongue in her mouth and I hear her sigh, and it was a sigh I'd never heard before, a sigh of desire.

When the song's over she pushes off me, sways in the middle of the room. I get one arm around her back, the other across her stomach and help her to the bed. She falls onto the midnight blue comforter. She rolls onto her back, her cobalt blue eyes look up at me. I look down at her, her skirt bunched up on her thighs, curvy legs luminous, tits sprinkled with sex dust.

"You want me so *much*, Michael," she says. "*Crazy* how much."

Her hair's an explosion around her head.

"I'm such a big fucking deal," she says. "To *you*."

She has a blitzed-out smile.

"Now to *me*," she says, and turns her face slow to the left, slow to the right. "Not that big a deal. Oh Michael, sometimes it's *too* much. You try so hard."

She laughs her Jean Seberg nervous laugh. "To *you*," she says. "I'm the *big prize*. Well I'm not a big prize. I'm not the Madonna or Kim Novak or some big deal. Just a girl, Michael, you know that?"

Lies there, and quick as she's laughing, she's not laughing.

"I think I'm ready."

"Yeah you are," I say.

"Oh Michael, you've been so patient with me. I feel something so strong in my heart."

She undoes the flowered skirt, pulls it down past her thighs, struggles to push it down further and kicks it off onto the carpet. She lies there naked except for her beige panties.

"After all my craziness, do you still want me?"

Her panties tight against her body, *you're the first boy who's ever cared,* her face flushed, and the mischievous smile from when she threw the tequila bottle. Her tits luminous in the flicker of the candlelight. *You care more than anyone.*

Elise. *My obsession.* My Visions of Johanna. I lie down next to her and I kiss her again and taste her warm boozy mouth. We kiss slowmo slow, and I don't wanna scare her, don't wanna rush it, don't want her to feel the desperation in my kiss, but she feels it. My tongue, her tongue, in my mouth, in her mouth, in my mouth, in our mouth.

We stop, get some air.

"Of course I want you, Elise, are you kidding?"

And in that moment I *know*. If Elise escapes her past and we fuck, experience the Forever Infinite Ecstatic, well her fear gonna split, the beautiful sadness gone forever, and she'll be free. The New Trip. A hesitation, and she moves her head same as a yes, only now there's some fear, not so much, not yet, but it's there. I don't want it to be there. It's there. I mean this is serious shit, her pussy isn't a prize. This is my life and this is her life, and we want so bad for it to be our life.

"I don't know," she says. "I want it, I just—."

Her breathing speeds up, and she lies waiting. I sit up, unzip a boot, and get my foot out of that Keith Richards snakeskin deal. I bet Keith fucks chicks loaded. Get the other boot off. Him stoned, the chick stoned. Unbuckle my belt. Keith probably fucked a chick after she passed out one time. Unbutton the metal button of my jeans. Probably fucked a bunch of chicks who were passed out. Unzip my fly. And I get my jeans off.

She watches me, sees my boner hard against my blue-and-green-plaid boxers. She sits up and her hand, her pale white artist fingers against my shorts, and through the cotton she feels the hard of me. I don't move, don't breathe, and I lie back and dig on her touch. She takes her hand off me, and did she change her mind? She takes hold of my shorts, pulls them down to my knees and gets them off. I'm total naked, my cock curving up and she takes hold with both hands.

"Some of those nights you stayed with me, I wanted to touch it," she says. "I was scared. I thought if I did there'd be no turning back."

Her Jean Seberg laugh.

"You know, Michael," she says. "I never touched a, a dick before."

We laugh that a cock has a person's name.

"Just think if your folks named you Richard," and it's weird-ass weird to be laughing hysterical while a chick got my cock in her hands. But then we're quiet and I lie there and she doesn't know what to do with it. My cock. So she lets go.

She lies back down right close and I kiss her again, her face smooth and luminous white and I climb onto her, my cock between her legs, against her panties. The hard of it presses against her pussy and I move down her, my lips on her right breast, her skin hot and salty in my mouth and I kiss it. She never felt it before, what it is to have a freakster bro she loves lick her nipple, and she sighs the ecstatic sigh.

After a while I get up, pull the beige panties off her and she has light golden curls. It's too fucking much. All of her luminous white naked in the flickering candlelight.

Oh man, this is the authentic real.

Elise naked, *and she wants me.*

"Got any lotion?" I say.

"Bottom drawer," she says.

She has some kinda hand cream and I unwrap a Trojan—I'm no fool—and get it on me, and I rub a ton of the lotion all over my rubber-sheathed cock, and I'm on her again, but something's wrong. Well this time there's nothing in the way, and though her body's tense, her hands on me, I get my cock right at her pussy lips and I start to push into them.

"*No, Michael,*" and I can feel them parting, feel my dick going into her.

Her voice is louder. "I *can't.*"

Her hands pushing against my chest.

Well Keith would do it. She's freaking, her face distorts into a horror show trip. Of course Keith would, and the monster ex-boyfriend, but I'm different. I'm a stand-up freakster bro.

"I just can't."

"Elise, it's OK," I say. "We've been here before. There's no fear in this moment."

Well she's not here, not in the moment.

"Breathe, Elise," I say. "Come back to me."

But she can't do it, and I'm not Keith Richards, my cock gone soft.

"Don't," she says. "Just please *don't.*"

I roll off her, get the Trojan off my dick and toss it onto the rug. I get my arms around her, and, oh fuck, her face broken, and her crying is a sad sound. I don't know how long we lie there. When I think she's asleep I start to get up but she has her hand on my arm.

"No," she says. "Don't leave me, Michael."

It's still hot in the room but now there's a cold shadow. Not a real shadow, of course, it's far worse, a shadow to chill the soul. Both our souls. Perhaps it's cast by those two Black Magpies, Doom and Gloom, 'cause for sure they're in the vicinity. I know Elise feels it 'cause she shivers and her nipples are hard, and it's not 'cause she's turned on.

We get under her midnight blue comforter and lie there and she wants me to hold her, the both of us naked, skin to skin. Maybe if we hold each other we can escape the cold shadow. You know how a person shakes when they've been out in the ice and snow for too long without enough warm clothes. Well that's how she shakes in my arms, so fucked-up.

Why's it so fucked up?

When I wake, where the curtains were open a little, the light on her, a wash of light across her chest, and her breath, her tits move slightly upward as she inhales. One of those beautiful moments, the way it would be with a chick the morning after in a groovy Paris walkup, a view of the Seine from the window.

Oh man, Elise as Renoir's "The Sleeper." But the longer I look, well she's not only "The Sleeper," she's Edvard Munch's "The Day After" too. Her hair has that tired look to it, matted and unbrushed, the way long hair looks after a night of sweaty dancing and too much booze. The sheet comes up to the bottom of her stomach, and her right arm coming out from her body, the hand open, palm up, and she has the smallest bellybutton, this tiny dark circle. The gentle rise and fall of her chest.

Oh man oh man oh man.

We agree to a break. To get some air, to decompress from what gone down. I wouldn't have suggested it, that's not me, but if she needs some time, that's how it's going to be. On day seven I leave a bouquet with a card outside her door. All it says on the card is "miss you," and my name. Nothing sappy.

A week later, a Wednesday morning, I find a note under my door. It says I should come to her room on Friday at 10 p.m. The rest of Wednesday, all of Thursday and Friday passes so slow it's same as months gone by.

We don't need the excuse of a party to get blitzed. We're far gone past all that, and there's nothing romantic or Lost Generation bohemian or Freak Scene Dream groovy about it. Too much booze and too much weed, *take me to the depths of absinthe. Oblivion, man.* Yeah I used to think she was so hip when she said that, some kinda poetry, but it's no different than a drunk asking for another bottle.

She returns from the bathroom, sits in front of her desk. It's the two of us, well past midnight. I get the demon jug, sit on the edge of her bed facing her, pour myself another.

"You OK?" I say.

Her hair's a mess, long strands across her face, eye-shadow smeared and lipstick gone, the tight black mini-skirt wrinkled and wine stains on her t-shirt and over her left thigh. She always looks groovy but tonight she's used up. The weeks we've been apart done nothing good. She gets a paper cup of wine too, of course she does.

"No," she says. "I'm *not* OK. I was sick. I mean *really* sick."

I'm staring the way I always do even after her telling me not to and I flash on this Otto Dix drawing, "The Suicide," this ghostly apparition sitting in a ghostly chair and next to it a dead body, hanging, and it's the body of the ghostly apparition, and under the dead body, a second chair, knocked over. Before and after, and it scares me that I think of that drawing.

"Too much wine?" I say.

"Fuck you, Michael," and the cup on her desk, the Kool pack in her hands, always the wine, always the cigarettes, as if each object is a talisman, and holding them will end the panic and the pain, and she tries to get a cigarette out.

"Maybe you could take a film of me naked," she says. "And you can watch it and play with yourself. Oh I have a better idea, paste a photo of my face on a blow-up doll. There were those kinda guys at the carnival. You would fit right in."

A cigarette between her naked lips. I toss her The Dylan, but she doesn't move, doesn't reach for it, nothing. It falls to the rug, and her foot jerks, kicks it away hard.

"What you've got here is damaged goods, Writerman," she says. "I guess I'm the *booby* prize."

She has matches, her cigarette lit, a nervous drag, nervous how that Patricia chick is when she's giving Michel up to the coppers, red-hot glow of that burning cigarette hovers front of her mouth.

"Maybe you can find some slut you can film *and* fuck. That Harper girl, what happened to her?"

Maybe if I'd said the right thing I might have saved us, but I couldn't let go.

"Let's try once more," I say. "We'll cool out a few days and Monday night——."

"It's all about you," she says. "What we're supposed to do. How I'm supposed to feel," and she drains her paper cup. "And when it doesn't work out, and it *never* works out, I feel so damn guilty and ashamed, like there's something wrong with me."

I've been looking at her face but my eyes slip to her chest, and I see the lines of her bra against the tight of her t-shirt, against a wine stain, and even then, amidst my own disarray, I can't not look, and I would die to touch her again.

"Bloody massacre, Michael, don't you look at my tits."

She hurries the cup onto her desk, wine splashing, cigarette on the desk, no ashtray, frantic to pull the shirt away from her body, and she reaches for the Egyptian sweater, pulls it on, that oversize wool sweater, and it's inside out, and the pounding blood loud. I want her, my heart a rush, so fucking bad I want her, those thin artist fingers trying to get the hair off her face.

"Maybe it isn't me at all," she says. "Maybe you're the damaged one. How could anyone ever relax with you *staring.*"

I smell the cigarette burning into the desk. She pours wine on it, sizzle of the cigarette dying. "I don't owe you," she says, and she's pulling one of those boots off, trying to get her foot out of it and I get up off the bed. "Stay away, Michael," but I take hold of the bottom of the boot, pull it off her.

"Elise, it's not true."

"Stay *away*, Michael,' she says.

She lifts the other boot, her knee bent and despite her words I reach to take hold, but before I do, well that's when she kicks hellfuck hard into my left thigh.

"*Goddamn goddamn.*"

"I hope it *really* hurts," she says.

She gets her boot off, throws it at me, the heel hits my knee, and the room changes, and there's an eerie quiet, such stillness.

We're Edward Hopper's "Summer Evening."

I already told you she looked all used up, but her face, oh I could tell she hated me then.

"The torment of you wanting too much," she says. "I don't have it to give."

I sit on the bed, rub my thigh, *the torment of you wanting too much,* and I pick up the bottle, fill my cup again, and suck that shit down.

"The hole in your heart is too big," she says.

The room starting to spin, barely, but it's moving. "Cool out, Elise."

I get the bottle, pour wine into my cup, but the wine's not gonna save me. "I know I'm an ass sometimes."

"Get *out.*"

"Elise, I--."

She comes at me. I drop the cup, wine on my jeans the bed the carpet, and she pounds fierce my chest, her thin artist hands, pounding pounding, the room gaining speed. I drop the bottle, it hits against her leg or something, on the rug, wine pouring out of it and she cries out, *you've ruined us,* and I have her wrists, *why, why, why,* her knee into me and we fall back on the mattress, her on me, she pulls free, her fingernails into my chest and she spits on my face, the salty taste of her.

I dig my fingers into her sides, get a grip on her inside-out sweater and roll us on that bed, the weight of me onto her, and I get her arms pinned, *I can't give you any more,* and in that moment I feel her slight chick body struggle under me, and through my jeans and her black mini-skirt my hard-on cock against her, and through my t-shirt and her sweater, my chest against hers, her face so close.

And I see the horror. I see what the monster ex-boyfriend must have seen while he raped her.

It's too much, man.

I get up off her, the walls swirling, stagger to the middle of the room, wipe her saliva off my face, and I'm on my way to the door but I can't leave, I can't face the nothing that is everything that isn't Elise.

She's lying on her side, curled up, arms around knees, head against knees. I see her naked Psyche legs and the beige of her panties against the black skirt, her face hidden, her long brown hair wild, and if the beautiful sadness has a sound, that's the sound I hear from her lips. She's broken, and that goddamn goddamn suicide chick on her wall, Picasso's whores lookin' out at me same as I'm scum, and the blackness everywhere. The crushed souls.

I gotta cry, man, but no fucking tears.

There is finality in the physical realm, death when it comes, the body up in smoke or left to deteriorate in a wood box. But heartbreak is an endless pain we inflict on ourselves and others and I know that so well. How I bled after what I did to Sarah and how Sarah never recovered from my betrayal, the pain tattooed on our souls more indelible than the true love scars. Now, because of what I've done, and who she is, I've lost Elise.

The white plastic reel of Super8 film. I mean sure I want to fuck Elise but I'll never fuck her. I'll never sit next to her on the carpet in her dorm room and talk about nothing and everything, never know the conspiracy of two when we laughed as one, never hold her artist hand with my writer hand or press my face against her flat pale luminous stomach. So much at stake and I didn't understand.

Nothing's worth shit, Harper said, *if you're not putting it on the line.*

Well fuck you, Harper. I put it on the fucking line. I risked everything, and I'm a goddamn goddamn ruin.

I get the projector, this heavy metal thing, set it on my desk. Get the film threaded and turn the projector on, but not the bulb. Gotta make sure the film advances right 'cause I could burn a hole through a frame of the film if the bulb is on and the film's not moving, and I don't wanna burn a single frame of Elise.

This is all I have, the film, and the nervous shakes, but the projector is working, so I turn on the bulb, and the frame is big, has to be four feet wide and nearly all of it filled with her face, moving on my wall, Elise's face, the motor whirring and the clicking of the sprockets turning through the holes in the film. I get the focus right, and this is before she began talking. I mean the beauty of her face, freckles on her nose, and her eyes. Her cobalt blue eyes, looking down, out of reach. She hadn't shown me her soul, not then, hadn't broken open yet.

I shake out a Pall Mall, reach into my pocket for The Dylan only it's not there, and I remember. On the floor in her room. Goddamn goddamn. Light up with a match, take a drag same as I woulda done sitting next to her, and I have a cup of red wine, Almaden, drink from it, woulda done that too. The whirring and clicking.

This is the part when I almost gave up. She's not gonna reveal nothing and I want to throw my wine at her. And then her face changes. And how could I think such a thing? The flickering light on my wall, and her defenses gone, and her face. Only the sound of the projector, whirring and clicking.

Elise stares right at me. On my wall her lips pressed together, this imperfect line running between those lips. Oh man, the quiver of those lips in her room that night, and I'll never feel them against my lips again. Never feel her soft hair against my face or touch the freckles on her nose.

It's weird 'cause she did something, maybe rocked back in her chair, and it's her neck in the frame, and her fingers touch the white pearls, Jaded's white pearls, something so beautiful about how her fingers move along them, and her neck, her beautiful neck, and it hurts so bad. Seeing those fingers brush the pearls, and right quick it's only her face in the frame.

She looks right at the lens, right at me, man, her Jean Seberg smile, her Jean Seberg laugh. I've lost her, my Visions of Johanna, but I have her. I'll have her forever. The essence. The beautiful sadness. The whirring and clicking, and her smile and her eyes, giving me her Visions of Johanna chick look, her face so huge and beautiful on the wall, in those cobalt blue million miles eyes.

3. THE NAKED KISS

JADED WAS NO ANGEL, and I was no true friend. I wish I could believe it was fate and I had nothing to do with it. But I wasn't a victim.

I was a ruin after Elise, and from inside me I heard Hank Williams' hard Alabama voice over those three downbeat chords sing the saddest of heartbreak ballads, "Alone and Forsaken."

Her love like the leaves now has withered and gone.

Over and over I heard it.

What happens next starts about three weeks after that final night with Elise. Me and Jim in the dining hall, heavy into our second cups of shit-strong morning coffee.

"By the way, old sport," he says. "*Her,* you know, the one whose name I must not speak in your presence, *that* girl. She left The Dylan with me."

The Pall Mall between his fingers, the smoke signals rising.

"Let me have it, man," I say.

"Was it like an engagement ring?" he says. "I must say I was tempted to keep it."

"This isn't a joke, Jim," I say. "Gimme The Dylan."

So he says he's got it safe for me, back at his room.

"Jade and I are going to see *that* film tonight," he says. "Why don't you join us, a jolly party of three. Get your mind off *that* girl."

That film is Sam Fuller's "The Naked Kiss." We were all taking
Wallace Wiley's *Film Noir* course. Wiley made a big deal about
the opening scene, and screened it in class. What a mindfucker.
No credits. Nothing to prepare you.

Wham, this hooker Kelly slams her black purse into her
pimp's face, and he staggers back into the room. Kelly—yeah,
Constance Towers—in a black blouse, short black skirt and
black heels. Fuller cutting fast between the hooker and the
pimp, her swinging the purse, the purse hitting the pimp's face,
the pimp backing away frantic.

She hits him again, he grabs at her blouse and it rips off her,
and she has on a black bra. She keeps whacking him, and he
grabs her hair, only it's a wig, and it comes off. Gorgeous bald
chick in a black bra and short skirt knocking her pimp to the
floor, hitting him again and again and yet again.

That's the film that's supposed to get my mind off Elise. That
was rich. When I stop by Jim's room around seven he's in bed
sick, a gray and blue plaid wool blanket wrapped around him.

"Jaded, *honey,* could you get The Dylan?" he says. "Top desk
drawer," and the way he said "honey," as if there's some kind of
ownership rights, and the look on Jaded's face, it was like she
was ready to hit him in the face with a heavy black purse.

She has The Dylan, and it's a shiny silver jewel. I reach out,
and her small hand on mine, the lighter against her icy palm,
against my palm, and she keeps her hand there too long.

Jim is into an ugly coughing jag. When it stops, when he
gets his breath, he tells me he's gonna skip the flick, gonna stay
there in bed and rest.

"I know you'll take good care of my girl, old sport."

It isn't 'til we're walking across the quad that I take my first
good look of the evening at Jaded. She's wearing a black skirt
and a black V-neck t-shirt and a short black jacket with a black
velvet collar, some '40s deal, and a black beaded purse hangs at
her hip from a thin black strap. And the white pearls. Every
time I watch my film of Elise there's that strange moment when

her neck is in the frame, and her thin artist fingers touch those pearls.

We get on the path to the theater, and in the darkness I barely see her grainy gray and black silhouette.

"I'm so sorry about you and Elise, Michael."

Usually she calls me Writerman, but not tonight.

"I probably shouldn't say this," she says.

Ghost of 'lectricity. Jaded's neck curving up into her pale white jaw, her naked body fluorescent white, her lips blood red, all of her a stain against the white marble.

"That girl took you for granted, Michael."

"I don't wanna talk about it," I say.

The smell of her Narcisse Noir perfume—a seduction drug.

"I don't mean to be mean," Jaded says, "but she seems—this is embarrassing."

Well there was no embarrassment on Jaded's face.

"Don't trash her, " I say.

"I think she might be a lesbo," she says. "Have you seen how Kate—."

We're still on the path when Jaded smiles the smile of Delilah. Only I don't know it's a Delilah smile. I take it at face value. *She digs me, man.* That's what I want her smile to mean and riding the rush of that smile I say something poetic about the light from the moon.

And more of her smile.

"It's the kind of thing a writer sees," she says.

She takes my hand and stops walking, turns to face me.

"You need a girl who digs you," she says. "*All of you.*"

I pull her to me, her soft body tight against mine and I kiss her, my lips against her cold lips.

Jaded knows how to kiss, I'll give her that. There's this way she nibbles my lip, and sparks run up my dick. Oh man, she marks me with her Barbara Stanwyck scent, and in her kiss the promise of so much more.

You have to take what you want, Michael.

And then it's over, but now it's different between me and her.

"I'm sorry she hurt you," Jaded says, as we continue along the path.

Right when she said "hurt you," my chest tight with the dread, as if my blood been drained and some noxious elixir of the lonely fills my veins, only that doesn't tell you the all of it. A sense of inevitability, no one will ever love me how I need to be loved. *The hole in your heart is too big.*

I remember what I'd somehow forgotten.

Her. *That girl.* She'll be at the theater. Elise never misses one of Wiley's noir screenings.

We're early, and in the darkness of the theater it seems as if no one is there. Well I'm wrong. There's two people already there.

Oh no, it's that too loud voice saying some shit about "The Naked Kiss."

"So freaky that she's bald," Sappho says.

She sits in an aisle seat maybe halfway between the back of the theater where we are and the screen, a wisp of smoke rising. The smell of weed, and the glint of something. Me and Jaded walk down the aisle, and the back of a brown fedora right next to Sappho's head.

Having a party, those two, leaning back into the velvet seats, boot soles against the metal seat backs. Elise takes a slug from a silver flask, pounding blood loud, and anyone ever had their heart ripped to pieces knows my pain.

I walk down the aisle to where I'm near Sappho, and she's wearing an invisible porcupine-quill coat, each quill has a sin-detection nerve end.

"Where's old Jim?" she says. "Old sporty sport sport."

"Elise," I say. "How are you?"

Her head jerks forward, and she's got a hoarse cough. Her boots drop to the floor, and she's bent over. She sounds worse than Jim, and her face has a hollow look. She's lost weight she can't afford to lose.

And in Sappho's voice I'm some Nabokovian creep, a Fowlesian collector.

"She doesn't want to talk to *you*," Sappho says.

Yeah I hear it. I'm a leper, man, Quasimodo of all lepers.

Sappho has her Modigliani-chick-possessed-by-the-Devil smile, looking right at me as she sings that "Out of Time" song. You know, the Stones, *that song*.

"Shut *the fuck* up, Kate," I say.

Elise coughs again, flask to her mouth. She clutches her trench coat around her as if it's protection. Sappho's voice, goddamn Devil smile, and something dirty in it.

"You two *ditch* Jim?"

Jaded, maybe a couple yards up the aisle from me, can't hide the distain she has for Sappho. "Jim's sick."

"On a little datey poo?"

The cough and the silver flask, they're both new, and I bet there's more 'cause Elise is moving in another direction and there's gonna be all kinda shit I won't know about her. Soon she'll be a stranger, as if we never have met.

"Such a drag Jim's sick," Sappho says. "I'm sure you're heartbroken, Jade."

Jaded won't look at Sappho, and now she turns, takes a step up the aisle away from us.

"You're a fucking cunt, Kate," I say.

"How gallant of you," Sappho says. "Defending your—well now what should I call her? Your female *friend*? The other woman?"

The shake of the flask, the hard sound of Beat Chick Elise's breathing.

"Oh, that's not right," Sappho says. "It's *you* Writerman, you're the home wrecker. The *other* man."

Elise gets up and looks up the aisle at Jaded, looks at me, and she *knows*. Oh man, she works her way past the seats, away from us, fast as she can move.

"Don't leave," I say.

"Bloody massacre, Michael, it's *done*."

She steps into the far aisle, oh yeah she wants to walk faster but can't.

"Elise, see you back at the dorm, OK?" Sappho calls out.

"Michael, are you coming?" Jaded says.

In, or out, love or lust, and I gotta do something. *Choose,* motherfucker.

Bitch Sappho steps out into the aisle.

"Finally Elise is yours, Kate," Jaded says. "You must be on cloud nine."

I figure Sappho gonna hit Jaded. Well she'll have to get past me first.

"You going to let him do you like a *dog?*" Sappho says.

"You'd be lucky," Jaded says, "to get any guy to do *you* like a dog."

Jaded walks fast up the aisle, stops and turns toward me. "Michael?!"

Right then Sappho throws something at me. Oh fuck, 'cause one of those small aluminum foil packets that contain a Trojan hits the rug.

I see it. Jaded sees it.

"You're a motherfucking riot, Kate," I say. "A regular Girl Scout."

I pick it up, as if, if I can make it vanish, all that came before will vanish with it. I look across the seats to the back of the theater and hear Elise's hoarse cough. And she's through the doors, gone baby gone.

"Thing is," I say. "'Be prepared' is the *Boy Scout* motto, Kate."

"I got news for you, Writerman," Sappho says. "It's also the *Girl Scout* motto."

I hold the lobby door open and Jaded walks past me.

"You're such a gentleman," she says, and she's trying to button her jacket, rushing it, can't get the middle button through the hole.

"I'm sick of these *noir* films," she says. "Let's go down to the Boardwalk."

She turns to face me, her Delilah smile and her amber eyes spark gold and lock in on mine.

"I want to ride the Ferris wheel, Michael," she says.

My hand on her hand, the hand trying to button her coat, and I take over, button it for her and she steps into me, her warm breath on my cheek and the *Narcisse Noir.*

"Maybe later this evening," she says. "I'll get you to be less a gentleman."

All my imperfections, all my sins, inked into me, but still I have no excuse. A human always has a choice. I'm not a victim, and there's temptation everywhere if you're looking for it, and Jaded asking me to take her somewhere, yeah, I'll take her wherever she wants to go. Straight to hell if that's what she wants.

Anything to forget.

Jaded behind the wheel of her Mercedes, me riding shotgun where Jim always sits. She's got the top down, and we bullet down the winding two-lane. It's one of those nights, a spring night only it's not spring yet. Quarter moon large in the sky reflecting the light of the sun down on us, only it's not sunlight, not after the moon gets done transmuting it, the air warm and the radio on. Van Morrison sings "Gloria" from 1964, back when he's fronting Them, back before he went solo, back when he's just another rock 'n' roll singer. That's the genius, he's so unselfconscious singing "Gloria."

It's found art that record.

"Gloria," another transmutation, music into sex. Van Morrison sings for every horny guy who ever waited on a chick, and she's walking down his street. His impatience, and she's at his house. His frustration, and she's knocking on his door. And then she's in his room, *an' she make me feel alright.*

Anything to forget.

Jaded pulls up in front of Liquor King and gets out a 20.

"Michael, be a love," she says. "Get us a pint of Johnny Walker Black and a box of Sherman's."

"I've got money," I say.

"Well now you have more."

Liquor Store sits behind the counter, his nose in Kant's "Critique of Pure Reason." That was rich. I bet he really digs Kant's trip about freedom—how there isn't any. He looks up, and whatever he thinks of me, he doesn't show it. Through the window he can see Jaded, already she's bored. If anyone needs proof of freedom, Jaded in her Mercedes 280se convertible is it.

"New girlfriend, Writerman?" he says. "What happened to the other guy she's always with?"

He's traded his surf t-shirt in on a forest green Walden Pond deal. There's a quote from Thoreau under the black line drawing, and it's as if smirkface been expecting me.

How vain it is to sit down to write when you have not stood up to live.
Motherfucker.

I tell him what booze and smokes I want, lay Jaded's 20 on the counter.

"Calls me *old sport*," Liquor Store says. "Like he thinks he's Gatsby. And the cane. God is that stupid. He's not a friend of yours is he?"

He has reeferized pupils, and whites streaked red.

"I've been in that kinda triangle," he says. "You seen that Truffaut film? It's hard when two bros are into the same girl."

"Save the sympathy, man," I say. "How's your hearing? I'm in a hurry."

"You mean peach brandy, right?" he says. "And you're the one who smokes the Pall Malls. I have a great memory. That rich girl, she's the one smokes the Sherman's."

"Look, I don't care if you have an eidetic memory," I say. "It's a simple request. You get me the booze and the cigarettes and I pay you and we don't have to have anything more to do with each other. OK?"

"You know what," he says. "I think you're the errand boy. Last time you're here with that other chick, the prick teaser with the glasses who's given up tequila for Southern Comfort, and now this one—she for certain has a tight leash on you."

An army of little men arrive inside my skull working the nail guns.

"Mind your own business, man."

Freaks me. First I hear of Elise drinking Southern Comfort. He picks up the 20, his nose twitching.

"Well Mr. Errand Boy," he says. "Unless you're into girly perfume, I'd say your sugar mammy gave you this when she patted you on the head and sent you in here. I guess you're the kinda guy lets the chick pay."

Now the army are beating on my skull with steel hammers, and I search for cruel words to burn his ass. But what rushes through me is Jaded paying, Jaded driving.

"Must be hellfuck tough to be in here reading Kant," I say. "Chained to that counter. Everyone else out partying. Bet it feels like shit."

Anger burns through me.

"Isn't gonna last," he says. "No writer can afford that chick in the Mercedes."

Oh I'm pissed, but I have it all under wraps. I get in and Jaded floors it, speed limit 40 but she's somewhere past 60.

"Cocktails, Michael?"

Johnny Walker Black. What grown-ups drink. What a man and a woman who are married to other people drink in the motel room before they fuck. In the moonlight there's more pink in the porcelain white of her face. I take a slug and pass her the bottle. The booze burns, but burns good, burns the bad into me. *Fuck you smirkface.*

There's still the question of Jim, and what Jaded's doing driving too fast to the Boardwalk with an open bottle and her old man's best friend on the passenger side. The burn's not so intense the fourth time, and that's when I decide I'll pretend Jaded's my chick, and I'm *really* not gonna think about Jim anymore.

Anything to forget.

4. THE FERRIS WHEEL

JADED PARKS THE MERCEDES, and she's got the bag, the bag with the bottle. The booze that's gonna sear the pain of Elise right outta me.

We hurry through the Casino, this wreck of a building that serves as the entryway to the boardwalk. It's full of pinball machines and pool tables and a bumper car ride and a snack bar with corn dogs and cheeseburgers and cherry snow cones. Once outside we walk south on the raised wood walkway that borders the beach, to our right the orange-gold flames from campfires, people in t-shirts and cut-offs stand in the sand, dance in the sand, gather 'round the fires.

Yeah, everything's burning tonight, man. Someone bangs out buzzing bar chords and a ragtag choir sing "Give Peace a Chance." A dog gone off on a barking jag, and a second dog adds its howl, and a third, and beyond them, the people and the dogs and whatever else on that beach, an immense dark presence.

Forever Infinite Pacific.

I take Jaded's hand, hold it tight. To our left, all along the boardwalk a carnival midway, which is funny. You know, after it's all over with me and Elise I end up in a kinda carnival deal. Oh fuck, flash on her coughing, and the beautiful sadness, and is she OK? Hard to forget her. *Bloody massacre, Michael, it's done.*

Me and Jaded walk slow past all the sucker games. "Milk Bottle Throw," "Test Your Strength," "Ring the Bell," and all the rest. We're in the flow of the crowd, all these people out for a good time, a kid crying he's lost his allowance playing "Ball

Toss," a white army guy and his black chick girlfriend with a
fancy Diana Ross kinda hairdo, the two of them sharing cotton
candy. It seems so innocent, only it's not innocent. Nothing's
innocent once you grow up.

The Golden Dragon Ferris wheel is at the end of the
boardwalk, past the Looff Carousel, past the Tilt-A-Whirl, past
the cotton candy cart and the Foster's Freeze concession, and
the corn dog stand, on the ocean side of the Giant Dipper
wooden roller coaster. It's at least 100 feet high, a gigantic wheel
set against the moonlit night, and it looms over everything same
as a metallic "War of the Worlds" creature. It slowly rotates as
we approach, the Chinese-themed gondolas rocking slowmo
back and forth, little twinkling lights on each, and we hear the
creepy turn-of-the-century amusement park music, and the
scratch of the needle in the groove. Could be one of the
original 78s. Hundred year old vinyl.

Jaded lets go of my hand, points to the top of the Golden
Dragon.
    "It thrills me, sitting up there."
    At the ticket booth she puts a fiver on the counter.
    "Come on, Jade. You bought the booze."
    "I'm paying," she says, but it wasn't true.

The Golden Dragon was completed in 1907 according to the
ticket seller, the year the Boardwalk opened for business. What's
unusual about the Golden Dragon are the enclosed gondolas.
They're nothing same as what you find on the newer Ferris
wheels. Seven feet tall, you can stand up in them, though you're
not supposed to when the ride's in motion.
    The bottom half of the gondola, going up about four and a
half feet and including the floor, is wood, this cool old black
varnished wood bolted to the gondola's steel frame, and there's
a wood door that hinges out with a Chinese gold dragon
painted on it maybe from the Zhou Dynasty, or anyway, some
old dynasty.

The upper section is a wire cage, hard inflexible steel wire rectangles, each one maybe two by three inches, so you can see out but no way anyone gonna fall while the ride's going. Each gondola has a peaked pagoda-style roof with a carved, metallic-gold painted wood dragon at each of the four corners.

There's a handful of people in line behind us when it comes to a stop. The Ferris wheel dude running the thing opens the door of the ground level gondola and this young chick and her guy get out. They're 15, maybe 16, she has straight blonde surfer chick hair, giggling at something her guy said. He's a Deadhead stoner kid. Fuck, they're the innocence, and I'd give anything to get it back.

It's our turn and Jaded gets to work, the Ferris wheel guy a victim, her Valentine's Day smile, you know, the one she gives Jim, *pretty please*, and she holds out a three buck tip along with the tickets.

"Could me and my guy," she says. "Have one to *ourselves?*"

Oh man, *me and my guy*.

The Ferris wheel dude has construction worker hands, rough and callused, slips the dough into a pocket of his denim shirt, the faded-blue tickets between his stubby fingers, tears both tickets, and Jaded takes the stubs.

"No problem," he says. "No kind of problem, Miss," and him calling her "Miss," yeah, that was rich. "Watch your step."

She steps into the gondola, the curve of her ass tight against her short black skirt. Yeah I see it, and the Ferris wheel guy sees it, and he gives me a sage nod kinda look. It's same as he said something crude, an us-men-appreciate-a-good-fuck-when-we-see-her kinda look. I stare through him.

Inside there's two benches, each wide enough for two, each with a pair of safety belts, the benches facing each other, the black glossy lacquer worn dull. We sit facing the ocean, buckle the belts, and there's something so wrong being buckled in next to Jaded.

The Ferris wheel guy tips his hat to her, but she doesn't

smile. We have a gondola to ourselves, and she doesn't need to waste another smile. She's learned how little she needs to give to get her way. But there's always a price. Her phony smile, her phony gaze. Her duplicity smeared on her.

R. Meltzer's right, we're all whores and everything's got a price.

The Ferris wheel starts up, and our gondola rises and swings, and the Ferris wheel guy lets a couple empty gondolas go by, and the whole deal comes to a halt and we're up at about 9 o'clock, maybe 50 feet above the ground. He has to get everyone into the gondolas before he can let the Ferris wheel go 'round and 'round, and when there's a big crowd it takes forever. He has to stop it, get the people out who've gone round, get four more in, and so on.

A light from the top of the Giant Dipper is coming in through the wire of the cage casting thin rectangular shadows on us. Jaded has the smooth glass neck of the bottle in her mouth, and I'm glad 'cause I want her to get drunk and wild and fucked up. Fuck true love, fuck Elise.

Anything to forget.

Ghost of 'lectricity. Jaded's smooth white skin against the white marble, one arm extended, the thin fingers with the black razorblade nails motioning me towards her, and without touching me, pulling me to her.

It's dark in the gondola, everything gray and black and grainy. We're locked in a cage passing the bottle back and forth. Three drunk motherfuckers in a gondola somewhere below are bellowing a sea shanty.

I'll go no more a rovin', with you fair maid. A rovin', a rovin', since rovin's been my ru-*in.*

The machinery coughs, and our gondola swings forward and back, rises past 10 o'clock, and the bottle tight in her hand and she's laughing, her red lips apart, her skirt high on her thighs. She sees me looking and she stretches out her left leg and I see her boot. She's wearing the boots Elise drew one time, the black boots with the pointed toes that were spikes and the huge stiletto heals that were knives.

"My favorite," Jaded says. "Is when we get to the top."

The drunk fucks down below must have a pint with them too.

Then take warning boys, from me, Mark well what I do say! So take a warning, boys, from me, With other men's wives don't make too free.

The pointed toe of Jaded's boot aimed toward the black ocean, and she has a Sherman and I have The Dylan, the blue gold flame flickering and her hand on my hand, and she's wearing a jade ring, a ring Jim bought her.

"On top of the world I can see everything," Jaded says. "I can see the ocean, and all this below is so small, they're ants crawling about, Harry Lime's dots."

Harry Lime's dots. The suckers and the mugs, Orson Welles' Harry Lime called them in "The Third Man," guys and chicks, little kids and old fucked-up geezers, families of three and four and five talking too loud. Her thin fingers holding the lit cigarette, she takes in all that's down below, the three-card Monte midway wheeler-dealers in the business of extracting quarters from those folks in exchange for the hope they can be winners.

"We're up in the sky, free from all of it," Jaded says. "All the *little* people and their stupid meaningless lives."

The glow of Jaded's cigarette, as if she's using it to burn out the dots one by one. Only the dots aren't dots, they're people, living breathing people same as us, no better, no worse. Each has their humanity inked into them. Though perhaps they are better. They're not thinking about fucking their best freakster bro's chick while she wears his ring, not laughing at the people who are just trying to get by, enjoy an evening of fun. Maybe win a stuffed animal.

When all the gondolas have people in them the Ferris wheel kicks into gear, the hum and whir of the huge motor and we start going up, the watery carnival music drifts over the motor sounds same as sonic soot through the air mixing with screams and laughter of little kids and teenagers and those drunk fucks below us still singing.

They call me hanging Johnnie, hooray, hooray!

Me and Jaded so close, and as our gondola rises it rocks back and forth, and we're at 12 o'clock, and the elation, as if we float in space high above the earth, come past the peak, the inflated rush from the booze. Elise and her fucking cold eye. Well she had her chance, she had plenty of chances, and Jaded's right. If she were a lesbo that would explain plenty.

The warm night air against my face, and the black sea, moonlight shimmering off the miles and miles of unseen waves.

"Have you ever seen anything so beautiful," Jaded says. "You wouldn't think of the undertow, seeing it like that."

"No I haven't seen anything," I say, and it was blasphemy, me echoing words I once said to Sarah as I look at Jaded's face, "so beautiful."

She drops the butt of her Sherman, grinds it with the toe of her boot, and there's other cigarette butts, and a crushed Michelob can. I look behind me and see those drunk sea shanty fuckers, the glow of their cigarettes and as their gondola keeps rising and ours drops, looks as if they have a match lit or a candle.

Jaded's grooving from the whiskey, her hand on my upper arm, icy through my cotton shirt. I get a Pall Mall, maybe that'll cool me out.

She has another Sherman between her fingers.

"Jim doesn't like Ferris wheels," she says.

And me too eager to please, The Dylan at the ready, light our cigarettes, and as I flip closed the lid, The Dylan a smooth silver object in my hand, her hand on my hand, her fingers slide around my hand, her palm against The Dylan, she wants to hold it, from my hand to hers.

"It was Bob Dylan's," I say.

We pass the lowest point, where we got on, and rise again, 8 o'clock and 9, the shadows of the wire cage on us.

"Jim told me," Jaded says. "How'd you get it?"

There's a light breeze, the air warm on my face.

"It's too long a story," I say. "A friend of his—"

"I want it."

That's when she slips The Dylan into her purse.

"Let me use it tonight."

The Valentine's Day smile.

"Just tonight," I say.

The fingers of her free hand through my hair, and she holds the black ends.

"I should dye it all black again," and she stretches out the other leg, her skirt even higher on her thighs.

"Jim's afraid of heights. He's never brought me up here."

Another drink and she passes the bottle but keeps her hand on it and we both hold it, my head back, I take a slug and I'm gonna bring it away from my mouth but she holds it there, and more booze gone down.

She sets the bottle on the bench, unbuttons her jacket, shimmies it down her back, a burlesque show jiggle, a quick look to make sure I'm watching. She takes it off, and even in the darkness I see her tits pressing against her t-shirt.

"Imagine. If I stay with Jim I'll never ride a Ferris wheel with my lover."

The Ferris wheel goes 'round five times, and while it does we share the bottle and smoke and look out at the blackness of the Forever Infinite Pacific. We reach the highest point again, and I see the pagoda tops of gondolas below us, the lights on the midway and the darkness out where the waves crash the beach.

We begin to descend, to 3 o'clock and then 4, laughter from a gondola above us and something falls past and a crack, loud as a gun shot, Jaded's fingers take hold of my arm, and a shiver of fear.

We reach ground level and up we go again until it stops at about 8 o'clock, two stops past the loading area, which means we're gonna go all the way up and then down, stopping each time a gondola gotta be unloaded before it's our turn to get out.

"I like a guy who's got some muscle," she says.

Her hand on my upper arm, and she wants me strong as I want her. I *know*.

"Jim still works out," I say. "Doesn't he?" and in the darkness *les fleurs du mal* cover the black floor of the gondola.

"I'm talking about you," she says.

The gondola rises to 10 o'clock and stops, and I swear I hear 'em, *caw caw caw*, Doom and Gloom somewhere above us, and I kiss her again, second kiss of the night, her icy cold lips, and this kiss is even better than the first one.

We stop to breathe, and I gotta be sure she knows what we're doing, and how stupid am I?

"Jim," I say, and her other palm covers my mouth.

"We're gonna fuck," she says. "Right now, right here."

The click as she unbuckles her safety belt and she's in front of me on her knees, knocks the crushed beer can aside. Across the 100 feet of night air to the gondola on the ocean side of the wheel, the backs of two people. Shit, all they gotta do is turn around and God-who-most-surely-doesn't-exist only knows what they'll see. She gets my cowboy belt unbuckled, and *Jim, coughing, lame-ass wool blanket around him*.

She zips down my fly, and what kind of trouble we getting into? Jaded doesn't care, her hand down my shorts, and if I did care, I don't any more.

Anything to forget.

I unbuckle the safety belt, and I lift my ass and I get my jeans and shorts down off my ass and out from under me, down past my thighs to my ankles and her cold hands, her fingers on my ass, and my hard-on curving up, and is that her Delilah smile? Screams of delight and terror from atop the Great Dipper, and the creepy "Phantom of the Opera" organ music, crude laughter of those boozed-up sea shanty jerks, and my ass cold against the cold hard bench.

Jaded's impatient. She stands and she's frantic unzipping those black boots, gets them off, pulls her panties down, and steps out of them. She doesn't waste a second, hands on her black skirt, bunches of it in her fingers, pulls it up and she's straddling me, her ass cold on my thighs. The light glints off her ring, the Jade ring, *Jim's face, lame-ass wool blanket.*

Her hand on my cock again and the soft of her pussy hair against it, and I'm an animal, I want what I want, and I push up and I'm in her. *Elise walks slow up the aisle, her hand holds her trenchcoat closed,* and I look right through her into Jaded's face, and the hunger in Jaded's lips and her hands under my t-shirt, her nails scratch into me.

"You better not be thinking about that lesbo."

Anything to forget.

She yanks at my t-shirt, pulls it up, and her getting it over my face, my glasses caught, and the t-shirt and glasses land on the gondola floor. Without my glasses everything a soft blur.

Up high above the earth, the dark night around us, my arms, my chest, my legs, the blurred lights from the Giant Dipper. So naked, so exposed and Jaded's not exposed at all. She rubs her tits through her t-shirt against my bare chest. She's rocking on me, attacking me with her mouth, and I get my hand under her t-shirt, and I feel her tit.

"Tear me apart," she says. "Tear me down."

The rush of the wanting, a horny current charging my body, and she pulls her t-shirt above her tits so it bunches between us. She arches back, pushes her tits up in my face, another burlesque show shake, pushes a nipple hard into my mouth.

"Don't fuck me like a gentleman, Michael," she says. "Make me feel your teeth."

Her nails dig into my ass cheeks. "You fucking do what I tell you," she says.

I bite into her and she twists, pulling her tit hard against my teeth.

"Harder," she says, "Fucking harder!," and the salt-warm poison of her blood.

The Ferris wheel comes alive again, jerks us, the gondola

swinging back and forth as it goes up, and it swings forward and I push into Jaded, and it swings back and she comes down hard around me, and we're at 11 o'clock and Jaded has her hands still on my ass, pulling me into her and rocking on me, and the insects inside my head, goddamn Jim, goddamn goddamn Elise.

"You wanted me," Jaded says. "Since the first day. I saw your desperation."

In desperation lies defeat.

Her hands still on my ass, razorblade nails, pulling me into her.

"You need it," she says. "You can't help yourself. Tell me!"

I let her tit slip from my mouth.

"Yeah," I say. "*Fuck* yeah."

The gondola swinging back and forth, rising to 12 o'clock, sittin' on top of the world, the soot of the creepy organ music falling on us. Jaded rocking, lifting herself up and down so I'm in her, out a little, in her again. A burning I always feel before I come, her pussy relentless, up down up down. I want her to stop so I can dig on what it is to be inside her, but she's not stopping, her teeth tear my lip, the horny current arcing bright, my blood and hers salty wet on my lips, and in that moment I'm free, free of every goddamn goddamn thing.

Her eyes are closed and her face sweaty, how a chick's face gets, how the skin is different, a luminous pink, and something else, you know what I mean, and she shivers. She jams down hard, her choked cry, her tits against my chest, her whole body a spasm, a jolt of orgasmic electric.

As soon as she's finished she gets her hand down there around the base of my cock and she lifts herself, pulls it out. It's still hard, but she's *done*. She doesn't play with it, doesn't give me a hand job, nothing. She's off me, picks up my t-shirt and wipes her hands with it careful to get the sperm off her. She rubs between her legs with the shirt and drops it back to the floor. Her hand against the metal cage to keep her balance as the gondola swings. So weird, how fast she ends it. Not that I've fucked that many chicks, but the ones I did fuck, even Harper, it's never been like that.

The gondola drops to 2 o'clock. Jaded pulls her panties on, lets go of the gondola and she's off-balance, as if she's on the deck of a boat. She regains her footing, tries to smooth her t-shirt and her skirt but that's hopeless.

The fucking rush, man, the fast beat of my heart, yeah I never fucked same as that before, never known that kinda danger.

I find my glasses, get 'em on, and get my internal balance back. Sperm is slimy weird stuff, it'll seep right through jeans, and I don't want a wet sperm spot near my crotch. I get out a handkerchief, jerk a few more drops out. Still sitting, pull my shorts and jeans on as the gondola drops to 4 o'clock.

"I guess you like me," I say.

It's supposed to be a joke.

"No," she says. "Not really."

I look at her, but she's ignoring me same as how she treated the Ferris Wheel guy. Fuck. My shirt's damp but I pull it on anyway. Jaded looks how a chick looks who's rushed to get her clothes on, black hair tangle in need of a brushing, red lipstick smeared, cheeks flushed pink.

"You and Jim?" I say.

"What *about* us?" and she takes a slug, passes me the bottle.

"You need this," she says.

I drink some, burning the guilt into me.

"Are you two breaking up?"

"Why would we do that?"

"I thought, I mean, what if he—?"

She gets her purse off the floor, and sits on the opposite bench. Gets out a compact, a piece of tissue paper, lipstick, and gets to work.

"You got me drunk."

She carefully applies the lipstick.

"Raped me."

The scratches on my chest from her nails sting, and my lip hurts.

"Like what you did to Elise," she says.

She drops the lipstick into her purse and brushes her hair, and except for the wrinkled clothes looks herself again.

"I didn't do *anything* to Elise."

"Really?" she says. "I guess Kate made that up."

She picks up her black jacket.

"Maybe I should ask Elise, just to be sure Kate was lying." My voice quiet. *"That's not what happened."*

Jaded buttons her jacket, no trouble getting the buttons through the holes now.

"Everyone remembers the past different," she says.

The gondola comes to a stop at ground level. The empty booze bottle is on the floor, and I hope the Ferris wheel guy doesn't find it 'til we're long gone. He looks through the wire cage at Jaded. I see his eyes check her out, and he looks at me, and he *knows*.

"We're in a hurry," Jaded says. "Unlock this thing."

"Sure miss," and he's opening the door when Jaded pushes it hard and she's out of the gondola rushing past him and I'm right behind. The Ferris wheel guy calls after her, "Tuesday thru Saturday, 4 'til midnight. Rides on me anytime, miss."

We're partway down the boardwalk when I hear the Ferris wheel kick into action. I turn to look up, the gondolas swaying, clouds extinguishing the moonlight. Huge-ass wheel in the sky, 'round and 'round it goes, never getting anywhere, and atop the gondola that's at 12 o'clock, two black birds. I run to catch Jaded, get to where I'm beside her.

"So how does it feel, Mr. Eagle Scout? Cheat on your best friend. You and Jim never will be the same."

Jaded turns into the Arts College lot, and we see him pacing the asphalt. He's got that plaid blanket wrapped around him, his bird's nest crazy outta control, and when he looks up toward the car I don't know if it's panic or anger or both. For sure *I'm* a panic. What have I done, and how's this goin' down?

"What the hell we gonna tell him, Jade?"

Oh she's cool, has her Valentine's Day smile in place as she looks in his direction.

"Keep it together, Writerman. Let me handle this."

We get out and Jim says, "How'd you like the damn movie?"

On the pavement where he's pacing, gotta be more than a dozen butts. He's more of a mess than the first day I saw him. He's gained back whatever pounds he lost, and his face puffy.

Jaded's voice has the tragic breathless sound.

"We were at the health center, Jim," her hand on her stomach. "Cramps so bad I thought I'd die."

I guess it wasn't until she said the first lie that I got it. This is the real deal. I *fucked* my best freakster bro's chick, and those men with the steel hammers goin' crazy.

"They started in so bad I nearly fainted," Jaded says.

He looks at her, looks for a sign, looks at me.

"What happened to you, old sport? Cut your lip?"

This is what adulterers do in the aftermath. They lie. They make up a story. And they hate themselves.

"Michael took me to emergency. He was a real Boy Scout."

Jim giving me the dotted-lines eyes, and I freak 'cause I can feel some dampness where my dick touches my thigh, and is there a damp spot on my jeans?

"So let me get this straight," Jim says. "You've been at the health center all this time?"

"That emergency room was ridiculous crowded, man," I say, and lick my lip. "Must have bit it during dinner."

He has the quizzical goin', trying to figure it out.

"Funny, I didn't notice a swollen lip when you stopped by the room."

"Oh Jim," Jaded says, and she's in his arms, gives him a kiss with plenty of tongue.

"It was awful in that waiting room, Jim," she says when they break for air.

He's still holding her, but something's not right, his whole body a clench.

"You two been drinking?"

He's looking at her, and oh fuck, there is a dark spot on my jeans.

"No," she says. "Haven't had a drink all day."

"Whiskey?"

"Don't be ridiculous, Jim," and yeah, this is what adulterers do. I pull at my t-shirt, but it's not long enough.

"Listen to your girlfriend, Jim," I say. "Your nose is fucked up from being sick."

You know how even when your senses tell you one thing, if the people you know and trust tell you something else you can doubt your own empirical experience, and when it's your chick, *especially* if it's your chick, and you have the wanting as strong as Jim has it, well he leaps, man, leaps the leap of faith.

Jaded gets a bottle of pills from her purse.

"They gave me Midol," she says. "I need to lie down."

I let my arm hang so my hand obscures the spot.

"How's your cold, Jim?"

He gives me his beatific Dean Moriarty grin, and that's when I know he's let it go. He can't believe she'd lie, can't believe his best freakster bro would bullshit him. Yeah, Jim's gotta believe, otherwise his whole world blown to pieces.

"It's amazing," he says. "The curative power of ganja."

He's got his arm around her, and she's saying how she missed him so, and my sperm still dripping into her panties. They walk across the parking lot same as I'm not there. I let them get ahead of me, and when they're a ways off I follow, keep my pace slow, and inside me I hear that scratchy Skippy James record.

Spectral steel string guitar and James' spooky voice, and by the time I get to the quad, Jim and Jaded are halfway across it.

The woman that I love, I stole her from my best friend, But you know he done got lucky, An he done got her back, again.

Nothing lucky about it. Fucking cunt. But I'm no better, maybe worse. Betrayed my best freakster bro in the whole wide world for a quick fuck, and I'm part of whatever sick thing Jaded is doing to Jim. Look down at my jeans and see the stain.

5. PERSONALITY CRISIS

WHAT GONE DOWN AT the top of the Golden Dragon didn't make me forget Elise other than in the momentary flash of orgasm. All the pain came rushing back, and I was a ruin those next couple months. As bad in its own way was the taut wire between me and Jim. He didn't know why but something had changed. Every time we were together the crew with the steel hammers were in my head goin' at it.

When spring break came I was so glad to load up the TR4 and head home, but what I found there was the same old bummerosity of my parents and their goddamn gray house. It was way worse than Christmas vacation 'cause there was nothing I could look forward to, you know, when I returned to The University. Not a fucking thing. I don't know why, but I waited 'til the last day to stop by The Pad on my way to The University, and yeah, of course I brought an extra large.

That day it was all wrong soon as I got to The Pad. The buzzer still didn't work, of course it didn't, and as I opened the screen door I heard laughter, high hard laughter, and it was in the ghost wind, everywhere and nowhere. Doom and Gloom laughing at me. From inside, James Brown cranked loud and as I knocked on the door I saw another chunk of veneer had come off. Everything falling apart, and where's the upside in being a rock critic? Sausalito Cowboy in all the groovy rock mags but he doesn't even have a doorbell that works, or a front door that doesn't have the veneer peeling.

The door swings in and that Wishbone face has a stoned

grin going. Sausalito Cowboy glad to see me, or more likely, glad
to see the extra large. Yeah well whatever, him welcoming me in
means I'm cool, I'm somebody 'cause of knowing him.

Which of course is ridiculous. I mean the truth of it, it
doesn't make me somebody. And more. 'Cause what he sees
right then is the *pizza boy*, and authentic real, I had to know it.

He looks at me from under the black Stetson, and he fills
even more of that doorway. Nothing stays the same. Beyond
him, Buckaroo drowsy Southern half asleep slouched back deep
into the couch reading the new issue of *Creem*, got faded wide-
wales and a plaid flannel shirt, sipping from a can of Bud.

Well it's not Sausalito Cowboy or Buckaroo I focus on. No
man, 'cause they have a guest, and fuck, it's "Rocket Reducer"
Harsh, the editor of *Creem*. He's this high-energy cat standing
behind Sausalito Cowboy near the wall of books. Well he
doesn't exactly stand 'cause if there's a line that separates
standing and dancing, he walks the line. A 5-foot-4-or-so
skinny-ass guy, Gregg Allman hair parted in the middle hanging
down past his chest, only it's dirty brown not blonde, dead-
serious expression pimpled-out face with a narrow chin.

He's wearing an oversize denim jacket over a black and
white MC5 t-shirt, singer Rob Tyner's Afro-topped mug on it,
the glow of a cigarette down by his thigh. Most of his weight's
on one leg, his other leg a little bent, scuffed-out black and
white Converse sneakers, whole body groovin' to "Papa's Got a
Brand New Bag," and his voice loud and certain.

"Grand Funk rocks it!"

Grand Funk? In the spring of '73 woulda been hard to find
another band lame as them. Well I mean that band America is
ass-backward and Black Oak Arkansas suck big time. Still. Take
a football jock, give him down-to-his-ass hair, a bunch of shit
songs and two beer-guzzling losers on bass and drums and
you've got Grand Funk.

This guy is Rocket Reducer for sure, and not only 'cause I've
seen a photo of him in an article he wrote for the *Voice*, "Yes,
It's True, Me and My Five Rock Critic Friends Tell America
What to Listen To," but because it's *so* Rocket Reducer, always

defending meat-and-potatoes working-stiffs rock even if it's not any good. For Rocket Reducer ideology *always* trumps everything—even the music.

"You're just in time, Writerman," Sausalito Cowboy says.

That day nothing I see in The Pad looks groovy. It all has a layer of downerosity, and exhibit one is Sausalito Cowboy. The black Stetson is dustier and more sweat grime, and he's collected a whole new batch of stains on the leather vest. And I hear the words Jim said to me in the quad first day we met: *Rock critics are parasites living on the backs of the musicians. Sucking their blood and writing about how it tastes.*

"Rocket's making a damn fool of himself," Sausalito Cowboy says. "Hyping Grand Funk, the most tone-deaf band since Blue Cheer."

It was a whole different scene at The Pad that day, the three of them over-the-top blitzed on beer and weed, and the first thing I noticed was their attitude. You know how guys are when they're together without any chicks? Teasing each other, talking about cars and sports and which chick in *Penthouse* they wanna screw.

Yeah that was the vibe.

I guess that was always the vibe, Sausalito Cowboy and Buckaroo being a couple stoned bachelor types, only I ignored it, me just glad to be in the same room with real rock critics. They might as well been gods, how I thought about 'em. Well, I can't ignore it anymore. The high hard laughter, it's in the walls, or maybe the ghost wind blows it through the pad, and I'm not one of them. Gods? What the hellfuck was I thinking.

Rocket's body synced to JB's funky beat, a hard half spin where he loses control of his feet and nearly falls into the Thorens' throne, and you *know* how Sausalito Cowboy feels about the Thorens. Fuck, man, might as well be the Golden Calf how he bows down. So of course he's in Rocket's face, gives him the stern *no one fucks with the Thorens* rap. Rocket does a mealy-mouth *yeah, yeah, sure,* and then he's back on his Grand Funk trip. He's got an advance promo of the upcoming Grand

Funk record, *We're an American Band,* and he makes sure we all know it's produced by Todd Rundgren. Boy does he want Sausalito Cowboy to play it.

"Please, Rocket," Sausalito Cowboy says. "Have a little respect. We're listening to James Brown, Mr. Please Please Please himself, the Godfather of Soul. Our savior."

What happened next, I still can't believe it gone down. Sausalito Cowboy is off in the kitchen when Rocket attempts some full-bore James Brown spin, total loses it, and one hand hits the Thorens' throne as he falls to the floor. Goddamn goddamn, never heard anything so ugly as the ugly-ass sound of the needle cutting a new groove across "Papa's Got a Brand New Bag."

There was a pain-sick howl from the kitchen, woulda thought a horse been shot, and right quick Sausalito Cowboy standing over Rocket, those two yelling at each other, and that was crazy. I didn't know what to think, I mean these guys were the top of the rock, you know, in the rock writin' world, and here's Sausalito Cowboy going on how the *Thorens is sacred* and *my James Brown record is fucked.*

Rocket knows he hellfuck blown it, but trying desperate to downplay the whole deal. That's not cutting it so finally, as if he's Rocket's mom giving him a time-out on the stairs, Sausalito Cowboy says, "Go sit on the couch Rocket. Long as you're in The Pad I don't want you anywhere near the Thorens."

I didn't think Sausalito Cowboy was ever gonna recover. He takes the James Brown record off the turntable and he's gonna have a stroke 'cause of the bad scratch cutting across the whole disc, and when he tries playing it, every 1.8 seconds, you know, each complete revolution, there's a loud pop. Rocket has to swear he'll get him a mint replacement copy before Sausalito Cowboy can get close to cooling out.

Eventual Sausalito Cowboy puts on a different James Brown record and goes back into the kitchen, and Rocket tries to act same as nothing unusual gone down, but he's talking too much, using too many words, saying 'em too fast.

"You understand," he says. "Right, Buckaroo? Grand Funk

down with the people, in tune with the vibe of the common folk. Right, man? Right?"

Sausalito Cowboy is back with paper plates and paper towels, takes a seat near the Thorens' throne, takes a slug of his Corona. He looks over at the Thorens, I guess to make sure it hasn't died.

"Hey, Rocket," he says. "You still screwing that Cynthia chick?"

Seeing those guys so out-of-control loaded, and Sausalito Cowboy bossing Rocket how he did, already they'd lost their glow, but what nailed it was Sausalito Cowboy talkin' crude about Rocket's girlfriend. That wasn't any way to talk about a chick, *any* chick. He coulda been asking Rocket if he still smoked cigars after dinner.

Pretty much anywhere a person goes, there's guys of a certain age who never got the underlying point of the libber trip, you know, that each chick is a unique human, and same as a freakster bro is more than a cock, a chick is more than a pussy and a pair of tits. Those three there at The Pad, five, six, maybe seven years older than me, they were those kinda guys. Even with John and Yoko putting "Woman Is the Nigger of the World" on *Some Time in New York,* they didn't get it.

"How does Cynthia deal?" Sausalito Cowboy says. "I can't see *her* getting down with Grand Funk."

"I'm the only guy I want her getting down with," Rocket says.

"You mean goin' down *on,*" Sausalito Cowboy says, and him and Buckaroo share a laugh. I don't dig it, and that awkward I-don't-wanna-be-here deal, only worse. It was the awkward and the anger and the embarrassed of when some guy says nigger, or spic or kike.

"Fuck you, Cowboy," Rocket says. "In June it'll be six months."

Sausalito Cowboy snaps his fingers as the finale to "Prisoner of Love" builds.

"You *care* about a chick?" he says. "Rocket, what's got into you? Your motto was always 'fuck 'em and leave 'em.'"

The four of us sit around eating pizza and drinkin' beer, Rocket making his case, telling us "the kids are hip to Grand Funk," and Grand Funk make "the music of democracy," and Buckaroo in solid agreement. Things woulda probably been OK if they stuck to music talk, but they didn't, and this time I'm the one the Sausalito Cowboy teases, telling Rocket he knows what I'm really doing at The University.

"It's all that teenage pussy," he says, and the laughter, only now it's all of them. "Moony-eyed Joni Mitchell fans living up on the hill trying to find themselves. The University has the sweetest poontang in the country. Right Writerman?"

I should tell him to fuck off. Only I'm silent and I hate myself for not speaking up.

"They must all be on the pill," Buckaroo says. "Oh to be a sophomore again."

I try to defend myself, tell them it isn't about chicks, I'm trying to learn something about film and photography and writing, and I dig the intellectual scene on campus, but that has 'em laughing harder.

"Of course you do," Sausalito Cowboy says. "Everyone knows the brainier the chick, the tighter the pussy."

For some reason that got Rocket going on about the time he interviewed Jimmy Page, and all Page talked about was screwing groupies. Rocket trying for a cockney accent.

"Them plebby tarts play the pink oboe *fab*, mate."

"Didn't you tell me Page likes to pull his dick out before he comes," Sausalito Cowboy says. "So he can 'give her the frigging pearl necklace.'"

Sausalito Cowboy doesn't sound anything same as a British rock star, but Rocket's got it down.

"'Give her the frigging pearl necklace, matey.' Page was in a randy mood that day. Told me, 'I lurv watching a peanut smuggler frig.'"

"Lord James Page the third," Sausalito Cowboy says. "The perfect gentleman."

Somewhere along in there, after we each ate another slice of pizza, the Sausalito Cowboy decided it was time to hip me to how rock critics don't have any status with the chicks.

"It's the sad secret truth, Writerman," Sausalito Cowboy says. "Damn little pussy."

"My ex-girlfriend thought it was far-out," I say. "Me writing about music."

"*Far-out?*" Rocket says. "The Sixties are *so* over, *man.*"

"She couldn't have thought it was that *far-out*," Sausalito Cowboy says. "'Cause she isn't your girlfriend any more."

So then they had plenty of advice about how a rock critic gets chicks. Buckaroo says, "Never tell 'em you're a rock critic," while the Sausalito Cowboy says, "Tellin' 'em you're a student works," and Rocket says, "When you get too old to pass as a student, like Sausalito Cowboy here, say you're putting the finishing touches on your *third* novel."

Buckaroo laughs when he hears that, and says, "Come up with some book title that sounds *real* intelligent."

"Like 'The Flowers Lied?'" Rocket says.

Oh man, Rocket and Buckaroo get a good laugh outta that one, and you know how when you been all tensed, grinding your teeth, holding your anger and upset and frustration, and someone tells a joke. Yeah, you got it, and I'm laughing with them, and it's contagious, harder I laugh, harder they laugh, harder they laugh, harder I laugh, and Sausalito Cowboy hellfuck pissed. Finally we can't laugh any more, Rocket has a coughing jag, Buckaroo takes a drink of his Corona, and I do my best to catch my breath.

"Sure, laugh," Sausalito Cowboy says, "but 'The Flowers Lied' is a great title."

One moment I'm laughing so hard but then I get total serious deal 'cause I remember *why* he called it "The Flowers Lied." It was when I'd hung at the pad during Christmas break and he told me what his book is about, and put down the whole Sixties trip, said it was nothing but a utopian pipe dream.

"You're wrong, man," I say. "That's why you can't finish your book. It's not the truth. Doesn't matter who paid the bills. That shit *happened*. The Freak Scene Dream. People living out those ideals. That peace mattered, and love was the answer, and life was a work of art. Everyone laid back digging the scene. It was a new way to live."

"It wasn't sustainable," Sausalito Cowboy says. "And there was a dark side. Chicks raped. ODs. Manson."

"We got a glimpse," I say.

And there's this feeling I get, I mean Sausalito Cowboy was maybe 20 when it all gone down, and now he's so fucked-up cynical. How can that be? I don't want to be cynical same as him or Buckaroo or Rocket Reducer. Not about the shit that matters. Never. And they're not so cool as they think they are, or how I thought they were, before what gone down. So fucking cynical, but there was a time when Sausalito Cowboy felt different, and how I know it, well what he says next, his voice is different, a sadness underlying the words, contradicting them, a sadness for what might have been, and remorse about the trip falling to pieces.

"The door got slammed shut, Writerman," he says. "Don't be a sap."

I want the New Trip to happen so fucking bad. I need to believe people can live for more than making a buck, that art matters, can trump everything, and we really can love one another. The high hard laughter stops, the ghost wind dies down, and I look from one to the other, and when I get to Sausalito Cowboy, I give him the cold eye.

"Not in my world, man," I say.

And that's when the UPS guy delivered the promos, including a box of *New York Dolls* albums—five copies.

"Holy fuck," Sausalito Cowboy says. "*This* is what Christgau's raving about? *This* is supposed to be the best album since *Exile*? These drag queens?"

"Paul signed them to Mercury," Buckaroo says. "And Ellen's a big fan. She's writing about them in her *New Yorker* column."

"It must be the smart shit," Sausalito Cowboy says.

Makes me feel cool, knowing "Ellen" is *New Yorker* critic Ellen Willis and "Paul" is former rock critic/current Mercury Records A&R man Paul Nelson.

The four of us check out the cover, I mean you seen it, right? It's a black and white of the band sitting on a couch, dressed up as ugly chicks, ugliest chicks you ever seen, uglier even than Jim in the gold lamé dress and the blond Marilyn wig. John Wayne in a dress or tight pedal pushers, and overdone lipstick and huge fucking platform boots. And the hair. Big-ass hair. Dusty Springfield hair, Ronnie Spector hair. Fuck, it was the mutant love child of the Stones and the Shangri-Las sitting on that couch.

"You'll love this, Rocket," Sausalito Cowboy says. "Produced by Todd Rundgren. I guess he swings AC *and* DC. In Studio A, the macho men of Grand Funk, and in Studio B, the drag queens. What kinda men call themselves 'dolls'?"

Me and Rocket and Buckaroo stood back from the Thorens as Sausalito Cowboy cranked the volume, and we could hear the static of the needle tracking the groove. Yeah, *that* loud. We were ready, but it doesn't matter, no way to be ready. There in The Pad inside a tsunami of broken bottle fuzz guitar, a furious Chuck Berry groove. It was immediate, total blew me into the stratosphere, a primitive groove more devolved than either The Stooges or the MC5, but when I check the react from the others, oh man oh man oh man.

Rocket's face total frownland, not his idea of something speaks to the common people, or *the kids*. Now Buckaroo didn't dig it either, but he was crafty, trying to figure out if it was the future 'cause if it was he'd have to feign digging it, nothing worse than an aging rock critic who can't relate to the New Trip.

And Sausalito Cowboy, he wanted to dig it *so bad*. If Christgau and the rest of his rock critic pals said it's the Holy Grail, well he didn't wanna be the one to trash it. Only he didn't get it either. And for the first time that day I was total groovin'. 'Cause I *knew*, man, it was the authentic real, the rock 'n' roll I'd been waiting for, and I was the only one in The Pad got ears to hear it.

The singer was yelling *yeah, yeah, yeah,* but not the pretty Beatles harmonies, this was losing your mind, a fucking *personality crisis,* and that's the name of the song but it's the *sound* of the song too, and *those crazy freaks in the nut house, and one of them is me, Sarah alone at the graduation party in the dark night sitting outside on the bench shivering, Elise's nails into my chest, Jim in the parking lot pacing.* The music of the blackest black, the crushed souls. The ghost wind laughing the high hard laughter.

This was the heavy shit.

Those three, I see 'em look at each other, and the sage nod, total and complete non-comprehension.

"What's Christgau been smokin'?" Sausalito Cowboy says.

Rocket's voice, loud and certain, only he's not talking about Grand Funk anymore.

"Future of rock 'n' roll, gentlemen," and he's laughing, and the other two join in.

Well I'd had it, and I told them they could go fuck themselves—stopped 'em cold. "What's wrong with you guys, man?" I say. "Don't you remember the first time you heard 'My Generation' or 'Mystery Train' or 'Gloria'?"

"What's wrong with *us, man!*" Rocket says.

"Shut up, Rocket," Sausalito Cowboy says, and I see the uncertainty, he knows he's losing it. How he's looking at me, I'm not the pizza boy anymore.

"I'm sick of your arrogant jive," I say. "You're goddamn parasites living off the throwaways of the music biz, holed up in here getting drunk and stoned and ego-tripping 'cause you get your names in the rock mags. Talkin' about the chicks you wanna screw as if they're blow-up dolls.

"What we just heard, man, it's Brando in 'The Wild One' and Dean in 'Rebel Without a Cause.' It's the MC5 and Iggy and the Stones in one motherfucker of a band. If anything is the smart shit, you finally heard it. Only you're deaf to anything that doesn't sound same as the past. Asleep at the Wheel? Give me a break. Well this isn't the past, man, this is the future."

I dug in my pocket, got out a fiver, laid it on the Thorens' throne and told Sausalito Cowboy it was for a copy of the Dolls album. He nodded slow and fucked-up, and with one of the five copies held tight in my hands, I split outta there. That was the last time I saw those guys, last time I went to The Pad.

6. LONELY PLANET BOYS

DRIVING ONTO THE CAMPUS I know things between me and Jim are wrong, but I don't know, or I don't wanna know, how heavy traffic serious wrong. With the Dolls album under my arm, *the smart shit*, I go to Jim's room to play him the future.

Still, the song off the Dolls album I hum is "Lonely Planet Boy," this melancholy melody so forlorn. It's been playing in my head since I split The Pad, and yeah, my unconscious gotta know. 'Cause that's who I am, the lonely planet boy, ain't got no one, and it's so lonely.

I haven't shaved, and wired from too much coffee and too many smokes on the road, and the excitement of the Dolls, the rush of what they portend, and the jolt of the wakeup, finally seeing those guys at The Pad for who they are, *total dicks*.

Get to Jim's door, knock too hard, too loud, and behind the door he can feel the too too jacked-up state I'm in. He must know it's me 'cause he takes forever. I mean what the fuck is he doing in there, and I'm about to split the scene when I hear him.

The door opens enough so Jim can see who the fuck it is, but when he sees who the fuck is me, no "Hey, what's happening, old sport," no "Glad you're back, old sport," no "Have a good vacation, old sport?"

"Yeah."

"Bad time?" I say, and the insects inside my head. "Busy? Hanging with Jade?"

There's a bare bulb behind him too too bright, his face a shadow, glow of a cigarette in his hand.

"What *about* Jade?"

Oh fuck.

Classical music playing in his room. That was fucking rich. And I never seen him so agitated.

"Still into that highbrow deal, man?"

Yeah, that highbrow deal.

I haven't told you how about a week before spring break Jaded showed up at Jim's dorm room, me and him in deep heavy traffic consideration of "Dazed and Confused," dazed and confused ourselves on a couple numbers, and she announced she was done with the *rock 'n' roll shit, all this kid stuff* and furthermore she was gonna listen to classical music forevermore, and really, it's time for all of us to put away our fucking *childish rock 'n' roll*, listen to it nevermore.

She had a pile of highbrow disks. Bach's *Goldberg Variations* and Beethoven's *Ninth Symphony* and Tchaikovsky's *The Nutcracker*. Bartók's *Eight Improvisations*, Verdi's *Rigoletto* and Mozart's *Serenade No. 13 for strings in G major*. And a half dozen or so more, and this was Jaded's New Trip, and no way could Jim fight that current, and so the deal was sealed, and if rock was lame and I still dug it, where'd that leave me?

Fuck, man, didn't Jaded remember?

Roll over Beethoven and tell Tchaikovsky the news.

That classical shit, our goddamn goddamn parents' music. Ancient history. Dead and buried. That's where I was at and I wasn't budging. Jaded and Jim could listen to their nose-in-the-air music, but not me, baby.

No fucking way.

Yeah, that highbrow deal.

Jim widens the opening, and what the fuck? *Thee* Freakster Bro had gotten a haircut. Stevie Winwood look-alike in the hair department, you know, long enough to be hip among a bunch of straights, but any freakster bro gonna laugh his ass off. Gotta be Jaded's doing. Turn Jim into a total dork before she gives him the heave-ho.

He's for sure done with the lipstick and nail polish, and face-to-face right then I'm glad I gave it up too.

Some of the hall light on his face, his forehead a clench, and it's the freeze out. I'm not certain about the why of it, oh come on *man,* fuck the bullshit, 'cause I know. For sure this is about Jaded, and how much does Jim know? Is he only suspicious, or did she come clean?

"What *about* Jade, old sport?"

Another few inches of the door opens, but he's blocking the way, doesn't move, smoke rings curl up from his mouth.

"Nothing, man," I say. "Just didn't know if this was a good time."

The insects biting. "You know, me stopping by."

Jim stretches out the burned rubber of the word *alone* and gives it a loony twist. "Jade's getting some '*a-looone* time,'" as if it's this big theater-of-the-absurd joke, "or rather," focus of his eyes tight on me, "to be perfectly clear about it," scanning my face for clues, "so there's no confusion," the insects eating me alive, "Jade is getting some 'away from *Jim* time.'"

So goddamn awkward, and I'm sweating man, feel it on my chest, and my hands, and is he gonna invite me in, or am I gonna have better things to do?

"Chicks are weird," I say. "They wanna be with you every second, but when—," and he cuts me off, his voice cold as his cold eye eyes.

"What do *you* know about chicks," he says. "Mr. all-I-can-think-about-is-how-I-*betrayed*-my-high-school-girlfriend. You got laid once this year and you have the big advice for me about chicks."

He has no fucking right, throw that at me, and I don't care what he does or doesn't know about me and his fucking chick.

"Jim, man," I say. "Major bummerosity. I'm splitting outta here."

That's when he swings his door open, and he's wearing a shiny black shirt and those black velveteen pants, raises his black-sleeved right arm and brings his hand down and out into the room, the glow of the cigarette leads it, waving me in with an imperial gesture. Yeah, and his face—the mustache and beard demonic—impassive as the cold, calm freeze-out of his voice, and the way he looks at me, same as Sarah, same as Bobby, same as Elise. Jim's lost faith in me too. I might as well be some second-story man, total cheap-ass hood or worse, a deadbeat freakster bro. And a deadbeat freakster bro isn't a freakster bro at all.

"Your shit about chicks," Jim says. "Keep it to yourself, *old sport.*"

Cigarette he's smoking, it's a Sherman.

"It's not wanted," he says.

"What do you want, anyway?" he says.

The Dolls' album, forgot about it, Jim so weird-ass weird, but his question wakes me the fuck up.

"You gotta hear this," I say. "It's the smart shit for sure."

I step across the threshold, my words a loud fast rush.

"Christgau's giving it an A+," I say. "That's what Rocket Reducer told me, and it was cool, man, I got to hang—"

Jim, 6 feet and 180 pounds of determined disinterest, walks to his desk, another drag of his Sherman, sucks my enthusiasm from the room.

"I don't read *Creem* anymore," he says. "It's, hmmm," and his fist to his chin, mocks "The Thinker," mocks me. "Teenage."

I sit on the edge of Jim's bed, maybe five feet from where he sits in the orange Eames, the chair Jaded got him for Christmas, and that's when I see his Rolling Stones poster, the one with the huge red tongue logo, rolled up on the floor next to some copies of the *New Yorker*, the goddamn goddamn *New Yorker*.

I look to the wall where he used to have the Stones poster and there's a shiny new Mozart poster. That's *fucking* rich. There's a mess of highbrow books—about classical music, opera, the Impressionists, Beethoven, and one about Matisse—piled on the desk. As if he can change who he is by trading out posters and records and books.

That dead asshole on the wall breathing down my back.

"As I was saying," I say. "I hung with Sausalito Cowboy yesterday," and I was gonna tell him what gone down, the way close friends confide in one another, the whole deal, what dicks they were, sexist and full of themselves and all the rest, only Jim is being too much of a dick himself.

"Aren't you the lucky boy," he says.

Well what I understood, finally, Jim wasn't my friend, not anymore, so I changed my mind, wasn't gonna tell him the authentic real, no man, instead I'd use knowing those big time rock critics to impress him and make my case for the Dolls album.

"Dig this, man," I say. "Sausalito Cowboy told me Ellen Willis is writing her column on the Dolls. So you'll get to read about them in your new favorite magazine."

Jim's cane is leaning against the desk, and the light from that bare bulb glints off the lion's head. His cigarette smolders in the heavy glass ashtray and he flips through this mess of albums leaning against his desk.

"I was listening to this earlier, old sport. I thought of you," gets the record out of the sleeve, and that's when I see the photo, there on his desk in a silver frame, the photo I took in the dining hall so long ago.

Jaded.

Took it the first day me and Jim met her. God she looked beautiful that day. So bright and, well, not innocent, Jaded never looked innocent, but shiny, same as the black shirt Jim has on. I guess me and Jim were both blinded by the light.

The high contrast of the print makes her skin so white, but what's a trip are Jaded's eyes. I caught the wildness, and the danger, only when I took it I only saw the upside of the danger. Now I see the downside. You know, kinda chick betray her boyfriend, fuck his best freakster bro.

Jim has the album on the turntable, and there's a smirk he's doing his best to contain and something about him, the smirk, yeah he's pulling a fast one on me, gotta be what's going on.

"It's a Beethoven composition."

"You're sounding so sophisticated," and I try for a stilted British accent, my version of Rocket's Jimmy Page. "It's a *Beethoven* composition, recorded by the London Philharmonic with Leonard Motherfucker Bernstein conducting."

"You'll never grow up," Jim says.

"Sure hope the fuck not."

The music begins, just piano, and it surprises me, it's the shimmering stars in Van Gogh's "Starry Night." *Thee* Freakster Bro stands by his desk, and I sit on his bed, and we listen. Three minutes it plays, maybe a few seconds more, and that shimmering stars sound makes my heart beat fast.

He has the self-satisfied smile of The Joker, you know, when he one-ups Batman.

"Thought you'd dig it, old sport," Jim says, and for a beat, a long beat, he's silent.

And the smirk, the smirk I've seen on Liquor Store's face, and that chick Rhonda, yeah that's the one.

"It's called 'Für Elise,'" he says.

"You motherfucker," I say.

"Oh, I guess I forgot," he says. "You and *that girl* had a falling out."

I have an unlit Pall Mall between my fingers, and I don't know why I don't get the fuck out of there. The photo of Jaded on the desk, and I flash on me and her in the gondola, want to tell Jim his chick took me where he's too scared to go, *and we fucked Jim, and her blood in my mouth, my cum in her cunt.*

"You got a light," I say.

"Actually," Jim says. "I do have a light," and he opens the top drawer, gets something in his right hand. "I found this in Jade's purse, *old sport.*"

He holds The Dylan, turns it so the light of the bare bulb reflects off it, and the light, bright as the bright bright sun, in my left eye. Squeeze my eye closed, blurry rings of light pulse. Fuck, get my hand up between the light and my eye.

"Stop that shit, man," the light jabs my right eye. I move my head, the pulsing afterimage. Jim a big hulking shape through the light rings.

"Now how exactly did The Dylan end up in my girl's purse?"

The reflection stabs my left eye again.

"You know," I say, "at the health center."

To me I don't sound so certain; to him I don't sound so certain either.

"Oh, the health center," he says. "I see," and a moment of silence deep and scary. "Your precious lighter. *The Dylan*. In Jade's purse."

He uses The Dylan to light another Sherman, serious inhale, and the light jabs me again.

"Fuck, Jim. Yeah, the health center. In the emergency waiting room. She had cramps."

"That's your story?"

Everyone remembers the past different. What about a past that doesn't exist?

"She stepped outside for a smoke, man," and I can't escape the goddamn light. "What's with the third degree?"

"It's more than disturbing," he says. "Your *precious* lighter in my girl's purse."

The insects biting the inside of my skull, the pulsing blur of my vision.

"Yeah, the health center, man," I say.

His fist closes around the Dylan.

"The *fucking* health center," and he throws it at me hard how he'd throw a hardball, and it hits my sternum hard as hard can be, but the hurt I feel, it's not from The Dylan.

Ghost of 'lectricity. I'm in Elise's room, on her bed, and she kicks The Dylan away, tells me to get out, *I hope this hurts, like the torment you've put me through.*

There in Jim's room, palms against my forehead, her voice, *the torment, the torment, the torment.* I shake my head, the crushed souls, gotta make it stop, *like the torment you've put me through.* The nail gun pummeling the inside of my head, the insects chewing me up, and I yell, "Fucking stop it, goddamn you." The nail gun and the insects and Elise's voice, again and again. "Goddamn you, Elise. Leave me be."

There's a silence in Jim's room, the silence of the undertow after it's pulled you under, and he's looking at me how a sane person looks at a crazy person.

"It's nothing, man," I say. "My head. Bad headache."

His anger is gone in the moment of that moment, replaced by fear, more than fear, he's horrified by what he saw on my face, and the sound of my voice, and whatever ghost wind blows through his room. And concern, yeah I guess I broke through to the place where he still considers me his friend.

"I'm going to smoke a doobie," he says. "You in?"

I raise my head slowmo jaw out, and lower it, a stoned nod though I'm not stoned. Not yet. The Dylan in my hand, in my left palm, covering the true love scar, the smooth silver finish, rub my fingers on the back of it, and what's that, a rough spot? Fuck, must have got scratched in her purse. Turn it over, and that's when I see a check mark. Jaded scratched a check mark on my lighter.

"You all right, old sport," Jim says. "You're looking a tad green."

I shove the Dylan into my jeans pocket. I oughta take it out to the beach to throw into the Forever Infinite Pacific. It's not silver anymore, it's stained black. The black of crushed souls, my very own bad luck charm.

He sits at his desk, his back to me, using the lid from a boxed set of *La Bohème*, yeah, and if I wasn't freaked it would crack me up, and rolls a fat one. Gets turned to face me. We pass the number from him to me and back again, smoke in silence, and soon I feel the soft gauze insulating me from everything.

"Jade's teaching me about these classical artists," he says. "Brahms and Verde and a bunch of others. Compared to rock, one could say it's the difference between addition and calculus."

"I thought you said Jade was taking a break from you?" and I look at him, you know, dotted-lines eyes deal, see if we got any kinda understanding, only he doesn't connect.

"Just for today," Jim says.

"Just today, man?"

"Well, a couple days, the rest of the week," he says, and he's embarrassed his chick needs a break. "Yeah, you know, absence —."

Yeah sure.

"So hand it over, let's give it a listen," he says. "This *Dolls* record you're so excited for me to hear."

"The vibe's not right," I say.

"The 'vibe' is *perfect*, old sport," he says. "Great time to check out your new favorite teen idols."

I look to that photo of Jaded again, *she's on me, her teeth into my lip*.

"You wanna look at Jade?" he says, picks up the frame, walks over until he's close to where I sit, too close, less than an arm's length away.

"Here," he says. "Take it, get a closer look."

I don't do anything, let him hold it between us.

"You can tell an awful lot," he says, "about the photographer from the photo."

I thought I was so smart playing so fucking dumb.

"What do you mean?" but I know what he means. Still he holds it out, but no way.

"This photo," he says, "is the blueprint for how you see Jade."

I move back on the bed, get my back against the wall.

"Just a photo, man."

"Yeah," he says. "The student health center," and he has the frame in both hands, turns it and brings it in close to his stomach and he's looking at it, at her face, at her crazy-wild eyes, takes a breath and I hear the lonesome in that breath.

And he's all bluster.

"Jade and I are getting a place together," he says, and walks back to his desk, sets the frame down. "Off campus. I'm sure Jade will want to have you over. We both will."

Jim lookin' right at me, and I try to avoid his eyes, and brief-like there isn't a sound in his room other than pounding blood loud and the too-fast-beat of my heart.

He sits in the orange Eames, still lookin' at me same as he's searchin' for clues.

"So let's give it a listen, old sport. Time's a-wasting."

I bring over the Dolls album, hand it to him. He checks the cover for the first time, sees those guys dressed as transsexuals.

"It's funny," he says. "A few months ago this kind of thing seemed so radical."

"So what's with the haircut, Jim?" I say. "Thinking about an MBA? Cut it a little shorter and you can work at one of those investment companies, Morgan Stanley or Fidelity or some shit. That's a *real* 'mature' thing to do. Ask my dad."

"You don't get it," he says. "That rebel-without-a-cause stance is so tired. Grown men dressing this way."

"I swear, man, future of rock," and then I figure I'll really piss him off. "You shoulda seen Rocket Reducer raving on and on about it."

"Rocket Reducer can shove it," he says. "I'm tired of hearing about your *groovy cool* rock critic friends. Sounds like a kids' TV show. Sausalito Cowboy and his sidekick Buckaroo and their robot friend Rocket Reducer. You're their little pet. 'Oh Sausalito Cowboy, tell me what to like.'"

How's it come to this?

"I'm outta here," I say. "Jade's brainwashed you."

"No, I'm putting this on," he says. "Let's see what the Dolls got to give."

He sleeves Beethoven, gets the Dolls on his turntable, and turns it up loud. Oh man. The fuzzed-out guitar slurring into a fucked-up Chuck Berry riff and singer David Johansen lets out that wild scream and the crazy-ass "yeah yeah yeah," follows it with a "no no no no no no no," and somehow in 21 seconds the Dolls nail the essence of rock 'n' roll.

Fucked-up tear-it-down-start-all-over again.

"Personality Crisis," it's a tidal wave rawer and cruder then I remember from The Pad, a car wreck in 4/4 time and by the end of the chorus, about a minute in, Jim can't help it. Gives up trying to sit still all adult-like, and he's rockin' forward and back in his chair and his hands do the air guitar deal. Yeah, yeah, yeah, and I'm starting to see traces of the old Jim. *Thee Freakster Bro.* If I were into betting I'd wager he doesn't realize he's doing it. His head forward and back keeps the beat. Gee-whiz wow, *rock 'n' roll* smile of his, and when the Dolls come around to the chorus a second time, goddamn goddamn he's singing along.

I'm a grinning fool to see him transformed after that highbrow shit. All it's gonna take is another song or two. The old Jim Costello making a serious comeback, ready to return for good. I figure "Looking for a Kiss" is the jailbreak. When it kicks in he'll be up on his feet.

Well that's when Jim gets a look at himself in the mirror, sees his hands doing that air guitar deal and his body moving all jerky, but what else he sees is me. Jim sees me watching him. *Caught.* Thought he was so cool with all his I'm-grown-up-now jive, but this rocking Jim is the authentic real. Yeah, he knows I've seen the hypocrisy of his trip.

And what's it gonna be, come clean or live the lie? Give in to the moment and embrace the authentic real of who he is, or keep up the front? Yeah well something clicks *off,* as if Jaded shown up to spoil the party. His foot hard on the brake, pulls himself together, remembers. Reaches over, dials the volume down to quiet and for the last 30 seconds of the song pretends he's not into it.

"Oh my God," Jim says. "The *second coming.* What do you call it, oh yeah, it's the *New Trip,*" and he opens his mouth, sticks his fingers in and leans over as if he's gonna puke. "Loser junkies who don't know an E chord from a D and shriek about their emotional life and the heavens open and Zeus, or at least Ellen Willis, stands at attention."

Already "Looking for a Kiss" is playing but the volume's too low and it sounds puny. Damn Jim's hypocrisy. Jim becoming one of *them.* I feel a sadness too, same sadness I felt the last time I went to see Sarah, when she closed the door on me and I heard her cry. 'Cause this isn't about the New York Dolls.

When the fourth song—the sad sack ballad I told you about, "Lonely Planet Boy"—starts, might as well be Jim's cue.

"I've got to study," he says.

"Lonely Planet Boy." That day that song was me, and it was Jim. I didn't have no one, and he didn't either. He thought he had Jaded, and would do anything for her including betray his best freakster bro. Me betraying Jim, Jim betraying me.

He took the record off his turntable and slid it into the cover.

"Future of rock, old sport?"

"Jim, man," I say. "Don't jive me."

"Rock is over," he says. "This is the dying embers."

He takes a couple steps, gets so he's standing right front of me, holds the album out, and I reach for it and for a moment we both have it in our hands, the cardboard connection. I'm gonna take it only he doesn't let go, hangs on and pulls it hard back outta my hand, stands there looking down at me.

"Listen up, *Mike*," he says.

Jim never before called me Mike.

"Stay. Away. From. Jade.

He looks at the cover, he looks at me. Spits on it, shit-ass loogie, got his self-satisfied The Joker smile going, and he spins the cover at me, same as a Frisbee.

"Old sport."

I catch the cover, and some of his loogie on my hand, I mean it's bad enough if a person gets their own slimy-ass spit on themselves, but someone *else's* spit. I wipe my hand on his bedspread, and use the bedspread to get the rest of it off the cover. Fuck, 'cause the cardboard's damp where he spit on it.

"Great," I say. "The cover's ruined."

He drops his Sherman on the rug, fucking thing smoking, grinds it in with the sole of his shoe.

"Oh isn't that terrible," he says. "What's that they say, if you've got a lemon make lemonade? When you look at the cover it can serve as a reminder to keep away from my chick."

His eyes on the rug, on what's left of that Sherman. Tobacco, brown paper and black ash.

"You need to keep her on a shorter leash, man," I say.

Well that's when he goes for his cane, his hand on the brass lion's head.

"Your chick's got the roving eye deal."

Oh he's mad, and he has the cane in front of him, but still I keep talking.

"You know that Muddy Waters song, man?"

His other hand on the cane, and he grips it same as a Kung-Fu master grips his boh and I quote from that old blues:

Picked up the receiver, voice said, 'Another mule kickin' in your stall.'

"You heard that one?" I say.

He raises the cane so it's about six inches off the rug, lets it drop so the metal ferrule hits the rug, grips it with both hands, raises it and lets it hit the rug, and again.

"*Get out.*"

And again. That's when he gets up fast outta the orange Eames, the cane in his hands, and panic rising inside me, the hard heat, and each of those insects has a drill bit, hundreds of 'em drilling into me.

"I'm sick of it all," he says. "You and The Dylan and your rock critic friends and your Dolls album."

He takes a step toward me, the cane a hard black line in his hands, something lethal in his eyes.

"And those *stupid* boots."

Yeah well I'm off the bed, gotta get the fuck away, and I back toward the door. Oh fuck it, and I turn. Yeah, hit me with that cane, motherfucker. Open his door, I'm out in the hall, bang it shut hard and loud.

Stand there in the hall, try to calm the pounding inside me, and I hear it from inside the room, the cane hard against the door, the crack of the wood, Jim swearing. And again, as if the door gonna break apart.

And is this how I lose my best friend? The last time I hang

with Jim Costello?

Everyone in my world jumping ship or I pushed 'em.

Sarah.

Bobby.

Elise.

Sappho.

Jaded.

The guys at The Pad.

And now Jim.

As I walk away, the muffled sound of Jim inside his dorm room, *fucking snakeskin boots,* and again, the splintering wood, and goddamn goddamn again.

THE FREAK SCENE DREAM TRILOGY

For Michael Stein that day, that sad sad day when he left Jim's dorm room and slammed the door on him, seemed like the end.

But that was not how it ended.

In the third book of the Freak Scene Dream Trilogy, titled 'The Moon & The Stars,' you'll find out how it all really ends.

Along the way, you know, before the end, you'll hear about 19-year-old Michael Stein's affair with 35-year-old feminist college teacher Susan "Simone" Braveheart, his unexpected reunion with Jim Costello, and a crazy road trip to Big Sur with Simone that signals the end of their summer fling.

And you'll be there when mysterious trouble girl Harper reappears, moves in with Michael Stein at Simone's beach house and causes all kinds of, you guessed it, *trouble*.

Michael Stein is obsessed with sex. Only the sex is more than sex. Sex is the door to intimacy, and transcendence.

For Michael Stein, the Sixties ended in the nut house. Where they put the crazies. His parents blamed his erratic behavior on drugs. Michael Stein just blames himself.

Aware. Michael Stein is aware he has lived through one of the biggest social changes America has experienced. The trouble is, Michael Stein's not aware that the biggest social change has already changed, moved on down the line.

The love is gone and all that's left is the drugs.

The Freak Scene Dream Trilogy is one long deep breath. The exhale is obsessive, transgressive. How macho meets feminism. How second chakra rises up to third. Through all the women: Sarah, Elise, Jaded, Simone, Harper, Eve. A puff, a party, a tragedy—from marijuana to angel dust, teenage heartbreak to addiction, from "All You Need Is Love" to the junkie garage rock of the New York Dolls.

How the dream died and what there is left after.

If you enjoyed, The Flowers Lied, come along for more of the ride as Writerman struggles to escape his past and invent a brave new life.

"The Moon & The Stars"
by Michael Goldberg

For more information about the Freak Scene Dream Trilogy, and "The Moon & The Stars":

www.themoonandthestars-thebook.com

If you want to keep up with what I'm up to as a writer and blogger, please sign up for the Days of the Crazy-Wild Communique at:

www.daysofthecrazy-wild.com/novel/email

ACKNOWLEDGEMENTS

If you checked out the Acknowledgements page of my first novel, True Love Scars, some of this will be familiar. And some is new.

Just sayin'.

I want to thank my wonderful family: Leslie, Joe, Anne, Norah and Sammy. You're the best!

And my good friends Pearl the dog and Barky the cat.

This book could not have been written without the help of the 2008-2009 version of Dangerous Writers in Portland, OR. And a hats off to Tom Spanbauer, the most dangerous of the Dangerous Writers. Thanks for listening, Tom, and for six years of support.

Thanks to the Writer's Cafe, September 2010 – November 2013, for your comments, support and advice.

My best buddy David Monterey is one of a kind for sure. They don't make friends like you anymore, Dave.

Thanks to Jolie Holland, Emme Stone, Brittany Flynn, James Cushing and Mark Mordue — you five were the first to read the Freak Scene Dream Trilogy, and your enthusiasm was and is appreciated.

Thanks to the following, in no particular order, for media coverage and/or reviews: Jann Wenner, Nathan Brackett, Simon Vozick-Levinson and Colin Fleming at Rolling Stone, Dennis McNally, Fred Mills at Blurt, Simon Warner, Roy Trakin at Trakin Care of Business, Paul Krassner, David Browne, Greg M. Schwartz at Pop Matters, Tyler Wilcox at Doom & Gloom From The Tomb, the folks at Book Passage, Denise Sullivan, Jack Boulware and the folks at LitQuake, JC and everyone at Down Home Music, Burtis Downs and R.E.M., Barney Hoskins at Rock's Back Pages, Brian Wise and Des Cowley at Addicted To Noise, Mike Foldes at Ragazine, Wallace Blaine at the Santa Cruz Sentinel, David Wright at Sterling & Stone, Sarah Burke at the East Bay Express, Paul Liberatore at the Marin Independent Journal, Holly Hooch at Cheap Hooch Radio, Andy Phillips at Wax Atlas, Norm Honbo, Jeanne Lavin and everyone at the Marin Vegan Meetup, Bill Lamb, Chris Scofield, Brendan Halpin, Adam Strong at Kronski Confidential, Michelle Swide, Alan Zoldan, Silas Valentino, Nicole Cohen, Jen Lemons, Frank C. Tortorici, Aria Mencken, Linda Watson, Melanie Hoist, Mark Cunningham, Darcee Kraus, Bradley Hanebrink, Jason Gross at Perfect Sound Forever, Karl Erik Anderson at Expecting Rain and Gigi Little at ut omnia bene. And I want to acknowledge the late Barbara Shelley, who said she dug "True Love Scars," and told me repeatedly she couldn't wait to read this book. I reget not having it completed sooner.

Thanks to my wife Leslie Goldberg for the amazing cover drawing, Emme Stone for the cover design and Mary Eisenhart for copyediting.

Thanks to Jeff Rosen and Lacey Chemsak for being so gracious regarding the use of song lyrics.

Thanks to Direct Action Everywhere (DxE) for all that you are doing for the animals, and for changing my life. Until every animal is free!

And to Bob Dylan, the Rolling Stones, Captain Beefheart, Neil Young, Jack Kerouac, Sam Rivers, Skippy James. J.D. Salinger, Richard Meltzer, F. Scott Fitzgerald, Jean-Luc Godard, François Truffaut, Robert Frank, Diane Arbus, Andy Warhol, Picasso, Salvador Dali, and all the other musicians, visual artists, film directors and writers who have been so much more than an inspiration.

— Michael Goldberg, August 2015

ABOUT THE AUTHOR

So what do you wanna know?

When I was a kid, rock 'n' roll and literature made life worth living.

Or rather, it was literature that rocked my world—"Treasure Island," "Crime and Punishment," the Hardy Boys books, the Oz books, all those sexy 007 novels—until I turned 12, and then rock 'n' roll—The Beatles, the Stones, Dylan, The Yardbirds, John Mayall's Blues Breakers—blew my mind, with literature a strong second.

Well girls trumped both, but that's another story.

I started writing my own stories in sixth grade and by high school I was certain that writing was my vocation.

So while my friends and I promoted dance-concerts at the high school (mostly so we could project psychedelic lights behind the bands), I was also writing for the school paper. And I did have one of those "Almost Famous" moments, writing *Creem* editor Lester Bangs and getting an encouraging letter back asking me to send him some record reviews (which he didn't end up using).

Fast-forward to 1975, the eve of the punk rock revolution, and I was in the thick of it, interviewing Patti Smith and The Ramones and the Talking Heads and Crime and so many more for stories that ran in the *Berkeley Barb* and the *San Francisco Bay Guardian.*

I had some close calls. The Clash nearly threw me out of the San Francisco recording studio where they were recording their second album, the Sex Pistols tried to break my tape recorder and Frank Zappa said if I was one of his fans he was in big trouble.

The life of a rock journalist.

Things did work out, and I spent 10 crazy years talking to everyone from George Harrison and George Clinton to Brian

Wilson and Stevie Wonder for *Rolling Stone* where I was an Associate Editor and a Senior Writer. My writing has also appeared in *Wired, Esquire, Vibe, Details, Downbeat, NME* and many more.

In 1993 I got hip to the Internet and by 1994 I'd founded *Addicted To Noise (ATN)*, the highly influential music web site. People said I was a distinguished pioneer in the online music space; *Newsweek* magazine called me an "Internet visionary."

I joined forces with SonicNet in 1997. I was a senior vice-president and editor in chief at *SonicNet* from March 1997 through May 2000. While running SonicNet editorial I interviewed Neil Young, Patti Smith, Lou Reed, Prince, Tom Waits, Metallica, the Smashing Pumpkins, Sonic Youth, Pavement, Sleater-Kinney and, and, and...

In 1997, *Addicted To Noise* won a Webby award for best music site, and a Yahoo Internet Life! award. While I was at *SonicNet* the site won Webby awards for best music site in 1998 and 1999, and also won Yahoo Internet Life! awards for three years running as best music site in 1998, 1999 and 2000.

I started writing the book that became the Freak Scene Dream Trilogy in the mid-2000s. The first book, True Love Scars, was published in 2014, and the second in 2015. You can expect the third book, The Moon & The Stars, to be available by August 2016. I currently write a monthly column, The Drama You've Been Craving, for the Australian version of *Addicted To Noise*.

And I publish the video-and-audio-intense culture blog, *Days of the Crazy-Wild* at www.daysofthecrazy-wild.com.

Any other questions?

PERMISSIONS

Made in the USA
Charleston, SC
07 December 2015